THE DIVINE OBLIVION

THE SECRETS OF THE SUN

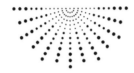

CLARE ARCHER

Hardcover: 979-8-9871628-2-8

Paperback: 979-8-9871628-1-1

Ebook: 979-8-9871628-0-4

Edited by: Jade Church

Proofread by: Roxana Coumans. 5Dogs Roth Book Editing

Cover Art by: Hanna Sternjakob Design

Character Art by: RomannaBoch & ColourAnomaly

www.clarearcherauthor.com

❀ Created with Vellum

To my daughter, Olivia. May you always look at the stars, dream the impossible then go for it! To my husband, Matt, who is always there to catch us when we fall from the sky.

CHAPTER ONE

The shadows surrounding me were unnatural for a sunny, July day in Arkansas. Squinting up at the relentless sun had me baffled as it seemed to gaze back down at me in mockery, providing no warmth. I shivered in confusion, double checking around the arcade's dumpster and each corner of the otherwise empty back lot, looking for anything out of the ordinary. Every inch of me tingled—a warning as if someone was following me, but there was nobody in sight except shadows that didn't belong. Where were they coming from? The rear of the arcade was an open area with no awnings or trees and yet there were clouds of darkness following me, just out of reach.

Crazy. I'm being crazy, pull yourself together, Cyra. Shaking my head in disbelief, I finally moved from my state of uncertainty as I threw the trash in the dumpster. I wasn't even supposed to be at work today since it was my birthday, but my parents insisted I didn't leave their sight on my special day. It was weird, but I'd agreed, not in the mood to argue and it didn't make much difference to me anyway. My parents' arcade and comic book shop, ARCADE-ON!, was my second home, if I wasn't working for them I was spending my free time there with my nerdy friends.

My inner child got the best of me and I kicked the dumpster in anger and paid for it, grunting in pain. It was clear my decision to leave the house in my ragged clothes and Darth Vader slippers was a poor one, but my parents claimed they only needed to make a quick appearance.

A small breeze caused papers to flutter in the dumpster and the comics section jumped out at me. Time stopped for a moment as I flattened out the paper and traced my fingers over some of the messily circled comics as tears started to form in my eyes. Grandpa Amrel was obsessed with the comics section of the newspaper and always circled ones he thought I would find funny. I never got the chance to see this one because he had just died a few days ago and I was still deep in mourning, unable to get past the fact that he was full of life one day and gone the very next. My parents must have thrown this out, not knowing I hadn't seen this edition yet. It was a sucker punch to my fragile emotional state, a cruel joke from the universe reminding me that my favorite person was gone. The paper crinkled in my hand as I gripped it tightly, anger and grief burning through every inch of me.

The elderly die every day, it's no great shock when they pass on. But grandpa Amrel wasn't just any old person. He was a force of nature with extraordinary golden eyes reminiscent of the sun he loved so much. Not only was he sharp as a wit and hilarious, but he was empathetic and kind. In the blink of an eye that behemoth of a man—simply ceased to exist. Grandpa was mysterious, but I knew he lived a full and gratified life, not having wasted a moment of it.

It made me ashamed of myself. I'd done a hell of a lot of nothing important, wasting away working at my parents' arcade with no true ambition or interest in going to college. Twenty-one years of time passed by with me not having savored every precious moment of it. If I left this world today, I would have made no lasting impact like he did. He managed to procure the love of anyone who laid eyes on him.

I laughed bitterly, shaking my head, but when I turned around the blood drained from my face and I couldn't breathe. In front of me was a man encased in shadows, seemingly made up of them. I always believed that if I ever found myself in a dangerous situation I'd imme-diately fight and defend myself, but that notion was a monumental fail. My feet were cemented in place while my eyes bulged out of my head. The only movement was the uncontrollable shaking of my body and any evidence of intelligence was nowhere to be found since my brain seemed to stop working. All I could do was watch him slowly drift amongst the unnatural shadows while I silently panicked. Only half of him was visible and he seemed to be an illusion, moving as if he was made of vapor and when he inched closer I finally came out of my stupor and began to run like hell. Since the pathway to the back entrance was blocked by the mysterious phantom I turned and ran around the corner to the front arcade entrance, nearly falling into the door in my haste.

"Crya! What's wrong?" Brendon asked, rushing over and taking my hands in his. I looked into his warm brown eyes and instantly felt safer. He'd always been my rock and a source of comfort, and in the safety of his arms I wondered if I had just imagined everything. Taking stock in my surroundings, I realized everyone in the arcade was staring at me. Rightly so.

The various lights of the arcade games flashed and sang to clashing tunes, mocking my obvious insanity.

"Um...I saw..."

"What? What did you see?"

"There's someone around the back," I whispered, not wanting anyone to know about my delusions. My reputation was at stake since I knew everybody in this store for my entire life. Brendon straightened and wasted no time rushing outside to slay my demons, no matter how ill-equipped he was to do so.

"Wait! Brendon don't go!"

My other friends, Jules, Mike, Ben and Rick, rushed over not wanting to miss out on the action. "What's going on?" Rick asked with a smile, his enthusiasm barely contained. The rest of them huddled together, hoping for some excitement in our otherwise lackluster lives.

"I don't know." I looked down to the floor and played with my braided strawberry blonde hair, not wanting anyone to see my hands still shaking.

Brendon returned quickly and shrugged. "There's nobody there. They must have run off."

I let out a sigh of relief. There probably wasn't anyone there to begin with. I didn't have the courage to tell him, but I had been seeing things for a few months. Phantoms half-existing for a few brief moments until they disappeared, people in hooded cloaks with faces I couldn't see, but there was no mistaking the evil aura around them.

I'd been paranoid and off my rocker for months and too afraid to tell anyone.

"No doubt it was an evil overlord coming to kidnap you and hide you away in his dark, magical kingdom in another universe," Ben teased.

I forced a fake laugh. "Obviously, what else would it be?" I thought I was playing it cool, but Brendon took my hand again, clearly seeing through my pathetic facade.

"So, we ready to play?" Jules clapped her hands together and rubbed with excitement. We had a standing game of Dungeons and Dragons a few times a week after I finished working at the front counter, and they likely assumed I was off duty.

"Nah, I'm only here for a few minutes today, I'm heading home now." My lips pursed to the side with false disappointment.

"Yeah, I'm out too. I'm going home with Cyra," Brendon chimed in. The group looked disappointed, but said their goodbyes and wished me happy birthday before going off to play on their own.

"Hey, Cyra! You look dazzling today!" I turned to see one of our daily customers, a little boy named Bart who I'd taken under my wing since he never seemed to have any adults with him. His large round eyes were full of hope, knowing it always worked in finagling free gaming coins from me. Never able to say no to that kid, I threw him a few and he disappeared before I could take them back.

I turned to Brendon. "Let me see what my parents are doing and we'll head out."

Bredon's eyes squinted, clearly still worried about me. "I'll come with you."

"No, it's okay. I'm fine, really, I guess I just saw something that wasn't there. The back of the arcade is a little creepy." That must be it. I was daydreaming, my heart was broken over my grandpa and I saw things that weren't there.

"Yeah, I guess you're right. If you're sure, I'll meet you at my car."

I gave him a sweet smile that seemed to appease him, but it disappeared from my face as soon as he left. I didn't want to worry him because he would make it his life's mission to make sure I felt better and I didn't want to be coddled–even though that was partly why I loved him so much. He was the fiercely protective brother I'd never had.

When I entered my parents' office, my mom was in my dad's arms and they were whispering with distraught expressions, their foreheads touching. They started kissing, and usually their amount of public affection made me nauseous, but at that moment it was grounding me, giving me faith that some things were unbreakable. And for my parents, their love for each other was as solid and true as the day they married, and it was the first time it really hit me and filled me with exactly what I needed—hope.

"Are you guys ready to leave?" They both jumped with alarm and tried to hide their bizarre behavior. My mom's eyes fluttered and she proceeded to act like she wasn't just crying. "What is going on with you two?"

"Nothing at all, dear," my father replied, rubbing my mom's back.

"We're ready! Let's go celebrate your birthday!"

I tried not to roll my eyes. It was my wish not to celebrate because of Grandpa's passing, but Brendon and my family insisted. Grandpa Amrel had made such a big deal about my birthdays that even thinking about celebrating without him made a knot twist in my gut.

We left the arcade and I let them know I was riding with Brendon and would meet them at home and, being the usual gentleman that he was, he stood waiting outside of the car to let me in.

"Shall we, my lady?" Brendon wiggled his eyebrows and I couldn't help but laugh. He led me to his gray, paint chipped, run-down car and opened the door for me.

"So gallant."

"Sixteen years of friendship and you're still surprised? Just call me your knight in shining armor who will forever protect you from your garbage can foes."

"What would I do without you, Brendon Braven?"

"Well, you're in luck because you'll never have to find out."

5

It was no surprise that my parents beat us home. They were speed demons and Brendon's car was a hunk of junk. I exhaled with relief when we entered our comfortable log cabin type house and my parents were already busy turning on the television and gaming system. Our golden retriever, Xenos, nearly bowled me over with an unusual amount of excitement like he knew it was my birthday. I scratched him behind his ears and he followed my every move.

"We were wondering if you wanted to 'duke it out' with a good ol' wholesome game of Dr. Mario?" my Dad asked with hope shining in his eyes.

I smiled back at him, trying to hide my repulsion at the idea. Owning a hybrid arcade and comic book store, our family was obviously a bunch of nerds, so we played games together very frequently. We also settled disputes and bad moods with video games as well, so when Dad suggested we "duke it out" he was trying to make me feel better. But the last time we played together was only the week prior, and Grandpa and I had tricked the controllers so that when my mom and dad fought over who was first player their fingers were zapped from pressing the buttons of both controllers. They were so shocked that they screamed and my dad passed gas so loudly we all fell to the ground laughing. Grandpa and I had high-fived in triumph, as was our custom, mercilessly pranking my parents on a weekly basis—it was one of our special things. The memory impaled me. It felt like it *just* happened yesterday.

"Um, maybe. Let me just change first and then we can talk about it."

My parents immediately began arguing who was going to be first player, my mom almost tackling my dad to the floor as Brendon looked on with laughter. A smile escaped my lips, feeling gratitude and love at the normalcy of my ridiculous family even though it was missing its brightest member. My grief seemed to be accumulating on my body and I rubbed at the pain in my shoulders as I climbed the stairs, already emotionally exhausted.

But my bad day plummeted to epic proportions when I entered my bedroom and was immediately slammed against the wall with the sharp sting of a knife pressed against my throat.

"Don't move or I'll fucking kill you."

This was *really* not how I imagined my twenty-first birthday.

Despite his warning, I thrashed against him, trying to break free even though it caused the knife to inch deeper into my skin. I felt a tiny droplet of blood run down my neck and I cursed the universe at this shitty week.

His hand was over my mouth so nobody could hear my screams and with my cheek against the wall I couldn't see the coward. When he tightened his hold on me I kicked my leg up, attempting to hit him in the junk.

I felt a small moment of victory when he yelled out in pain. "Bloody hell, woman, did I *not* just tell you I will *kill* you if you move?"

My words were garbled since he was still covering my mouth. "It's you! You've been following me, haven't you? What the hell do you want from me!"

"Screw this, I don't have the patience for this shit." My attacker sheathed his knife and whirled me around. My eyes bulged and I screamed in fear at the person before me with glowing silvery-gray eyes and light, slate gray skin. He slapped his hand against my forehead and hundreds of emotions and visions started flipping through my mind in rapid succession. The sensation was overwhelming and unbearable, making me physically ill. Everything around me began spinning and my sight started to sputter until everything went black.

CHAPTER TWO

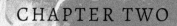

Groaning in pain, I pressed my hands against my head as if trying to keep it from bursting apart. I slowly opened my eyes and the brightness around me made me hiss, doing nothing to help my splitting headache. As my eyesight adjusted, I noticed a whistling sound and when I looked toward the source I jumped from my seat and tried to run in the opposite direction, but there was nowhere to go. I was on a...*spaceship*. A small one, no bigger than an SUV. *What the actual fuck?* I was extremely groggy and confused, unsure of what was happening to me. Wasn't I just about to play video games? Was I dreaming? Because spaceships and shadowy gray colored men weren't real. *Right?*

As I tried to slow my breath, I became more coherent and to my dread I realized this must be real. Pinching myself hard enough to draw blood also confirmed it. I looked around, trying to find a weapon to protect myself from this stranger, but there was nothing that looked threatening and the seat was firmly attached to the floor. And even if I did find a weapon I couldn't kill the fucker because *I don't fly spaceships.* It was just me and him, so I was stuck until he landed this thing.

My abductor's energetic whistling continued as if he didn't have a care in the world. I turned around and peeked out of a small window, and almost choked at the intensity of what I was seeing.

I didn't know how long I was unconscious, but I was definitely witnessing the splendor of the Milky Way galaxy and it looked like an insignificant thing I could encompass in my arms.

But its beauty was still beyond comparison. The spiral arms and dust clouds spread throughout countless sparkling stars that I had once dreamed about while looking through a telescope. Brendon would absolutely lose it over a view like this.

My parents and Brendon! My friends, *my life*. Beads of sweat began to form at my brow as I lost control of my breath again. They had no idea where I was. Oh God. Would I ever see them again?

I doubled over clenching my stomach, the confusion and feeling of loss becoming a physical pain and I spoke through my sobs. "What do you want with me? Why did you kidnap me?"

He finally stopped his irritating whistling and swiveled around in his chair, completely ignoring my tears. "Ah, you're awake. What a shame, I thought I'd get more than thirty minutes of peace."

Thirty minutes? That's all it took for my loved ones to be thousands of mortal lifetimes away?

"Take me back. Now!" It was an absolute command, I left no room for negotiation.

"No." His lids were low and his voice monotone with boredom. It made fury blaze in my core.

"Take me the fuck back now!"

"Or what, princess? You'll do what, exactly? Sit down and calm down or I'll gag you and tie you to that seat."

What a dick. But he was a dick who had the upper hand. I had no possessions, no weapons, no means of escape. Maybe I could reason with him or appeal to him that I wasn't worth taking. "Look, I'm nothing interesting or special. You have no use for me. My family has some money, I'm sure they'll pay handsomely for my return."

"Just save yourself the energy of begging. Your parents knew all about this. You're stuck with me."

My blood turned icy cold in my body and my heart sank at what he was implying, especially because of their strange behavior. It made me sick when I recalled how unusually anxious and sad they were all day because it all made more sense if they did actually know about this. But I couldn't accept that, not about the people I've known and loved all my life.

"No. They wouldn't let me go like that, they're the kindest people on Earth, everyone loves them. They would never accept this."

He huffed in dramatic annoyance. "It'll be better for all involved if you accept it sooner rather than later because you know in your heart of hearts that I'm right."

I rubbed at my temples as more tears fell down my cheeks. It was too much to take in while still having a splitting headache, so I blurted out the obvious. "You're not human."

If I didn't know any better, I'd say he looked like a dark elf, but with no blue tint to his skin. His black hair fell to his shoulders, and his ears were slightly arched to a point, but most striking were his eyes that were reminiscent of a bright, shining moon.

"What an astute observation, you're quite the clever one, aren't you? I'm still not convinced as to *why* Amrel insisted you were some special 'chosen one'."

I gasped, shocked that this being would know anything about my dead grandpa and him even talking about such a wonderful person fed the well of anger even further. "What do you know about me and my grandpa?"

"Oh, I know a great many things about you, Cyra Fenix, and I've come to take you home."

"That's not my name," I said stupidly. My last name was Fela, but I had a sick twisted feeling in my gut that he was right and my name *was* Fenix. What was happening to me? Why did Fenix sound right?

He rolled his eyes and let out an exasperated groan. "Use that over-worked noggin of yours and *think*. Does the name Adelram ring a bell?" he said, floating his hand from his head to his chest as if putting himself on display.

No, it absolutely did not. If I did meet him it was no surprise to me that I buried the memory of him deep down where it was lost.

"I took your memories sixteen years ago and altered them a bit to give you a memory of a human past. Amrel brought you to your Earth parents who were looking to adopt, and they raised you knowing that you'd have to go home again one day."

No, this couldn't be true. Grandpa and my parents were all in on this and they'd never told me? We told each other everything, they couldn't have kept something so monumental from me.

"Did Brendon know too?" There was a little more venom in my tone than I liked, but I couldn't help the overwhelming feeling of betrayal and hurt.

"Your little boy toy? No, he had no idea."

"You're such an asshole."

Adelram waved his hand, casually dismissing my comment like he couldn't care less. I supposed he heard that on a regular basis. "I just returned your memories to you in your bedroom. They are all back, but they'll come to you sporadically. It will take some time to feel whole again, you'll get flashes of memories here and there not realizing they were missing. You could experience some confusion."

"Are you kidding me right now? If this was all *supposed* to happen why the fuck did you have me at knifepoint? I highly doubt that's what grandpa Amrel had in mind."

"Likely not, but he didn't specify the manner in which I had to bring you back to Solis."

"Solis," I said aloud. Yes, to my shock and dread, it did feel right.

"That was more fun than I've had in years." He swiveled his chair so he spun around in a full circle with a sickening smile on his face.

He was having the time of his life while my world was turned upside down. I was seconds away from scratching his eyes out, but got sidetracked when I doubled over in pain again as a sudden flash of memories of two smiling faces hugging me tight appeared in my mind, followed by their dead bodies lying on the ground. They were… my birth parents.

Oh God. I almost wished I could give the memories back, because recalling my Solian parents and their death felt like I was being stabbed in the heart. It was still hazy, but I knew without a doubt that before my life on Earth I'd witnessed my Solian parents' death. And my grief was stolen from me when my memories were taken. I never got the chance to say goodbye, just like with my parents from Earth. My anger toward Adelram grew exponentially by the second.

"That says a lot about you and how miserable you must be if that was the only fun you'd had in years." I spoke through clenched teeth, unsure how to process the multitude of violent emotions coursing through me at once.

"Doesn't it just? Anyway, we digress, let's get to the point, shall we? We are in this mess because the High Oracle, Siare, had a prophecy that Amrel believed was about you. *The girl with the divine mark shall deliver balance back to the Eredet galaxy with a king blessed by the sun.*" He delivered the speech with mock flair like he'd heard it a thousand times and looked at me with boredom. As if he couldn't be bothered that I existed. It was safe to say I wasn't his biggest fan.

"What the hell is wrong with you that you couldn't let me say goodbye to my parents and my best friend, Brendon? They were downstairs in my house. It wouldn't have taken much time out of your precious schedule. Not that I even believe anything you're telling me." Though to be honest, I looked down and rubbed the birthmark on my wrist, starting to remember my mother from Solis telling me bedtime stories about a girl with a special destiny that had a mark like mine. *I was grieving for two mothers at the same time.*

"Yes, yes. I'm a heartless bastard, woe is you. Before you go on an epic monologue about how hard you have it, just know that our people and our galaxy is dying. The natural energy supplied by our sun is being siphoned so that those who rule our lands can manipulate it and distribute it to their will. Once it was an abundant free supply that anyone with magic could absorb and wield but, since the curse, those able to use magic are few and far between. Our sun is dying and we're close to mass extinction."

That was a lot to process for someone who an hour ago thought they were an average, nerdy human who worked in an arcade. "That is all tragic, but I don't understand how I can be of any help."

Adelram looked me up and down with the corner of his lip raised in a sneer. "Yes, I don't either, but here we are."

What an overwhelming, repulsive ass.

"If you're so mighty and powerful, why couldn't you save grandpa from dying?"

"Keeping Amrel in his full immortal form would have required a tremendous amount of power and energy. There's a reason why Earth has no innate magic. Amrel and I could have used magic on Earth with our ability to access energy, but it would have destroyed the sun and the Milky Way galaxy in a matter of months. Amrel was convinced you were able to save us so he decided to come to Earth and take human form, to give you the education you needed, the life you needed to experience, to fulfill your destiny."

"Again, I don't trust you. Why should I believe what you're saying or even that prophecies are real?"

"I could care less what you think of me, but our prophecies aren't just human ideas of divinations, it's based on science, magic and Amrel's knowledge of the way our cosmos works. You don't need to trust me because you will see first-hand the devastation the curse has brought on our galaxy. Your family were rulers of Solis, and you need to take your rightful place. Why do you think Amrel chose to take a mortal body and die on Earth to make sure you would live and thrive? He ended his own life so you could fulfill your destiny."

My heart sank to my gut and my mind whirled with sickening disbelief. He was insinuating that grandpa Amrel's death was on my hands. I covered my mouth with my hand and tried to choke back the acidic nausea. Adelram knew just what to say to cut me down to the smallest size and even possibly accept what he was saying. Grandpa chose my life over his? He *chose* to lose who he was and take a mortal form knowing he would die. I felt utterly sick to my stomach. The guilt was a vice clamping down on my core, suffocating me.

"I don't understand, why would he *have* to die? Who exactly was Amrel?" He had to be somebody incredibly important if he had some hand in all this.

I rubbed the bridge of my nose, my sinuses now aching and backed up from so many tears. Grandpa and my Earth parents knew about this for sixteen years and never told me. Why couldn't they have just confided in me?

Adelram sneered and I swore I saw a flash of genuine pain behind his cold eyes. "I don't know why he died, he never told me. And as to who he was, that's a story for another time."

Since I couldn't escape his brooding self, I childishly swiveled my chair toward the wall so I didn't have to look at him and we sat in silence for quite a while. I truly didn't know what to say anyway. My reality was still catching up to me and I didn't know what to expect on the other side of it. My hurt—my grief was overwhelming, and it took effort to breathe.

I looked at Adelram and realized he'd been cradling Grandpa's urn like a piece of cherished treasure.

"Why did you take Grandpa's urn?"

Adelram hissed that I dared to speak again. "You can stop with the grandpa shit. Amrel will do."

"I'll never stop calling him Grandpa. That's who he was to me, and you can't belittle what we were to each other. And that doesn't answer my question."

"Not that it's any of your damn business, *princess*, but I want to secure his remains."

"Well, then I guess you'll be disappointed." He whipped his head back with an unmistakable wrath and his eyes brightened with a fierce glow.

"What are you talking about?"

"I released his remains with Brendon yesterday."

All the sound from the ship seemed to seep from existence and the light dimmed to almost nothing. A rumbling sound vibrated from his chest that sounded eerily similar to a growl. "You did what?" His face contorted in rage and as he stood, he bared his teeth, showing his very slightly elongated canines.

I ignored his show of theatrics and pretended that I wasn't thoroughly scared of him. "Brendon and I went to the summit of Fog Mountain before dawn. I released them as soon as the sun rose. It's what he would have wanted."

Adelram's fists bunched so tightly they started to whiten under his gray skin. "You're lucky I need you unharmed. You have no idea what you've done."

"So why don't you tell me instead of being cryptic?"

The muscles in his jaw pulsated as if he were grating his teeth and he took a deep breath trying to calm himself down and the light and sound of the ship returned to normal. I wasn't going to feed his dramatics so I changed topics.

"I'm surprised you speak English. Will I have to learn another language?"

He huffed, rubbing his eyes but answered. "Everyone from Eredet

—The Creation galaxy—can understand and seamlessly translate eighty percent of languages. Our own galaxy's languages have evolved many times over the years, but you don't need to worry about that."

I suppose it made things easier. "How long will it take to get to Solis?"

"A few more hours," Adelram grumbled.

I gaped at him. "I thought you were going to tell me I was stuck in this tiny ship with you for a year." Thank God for small miracles.

"Oh, the princess has jokes. A little souvenir from Earth I'd imagine since your people are painfully droll. Don't worry, princess, I wouldn't be caught dead with you in this small space for more than was necessary."

The feeling is entirely mutual, asshole.

"Fine. Here's an olive branch, I'll explain how it works. Eredet is far. Approximately one hundred million light years away. With magic we're able to pinpoint our sun's location and lock into its gravitational pull. We create a magnified suction where we stretch the connection like an elastic band which creates potential energy, and the pull back to the source of the gravity is amplified and we are propelled toward our sun. Once released, it's like a slingshot effect thrusting us through space. We can also use other planetary bodies and natural satellite's gravitational force as supplements to accelerate the process. Since we're so far away we'll be utilizing that method."

He kept looking at me like I was the biggest nuisance to ever grace his presence. "If this is such a burden for you, why didn't someone else come for me?"

"I'm the one who took your memories, I'm the only one who could give them back."

"If you were dead, how would I have gotten my memories back?"

"Your memories would have died with me. Don't forget that, or I'll steal more from you as insurance, so quit with your fantasies of killing me."

Damn, he was too clever for his own good.

He took a flask out of his back pocket that looked tarnished and well used, and chugged about half of it, the unmistakable smell of alcohol wafting toward me.

"Are you out of your fucking mind? You're drinking while operating a spaceship!"

He acted as if he didn't hear a word I said as he took one more chug and put it back in his pocket. "Okay, hold on, princess, we're about to initiate the pull."

"Ugh, stop calling me that!"

He turned to look at me, unamused and almost disgusted, and his eyes flashed in a moonlit glow. "That's what you are, aren't you?"

Fuck, was I? The thought hadn't dawned on me even though he said my family were rulers of Solis. I didn't get a chance to think it through as I was instantly smashed into the back of my seat. Sickness overcame me, my stomach lodged firmly up in my throat. I couldn't imagine how fast we must have been going, and my inhales were unsuccessful hiccups—it was as if I was frozen in time and my breath was suspended as well. My eyes were glued in place, but I could tell Adelram was completely unaffected by the sudden debilitating force. Just when I thought it was going on for an eternity, we stopped, and I fell forward and hit the chair in front of me. I didn't care about my bruised ego, I was just glad I could breathe again.

Adelram swiveled in his seat and said with a nasty smirk on his face, "Good thing you're going to be a ruler since you're shit at taking orders. I told you to hold on, the marks on the seat would have protected you from the forward thrusting. Maybe next time you should listen to me." He had an odd look on his face like he was deadly serious. This man was baffling, and I couldn't wait to get off this ship and as far away from him as possible. But I looked off to the side and saw a beautiful glowing cluster of stars and a *massive* burning sun in the distance.

I only got to witness the beauty for a moment before an unexpected darkness befell us, and I felt a squeezing sensation until I could see again. With no warning we were in front of a large planet.

"What just happened? How did we get here?"

Adelram shrugged nonchalantly. "We *drove* closer."

"Okay, but we were just outside of the galaxy. You can't *drive* that fast, can you?"

"It's what we call instant travel. In a crude explanation, we can create doors to step through locations in our galaxy. We're not able to do it outside our galaxy on this scale, hence the need for a ship."

Wow. Instant travel. Would I be able to do that now? We were finally adding a 'check' in the pro column. I looked down in awe at a planet that looked shockingly similar to Earth, with blue waters and two large land continents—it was lively and bright, but within it held more power and secrets than the planet I just left behind. From what I'd seen so far it was hard to believe this galaxy was dying.

As soon as I heard Adelram's voice my annoyance grew to an ugly level. "Welcome home, princess. Here lies the horribly jubilant planet of Solis – my prison and my own personal hell."

CHAPTER THREE

*W*e started the descent into the planet's atmosphere and I expected some kind of blinding light threatening to destroy us. Turned out movies weren't always right, and I wasn't about to ask Adelram about it. It took mere minutes to reach the surface and the view was spectacular. I was glued to the windshield the whole way down, taking in the white stone architecture and the glistening clear blue waters – the first glimpses of life, of my true people. This was where I was born. This was where my parents died. *This was where I'm supposed to belong.* It was a bizarre mix of emotions, excitement, confusion, anger and overwhelming grief.

The moment I stepped foot off the ship and onto the ground I felt a surging force blast through me that almost knocked me to the ground. I stopped as I felt an electric tingling in every part of my body, intense and euphoric, and I breathed through it as I felt energy binding with every molecule in my body. It was as if I was fully alive for the first time in my life, and for just a moment my troubles took a back seat as I relished this strange feeling of power. Everything looked brighter, my mind felt clearer and sharper and, I didn't know how, but I felt physically stronger. Had I really been living in a mindless fog my whole life on Earth? A veil was lifted that I didn't have the faintest clue was there. Despite the sadness of leaving my family and friends behind, I couldn't deny relishing this feeling of empowerment, like I could do anything. When I looked down my confidence instantly melted away as I gasped in horror, realizing how I still looked.

"Oh my God." Panic alarms blared in my head as my mouth parted in a stupefied expression. This couldn't be happening. These strangers that I was supposed to *lead* were going to see me for the first time with morning hair, ancient baggy sweatpants with holes, my grandpa's oversized novelty t-shirt and Darth Vader slippers. Why didn't I change like a normal person this morning before I went out in public?

I looked to Adelram and pleaded, "You're going to *drive* us in, right?"

"Oh *no*, princess," he said, tickled with delight, "everyone we pass will get to see you in all your majestic glory. Watch out everyone, here is your savior, returned!" Adelram busted out laughing and I had never been so filled with the desire to incite violence.

"Are you like this with everyone? Or have you been saving this attitude up just for me?"

"Ouch, those words hurt my tender feelings. But regardless, we have no choice but to go in by boat. Those who have never entered the castle before have no access to *drive* in. They must be greeted at the port and given clearance to enter. This is the closest I was able to land the ship, which is a small island right across from the Eluroom port. You'll need approval to drive into the walls of the castle in future."

"But I've been in the castle before." It was shocking to me that I was starting to receive glimpses of stoney castle corridors and staff dressed in finery. It was painful to admit to myself that everything Adelram had said was probably true. Being here felt right.

"Not as an adult with magic you haven't."

Magic...I have magic...

In quiet disbelief I turned around to inspect the ship from the outside. It had an opalescent shimmer to it with hints of lavender and pink and the rear held two blue glowing circles which I assumed powered the ship. It was stunning, but I wondered how something so small and delicate looking could weather a trip through the galaxies. Walking its perimeter, I noticed there were designs embossed into the glossy surface – a forest with a winged creature flying over a moon and I wondered if it held any significance.

"Stop dawdling," Adelram said, pulling on my sleeve with a grimace then wiping his hand. With no other choice, I sighed and reluctantly followed him.

We walked for about five minutes through the deserted green island to a dock lined with small row boats. They were simple, but the detail on them was intricate and carefully crafted. The man guarding the boat looked like no more than a low-level guard based on his simple garb, but he did have a sword strapped across his back. He nodded his head slightly. "Adelram, good to see you again, please take any you like." Then he looked to me and his eyes bulged. "What is *that?*"

"*Excuse* me?" How rude. The first Solian I meet thinks I'm disgusting, we were off to a great start. Wonderful.

Adelram belted out a satisfied laugh and answered, "I'm really not quite sure myself, dear fellow," he pretended to whisper to him, "but wish me luck! I'll obviously need it."

They continued to chatter, but I walked away, thoroughly sick of the sound of his voice. I took a moment to really observe my surroundings. The first thing I noticed was the soothing smell of the air. Closing my eyes, I took a deep breath and I could almost remember the intricate flavors that tickled my nose. It was a more organic, cleaner, smell than Earth, but I was surprised to realize that it did feel like home.

I didn't recognize the fields, the exotic, bright flowers or the body of water in front of me, but the bouquet of the air jostled something within me. I couldn't explain it, but despite my unrelenting desire to go back home to Earth and cling to my parents and my best friend, Brendon, I felt like I was *supposed* to be here.

Adelram waved his hand in front of my face. "You're not losing it already, are you? I promised Amrel I'd get you here in one piece. Although I can't fix what's already mentally broken. My gifts don't go that far..."

God, he was an ass. Maybe if I ignored his antics he'd stop. "How did you know Grandpa?"

He stilled, clearly not comfortable with my question. "We don't have time to get into it, let's just survive the trip to Eluroom dock, shall we?"

"Eluroom?" More memories jumped into view with the word on my tongue. A large home with never-ending halls. Castle staff who played with me and nurtured me. Kitchens where they let me bake cookies and cakes. *Oh my.* That's where my love of baking came from. I remembered my parents tucking me into bed. I remembered water. The images weren't fully vibrant, but they were there. "Eluroom is my home," I tried out loud to see if it fit.

Adelram looked at me like he was appeasing a small child. "Good job, gold star for the head of the class. Now, the Guardians will question you. They will ask how I came to find you. Be a good girl and repeat my story – I've been looking for you for many years in places around the galaxy and I got a tip somewhere about Earth. I went looking there a few times and got lucky this time around. I immediately returned your memories, and you were beyond thrilled that I saved you and brought you home to where you belonged, and you live happily ever after in eternal gratitude to me. You know nothing about Amrel. Got it?"

And he called me the crazy one. "It might be kind of hard to lie about the bit where I'm thrilled you came for me or anything about you in general, and that you didn't practically drag me here by the hair."

The mocking smile dropped from his face, and he looked so deadly that it gave me chills and made me want to hide in a corner somewhere. When he wasn't being a sarcastic bastard, he could be genuinely terrifying. His voice had slightly changed, and the air around us darkened which made me look for places to jump and escape should he attack me. He said with the venom of a deeper, darker voice, "If you have any hope of surviving this, of *any* of us surviving, then you'll keep your fucking mouth shut and do what you're told. This isn't Earth, there are people here who can obliterate you from the inside out in under a second and the pain of it would feel like five minutes of pure suspended agony. This isn't a game, little girl. For some insanely unfathomable reason the powers-that-be have given you the chance to destroy us all. One wrong step and you will be responsible for the extinction of life. *All life everywhere.*"

He looked me up and down at my ludicrous state and continued. "You don't at all seem like the savior of my dreams, in fact, I've already started preparing myself for your inevitable failure. You're an utter disappointment."

It felt like all the breath was knocked out of me at his words. They were heavy accusations and an even heavier weight he put on my shoulders. I wanted to yell at him for talking to me like that. I wanted to scream that he'd come to get me at all. Mostly, I wanted to cry, but I refused to do that in front of him after everything he'd said to me. Instead, I stayed silent and didn't talk to him again.

You're an utter disappointment.

CHAPTER FOUR

*B*oth of us sat pissed off and frustrated as we sailed above the clear turquoise ocean on a water bridge, wide enough to fit only two small row boats side by side. We traveled upward for some time until we finally crested and I gasped at the breathtaking view. I could see the castle in the near distance, reaching up to the bright sunlit skies, and then did a double take at the sky when I noticed the subtle pastel rainbow color nestled within almost every cloud. I had heard of that phenomenon on Earth, called iridescent clouds, but had never witnessed it myself. It seemed to be a staple in Solis's sky and it was spectacular.

Sailboats cruised in the clear waters around the castle docks and I could hear the faint sounds of chattering and movement from the sailors. The water bridge we sailed on was supported by a larger-than-life statue of a knight with one knee bent on an orb that resembled the sun, and his arms were raised holding up the bridge. It was both menacing and extraordinary and I imagined the skill and craftsmanship required to erect such a piece of functional art. Was it made by magic or by hand? I was blown away by the talent and beauty.

On the shorelines were scenic, vibrant trees blooming with flowers of almost every shade—pink, lavender, emerald, orange, white and amber. It was a canvas of natural art, spread throughout the borders of the land. As we neared the stronghold, petals from the various trees sprinkled through the water and we sailed right through them in a collection of color. If I was sailing with literally anyone else in the universe other than Adelram, it would have been incredibly romantic.

Unfamiliar species of birds flew overhead and their chirps were soothing unique songs that echoed in the atmosphere. Ships continued to sail beneath the bridge and I tried to get a look at the occupants, but I couldn't see much detail this far up. It was as if we were floating in the heavens, sailing toward a magical palace.

Adelram started to look somewhat anxious the closer we came to the citadel and I didn't know whether to feel smug at his discomfort, or worried by it. How could all this wonder and beauty surrounding me be so close to dying?

I also couldn't understand how Adelram hated Solis. With all this sunshine, brilliance and color, Adelram looked like a fragmented shadow threatening to be extinguished by the solar rays.

Once we sailed over the gargantuan knight sculpture, Adelram advised that we were officially in Eluroom. The flowering trees hung over the edges of the path, shading us from the sun as petals softly fluttered through the air around us before falling to the water. I picked up a lavender petal that fell in my lap and delighted in the soft, satiny feel of it. The air was saturated with a wonderful floral scent that was bold and fresh and reminded me of the smell of gardenias.

Despite my own melancholy and my miserable companion, I couldn't help but smile, overwhelmed by the sheer beauty of this place. But it was short-lived. My parents and friends had no idea where I was. Did they already notice my disappearance? Would I ever be able to contact them again to tell them I was okay? I closed my eyes and breathed deeply again, letting the soothing gardenia smell calm me just a little. The smells were as evocative as the sights and I somehow felt connected to all of it.

We approached the dock and Adelram leapt off the boat as if he couldn't wait to be rid of me. He started to reach his light gray hand to me to help me out, but someone else reached me first.

With all the trees now behind us, I looked up and was slightly blinded by the light, obstructing my view of the owner of the hand.

But the voice spoke, and the music that it made sent shivers over my skin.

"I am Theo Beaurdlaux, Karalis of Meri Kardem, but you'd know me as a prince. Please, allow me."

With his head now bent toward me and blocking the sun, it lit up his whole body like he was emitting the aura himself and I witnessed one of the most endearing male faces I'd ever laid eyes on. I gazed at his welcoming smile which reached all the way to his turquoise eyes.

"I've come to personally greet you! When news arrived of your return, I wanted to be the first to welcome you," he continued while I awkwardly stared in silence before clearing my throat.

His smile left you without a doubt of his sincerity and connected to it were two adorably attractive dimples. After being dumbstruck by his killer smile, I looked down at his widespread hand. His fingers were long and gentle, and his skin was smooth and flawless. I was like a moth to a flame, craving to grab hold. "Uh, thank you." My voice cracked and I winced.

Theo looked strong and muscular, but not overly built and when he grasped my hand to pull me out of the boat he towered over my smaller frame. I instantly liked him.

With no apparent control over my faculties, I gave him a dopey smile, freezing when I remembered what he must be seeing as he took me in.

Oh God. *Oh my God.* My cheeks burned until I thought they might turn to flame and I'd die from burning alive. It would probably be preferable to this. I was meeting a prince of Solis with Vader slippers and decrepit sweatpants, not to mention my disgusting mop of hair! Forget fulfilling some stupid prophecy and saving lives, I was going to perish from embarrassment before even making it to the castle.

If he noticed my horrendous appearance, he didn't say anything and I fought the urge to hide my face.

"I've been looking for you for years to no avail. I'm so glad you're finally home." He pulled me in for a hug and the humiliation only intensified as I realized I must have smelled atrocious compared to his hypnotic, fresh jasmine scent. Oh God, *why me?* Adelram gave me a seething look over Theo's shoulder that said, *do not test me.* I didn't need to hear his nasty sermon again, I wouldn't dare stray from the story he'd given me.

"I'm happy to be home," I managed to reply. Adelram looked pleased. Whatever, he could go to hell.

But Theo looked more than pleased, and that made my insides go all soft and gooey.

"I can't wait to show you all of Solis. We'll be spending a lot of time together, I think. I already have your quarters situated for you, which of course you can change however you like once you're settled."

Theo's enthusiasm was so refreshing after dealing with Adelram. He gently took my arm and led us across a walkway that took us from the port to the castle doors. Twelve more large knight statues, framed in silver armor with gold accents, lined the pristinely clear cobblestone pathway, encased by a small gate that emitted fire on all sides. They were a fierce welcome to anyone entering the pathway to the castle.

"Ah, those are thought to be the first protectors of the galaxy, the Sun Guard. I'll walk you through them later so you can read all the tablets on their history, or at least what we think is their history. Solians were known to be great warriors once upon a time," Theo said when he saw me admiring the gigantic effigies.

"Not anymore?"

He looked straight ahead and I had the sense that I'd said something wrong as his smile dimmed a little. "No. Not anymore." Adelram cursed from somewhere to my left and Theo frowned as we witnessed five cloaked figures spilling out of the castle doors. "I was hoping to avoid this, but it seems the Guardians already found you."

I couldn't believe it. Walking toward me were the beings of my visions and nightmares. Sound seemed to pause around me and my breath increased too quickly as the Guardians drew closer. Everything started spinning and my sight sputtered as the world moved in slow motion. A hand touched my shoulder, but my eyes stayed on the approaching darkness until everything went black.

CHAPTER FIVE

I awoke with a gasp, shooting up in my bed and panting. I looked around me in confusion and had no idea where I was, which only made me panic even more. My hands clung to sheets that were softer than I was used to and the bed was double the size of what it should be. I clutched my chest trying to even out my breath, but a hand touched me from my left and I screamed.

"Woah! It's just me, Cyra." Theo carefully stood from a chair that was placed next to the bed and I tried to force myself to calm down. "Are you okay?"

"What were those things? The Guardians?" It might be irrational, but it felt as if I would never be safe again knowing those beings were real and it only added to my rapidly growing list of trauma.

Theo frowned. "That is a loaded question, but that was a pretty strong reaction to them."

"What are they the guardians of, exactly?" My fear and doubt were probably etched into my worry lines, but at the moment I didn't care.

"Of our realm, our magic, our way of life. They're the ultimate judge and jury of Eredet. They make the rules and they keep us… safe," Theo concluded. I searched his face, waiting for more information, but he looked down, wiping a non-existent spec from his exquisitely tailored, blue brocade vest.

"Why were they there to see me?"

"There are two realms in Solis and you're the rightful heir to Eluroom Reindem, or Solis West. It was always the greatest ruling power in Eredet so your return is monumental. I imagine the Guardians wanted to question where you've been and what happened to you."

"Two realms—so you rule over Solis East?"

"Correct. I am responsible for Meri Kardem. It's a smaller realm in people and power, but there's more land. When you're settled, I'll show you everything."

His easy, friendly demeanor made me finally relax and let go of some of my anxiety. "Thanks for being so kind. This is all a little overwhelming. A *lot* overwhelming. I was taken from my home and everyone I loved and told a fantastical story about being some chosen one. I don't know what to believe."

Theo's eyes filled with compassion and he gently took my hand. "I can't imagine what you're going through, Cyra, but I am here for you. I know Adelram is – how do I say this…a hard pill to swallow, but he is right. We do need you here, and we can talk more about it all after you've had a chance to rest. Can I do anything for you right now? Do you want to see any of the castle, or meet anyone? Are you hungry?"

"If you don't mind, I'd just like to be alone for a while. I need to… come to terms with some things."

"Of course. I'll check on you in a few hours to see if you need anything. Take as long as you need. There will always be a guard down the hall or down the stairs if you decide you need something."

"Thank you."

Theo nodded and I heard him exit from the other room. I exhaled in relief that only lasted three seconds until there was a knock at the door. Reluctantly, I left the bedroom and walked to the door in the grand main chamber and Adelram burst through without waiting for an invitation. Possibly the last person in two galaxies I wanted to see. My reaction must have been visible because he said, "Yes, I'm so over-joyed to see you again too."

"Then why are *you* in *my* room?"

Adelram ignored me as per usual and spun around, pinning me with a look I couldn't decipher.

"What?"

"Why did you faint?" Adelram demanded, folding his arms.

"Why do you care?"

"I know you're such a precious, delicate, little flower and all, but you survived an abduction and yet you took one look at them and fainted? Explain."

I clenched my jaw, figuring it was probably faster and less painful to just answer him to get rid of him than drag this out. "I've had nightmares about them since I was little. I had forgotten all about it until a few weeks ago when it started happening again. They were always trying to capture me. I know it's stupid, but when I saw them today it felt like I was still stuck in the nightmare and they had finally caught me."

Adelram looked almost... scared? Nervous? Shocked? I couldn't even try to guess what was going on in his head since he was so excessive. For all I knew, maybe he was just constipated. It was a possibility.

"You *remembered* them before I restored your memories?"

"I wouldn't say I remembered them. I dreamt of the feeling and the fear. I didn't know who they were or even if what I dreamt of was real. I still don't, it was just a reaction."

Adelram glared at me with suspicion and shook his head. "Here. Amrel left this for you."

That's all he said before turning around and rushing right back out of the room again, slamming the door without another word. What the hell was *wrong* with that guy?

Good riddance.

I took a moment to survey my massive quarters while I stood in the main chamber. Off to the right was the bedroom and an impressive study with an elaborate wooden desk and a sinfully empty bookshelf. To the left of the main living area were the bathroom and another sitting area. All the decor was accented in gold or citrine and carnelian crystals, and I admired the many beautiful paintings of angelic, winged beings, cathedrals and ocean backdrops. I wondered at the story behind them and if they contained any Solian history in the art. Everything was bright and pristine and while it was beautiful it didn't feel very homey to me. It only made me miss my warm, log cabin type home even more.

I opened all the windows and the hot briny air hit me immediately. Each floor-to-ceiling window had a stunning view of the beach and the ocean, but I was too tired, lonely and broken to appreciate it. I sat down at the desk and eagerly studied the ornate box grandpa left for me. It appeared to be a hand painted war scene, with a group of people fighting against an obscure darkness. Gray figures reminding me of Adelram had sparks of various colors bursting from their hands that I assumed was magic, knights that mimicked the armor of the statues, and beautiful winged beings, flying above the battle. The magic wielders and the Solians I could discern, but I couldn't guess who the angelic beings were. I turned to the back of the box and was drawn in by an inflamed girl with reddish purple hair. A brilliant sparkling ruby caught my eye and I studied the large red jewel on the top of the box. I could see a symbol that looked like a constellation in the depths of the radiant stone. I opened the incredible box and found a letter inside. My hands began to tremble when I saw Grandpa's unmistakable handwriting.

My dearest Cyra,

Watching you grow into the woman you are today has been the greatest, most rewarding experience of my long life. You've given me the confidence and utter peace that my legacy will live on in your capable hands. You'll face many challenges in the future to come, but just know I'll always be a part of you. The light I had in me shines just as bright in you, don't ever forget that. Keep those you love close, and they'll be your guide and support. Don't close off your heart in grief as it is your biggest asset and will show you the truest path. There will be many things that will become clearer in the near future, but time needs the right conditions to reveal its secrets. But trust what Adelram has told you, you are needed back in Solis.

I have enclosed some of my most cherished things. A necklace and ring which are family heirlooms. Keep them safe as it will hold a piece of me close to you and you will receive necessary information through the crystals. The ring is for you to give to someone very special. Make sure not to give it lightly – you will know when.

Lastly, the goodness in you will bring many peace, and for that I am eternally grateful, more than you could ever know. I love you more than the cosmos and all that is held within it.

Love,

Grandpa Amrel

TEARS FELL as I immediately put on the gold necklace he left for me. I touched the clear crystal in the center that rested right between my collarbones and was so thankful I had an heirloom of his to keep with me, always. What did he mean that I would receive necessary information? Grandpa backing Adelram's lunacy terrified me. This letter didn't appear to be a forgery, so I had to conclude that he believed in this destiny of mine? I folded the letter and placed it back in the box with the ring.

I prayed that I'd be able to live up to these expectations Grandpa had for me. How did I go from a human nobody who worked in an arcade in Arkansas to an heir of a magical kingdom on another galaxy destined to save millions of people? And I was beyond confused, my thoughts not yet able to catch up to my devastating emotions. It felt like my Solian parents had just died since my memories were taken immediately after their death. I was still mourning the loss of grandpa Amrel and now I had to face the fact that I would never see my wonderful adoptive parents Jeff and Sarah Fela ever again. And Brendon...there wasn't a day that went by that we didn't share together for the past sixteen years.

I walked back to the bedroom and hid the box under the spring of the bed, then laid down with my legs to my chest. I stayed there for hours, silently saying goodbye to a precious life that was never truly mine.

A KNOCK at the main door was the only disturbance for hours and I heard a hushed male voice. "Cyra? I'm so sorry to bother you, but I'm going to come in and check on you for a moment."

It was Theo. With my back to the door, I didn't bother to turn around and look at him, the effort felt like too much. I was stuck in a stupor, clearly broken by the events of the day. He walked around the bed and stopped short in surprise. "Oh good, you're awake. Wow, I swore you were sleeping by...ah, never mind."

He approached with caution, very aware of the state I was in. "Cyra, I can't imagine where you came from and what happened to you, and I won't pretend to. I just want you to know that I'm here for whatever you need. And when you're ready, there is a surprise waiting for you down the hall, hopefully it will lift your spirits a little." He grabbed my hand and squeezed gently, and the kindness in his eyes eased a little of the pain that had me in a chokehold. He left me alone again, and I quickly fell asleep with my thoughts rooted a hundred million light years away.

AFTER A SHORT WHILE, I awoke to the darkness. Only the soft flickering of lights floating along the walls provided illumination, obviously powered by magic. It only served as a reminder of my bizarre abduction and that *magic was real*.

I didn't feel rested or rejuvenated but I wanted to roam the halls and see what Theo had left for me, and if I could find a weapon to hide in my room that would be a bonus. It was hard to hold trust for anyone or anything when you were lied to your whole life, then kidnapped to a world where I was supposedly an alien. I wasn't amused with this mind-fuck of a lifetime.

Frustration grew when I looked down at the state of my dress. My very human, lazy girl, comfort-wear which I'd been in for far too long and I didn't want to run into anyone looking like the hot mess express.

I rubbed my throat, realizing I was extremely dehydrated and greedily downed the glass of water that someone had left for me on my bedside tray while I slept. As soon as I put it down it filled back up again on its own. Okay, that was neat. I could get used to small conveniences such as that.

The food on the tray smelled heavenly, like freshly baked bread and roasted meat, but I was sickened by it at the same time. Still stuck in a state of fight or flight, I figured food would only be a bad idea, so instead I checked out the bathroom situation. I couldn't help but inwardly laugh at the toilet that looked like some kind of small throne with intricate sculptures of suns and gaudy designs around it. I rolled my eyes and did my business. When I stood to see how to flush, the contents simply disappeared. *Well, that was easy.* At least there were some perks to being kidnapped.

The bathtub was a major draw, massive and inviting with a recliner built in that you could lay on with a pillow rest. I leaned in to turn on the water, but there was no handle. After about ten minutes trying to figure it out, I cursed the ceiling at my inability to complete such a simple task. The sore loser in me had me fuming and kicking the side of the tub in retaliation–I really needed to stop doing that. Reluctantly admitting defeat, I returned to the bedroom to check the closets, but there were no clothes in them. However, I did find some nightdresses and undergarments in the armoire. I searched each one and took out the *least* sexy and revealing one. Who did they think I was dressing for? Some of these garments I would never wear in a million years. If you looked up modesty in the dictionary, you'd find my puzzled face in it clenching the neck of my collar since I was accustomed to jeans, t-shirts and sneakers. I undressed and took off my ratty old t-shirt bra and put on a long, white nightgown made of semi-sheer cloth with white lace appliqué. It had a low sweetheart neckline with illusion mesh above it to give the appearance of bare skin and was unlike anything I'd ever worn before – but it was a huge upgrade from Grandpa's t-shirt and ripped sweatpants. The change made me feel almost human again except... I supposed I hadn't ever been human to begin with. I sighed at the paradox of my life and started to pace the room, feeling restless and anxious, like a lion stuck in captivity.

Deciding against putting my Darth Vader slippers back on, I found the iota of courage I had and left my room to walk the halls barefoot and could hear the soft taps my feet made against the shining marble.

The castle corridors were dark, and the candle-like flames flickering every few feet didn't help much. The moving shadows had me on edge, thinking every little quiver of light was an unknown threat, ready to strike me down. I decided then and there that castles were fucking creepy, especially when the only sound in the halls were my breath and my footsteps. The mystery and danger of an unknown dying galaxy only added to my growing sense of unease.

I stopped when I reached a set of ornate double doors carved with different symbols. My birthmark was one of the etchings on the door with slight variations. What did this birthmark actually mean? Looking down at my wrist, I was astonished that it had changed and now matched the design on the door exactly. It was more vivid than it was before, and there was now a solar flare design around the circle, clearly resembling the sun. The small random orbs were now connected by lines that looked like a constellation, which also matched the design in the red jewel on the box grandpa Amrel left me. What did that mean? Was I the girl represented on the box? Did it have anything to do with this supposed destiny of mine?

I stepped into the expansive room with a cathedral-like ceiling and wondered if it had ever been used as a small ballroom. The stunning floor was adorned with intricate connecting designs that spanned the whole room and held a slight shimmer to the marble when it caught the dim light, so everything appeared to glow.

But I was floored when I saw what was on display in the center of the room. A beautiful, expensive-looking cello. That must be the surprise Theo had been talking about and I was beyond touched, but how did he know I had played the cello since I was a child? That it was such a big part of my life and I thought I would never get the chance to play again?

First, I walked the perimeter of the mostly empty room, and found what looked like a fountain pen on a writing desk. Score! It looked sharp enough to plunge into someone's jugular if used with enough force. I grabbed it to take back to my room since there was nothing else but the chair and cello in the room. It would have to do.

With eagerness, I quickly walked to the beautiful instrument and plucked the strings to see how they sounded and was astonished to hear that they were all perfectly in tune. I didn't know if someone sat here and tuned it or if they used magic, but it was ready to be used.

I knew exactly what I wanted to play, so I closed my eyes and began the last song I performed, one of grandpa's favorites, *Suite No. 4 in E – Flat Major: Prelude.* The song I played at his funeral.

As I performed, it felt like I was home again, and I was transported to the moments connected to this music. Grandpa's teary-eyed face as I played for him was my first memory.

I saw Brendon's face of shock when I made it through my first complicated song. He joked about not being surprised at choosing an instrument that would dwarf me in size. Sometimes he would sit and do homework or play games, listening to me play for hours with neither of us needing to speak, relishing the comfort of each other's company.

When I was a child and I showed an aptitude for music, my parents didn't balk at my choice of instrument. They bought it for me on the spot. Even at that young age, I thought it made the most beautiful sounds in the world. Warm, soothing, melancholy and transcendent. When they gave me the half-size instrument on my birthday with lessons for as long as I wanted them, I could barely contain the excitement for the potential of what I could make of it. Their look of pride at my progress along with my own love for the instrument kept me going. For my sixteenth birthday they gave me an expensive, full-sized cello and I was in love. There was no comparing the sound that came from my fingers and bow. My parents would be comforted to know that I had something from our lives together that I could cherish on this planet.

I came back to the moment, taking in the song that now meant so much to me. When I finished, I sat in silence for a while, appreciating this link to my past, but I slowly started to notice that I felt off, like my body was buzzing—not just my skin but every molecule inside me seemed to vibrate with strange anticipation. When I looked up in confusion I saw a dark figure in the large doorway, filling most of it. I leaned away in shock and my voice cracked as I demanded, "Who are you?"

The figure stalked closer until I could just barely see him. His footsteps were heavy, and I could swear I felt the marble shake under his bulk. The stupid creepy as fuck flickering castle lights didn't help shed enough illumination through the room so it only added to the fear. He stopped right before me and it took everything in me not to gasp. I attempted to swallow, but my throat was too dry so it felt like sandpaper rubbing me raw. My God, this person before me was...intense and insanely beautiful. He had similar coloring to Adelram but was a few shades darker, and he looked like he could kill me without hesitation. He was huge, even taller than Theo, with a full, chiseled physique. He wore what appeared to be a deep hunter green sleeveless leather vest with matching arm cuffs and his satiny onyx hair was trimmed short on the sides, but full on the top, so pieces of hair fell below his eyebrows. I must have been struck dumb with insanity because I had a strange urge to tempt death and touch a piece of his hair.

I came back to reality when I saw the veritable armory he was carrying on his person. There were two swords crossed behind his back and three daggers holstered at his waist, and I could tell there were more hidden judging by the bulging in his pants.

Don't look at his bulging pants.

Don't look at his bulging pants.

Fuck! I looked!

His gravelly, deep voice echoed in the vast darkness, giving me chills from head to toe. "Beautiful."

I lost the ability to use words from the fact that my brain was short circuiting. "W-what?"

"The music you were playing. I heard the sound from a distance and had to see what it was. I've never heard music in this castle before."

Of course he was talking about the music.

My eyes flew wide. "Never?" I had the vague memory of music and dancing buried in my mind – how could there never have been music played here?

He ignored my question entirely. "So, you're the Reina come home."

I didn't bother asking him who Reina was. It was dark in the room and yet it seemed like he was squinting, which was strange. My heart started racing out of control as he stepped closer and I tried and failed to keep my breath even. If this stranger kissed me right now, would I be able to refuse? *Why was I even thinking about him kissing me!*

A strange static sensation seemed to be pulling me towards him, but I didn't dare move even as the electric pulse grew the closer he got. I'd never felt a sensation like that before and I'd *certainly never* physically reacted this irrationally to a man. I dismissed it from my mind, reminding myself I was crazy and delirious from lack of food and restful sleep.

When he was a mere foot or two away from me, he folded his arms and said, "I'm Kaanan. It's unwise to be unattended with no training on how to defend yourself. Who knows what really hides in the darkest shadows of this castle in the dead of night? You'd certainly make the sweetest morsel of prey. Especially in that sheer nightdress." His eyes slowly moved over every inch of my body, and it was as if I could feel the impact of it on my skin, like a laser searing into my flesh. When his hooded eyes locked with mine I was sure they were penetrating through me, like he could see the darkest secrets hidden away. When his nostrils flared I realized with horror that I was drenched with desire. There was *no way* he could scent that... right? I shifted my legs nervously around either side of my cello, my sheer panties doing nothing to hide what was happening beneath the scant nightgown as I tried to unsuccessfully clench my thighs together. The open air teased me as the closeness of Kaanan made goosebumps rise on my skin. All this in response to his mere presence. He hadn't even come close to touching me.

I blushed profusely, finally thankful for the poor lighting, and blurted out the first thing that came into my head.

"Please leave." That was the only logical solution. If he was gone I would return to sanity.

Kaanan gave an almost imperceptible smirk and that was all it took for me to officially need another pair of panties. No wonder the armoire contained so much scandalous underwear. The men here were built for women to have spontaneous orgasms.

"Very well," he said in his bass voice. "Don't forget to lock your door when you're alone in your bedchambers."

To my horror, him mentioning my bed made me shudder and I bit my bottom lip imagining him in it – and that was before he turned to leave and I got a view of his unspeakable backside.

But something about him was familiar. I opened my mouth to call him back, to tell him to wait until I could figure it out, when it hit me. He was one of the other people I'd seen in my dreams on Earth. I didn't know what that meant or if it was a bad sign. My other strange dreams were of the Guardians, so it didn't bode well that he was lumped into that.

As soon as the sound of his footsteps faded away, I put my cello back on the stand, grabbed my pathetic excuse for a weapon and ran back to my room as fast as I could, locking my door behind me as I went.

CHAPTER SIX

*D*espite my bizarre encounter with the painfully gorgeous but mysterious stranger, I fell asleep immediately that night. I think the lack of self-care and the sheer draining emotional turmoil had finally caught up with me, and I didn't stir once all night. I only woke once I heard a knock at the door, making me shoot up in bed with drool all over the side of my face and pillow. My hair was half out of my hair tie, and, *damnit*, I think there was drool in there too. *Yes, here I am in all my glory, princess of the immortal magical people. Don't worry, everyone, I've come home to save you! And from what? I have no idea! Thank goodness you all have me!*

Hastily wiping away the drool, I got up, grabbed my death-pen for reassurance and opened the door, stopping short, thinking maybe I was still dreaming. It was Kaanan. And goddamnit if he didn't look even more stunning in the daylight. He put his fist to his mouth and cleared his throat as if he was trying not to laugh at the pitiful sight of me. It made me clench my pen tightly in annoyance, as if something so ridiculous could kill such a man.

Just fucking marvelous.

"Get dressed and meet me at the last classroom at the end of the hall on the second floor. You'll be getting your first training lesson." His eyes lingered on my painfully sheer nightgown before my eyes bulged and I crossed my arms. A small, devious smirk grew on his face before he turned and quickly walked away.

"Wait, what are you talking about? Training for what!" But he was already gone.

He was...training me? What about Theo? Sweet, docile Theo seemed like a safer bet.

I weighed my options. I could stay here, alone, getting nowhere or I could do what I was told and attend the lesson. It pissed me off to no end to blindly follow his order, but I needed more answers. It was imperative to understand why I was here. And it was possible that I was slightly curious.

Shit. I obviously needed to find some acceptable clothing, so I walked back into my bedroom to find a dress already waiting for me. Who the hell had put it there? I put it on quickly, and felt a small moment of triumph when I discovered it had pockets so I could take my super stealthy and powerful implement of death. At least it would provide some modicum of peace of mind.

I made the extensive trip down the castle steps from my wing, asking for help from some of the guards. The palace was a massive labyrinth that would take me forever to learn even though some of it felt familiar.

My nervousness grew the closer I got to this lesson, not knowing what to expect. Yesterday I was a human on Earth, spending time with my very normal human family. Now I was some prophesied immortal ruler going to training lessons? I still wasn't convinced this was really happening, but I continued my journey anyway.

As Kaanan mentioned, the various rooms were empty except the last one. I peered inside and my heart stopped beating for a moment. There were six children in the room attempting magic. I didn't know I was attending a class—with *children.* Here I was, twenty-one years old, and most of them looked between eleven to thirteen. Two students were between the ages of six or seven. I felt like an inadequate idiot and Kaanan was nowhere to be seen.

The teacher looked up at me and beamed. "Come in, Reina! You're most welcome! Children, please greet Reina Cyra." There's that Reina stuff again, but I was too self-conscious to ask her about it.

I received a mixed response of high-pitched greetings.

"Hello, everyone," I replied self-consciously, rubbing my arm. "I thought Kaanan would be teaching me one-on-one."

"Oh, Kane does usually teach this class, but I've filled in for him the past few lessons."

I was taken aback. Kane taught...children? I found it odd that the stoic and warrior-like being spent an extended period of time around tiny, innocent people. I guess it was a better thought than Adelram teaching children and giving them nightmares.

"Come to the front, Reina," the instructor said.

I walked to the front of the room with all the kids watching me, trying not to blush for the whole class to witness. On display were a bunch of bowls and containers atop a plain table. I stood by the teacher's side as instructed and tried to observe the contents. There were a few bowls that held water, fire and dirt. Next to them, electricity buzzed within a clear box, trying to escape, and the last two boxes were pitch black inside.

"As I was just explaining, this is an introductory class for new magic students, so first we need to figure out your magical strengths. You will each get a turn to focus on the objects in front of you to see if you connect with it. These are some of the most common magical gifts and it's likely your powers will stem from one of these elements or energies. In our galaxy almost everyone can wield at least one elemental power, but our abilities come from energy, so our gifts are as varied and numerous as the stars in the sky. Those with more power can have more control over various elements and energies, while those with less power might only be able to wield one element or hold small energetic abilities.

"We have two levels of magic – low and high vibrational magic. Everyone in Eredet has the ability to use small magics that require low vibrational energy, such as dimming or brightening lights, opening doors, household tasks and so much more." Lights flickered on and off in demonstration while the instructor wiggled her eyebrows, making the children respond with excited laughter.

"High vibrational magic is where we see our strengths come into play. I can only brighten that light so far until I lose a connection with it, but someone with fire or light magic could blind us all or engulf the room into flames. My magical strength is earth – so while I could

41

create an earthquake in this room, try as I might, I cannot burn it down. We hold intermittent group classes for all children to learn the daily workings of low vibrational magic and small targeted classes for high vibrational magic based on the children's power level." She motioned toward the table and we all closed in a little to get a better view.

"On the table before us we have the natural elements: fire, water, earth and air—air has no bowl since it's all around us. There's electricity, dark matter and dark energy. Dark matter and dark energy are not common gifts, in fact I only know one being who is thought to be able to wield them, but it's a dangerous gift, so it's a test requirement. I'll be testing your telepathic ability, and towards the end of the session we'll be doing private one-on-one testing required by the Guardians."

It greatly interested me to know what magical gifts the Guardians were searching for and I hoped I didn't have any of them. I didn't want anything else tying me to them.

"Magic is all around us in the energies our universe provides. We borrow that energy to wield our magic and it is released back to the universe in a delicate balance that protects our way of life. Why does life exist at all? Some would say, life only exists to supply a level of entropy. Our galaxy has an extraordinary amount of power, so we have it at our disposal to deplete not just with the plants, animals and beings that inhabit it, but with our magic as well. That's why our people have strengths in many different areas, it keeps our balance in check. In most circumstances, energy and power is depleted, then it must be returned in a give and take as we see in our symbiotic relationship of life and the cosmos. If we used too much energy, the system would collapse, and our planets would die."

Interesting. I wondered if that was what was happening in Eredet. Was this supposed curse draining the energy supply to the point of destruction? It was still hard to picture this planet dying from what I'd seen so far, which admittedly wasn't much.

"Now for the fun part, let's see where your strengths lie!" the teacher concluded.

A little boy raised his hand. "Who decides what power we should have?"

"That is a very good question, and it is not entirely known. Some say it is The High Creator who decides where our powers should lie. Others believe our galaxy protects itself, gifting powers to protect the balance, intrinsically knowing how to disperse magic. Some say it's simply hereditary."

She lined everyone up, and one by one they took a turn standing in front of each item on the table to connect with it.

"Usually our magical strengths are the initial powers to manifest and the first time you connect with it is when you begin to unlock your magical abilities. So we'll be able to easily determine your gifts versus simple low vibrational magic wielding. You'll also be able to feel the difference in energy, a deep connection to a particular element that feels as easy to manipulate as breathing."

She spoke to the first student in the line. "Now, look at the water and zone in on it. Try to see beyond it to the oxygen and hydrogen atoms within the water, and then attempt to venture even further to feel the protons and electrons that make up the atoms. If you can feel them, try to make them move, slowly increasing their speed. Moving the molecules within the water will increase its energy and you'll be able to bond with it and manipulate it to your will. Once you're in control of the movements of the water, the energy will increase, and you will be able to do anything with it. This is the same strategy you'll be using for every one of these items."

The first child focused on the water for quite a few minutes, but nothing happened.

"Okay, water is probably not your strength. You will most likely be able to create small ripples or movement as low vibrational energy one day once your true power is unlocked. Let's move on to fire, and the next student will step up to the water please."

Both children took their places focusing intensely on the object before them, and this time they both got a response. The fire started to grow brighter and larger, and the water started to slightly bubble.

"Excellent! These are probably your magical strengths, but you will try all of them to make sure there's nothing else that you can wield even easier. Many of you will have other abilities that will emerge over time."

The process continued all the way to the last child. Some had a bigger, more obvious effect than others, but every one of them was able to make at least some small interaction. Nobody was able to wield the dark energy or dark matter.

"Great job, students! Cyra, would you like to give it a try?"

I couldn't wait to try for myself. If I was going to be of any use as a 'chosen one' I would need to master any power I had, and the fact that I still felt like a human mortal made the thought that I would be able to use magic beyond exciting. I stepped up to the table and started with the water like all the children before me, and I tried to focus on it as hard as I could. I felt absolutely nothing. No connection, no mystical microscopic molecules—nothing.

"Let's try fire, Cyra. The Fenix line has always held fire as their strength," the instructor offered encouragingly.

Oh great, that must be it. I eagerly approached the bowl with flickering embers and focused on it like there was nothing else in the room. I wanted more than anything to find the power within me—to feel like I could be worthy of the confidence Grandpa had in me. I tried to envision what lay beneath the flames, to feel some kind of energy they emitted. After standing, unmoving, for what felt like ten long, painful minutes I began to panic. The teacher didn't interrupt me because this was *supposed* to be my strength and the small children were able to wield their power in a matter of a few short minutes.

Eventually the worried instructor led me to the next bowl of earth. I tried air, electricity, dark energy, dark matter, I even tried telepathy and empathy. I had *nothing*. I might have no magic in me and I had never felt so defeated in my life. It made me walk over to the flame bowl again and I attempted to will it to move where I commanded, but it still didn't respond to me. I was terrified Grandpa had made a mistake and I was not the one of the prophecy.

The instructor tried to look supportive, but I saw the doubt in her eyes and it damn near crushed me. I had felt like a failure since the moment Adelram had me in his grips and stole me away and there wasn't a damn thing I could do about any of it.

"You might need some kind of emotional reaction to get your first flame. We don't always know what triggers our magic, sometimes it's something I can't teach." I gave the instructor a small smile but her words were not at all comforting for someone who was supposed to be a powerful ruler.

Not a moment later, Kane sauntered in like a beaming, dark god and a tiny flame ignited on my index finger. Looking down in utter shock, I began freaking out that my finger was on fire while all the children laughed at my idiocy. Step right up, folks! Get your ticket to witness the savior of the century in all her sophisticated grace!

When I realized I didn't feel it at all, I calmed down. In fact it felt like a soothing warm bath that I wanted to relax into and explore. I played it cool and pretended like I didn't just make an ass of myself.

"Ah, looks like we found your emotional reaction." The teacher's presumptuous grin annoyed me and I couldn't stop the crinkling of my nose.

Kane walked past me in an intentional show with a smug smirk in all his infuriating grace and overflowing muscles. I rolled my eyes and closed my hands for the flame to die out.

"I'll be finishing your lesson," he said tauntingly with his rumbling voice.

The teacher replied, "Great, I'll finish the one-on-one tests with the students."

"Nice of you to finally show up," I said, glaring at him. "The teacher mentioned you usually teach these classes?"

"I often do, yes."

"Why?" I folded my arms with defiance, still sore about my lack-luster performance.

"Because I'm the most powerful being in the galaxy after Orphlam, they think I'm best suited to teach it."

Shivers overtook me at the thought, not expecting his answer, but also not surprised. I could feel his power like a constant hum tickling my skin. What made him so powerful? And if he had all this power, why was he working for Solians? There was a lot about him that was suspicious.

"Now, try again," he commanded.

I fumbled a little, suddenly unsure what to do with my hands or arms, trying to concentrate, but I didn't get far before Kane said, "You'll need to try harder and learn faster than that."

"I am trying. I'm doing everything I can!" This was my first attempt, what the hell did he expect from me?

"If you want any hope of protecting yourself, you'll do it now." He slowly approached me with a menacing gait, his eyes darkening to a deep (and beautiful) hunter green. He looked absolutely deadly as he grabbed my arms and a shock so strong ran through me that flames erupted from my hands in response, and he quickly stepped back.

"Interesting," Kane mumbled, tilting his head in surprise.

"What?"

"Your flame hit me."

"Sorry... you're the one who told me to try then practically attacked me."

"No." He shook his head. "I had a shield up and you penetrated it. That's usually...impossible."

I wasn't sure how to answer so I moved on. "Why does my flame look different from the other students who had fire strength? They seemed to summon the fire to them and held it in their hand, but mine seems to come out of me and my fingers *are* the flame."

"I'm curious about that myself. I don't know why. Your gifts could be something we've never seen before and it takes some individuals years to reveal all their magical talents. None of us know what powers we'll have until they start manifesting, even though there are some families that have abilities passed through the line— like the Fenix family and fire. Adelram could wield lightning as a child, but his mental powers didn't manifest until much later. Powers of the mind are very rare and not a gift that can be predicted."

I wasn't exactly comforted to know that Adelram was even more powerful than I thought.

"Is there something wrong with me that it's so much harder for me to connect to my power than the children? It doesn't come easily to me at all." My insecurity got the better of me and I had rubbed my arm so much recently it was beginning to chafe.

"It's not something you can always learn in a classroom. We hold these classes to help control power and give guidance, but each person's journey will be unique and we can't always advise what will work for everyone. You'll get there eventually, and if you have powers we've never seen before it might take even longer. Maybe fire isn't your strength," Kane shrugged.

"But you and the instructor said the Fenix family always had fire strength." I wouldn't admit to him that I didn't *want* to be different. It was bad enough that I thought I was human for sixteen years then lost my sense of identity.

"There might be something we're missing." He said it so nonchalantly that I let myself relax a bit at my deficiency.

"What is the instructor privately testing the students on? What are the Guardians looking to find?"

"They keep track of special powers, like healing, initiating growth, reviving dead plants and beings, and turning inanimate objects into live ones. But the very rare children that do show any of those abilities are never seen again. If I find any, I tell them to hide their power and keep it secret from everyone—forever."

"Why are those powers so special to them?"

"I imagine it's the same reason they want Amrel so desperately. He had similar abilities, and whatever they have planned, those powers seem useful to them."

The sting in my heart continued to grow the more I heard about my grandpa and how little I actually knew him. We were inseparable and I thought we confided everything to each other, and the betrayal I felt was like a poison festering through my fragile psyche.

Kane pointed to a table with various knives and daggers. "Go pick something."

My inner child seemed to be taking a front row seat on a permanent basis and I pouted as I made my way to the table full of worn down weapons that looked more like props than tools of death. I was already plotting what I might be able to steal away so I had something more substantial than a pen in my pocket.

Initially I grabbed the throwing knives in excitement, but I figured I should err on the safe side before my inexperienced self attempted to chuck weapons in a room with children. So I chose an ugly rusty dagger.

"These weapons look a little worse for wear."

"Unfortunately there's not much left in terms of weapons here on Solis." Kane's lip curled in disgust. "Most of the advanced and fine weaponry was destroyed." He saw I was going to ask more questions but cut me off, history not the lesson he was interested in. "Do you know how to use that thing?" His eyebrow was raised in doubt and it was amazing how one tiny movement could make me feel so incapable.

One of my favorite quotes from the series *Game of Thrones* popped into my head. *"Stick them with the pointy end,"* Arya so eloquently put. But knowing he wouldn't understand the reference, I lifted my arm in a pretend thrusting motion and said, "Stabby, stabby."

Kane rolled his eyes, unamused. "Okay then. Come stabby, stabby me." I stood there awkwardly holding the knife completely at a loss with what to do with my body.

"Well? Let's get this over with," Kane scoffed with boredom.

I looked around in confusion and felt the need to whisper. "What if I accidentally cut you?"

He let out a boisterous laugh and it sent chills of–something– throughout my body. "You won't come close to touching me. That's cute though."

Cute? Anger started bubbling within me at his quick dismissal. What the hell did he know? I had a fire within me to fight and protect myself, I could absolutely do some damage. Rage was still freely flowing within me for the fact that I was taken from my home and those I loved, and I was still processing the death of my grandfather and my Solian parents, however hazy the memory.

I used that fury to run at him with my knife raised, and with no effort at all he knocked it out of my hands, lifted and pinned me to the ground in a movement so fast I didn't know what happened until he was on top of me. I wriggled and thrashed, and he only tightened his hold on me until I couldn't breathe. When attempting to summon my fire, nothing happened. I tried with everything I could muster not to cry at my inability to do anything useful. The fight within me was *so strong,* but my outside could not match my determination.

"My provocation is intentional and I'm glad you see now that you need more training. It's clear you have the desire to learn and that is the most important first step." His voice was a deep, soothing song and it annoyed me that it lessened my resentment toward him. Kane was still on top of me, only inches from my face and the green in his eyes was multifaceted and entrancing. I had to look away to regain my ability to breathe. When he stood and reached his hand toward me to help me up, I ignored it and stood up on my own and brushed myself off. I could handle that much, thank you.

He proceeded to instruct me on techniques I didn't even know were relevant to using a dagger. He demonstrated how to change the position of my grip on the knife from outward to chambered positions lithely and without ever taking my hand off the knife or needing to change hands. He showed me some defensive stances and how to block someone coming toward me with a dagger and disarm them while hurting them in the process, so I could either use my own knife or escape. And lastly, I learned some knife attacks that would use the least amount of effort and what to anticipate from my opponent. We must have trained for a few hours, and between the self-defense and magic training, it seemed like I'd have a long road ahead of me if I wanted to master any of it. It was somewhat discouraging, but I was determined to prove myself useful if this was all actually real.

"You know, one day you might be able to turn your weapon into a flaming dagger, or you could melt away your opponent's weapon if your fire was strong enough to get that hot. You have a lot more training to complete, but it's a good first start. Let's try your fire one more time before we break for today. See if you can expand it further than just your fingertips."

I reached inside myself and attempted to focus on the fire in the bowl in the room. Again, I felt nothing.

"You're not trying hard enough," Kane said simply, making light of my efforts.

"Yes, I am. I'm *trying*."

"No, you're not." He raised his voice, and I couldn't help but hear Adelram. *You're an utter disappointment.* "You're a Fenix and you're a ruler of Solis. Fire should be shooting out of you accidentally multiple times a day. You must be suppressing it."

"You don't know me. Don't tell me what I'm doing. I *am* trying!"

"Then why don't I see any evidence of it?" Kane walked toward me with the muscles flexing in his arms as they swayed and he stopped when he was inches from my face. His voice was gravelly, a song of power and dominance. "Prove it. Because I don't believe for a second that you're trying your hardest."

Anger boiled inside me. I tried to blow him up with fire, with no result. He grabbed both of my arms and shook me.

"Fight, Cyra!"

The static tingling from his touch was unbearable, and my hands became engulfed in flames, and I was pretty sure my eyes were emitting some kind of fire or light as well.

"That's more like it," Kane purred, mere inches from my face and not letting me go. He inched down slightly closer and my whole body was electric from his presence. My hands *were* fire, and they grew in flames as his green eyes glowed with some sort of emotion I couldn't exactly ascertain. His breath intertwined with mine and I inhaled him into me, the scent of pine soothing my senses.

My body thrummed and came alive with energy with him so close, and I could swear that I could feel the pulse of his power floating over my skin in a sweet caress as if it wanted to lend itself to me. It was overwhelming, so much so that a force rushed through me and flame haphazardly burst and singed most of my dress until I was nearly naked. An embarrassing squeal escaped my lips.

"My clothes!" A tiny thump interrupted my tirade to find my pen on the ground since my pocket was disintegrated.

"Why are you carrying a pen around?" His voice was even keeled, but the small upturn of his lips gave him away.

"In case I have any important and urgent correspondence. You can never be too prepared."

"I see." Kane's eyes flashed with wicked amusement. "I'll make you a deal. If you can slice me once or block one of my attacks I'll restore your clothing."

I growled and ran at him at full force, but I ended up on his shoulder, flailing and screaming at him to put me down.

"I think that concludes our lesson for the day. I'll walk you back to your room."

Luckily, we were near the weapons table, so when he bent down to pick up my pen I snatched a small switch blade and shoved it between my cleavage since my pockets were obviously useless. There was just enough clothing that it was hidden from view.

He handed me the pen with a knowing look on his face. "Don't forget your pen. It's actually most likely sharper than most of the knives on that table." I took it from him, and my world stopped for a moment when our fingers touched and I felt a surge of adrenaline. At least that was what I was calling it. My betraying body would probably call it something else that I refused to acknowledge. I broke our contact quickly to regain my sanity and he started to leave.

"Are you seriously going to make me walk through the castle like this?"

"Oh, without a doubt. You have to earn your rewards with me." Mischief twinkled in his eyes that looked down at me with smugness.

Gah! He was just as fucking wicked as Adelram. As if he could read my thoughts, he chuckled to himself and I tried to pretend I couldn't feel his eyes over my skin as we made the grueling trek back to my room. As we walked, onlookers kept a wide girth, assuming they didn't want to get too close to the powerful man next to me.

"Don't expect me to take it this easy on you for long."

"That was you taking it easy on me?"

"Until next time." Kane turned and stalked out of sight and my jaw stayed wide open long after he was gone. What the hell had just happened? Why did that man drive me mentally and physically crazy? I'd known him all of one day yet it felt like a lot more. I tossed off my flats and let the soft, extravagant rugs tickle my feet while I retrieved my switchblade from its hiding spot. Kane had given me the pen back, knowing what I carried it for, yet I still wanted to keep the switchblade secret. My ability to trust was quite possibly irrevocably damaged and these small items gave me some semblance of comfort.

Grandpa's beautiful box would be the perfect spot for these until I needed them, so I went to my bedroom and dug it out from under my mattress. I looked into the depths of the red jewel that seemed to be endless, and couldn't help but wonder what Grandpa would think of all this. He was a firm believer in peace, kindness and empathy. What would he say about me learning to fight? His kind but fierce gaze entered my mind and I pictured how sorry he'd look if I had the opportunity to give him shit about never telling me about this curse, this prophecy and an entire other galaxy I was apparently born to. It was a profound feeling of loss that I would never get to see that apology in his blazing golden eyes. And the reason I craved it so intensely is because I wanted to forgive him, more than anything. And it was hard to do so without it.

I stored the items in the box and quickly hid it as a knock at the door mercifully put an end to the spiral of depression I was about to fall into. When I opened the door I was dumbstruck by one of the most beautiful women I'd ever seen. She smiled and said in a soothing magical voice, "Good morning, Reina. My name is Meili and I'm your *criada*. I'm here to help you get ready for the rest of the day, may I come in?"

Great, this goddess before me made me feel even more pathetic for not having showered in who knows how long, not to mention the state I was in after my first *easy training*. Whereas her long, full and wavy, golden blonde hair actually emitted a soft glow just like her flawless ivory skin. She had enchanting cerulean eyes and a cherub face. She was simply stunning.

"Oh dear," she frowned in response at the state of my singed scraps of clothing.

I realized I had my mouth open gaping at her, so I quickly shook off my stupor. "Yes, of course, please come in. But my name is Cyra, not Reina, and what is a *criada*?"

Meili giggled, brightness exuding from her. "Forgive me, Reina, I forgot that you've grown up elsewhere and will need some guidance. I am here for whatever you might need so please never hesitate to ask me anything. Reina translates to...I believe on Earth you call it... Queen? Ruler? Any castle worker or citizen of Eredet will call you Reina in respect as your status demands. Just like we all call Theo Karalis, or Kara for short. Kara Theo and Reina Cyra. I think it has a nice ring to it. *Criada* translates to...not servant, but one who helps a Reina. Oh, handmaiden? I'm sorry, Reina, I'm not well versed in Earth affairs like the Karalis is. It is not required education so only those who are interested know about Earth culture. When I realized I'd be serving you I started reading up on it."

"No, that answers everything perfectly, thank you, Meili. And...I'm sorry for my appearance, I wasn't able to figure out how the bath worked so I know I'm a mess."

"Please, never apologize to me, Reina, there is no need. I am here to serve you. And if you check in the cabinets now, you'll find some garments there."

I walked to the cabinet dubiously since I just checked it mere hours ago, but just as Meili suggested, there were a few gowns hanging on the rack. "Wow, how did these get here?"

"I sent them on ahead knowing you would need something to wear today. Kara Theo has asked for you to join *Sun Eine* this morning so I will make sure you look your very best for your first public appearance."

"What's *Sun Eine*?" I started to rub my arm with my hand—my nervous tick returning.

"I think on Earth you would call it breakfast, but it's a big deal here. We celebrate the return of the sun with feast and friends. The castle hosts it daily for any nobility who wishes to attend and the working class celebrate in their homes, often times with a group. It's not mandatory, but most of the nobility try not to miss it."

My nerves were definitely getting the best of me now. I didn't know what to expect at this event or how I would be expected to behave. The concept of starting your day with a communal celebration was interesting to me, but I wasn't sure I was ready for this. It had been a whirlwind of insanity and I still hadn't accepted this supposed fate of mine, but I didn't have much option but to play along for now.

Meili started walking away from the bedroom and I ran to catch up with her since I felt like a fish out of water. I already knew Meili was going to be invaluable. She held her hand toward the faucet of the bathtub and water came flowing out.

"How did you do that?" Yep. I knew she'd hold all the secrets to Solis. Little did I expect the bath faucet would be such a stumper.

"I used my magic, Reina. You'll find most things in the castle are run by magic, not actual controls."

"I noticed that there doesn't seem to be electricity." I pointed to the perimeter of the walls where the balls of light appeared at night.

"Our world revolves around energy so we have no need for it. At least until recently. The lights come on automatically at night, but we can make them brighter or dim them as needed with our power. Everyone can do it since it's a low vibrational magic."

"Can I try?"

"Of course! We have a pipe system where the water is ready to be released, you just need to open the stopper to let it in. Just reach inside yourself and feel your power and expel its energy. Visualize opening the stopper in your mind and you should be able to do it." She stopped the water from running so I could try it myself.

"How do you visualize something you can't see?"

"When your energy interacts with that of the water, you'll be able to feel it. Use the water to push the stopper or feel the metal and tug on it."

I tried to do as she said, but yet again, nothing happened and it took everything in me not to scream in frustration.

"Oh great, I'm screwed. I don't want to have to call you every time I want to take a bath or turn off the lights."

Meili gave her sweet giggle again. "Don't worry, Reina, we'll figure it out. We have all grown up with magic so we knew what to expect when it manifested. It's no surprise you might struggle for some time. I will be just outside here and will turn it off when it's done."

"Thank you."

"It is my true pleasure, Reina."

Sinking into the hot bath water felt *divine*. I breathed in deeply, melting into the relaxing scent of lavender which I'm sure was Meili's doing as well. I hadn't felt this good, or this relaxed in quite a while. Fully submerged myself into the water, I soaked my hair and started the process of erasing the dirt and despair of the past few days. With the quiet calm, I couldn't stop the violent flashes of my parents' death, and even though it happened sixteen years ago it felt like it happened yesterday. I wiped the solo tear off my cheek and wished I could talk to my adoptive parents just one more time. Tell them I loved them and was grateful for the amazing life they gave me and that I forgave them for not telling me about this insane destiny I still wasn't convinced of.

After I finished washing and soaking up the quiet, I asked Meili where the towels were. One immediately appeared in front of me, hanging midair. I almost laughed at the foreign sight, but I took the towel, dried myself and wrapped it around my torso. I joined Meili in the main room where she already had a gown and undergarments prepared for me. Gown might even be the wrong word since it looked more like a piece of art on a hanger. "Wow, this is a really fancy breakfast."

"It's for all day, Reina. This is your first appearance for your people, and you should look the part. I think Kara Theo has some plans for today, so you won't have a chance to change."

"Well, it's beautiful, where did you get these dresses? Is it the fashion in Solis?"

Meili hesitated a quick beat. "I made them, Reina. I sewed them myself without magic, but if they're not to your liking we can find you other styles or other designers."

"You *made* this incredible gown?" I gaped. It really was phenomenal, made of pearl-gray tulle overlay that deepened to a slate gray in the back with a bodice that was adorned with white flower and leaf appliques. Meili helped me put it on and I looked down at myself in disbelief. My favorite part was the tulle off-the-shoulder straps and I shimmied a bit to watch the sparkling lights shine from small crystals in every flower. It was absolutely stunning, fit for a princess. Or Reina.

"Designing and making beautiful garments is my passion. I truly love doing it, and if you'll allow me, I will keep creating your wardrobe, Reina."

"I'd hate for you to go through so much trouble for me, Meili. It seems like an incredible amount of work, especially if you're not using magic, but if you love doing it then I will *of course* wear whatever you make. This is the most beautiful dress I've ever seen."

Meili looked relieved and blushed prettily when I gave a small twirl. "Thank you, my Reina. I could never receive any higher compliment."

As I looked down at the intricate finery my smile disappeared. My mother would have fawned over seeing me in such a dress. She always tried to get me to wear something other than jeans and leggings, and now that I was–she wasn't here. The aching in my chest was overwhelming and my eyes stung from the increasing burn. I continued talking to avoid breaking out in tears.

"Is there a reason you make this by hand? Do all dressmakers?"

"I do it because I enjoy it. I could easily make them with magic, but to me it doesn't have the same intricate quality like it does when I've done it by hand. The dressmakers in Solis use magic whenever they can, but since our energy supply is dying, more and more tasks are being done by hand."

Meili took out a chair and motioned for me to sit. She dried my hair instantly and created an intricate braid in the front of my head that trailed down to one side and behind my ear. I imagined it looked like a braided coronet since I couldn't see it, then Meili created a few ringlets in the rest of my hair that trickled down.

She brought me some silver sparkly heels that matched the dress and I nearly choked at the audacity. "Oh, Meili, I've never worn heels this high before... I don't think I could manage it without falling over myself. I'm not the most graceful person in the world."

Her answering smile was infectious. "Please just try them and see for yourself."

I couldn't disappoint her. You don't say no to someone that sugary sweet. I put my feet in each shoe and was immediately dumbfounded. It felt like I was wearing sneakers and I looked up at Meili with bulging eyes.

"I've mastered the art of the truly comfortable heel."

"Meili, you'd be a gazillionaire on Earth."

She lit up with excitement, standing on the tip of her toes for a moment. "Thank you, Reina. Oh! I do apologize, I see you have no mirror here, you can't see the final result!" She waved her hand again and a large full-length mirror appeared against the wall.

"Wow, that's impressive. How are you able to do that?"

"I'm able to conjure items from other places or even create objects on a smaller scale." She held out her hand toward the mirror and said, "Please."

I was about to comment on the fact that it seemed like she had a tremendous amount of power for a *criada*, but when I caught my reflection, I screamed.

"Oh my God! I look different! My hair is a different color, and my eyes! My eyes have changed color!" What the hell was going on? I barely knew who I was anymore and now I physically looked like a different person too? I was really going to lose it in a convoluted identity crisis.

Meili initially looked horrified that I didn't like her creation, then relieved when she realized I wasn't talking about her clothing. "It was likely the change into your immortal body when you came home."

I recalled the surging energy and power I'd felt when I landed on Solis. Had I looked different this whole time and just been oblivious to it? My skin had a faint glow and my hair was now a deep purplish red, a color you'd never see on Earth unless it was from a box with a name like *berry* or *deep burgundy*. And my eyes were truly bizarre. Blue-gray toward the edges with flecks of gold and amber running through them, and russet-colored specs toward my pupil, all encased in a dark gray circle. The gold flecks made it seem like my eyes slightly glowed, or at least reflected light. I was floored by the foreign beauty that looked like nebula emissions and it reminded me of grandpa so much that I had a sudden urge to cry.

It would take me a while to process the change in my physical appearance, but I could appreciate Meili's work. I had never looked so good in my life. I was always the nerd-friend in hoodies, ratty jeans and sneakers with her hair in a messy bun. Looking at my reflection now, I actually *felt* like I could be a leader of a galaxy of people.

"You have a real gift, Meili." I smiled through my doubts and confusion. "Thank you."

"Your elegance reminds me of your mother," Meili said.

My wide eyes met hers in the mirror. "You knew my parents?"

"Oh, yes. Your mother saved me from a fate worse than death. She brought me here to be her *criada* not because she needed one, but to keep me safe. There's no way I could ever repay what your mother did for me, but I will try by continuing to help her daughter. I deeply mourned her death, and I still do to this day. I will always be grateful, so now I am in your debt, Reina."

My mouth opened to ask a million questions, but a knock at the door interrupted us. Meili rushed to open it, and the last person I wanted to see in the entire galaxy walked through the door.

He gave an elaborate, exaggerated bow and said, "My great and powerful liege." When he stood up straight, he gaped at me. "Well, who knew you could look like more than a homeless beggar off the street." He bent closer and loudly sniffed the air. "And you don't smell like ten-day-old garbage anymore either. Maybe there's a molecule of hope for us after all. I've been sent here to man-handle you should you refuse to come out of your room, but it looks like I'll be denied the pleasure."

"Don't you have to be a *man* to be able to do that?"

Adelram slapped his hand against his thigh and yelped. "Ha! And the little jokester princess keeps on showing up for practice. Shall we go, or do I get to throw you over my shoulder and drag you there after all?"

Ugh. I rolled my eyes at him and turned to Meili. "Thank you for everything, we'll talk later, okay?"

Meili had dropped all signs of her friendly, bubbly personality and didn't say a word or meet my eyes. She kept her head bent to the ground, curtsied and left the room. Reluctantly, I accepted my fate.

"Just give me a second," I moaned, running as quickly as I could to the bedroom. Since this dress didn't have pockets, the switchblade would have to go back into the bosom. I wasn't going anywhere with Adelram without being prepared and I had to do everything I could not to use it on him when I saw him tapping his foot with impatience, waiting for me.

CHAPTER SEVEN

*W*e took a right out of my room at the intersection of halls and down the disgustingly long staircase. I was ready to lodge a complaint with management that there was no shortcut to get to the bottom of the castle. Elevators, people. It's so simple that mere humans had even invented and executed it.

When I was about to collapse from fatigue, we reached the ground floor and found others heading in the same direction as us. The passersby looked at me with curiosity and I imagined these people knew everyone who frequented the castle. I was an outsider in a dying world, there probably weren't a lot of newcomers. The grand ballroom we entered was overflowing with the upper echelon of Solis. I couldn't believe how many Solians were in the castle just for breakfast. On Earth I was never able to get out of my bed in the morning to give a damn about breakfast, much less make an effort with my appearance.

The largest banquet table was straight ahead and right in the center of it sat Theo, beaming a joyous, dimpled smile directly at me. It relaxed me a little and I couldn't help smiling back. He promptly stood and walked toward us while Adelram thankfully rushed off, grumbling under his breath.

Theo took both of my hands with an abundance of enthusiasm

shining in his eyes. "You look absolutely stunning, Cyra! I'm so glad you came. You're really going to impress our people."

It hadn't really been my intention to impress anybody, I just wanted to survive the day. I tried to brush off my self-doubt by straightening my back with an air of confidence as Theo took my arm around his. Fake it 'till you make it had always seemed like a valid strategy and I was willing to play along until I knew the real reason I was here.

The ballroom hushed into silence and my heart started to beat in my throat so that I couldn't swallow. I had never suffered from anxiety before, but with hundreds of pairs of eyes on me, I could only hope that it wasn't obvious that every part of my body was shaking. He led me down the aisle that held numerous tables on either side and most of the women there were whispering to their friends with their lips curled, or metaphorical lasers beaming from their eyes aimed right at me, no doubt because Theo was an insanely handsome prince and they were all hoping to claim the spot by his side that I now occupied. I had no interest in playing their games. I didn't ask for this, it just happened to me, and this was my home now. For better or worse.

Letting the sea of envious women surrounding me fade into a blurry background, my nerves faltered when I felt a familiar humming energy rising within me. I looked toward my left and noticed Kane sitting at the very table I was headed to. He was turned around in his seat, watching me intently. His green eyes were unblinking, locked right onto mine as if there was nobody else in the room and it sent a shiver down my spine, twirling into that static tingling force. It was *impossible,* but it felt like it was pulling me toward him and it was an effort to remain walking straight ahead. I forced myself to pull away from his gaze and focus on where I was going.

When we made it to the table, Theo stopped and turned us around to face the ballroom. I couldn't tell if it was the social anxiety overcoming me from all these people watching and judging me, or the frantic pulsing energy coming from my back where Kane was sitting, but my whole body continued to tremble. Theo noticed and put his hand gently over mine. His tender but understated action calmed me a little, knowing he was there for me.

The loud authority and confidence of Theo's voice made me flinch a little when he began speaking. "Good morning, Solians! Thank you all for making it to *Sun Eine* this morning. As you all know, we gather together to celebrate the return of our sun and our power. The return of our precious source of life. But this particular morning we are celebrating the return of another light in our lives. Today the light shines even brighter than it has for the past thirty years."

Thirty years? I had only been gone for sixteen years.

Shocked faces and whispers erupted from the ballroom, and in that moment, I wished I had the power of invisibility so I wouldn't be the center of attention. I gazed off to the side and noticed Kane's face had softened and a foreign, soothing energy molded into me that eased some of my nerves.

Theo continued, "Friends! It is my great honor to introduce to you, Reina Cyra Fenix back in her rightful home!"

The room exploded with voices, questions, and general disarray. Solians began approaching the front to greet me and I inwardly panicked. I didn't expect *quite* this much attention. "If you'd like to welcome the Reina back home, please do so one at a time. Enjoy your feast!" Those who were approaching listened to Theo and went back to their seats.

Every banquet table in the ballroom instantly filled with an abundance of food and everyone sat, the room echoing with chatter and utensils clanking on plates. I was glad that most of the attention had moved away from me, but I still had plenty of curious onlookers.

Theo led me around the table to our seats. "I want to introduce you to my right-hand man and best friend – Ovishkar, this is Reina Cyra. Cyra, this is Vish."

Vish took my hand and bowed. "It's an absolute pleasure to meet you, Reina, I've heard a great deal about you. If I can ever be of service, please don't hesitate to ask."

"Thank you, Vish. Please just call me Cyra. I'm not comfortable with all this 'Reina' stuff."

Vish looked at Theo for approval and he gave a small nod. "Well then, Cyra, I'm at your service."

Theo motioned toward four other men I hadn't met yet. "These are the Masters of Solis." He gestured to the furthest man away from us first. "That is Elric, Master of Fishing & Agriculture."

"Welcome home, Reina." His voice was gentle and his welcoming smile reached his brown monolid eyes.

"Next to him is Hugh, Master of Commerce & Trade."

"Reina." Hugh's nose rose to the air a bit and I could tell he wasn't happy about my return. Theo took no notice and continued his introductions.

"Next we have Jacob, Master of Magical Utility."

"Good morning, Reina. I'm so glad you're back! Likely, you've noticed how all our utilities and facilities are run by magic. My team and I make sure everything runs smoothly, including this feast you see before you! Anything that is a regular recurring task for Solis, especially the castle, me and my team are in charge of. I'm able to program tasks through siphons that hold energy."

"How interesting. I'm so used to everything running on electricity on Earth."

"Ah, yes that would be one way to do it. But our system is easier, more consistent and reliable. So if you have any concerns on how utilities are performing, I'm your man."

"And lastly, we have Serin, Master of Public Health. He's the most talented healer I've ever met," Theo said, pointing to the man right across from me.

I was instantly drawn to him and his kind, light brown eyes. His aura was soothing and his movements were smooth and gentile. He stood and extended his ebony hand to shake mine and he had a lovely golden shimmer to his skin that glistened when he moved.

"It's wonderful to have you back home, Cyra." I also loved how he didn't call me Reina. "I delivered you, you know. You were my favorite patient as a little girl and wanted to know all the tricks to my trade. You spent a good amount of time in my infirmary trying to help people."

"Pleased to meet you, Serin. I'm afraid I don't remember that, but it sounds like something I'd do."

"And in more happy news, now that you've returned we can finally see the royal wedding we've all been waiting for!"

I choked on my juice and slowly turned to Theo who forced a laugh, rubbing the back of his head.

"What is he talking about, Theo?"

"Oh, dear. Me and my big mouth, I do apologize." If it weren't for my utter shock I would have laughed at Serin's sudden awkwardness at letting the cat out of the bag.

"We are betrothed. It was both our parents' wish that we marry and rule Solis together. I promise I will explain more later." He brought my hand to his lips and kissed me.

Would the mind-fuck of shocking information ever stop? I felt an all-consuming anger that made me shake and burn, but it was originating from somewhere off to my right. Kane was staring at me again and I wondered why he was so far away, separate from the Masters and Theo. I broke eye contact and the anger instantly disappeared. Was he using some kind of magic on me?

"Serin, fill us in on the triage situation. Hopefully it's good news," Theo commanded as if he hadn't dropped a bomb of information.

"I'm afraid not, Karalis. Another has succumbed. He's in the village infirmary." Serin spoke softly like he didn't want to be overheard.

"Damnit," Theo muttered with his fingers rubbing the bridge of his nose. "Any closer to finding a cure?"

"No, Karalis. The only thing that helps is what you've been providing."

Theo nodded. "Very well. I'll stop by later to supply more."

"You cannot keep giving up so much, you'll soon start to suffer," Serin said, his eyebrows pulled together with concern.

"You worry about the sick." Theo looked at me to explain. "There has been something making Solians sick for a few years and it's starting to get worse."

"It's very unusual for individuals in Eredet to get illnesses, especially at the rate of what we've been seeing," Vish offered, concern etched on his face.

"I'll bring you to the site so you can see what's happening," Theo said quietly.

I would hold him to that. I wanted to witness everything first hand so I could try to figure out my role in this prophecy. And when a lull in conversation hit I used that opportunity to address my concerns with Theo. "This is all very strange to me. Do you know about this prophecy? Some small memories are coming back to me about Solis, but I have serious doubts that I have some kind of destiny that will help save the galaxy."

Theo swallowed the bite of eggs he was eating and leaned in close to me. "I know all about it, why do you think our parents arranged our marriage? I have not one shred of doubt that you can do this—that we will, together." He winked at me with a one sided grin and I recalled Adelram's words. *The girl with the divine mark shall deliver balance back to the Eredet galaxy with a king blessed by the sun.* It was true that whenever I saw this stunning man the sun seemed to provide a warm glow just for him, as it was now. I looked over my shoulder at the massive bay windows letting in the sunshine and Theo seemed to absorb it all. There was some small comfort in knowing that my parents also knew of this prophecy and had a hand in trying to see it come to fruition.

"Does everyone know about it, or just a select few?"

"The prophecy was spoken by the High Oracle, Siare, many years ago and spread by word of mouth, so while it is widely known, many think it a mere story. But the royal families have kept this information close, passing it down through the generations to prepare ourselves for the day it was needed. Our families knew it would be our generation that would face the threat of destruction of our galaxy and they prepared for it."

"If this was foreseen so long ago why wasn't anyone able to stop the curse from happening?"

Theo looked prepared for my question and gave a sad smile. "It is one thing to know the ending of a story, but another thing entirely to live through the trauma of it. All our best laid plans to avoid an outcome more often than not feeds right into its fruition."

As someone who grew up on a mortal planet whose greatest concern was the rising price of video games all of this was beyond me. I continued to eat in silence, absorbing his words and wondering if I really would be able to make any difference in this world, until Vish spoke for everyone to hear.

"I used to be Master of Defense, before many other Master's Boards were disbanded."

"That seems like a crucial role that should still be upheld," I responded with confusion.

Elric knowingly nodded, his brows raised. "The Guardians disbanded many Boards that they declared were no longer necessary. We once had a Master of the Divine, Master of Education, Master of Governance and Law Enforcement and Master of Technology and Sciences just to name a few. There was a time you could look at the sky and see numerous spaceships flying to all reaches of the cosmos. But things are simpler now."

Hugh shook his head, his disappointment showing on his face. "We also once had large, thriving cities and elite schools that were the envy of the galaxy. We have devolved greatly."

"Why hasn't anyone challenged the Guardians?" I didn't understand why anyone hadn't simply detained them if they were the cause of Eeredet's suffering.

Jacob gave an incredulous laugh but spoke softly. "There is nothing that we haven't tried. The Guardians are all-powerful for a reason. They're invincible."

Well, that's one of the things I would need to focus on then. Everyone had a weakness—a vulnerability. And if I was stuck here, I would make sure we found theirs. I surprised myself when I realized I was slowly becoming more invested in this world and their plight.

I turned to Theo. "You mentioned earlier that I'd been gone for thirty years? I was only on Earth for sixteen years."

"Earth moves at a different rate than Solis, so I'm not surprised. You will probably be in time-shock for a while. Our days are longer, but our year is shorter. You'll get the hang of it eventually when your body adjusts."

Bloody likely I'd get used to it.

Theo leaned in so only I could hear him. "I'm so glad you're feeling lighter this morning, I could feel your turmoil from everywhere I went in the castle last night."

"W…what do you mean?" He *felt* me?

"I'm an empath. One of my gifts, anyway. I can feel others' emotions, and for a while there I wasn't feeling much of anything from you except some bouts of terror and sadness. When I came into your room, I thought you were asleep because there was an empty stillness in the room. I can usually feel at least a small hum of emotional energy."

That spiked my creep-o-meter and my self-consciousness grew. I'd always been a very private person, the idea of someone reading me when I didn't want to be open made me uneasy.

"Oh, sorry, now the discomfort is back. I try to turn it off when I can. It's not easy to do, but I do make an effort not to impede on others' privacy. Most people don't know I'm an empath, so, if you don't mind, would you mind keeping that between us?" Theo endearingly wrinkled his nose which made me relax a little. I wondered if he had the ability to mess with people's emotions as well. That was something I couldn't tolerate.

"Don't worry, I can't alter your emotions in any way. Even if I could, I would never do such a thing to you."

"And do you read minds too?" He laughed and I was struck dumb at the wonderful sound and the way his turquoise eyes shined with pleasure. Even in my emotional turmoil he could affect me in a way I was not at all used to.

"No, I'm just more in-tune with people's thoughts and reactions because I can sense their emotions."

"Why do you keep it a secret?" I was curious since Theo seemed like an open book.

"It gives me an edge over others, if people don't know I can feel their emotions they won't try to keep them in check. I get a lot more information that way."

"Then why would you tell me your secret? You don't even know me."

Theo tilted his head slightly like he was surprised by my question and gently touched my chin. "I trust you." It was a small confession, but I found that I was pleased that he wanted to confide in me.

"There's something I wanted to ask you." Theo became serious, which made my stomach drop and I braced for impact. "Were you kept as a servant on Earth?"

"A what?" My forehead wrinkled in utter confusion.

"Your attire when you arrived...were you kept as a servant? Were you mistreated?"

My hand clapped over my mouth and I laughed at his grave concern. "No, I was treated very well. I perhaps made a poor decision in clothing not knowing I'd be seen by others."

Theo's shoulders lowered in relief and he continued eating. That was immensely adorable and embarrassing at the same time and I tried to will away the heat in my cheeks.

I turned back to Vish and spoke, so people could hear us again. "How long have you known Theo?"

"Hmm, that's a good question, I guess I haven't thought about that before. Maybe...fifteen hundred years?" he threw out with a nonchalant shrug.

Theo saw my look of disbelief and laughed. "Humans on Earth take time very seriously. They measure everything in their lives down to the ticking second. I'm just fascinated by hearing your experience which is so varied from mine. It makes me think about things differently which is refreshing."

He put his hand on mine and I felt that strange prickling force from before twice as strongly. I looked up and did a double take when I found Kane intensely glaring at me. I quickly looked away, ignored him and squeezed Theo's hand.

"We met when we were both young and I liked him so much I went into service for the crown. Theo made me his right hand. As you heard before, I started off as Master of Defense, but now I oversee his affairs when he can't and help wherever I am needed." Vish's eyes creased from his grin and I tried not to stare. Vish had boyish good looks under a warrior façade, but I had no doubt he could manage the affairs of this golden planet and I liked him as much as I liked Theo even just from our brief conversation. I could tell why they had been such great friends for so long.

From the corner of my eye I noticed someone approaching the table and I braced myself. I wasn't sure why I was still anxious, but everything put me on edge. In anticipation, Theo respectfully put his utensils down and wiped his mouth on his napkin. He was so graceful and attentive. He was *born* for this and he did it so well. He couldn't have been more at ease during his speech in front of hundreds of Solis's elite.

"Karalis," the man said and bowed to Theo before turning to me. "Reina. I'm honored to be the first here to welcome you back home. I don't know if you remember me, but I used to be great friends with your father, Rhythen. My name is Halmar."

"I'm sorry, I don't remember you, but my memories are a little fuzzy. Thank you for your kind welcome."

Halmar looked a little disconcerted, but said, "Well, come by anytime. My *vordne* would love it."

He sauntered away and I looked to Theo. "I feel terrible I don't remember him. Was he really great friends with my father?"

Vish laughed and said, "You're going to get a lot of that."

"What?" I asked.

"High society looking to get higher. Don't worry, Cyra. I don't think that man ever had a conversation with your father," Theo assured me.

"What's a *vordne?*"

"It's a partner, or spouse," Vish offered.

There was so much I still had to learn about this world, but as breakfast came to a close, I was already mentally exhausted. Theo delicately laid down his napkin and I caught a glimpse of a thin, golden cuff on his wrist that matched the one I'd seen on Adelram. Through the braided design, I could see a faint swirling light peeking through and when I looked through the crowd I noticed that everyone was wearing one of the glowing bracelets. The only person whose wrist was bare was Kaanan.

"Cyra, after *Sun Eine* you must visit the Guardians' temple so you can meet with them. I wanted to tell you now so you can prepare. Adelram and Kane will escort you safely there. Unfortunately, I have a personal matter that I must attend to on Solis East, but say the word and I will cancel it."

My heart sank. I never wanted to see those creatures again, but I supposed it was unavoidable. It was time to face the source of my fears. Theo looked hopeful that I would ask him to stay with me and cancel his meeting, but I said, "No, that's okay. I'll go with Adelram."

"Okay. Just be careful around the Guardians. Say as little as possible and you should be okay."

I know he was trying to make me feel better, but it only increased my fear. I supposed I would have to hold onto my verbal diarrhea even though something deep within me wanted to test the boundaries and see how bad these Guardians actually were.

Vish stood when Theo did, pulling my chair out for me. I followed them and held my hands together to stop them from fidgeting as the static grew stronger the closer I got to Kane. I jerked my head up as we approached, not even realizing it had slumped down as I walked. I may be inexperienced and an outsider, but I didn't need to look like I felt it. *Fake it 'till you make it.*

Kane rose from his chair to display his full glory and I had to look up to meet his eyes. "*Reina.*" Was that sarcasm hidden in his deep, melodic voice? He reached out his shadow gray hand and I stood there hesitantly. I wanted nothing more than to touch it, which is what gave me pause. When I did finally put my hand in his, a force jolted them together and when we touched, we both flinched at the sharp electricity. Kane's brows furrowed and his jaw pulsed in a grating motion like I'd shocked him deliberately and Adelram looked back and forth between us with a raised brow. Ugh, this was going to be an *excellent* few hours.

Theo looked confused, but brushed it off. "Cyra, I will meet you as soon as I'm able. Be careful." His hand gently caressed my face and I closed my eyes as his thumb rubbed my cheek. I could hear Kane sighing impatiently behind me.

"See you later, Cyra. Good luck." Vish followed Theo out of the ballroom, both embodying confidence and congeniality, chatting idly to people as they left.

Much to my dismay, Adelram had a huge, fake smile plastered on his face. He rotated his hand in a circular motion and gave a full body bow until his head almost hit his knees. "My *Reeeina.* Shall we depart, oh great and powerful liege?"

"You're repulsive." I turned and walked toward the exit with every eye in the room glued to me. I didn't need to look back to make sure Adelram and Kane followed, knowing from the incessant tingling that traced over my skin that they were behind me. Was that a normal part of being immortal and having magic? Was everyone else simply used to it?

Coming to a stop outside of the banquet hall, I waited for them to react. "*Well?* Aren't one of you going to drive us there?" I asked after they both stood silently staring at me.

"As usual, our esteemed Reina has the astute observational skill of a doorknob. You cannot drive outside the castle, you must *exit* it first," Adelram spat.

"You know, Adelram, I might have been born here, but you eradicated my memories and then I spent my entire life somewhere else, believing I was someone else. I've been nothing but a pawn in someone else's agenda my whole existence, so you can quit talking to me like I'm an idiot."

Adelram threw his hands up in the air dramatically and my gaze zeroed in on the bracelet flashing on his wrist.

Nobody had ever tested my patience so much, and if he continued to rattle me, I would have to hurt him. This motivated me more than *anything* to learn some magical skill. Since I couldn't look at Adelram anymore I turned to Kane. "Why did everyone in the ballroom have one of those bracelets?" I pointed towards Adelram's wrist.

It felt like I'd asked something forbidden by the uncomfortable look on Adelram's face and the air between the three of us seemed to chill by several degrees as we resumed walking toward the castle doors. I touched the cool, fiery orange carnelian stone pillars as we passed them and marveled at the clean white and gold decor as we walked.

"They're given to us by the Guardians. They supply a power boost to whomever is wearing them and increases their energy stores. They're considered a staple and a true mark of a Solian noble," Kane explained. His tone made it sound like he thought the whole notion was ridiculous.

"The Solian nobles live and die by those bracelets. They would never be caught dead without one on, and if you don't have one you don't exist to them," Adelram offered. "Their power would be severely reduced without them and heaven forbid they allow that to happen."

"Well, I'm glad to see you're finally trying to fit in with the cool kids," I rebutted.

Adelram hissed at me. "I am forced to wear this garbage so the Guardians can keep me on their leash. Do you think I relish being chained like a dog in a land I detest?"

Kane saw me looking down at his empty wrists and anticipated my question, but he allowed me to ask it anyway. "And why don't you have one?"

"I do have one, but I don't need or want it," he said simply.

"Why do they force Adelram to wear it and not you? Why do you both work for the Guardians?" I asked in a hushed volume. Warning bells went off in my head and I didn't know who I was supposed to trust. I knew the Guardians were dangerous and it made me suspicious of Adelram and Kane.

"They made us an offer we couldn't refuse. Literally," Adelram spat, indicating he was done talking.

We reached the mammoth front castle doors that were carved with knights and radiant suns and the guards opened them for us to exit, halting the questions I had building up about the bracelets and why Adelram and Kane were even offered them if they weren't Solian. The incredibly large sun was shining so brightly outside that Adelram and Kane were squinting in pain, but it didn't really bother me. In fact, it seemed to tickle my skin with healing energy as if it were an old friend giving a warm hug.

Adelram turned to Kane, shooting me a glare. "She's your problem. I've had enough of the Earthling this week, I'll meet you there." He disappeared without waiting for a response.

I've never hated anyone before, but Adelram was becoming a close contender. Kane turned to me and sighed. "Come here. It works better if you're right against me, the further you are the more resistance there is for someone hitching a ride." Kane grabbed my hand and it shocked both of us once again.

"What the hell is that?" I asked, rubbing my hand.

Kane shrugged. "Probably some of your pent-up energies from lack of use. You'll have to learn to stop doing that."

"I'm not doing anything!"

He sighed like I was a nuisance and avoided my hands, jerking my back to him quickly. He smelled ridiculously good and I tried to breathe shallowly to avoid basking in the scent of evergreen trees. The charged buzzing over my entire body was becoming a familiar thing, but as we drew closer it faded to a pleasant background hum and I melted into his solid chest. He looked down at me with those piercing emerald eyes and my brows furrowed in confusion. I wondered if he was feeling the same sensation, or if he was causing it. I couldn't help but be suspicious.

Saying nothing, I simply took in his beautiful, slate gray face. A few strands of his onyx hair fell loose right below his brow and I had the unwelcome desire to move it from his face. For a moment I thought Kane was going to lower his head further to mine, but he quickly straightened and a second later it felt like my body was being sucked into a small crack through a wall with a great deal of pressure —and then it was gone. The sensation only lasted a few seconds, and then we were in an entirely new place I'd never seen before.

Like everything else I'd seen so far on Solis, the temple ahead was stunning. The stone was a pearly white that glittered when it caught the light of the sun and each tip of the structure was capped with what looked like solid gold. A kaleidoscope of flowers and trees made this place seem serene despite Theo's warning and my own nightmares. Behind the temple was the impressive backdrop of the turquoise Solian seas. We walked toward Adelram who was already at the steps leading up to the temple entrance.

"It's about damn time. Let's go. The sooner we get this over with the sooner we can get the *grof* out of here and I can finally get a stinking drink," Adelram whined.

Finally? I didn't freaking bother bringing up the fact that it was early afternoon. "What's a *grof*?" I asked instead.

"You don't want to know." Somehow, I believed him.

We ascended the stairs and lining the walkway were guards with gold masks covering the entirety of their faces with small spikes which hopefully represented sun rays and not instruments of death. Each mask held a different emotional expression and, just like the trimmings of the temple, they looked like they were pure gold. As we approached them, they turned their heads to look at us. Once we passed them, they faced forward again and didn't pay us any more attention. They were *extremely* unnerving, and I desperately wanted to run before we'd even seen the guardians. Perhaps I didn't want to test the boundaries of their evil after all.

The last guard directly before the entrance wore a mask which was contorted in an angry expression. I didn't know if the laughing mask of one of the other guards or the angry mask before us was scarier. *Why* was I taken from my safe haven of Earth for this shit?

"We've been expecting you. Only Cyra is to enter. The Guardians do not like waiting, so make haste," the angry faced guard relayed in a disconcerting, unnatural voice.

Okay, I resented Adelram and was wary of Kane, but they were absolutely preferable than going in there alone. My fake fortitude rapidly crumbled and my heart began beating out of my chest. Kane walked up to me and touched my back, which set every inch of my body quivering and alert. "We'll be right here."

I nodded like I had my shit together and walked inside. The door immediately slammed behind me and I was still visibly shaking from head to toe as I struggled to breathe. Unlike the castle, the interior of the temple was dark with gray walls and black marble floors. A pair of grand black double doors opened on their own, inviting me into the unknown.

My eyes fluttered shut and I thought of grandpa Amrel and his unwavering bravery. He was abundantly kind, but never one to shy from injustice. If he were here he would stand his ground and fight for those who needed it, no matter the danger to himself. He proved that fact by accepting his own death to protect me because of his belief. He must have seen something within me that was able to handle this and help people here who needed it. Even though I was still angry at him, he was the person I had trusted most in my life and if he believed in me with that degree of conviction, I could attempt to muster the courage I needed.

"Enter, Cyra Fenix!" an unknown voice bellowed from beyond the open doors. I straightened myself up, and marched through the doors to see the five beings of my nightmares sitting in an open, round room. There was clear glass from floor to ceiling so you could see the ocean and Eluroom castle. In fact, as I walked toward the Guardians, I noticed that they had a direct view right to the citadel.

My stomach flipped and I was overcome with nausea when I caught sight of a grotesque painting that spanned the entire length of the back wall depicting a bloody war with too many dead and mangled bodies among the battlefields.

The room was completely empty besides the Guardians themselves which I imagined was an intimidation tactic. They sat in a 'V' formation with the leader at the apex and the four Guardians behind him had their hoods on, so you couldn't see anything underneath. The

Guardian in the front wore a large, ornate gold mask that had half a disc representing a sun that came to two downward points. In front of the disc connected to the forehead were seven long, pointed spikes that looked like daggers. I couldn't make out his eyes through the hideous eye slits, only two glowing red-orange lights which made my skin crawl at the unnaturalness of it. His hood sat behind the mask, so you couldn't see the side of his face or his neck. He was truly terrifying to behold, and I was stuck standing before him—alone. I crossed my arms to feel the small comfort of the hidden switchblade that I knew would have absolutely no effect on these beings, both from the feeling of power they exuded and the Masters' mention of their invincibility.

"I saw you admiring our little piece of art." I was about to spew a response telling him it was a vile piece of garbage, but I held my tongue, remembering Theo's advice. "It's a depiction of the Great War, just a little reminder to all what happens when there's no order and chaos rules."

His voice grated against my soul like nails on a chalkboard. "We are the Guardians of Eredet, and I am Orphlam. We keep the order of the galaxy in check and protect our power. Being able to harness our magic, we graciously gift our people with an abundance of that power and energy. In exchange for our gifts, we expect our people to keep the peace. It is all we ask of you now."

Without showing any movement whatsoever, Orphlam floated a gold bracelet in my direction. I took it, but deliberately did not put it on, not trusting anything coming from his hands.

"We have some questions."

He paused as an uncomfortable silence enveloped us. Something about this…person, seemed wrong – and it was separate from the fact that he hid his face behind a horrendous mask. I hadn't recognized much magic since I arrived other than Kane, but I felt an overpowering strange energy vibrating off him in pulsating waves. I held my stomach, trying to relax myself to avoid vomiting. His presence made me physically ill and I started to sweat trying to hold myself together.

"What were you doing on Earth for thirty years?"

"…I…I was just living with my adoptive parents. I went to school and lived a normal life," I mumbled out, unable to control my nerves.

"How did you get to Earth?"

Shit. Shit, shit, shit. *Why* didn't Adelram go through more details with me? The story he pitched me was absolute *crap* which, really, was no great surprise.

"I don't remember. I thought I was born there."

"That sounds like someone meddled with your memories. Did Adelram do this?"

I couldn't stand Adelram, but I didn't want him to suffer any punishment this Guardian might deliver. "I don't know."

"Where are Amrel and Xenos?" Orphlam asked coolly, eerily tilting his head to the side. His easy mention of their names was like a sucker punch to my gut, but I had never tried so hard in my life to keep my cool despite my crippling anxiety.

I somewhat understood his interest in Amrel, but why the fuck was he asking about my golden retriever, Xenos? "I don't know who they are." I was always a bad liar and I hoped I didn't screw this up.

Orphlam inched forward in his seat and his movements were otherworldly. They reminded me of Earth horror films where a ghost moved in a chopped, non-fluid manner, and I thought I might actually pee myself in fear. He jerked his head to the side again which made him look even more gruesome behind the mask.

"We have great interest in finding Amrel. If you had any information on his location, you would be handsomely rewarded with as much power as you desire. Or...if we find you are hiding Amrel's location, we can give you something for that as well."

Orphlam awkwardly flicked his hand, and out of nowhere Brendon and my parents appeared in the center of the room. They looked around in confusion until they saw me.

"Cyra!" Brendon cried with a smile on his face.

"Oh honey, we've missed you!" My parents beamed in my direction.

My eyes bulged and I nearly jumped out of my skin in excitement and relief. "Mom! Dad! Brendon!" I yelled in pure joy. My God, I had missed them *so much* and the pain of it exploded seeing their faces. I smiled and began running to them, but I was stopped when two of the Guardians behind Orphlam disappeared and reappeared before Brendon and my parents. They punched their fists right into their chests with ease and ripped out their hearts, and time ceased to exist.

A scream reverberated throughout the room and it took a moment to register that it was me, feeling a gut-wrenching anguish only matched by the memories of my Solian parents' death. But this was worse, because the love and memories for these people were fresh and strong as steel.

I fell to my knees and kept screaming as I grabbed for Brendon, his blood seeping into my dress as the pool around my family grew. Their mouths were locked in shock, mimicking my own. I laid in the growing pool of blood in complete and utter horror. Orphlam stood and slowly stalked toward me and it looked as if he was disappearing and reappearing like a hologram...but I knew he wasn't. He was all too real. Some force picked me up off the ground as I continued to fall apart and lifted me directly in front of his mask and glowing, putrid red eyes. Blood dripped down the eye slits and he emitted a foul odor that I could only compare to death. I had never felt so repulsed in my life.

"This is just an infinitesimal taste of what I could do to you should you think it wise to hide anything from me."

My cries didn't subside as I looked down again at the blood still spreading on the ground, my innocent family in a state of gore.

The door was knocked down with a boom of splintered wood and Kane stepped through the billowing dust of the wreckage like a powerful deity. I couldn't fathom the strength required given how reinforced it was. I was violently dropped to the ground with nothing softening the blow of the hard marble. My face was glued to the floor, unable to get up as shock rendered my limbs useless. I felt a tingling energy approach until Kane and Adelram were by my side.

"What happened?" Adelram asked with disdain, but no sarcasm.

"You may take her and go," Orphlam offered casually. "Oh, and Adelram, don't forget what we discussed at our last meeting."

Kane picked me up off the ground and rushed me out of the room. When we were outside, I felt that squeezing pressure again until we were on a beach filled with trees.

"He killed them. He killed them," I panicked, clenching my sticky, blood-soaked hands.

"Whatever he showed you, it wasn't real," Kane said. I looked around and Adelram wasn't with us, Kane and I were alone on the beach.

"That's impossible. Everything was *very* real. I could smell the metallic odor of blood everywhere. Look!" I threw out my hands to provide the evidence, but they were clean. How was that possible?

"Orphlam has the power to sense your fears. You can guard against that if you hone your powers."

It had looked *so real.* The sounds of cracking bone, the smell and feel of sticky blood...

What kind of monster would put you through that just to make a point? My blind fear of the Guardians turned out to be valid. And I'd thought I disliked Adelram? I guess I had been lucky enough in my life to have never experienced what true hatred was.

"Where are we?" I asked as I looked away and out at the ocean, wiping away my remaining tears.

"We're at the rear of the castle. This is your private beach, it's the closest entrance to your bedchambers with a secluded entrance in and out of the castle."

I was grateful to Kane for bringing me close to my room since he couldn't drive me in. But for now, I sat on the sand and looked up at the trees and rocked back and forth, unable to calm down. I gripped the blazing hot sands and let it burn away some of my fear as it sifted through my fingers.

A sudden gust of wind bristled through the trees making them sway and I closed my eyes to take in the tranquil sound. When I opened them, Kane was watching me with concern.

"Did you do that?" I looked around me in wonder, still watching the trees sway with appreciation.

"One of my powers is wind. I thought it might soothe you."

"How did you know? It's one of my favorite sounds." For a moment we were silent as we simply listened to the breeze and I calmed myself down. "Thank you, it does help. Can you do it again?"

Kane sat beside me and the tingling energy in my body grew at his proximity. He gave me a small, friendly smile that made my heart skip more wildly than I wanted to admit, but the unmistakable pity in his eyes fueled my anger again. I hated that Orphlam was able to reduce me to a whimpering mess with such ease.

"He's a monster. There's no way he's protecting anything but his own interests," I spat with venom.

Kane nodded, exhaling loudly. "Pretty accurate description. Adelram and I don't work for them out of the goodness of our hearts, but because we have to." My interest was instantly piqued, wanting to know more behind Kane and Adelram's agenda.

"What kind of things do they make you do?"

Kane shifted and my heart broke at little further at the pain pouring from his eyes as his brows pinched together. "They captured me many years ago and did...unspeakable things. I was their prisoner for many years until my father made a deal with them for my release. As you can imagine, his mind powers are extremely helpful in making people forget things that would cause an outrage. And I do various tasks, like being forced to beat people for scare tactics and teach classes to find and abduct special children. Orphlam's starting to become suspicious that I haven't found anyone out of the ordinary, but I'll be damned if I give up an innocent child to that filth. Luckily my only priority now is to keep you safe, which is aligned with what Amrel wanted from me and Adelram."

And Orphlam's horror show continued. "They make you beat people?"

"It's another tactic of theirs. Solians and the Varjun people have a bunch of bad blood through history, so using me as a Solian's punishment is a huge 'fuck you' to them and as a result I'm hated around here even more."

It was as if he was being punished for being strong and powerful and his quiet acceptance made me despair for his predicament. I cleared my throat. "So, you mentioned you were the most powerful person after Orphlam. What other powers do you have?"

His eyes shot down and he turned his head for a moment, looking away. I was surprised that he seemed uncomfortable with my question.

"I have the ability to wield dark energy."

My eyes widened in shock. "The teacher from this morning said there was only one person who could wield it. She was referring to you? What is dark energy, exactly?"

"Dark energy makes up the majority of the universe. Think of all the 'empty space' in the cosmos. Most of that is comprised of dark energy. It's a negative pressure that pushes objects away from each other. Energy is gained from that pressure since it takes work to expand the space between those objects. I'm able to wield that energy on a smaller scale to perhaps rip an enemy in half."

"Fuck, remind me not to get on your bad side."

"That would be wise." He playfully bumped my shoulder with his and I had to mentally berate the treacherous butterflies that bloomed in my gut. After all, I apparently had a fiancé who I was fated to be with to save a galaxy. There was no room for anything else, but I could still cling to the comfort Kane brought me.

"I wouldn't mind if you used that power to rip Orphlam in half."

"He's too powerful. He can block my attacks and there's too much at stake to try to attack him and fail." I could sense that there was a lot more behind that statement, but I didn't want to make him feel worse than he already looked.

We sat silently for a few more minutes as I soaked up the gift of Kane's breeze and listened to the leaves dance in the wind until I felt okay enough to head back inside.

Kane walked me back to my room and Theo was already waiting outside of it, looking frazzled. My first emotion was anger that he didn't prepare me more for the Guardians' meeting, but when I saw how freaked out he was I calmed a little.

"Adelram reported that your meeting was a...'shit show.' Are you well?" Theo approached and caressed my face.

An almost inaudible growl escaped Kane, and Theo turned to him with his lip curled. "You're dismissed. Thank you for bringing Cyra back safely."

Kane took a menacing step toward Theo and I could tell it took him everything he had to stay still and not back away at Kane's intensity. "She's safe, no thanks to you."

Theo bunched his hands into fists and straightened with venom in his eyes. "I don't need to explain my actions. As I said, you're dismissed." It was strange that I felt oddly protective of the way Theo was speaking to Kane, but I had no right to feel that way so I said nothing. Nothing made sense to me anymore.

Kane huffed and gave a small, dark laugh, shaking his head. He looked at me once more before storming away and I opened the door to my room while Theo followed me in.

"I'm so sorry about your meeting."

"A little more warning would have been nice. They are *vile*. Did you know what they would be questioning me about? I wasn't prepared."

"No. I only knew that they wanted to give you your bracelet and question you about your time on Earth. I didn't think they would go that far. I can't believe they feigned killing your family." At his mention of the bracelet I took it out of my pocket and threw it onto a table.

"And what about us being engaged?"

"Oh, Cyra, please forgive me. I meant to speak to you about that when the time was right, I just haven't had the chance yet. I had a whole grand scheme to show you our world and our places within it, and I was going to start with your lands in Solis West. If you come with me, I'll explain everything." He reached out his hand, and his face was so hopeful that my anger melted away as I took his hand.

"Fine. But not today, I'm too drained. Tomorrow?"

Theo's clear aquamarine eyes beamed with pure delight, and it could charm the pants off just about anybody. And I did mean that in the literal sense.

"Then let's go see the world, my Reina. Tomorrow."

CHAPTER EIGHT

*E*ager to get more training in after the horrifying meeting with the Guardians, I awoke early. I got myself ready and made my way to the second-floor classrooms hoping to find Kane. I needed to get a better handle on my power and I really wanted him to teach me how to drive, so I could escape the Guardians if I ever needed to. It was clear a pen or a switchblade in the bosom wasn't going to cut it, although it wasn't going to stop me from stealing another weapon when I got the chance. I wouldn't be happy until I was surrounded by an armory protecting me at night.

As I approached the classroom we used before, I heard voices already occupying it, so I slowed down to listen. The buzzing sensation was already strong and I could place Kane's seductive timbre anywhere, but I was shocked when I heard the voice of a small child. I peeked around the door and saw a little boy around five or six years old sitting on Kane's lap on the floor. The boy appeared to be crying and Kane was holding him close in an embrace, comforting him. My heart skipped a beat at the sight. Watching this tender scene of a warrior god-like being gently reassuring a crying child was not something I was prepared for. But it made me ache to keep watching, transfixed at the beauty of it. Ugh! Why couldn't I control myself on this damned planet.

"I know you're there," the addictive voice purred. "You might as well come in."

I turned the corner of the door frame and waltzed in like I'd only just arrived.

"Oh hi, good morning—it's you." *Smooth. I'm so smooth.*

"Who's this? I thought we'd be training alone today," I said pointing to the boy.

The boy let out a huge gasp and said, "Cyra! I've missed you!"

He leapt from Kane's lap and ran at lightning speed to wrap his arms around my legs. He was so fast I didn't get a good look at him.

"You know Oliver?" Kane asked suspiciously. "How is that possible?"

"I don't know who he is," I said, dumbfounded.

"Cyra! Don't be silly, it's me! I see you all the time!" The boy grinned and looked up at me with his eyes still red from his tears.

I studied him and—no, it couldn't be. Could it? It appeared that in Eredet galaxy anything was possible.

"Bart? Is that—you?" I asked with disbelief.

"Yay, you didn't forget me!"

"Who's Bart?" Kane demanded.

"Bart was a boy I saw frequently on Earth at my parents' arcade. Only he wasn't this young. He was about ten years old. Bart, how did you get from Earth to Solis? And why do you look younger than you did on Earth?" I asked cautiously.

"Bart is my pretend name because I like The Simpsons pinball machine. And you wouldn't have let me play alone with no parents if I looked like this, would you?"

This was unreal, and it finally explained why he was always on his own in the arcade. "… No. I wouldn't have."

"You can call me Oliver now. And my two best friends are finally together! Can you both be my parents now?" he asked innocently.

"Woah, woah, wait. Where *are* your parents?" I asked.

"He's an orphan," Kane offered. "He has some special powers, so I tutor him alone and frequently. But it appears he has some *extraordinary*—and secret powers." Kane looked down at him uncertainly with one eyebrow raised.

"I surprised everybody! Can I be like an Earth superhero, Cyra?"

"Sure, you can. But superheroes always tell the truth and do what's right and they get extensive training so that they can use their powers for good. We need to make sure you can control your powers correctly. So, no more secrets?" I asked Oliver.

"Okay, fine. I promise."

It was bizarre reasoning with a small child when I used to jokingly toss Bart around like a younger menacing brother.

"Ba—Oliver, how old *are* you really?"

"I'm five and a half!" Everything he said was with excitement and enthusiasm.

"How did you find me on Earth? How did you know about me?"

"I had a dream about you! Mr. Amrel told me you were my distant cousin and we'd be good friends. I made another version of myself to visit you on Earth. It was easy! I can see what's happening in both places. Bart disappears when I don't need him." Oliver went rigidly still with a vacant expression on his face.

"Oliver?" I asked, waving my hand in front of his face. "What happened, is he okay?" I looked at Kane.

"I don't know. Oliver, what are you doing?"

"Don't have a cow, man!" a voice said from the other side of the classroom.

Kane and I both jumped at the sudden appearance. There stood Oliver—or Bart—the version I'd known from Earth. Both versions were in the same room.

"I still go to Earth to play video games. Brendon gave me free game credits since he knew you used to do it for me. He and your parents are sad all the time, I listened when they told him about why you were gone and he was shocked. It's not the same without you. Brendon just quit so he gave me his permanent access card," Bart said.

"Brendon quit ARCADE-ON?" I whispered.

"Yeah, and your friends post flyers around town. They said you would never disappear, and they won't stop looking for you. It makes Brendon even sadder since he knows you're not coming back."

I sat down at the closest chair unable to hold my own weight anymore.

"I had no idea." I didn't think about the other implications of my disappearance. The fact that he couldn't tell our friends and he had to watch them search for a ghost. That he would have to look at my parents' devastated faces every day. How his place of comfort and escape from his complicated life was now his greatest torment. A reminder of a life he lost.

"Do you know what Brendon's doing now? Where he's working?" I asked Bart.

"No, I don't see him anymore."

I put my hands over my eyes and felt four arms hold me. When I removed my hands I saw Bart and Oliver hugging me. A genuine smile formed on my lips as I hugged them back until Bart disappeared.

"Sorry you're sad, Cyra. I was sad too this morning, that's why I wanted to see Kane."

"You seem very young to have so much power, Oliver. I thought most people don't come into power until puberty."

"Oliver is extra special, so that just means we need extra training," Kane said.

"Then let's get started," I said, putting my hands to my hips. "Can either of you teach me to drive?"

Kane laughed at me. "You have to crawl before you can fly."

"Cyra is extra special too. She can do it. I can feel it," Oliver said.

"I'm taking lessons from him for now on," I said to Kane. "Can you tell me how, Oliver?"

"You have to have visited the place before and picture it in your mind. You have to close your eyes and squeeze yourself to the space between and force yourself there."

Oliver demonstrated for me by closing his eyes and clenching his fists. "Now you try it." Oliver walked to the other side of the room, then looked frozen and blank again for a few moments and Bart appeared beside him.

"Cyra—help!" Bart said, putting his hand to his neck.

Kane started walking to him, but was blocked by an invisible barrier. He started banging against it with no yield. It appeared that Bart couldn't breathe, and Oliver stood there waiting for my action. Bart fell to the ground still unable to breathe so I walked forward, but hit the invisible wall as well. I started to panic as my sweet little brother-like boy started to turn blue. I heard a voice that made its way inside my head.

"Just squeeze yourself into the hidden space between us and come get Bart or he will die," Oliver said without moving his lips.

I knew Bart wasn't exactly real, but I was panicked nonetheless. I did exactly as he instructed. Closed my eyes, clenched my fists and I tried like hell to feel that pressure I usually did when I was hitching a ride, until I actually started to feel it closing around me, propelling me forward. When I opened my eyes the pressure lifted, and I expected to still be stuck behind the invisible wall, but I had actually done it. I was right before the two children so I knelt before Bart trying to save him, but before I could touch him, he disappeared. What the *hell* just happened?

Kane appeared before me and said, "You still want him to train you? Oliver, how did you block me from moving?"

"I don't know *how*, I just knew Cyra needed help. If you came for me yourself, it wouldn't have worked so I made sure you couldn't."

Kane and I looked at each other in slight fear. I didn't know much about this world's power and abilities, but I *knew* that his far surpassed most adults, if not *all* the adults I'd seen. It was somewhat terrifying that a five-year-old could wield that amount of abnormal power.

"You don't have to be afraid of me, Cyra," he said with an endearing smile that melted my heart. "I will never hurt you and I like to be happy, not mad. And you have much, much more power than I do, you just haven't found it yet," Oliver said pointing to my heart with his tiny finger.

Again, Kane and I looked at each other awkwardly. I hadn't seen Kane look uncertain before, and the sight unsettled me. This whole short, bizarre morning blew my mind. Just when I thought I was starting to figure things out, ten more doors of confusion opened before me.

We only spent another fifteen minutes trying to practice my fire magic with no real result when Theo and Ovishkar walked in. Neither of them even acknowledged Kane. In turn, Kane ignored them and pretended he didn't even see them. It appeared Oliver was more of an adult than all of us combined.

"Good luck with the rest of your lesson, Oliver."

"Bye, Cyra! I'll be seeing you again." I got the sense that he knew that for a fact and his uncanny power made a shiver crawl up my spine. Kane gave me one last lingering glance before he took Oliver's hand and headed to the far side of the room.

Theo took my arm and led me out of the classroom and we walked the halls of the castle toward the exit so he could show me more of Solis, as promised. My mind was whirling with how much my life had changed in such a short time. A child who could duplicate himself on multiple planets? I shook my head in quiet disbelief. It was another crush to my ego that he was able to do so many incredible things while I struggled to light my finger on fire.

When we exited the castle, a clear rectangular vessel with two luxurious seats was waiting for us. Theo rubbed my hand to bring me out of my internal thoughts. "This will give us the best view since you can see from every angle of the ship." We both took a seat and when he touched a spot on the base of the chair, a clear tablet emerged. Theo input some information and we started moving.

The first thing we did was float up and circle the castle so I could witness every splendid detail.

"This has been your family's home for as far back as we can remember, probably since the origins of Solis. I've always loved coming here as a boy because it was so opulent and grand." He wasn't wrong. On closer inspection the gold adorning the tips of the stone were full of carvings of sun motifs and angelic creatures. This fortress was lovingly forged to capture the full beauty of the sun so it was reflected in every tiny detail.

"When your parents were killed and you disappeared, there was a great deal of panic from the people. My parents were also killed that day, we still don't know the full details of what happened or who killed them, but whomever the murderers were clearly wanted to wipe out the current regime of Solian royalty. I stepped in and did what I could to quell the fears and keep the peace of our people. Things just started getting back to normal a decade ago."

"Theo, I'm so sorry about your parents, and thank you for looking after all of Solis. It must have been terrifying stepping into that role after our parents were killed knowing that you could be a target."

He gave a small, vulnerable nod. "Before you were born, there was a division in Solis between east and west continents. The Guardians had come into great power and the citizens of Solis West backed their authority while Solis East did not. It was a trying time and, in an effort to unite the world, our parents arranged this marriage for when you reached adulthood. There are some who believe that we were also uniting to eradicate the Guardians, and that our union would be the answer to their demise. Your parents and mine believed we would save our people as the prophecy decrees."

"I have to be honest. I don't like the thought of arranged marriage, what if I choose otherwise?"

Theo shuffled in his seat looking slightly panicked. "I will not force you to marry me. All I ask is you just take some time, think over what it will mean to our people to be united and working together to restore the balance."

That seemed reasonable enough, but something still bothered me. "Are there any other royals in the galaxy?"

He pursed his lips and shook his head. "There is nobody left but us to rule." Theo searched into my eyes with hope and I nodded in response. If I was going to be a ruler I'd have to start thinking beyond my own happiness and consider what's at stake, and I didn't want to make a rash decision. "I'll think on it."

That seemed to relax him and his dimples made a charming appearance.

I grabbed his hand to brace him for my next question. "Did the Guardians kill our parents?" Sadness filled his eyes as he squeezed my hand back. "There is no evidence of who killed our parents."

The look on his face told me that he assumed the Guardians were to blame and it made an overwhelming anger rise within me to the point that I could feel the burn of my fire desperate to escape. It was obvious to me that the Guardians were guilty. They literally wore villain outfits for Christ's sake.

"I believe in this union, Cyra. I think our parents were right, and we could rule *all* of Solis together as a united world. I realize you only just met me, and I would *never* force myself on you. I am a firm believer in free will and choice. If you do not want to be with me, I will never make you. I *will*, however, try to win your affections any way that I can... and I am extremely confident in my abilities."

His eyes glowed with anticipation as he gently ran his fingertips up my arm. I was, without a doubt, obsessed with his strong but delicate hands. And when they touched me even for a moment, I was already hoping for more. Good lord. Any woman would kill to be in my position, a drop-dead gorgeous prince making it his mission to be with me. And as for me, I somehow inherited this glittering castle by the ocean along with a continent of people. Both of our parents had wanted this for us, and I couldn't deny the way I squirmed when he was in my presence.

One thing he mentioned did need to be addressed though. "Wasn't it odd to be engaged to a baby?"

Theo laughed. "You forget time doesn't mean the same thing for us. We're immortal, births are few and far between and our years are fast. It happens much more than you'd think, and for us it's part of the culture, especially for royalty. Waiting twenty or even fifty years for you to mature is a mere blink of an eye."

I supposed that made sense. The ship started moving away from the castle and I returned my focus to this stunning world I was born to.

"Eluroom belongs mostly to you, besides the Guardian temple grounds."

I shuddered at their mention. "I don't need to see that hell hole again, let's move on."

Theo gave a knowing nod. "As you wish. Lower Eluroom has a few private residences that belong to your family in which only someone with Fenix blood can access. I'm not even sure how to gain entry. It's a considerable amount of unused land. I've been told there are gardens, ponds and houses, but beyond that I couldn't say. Nobody else has been in the grounds since it's strongly protected by magic. I can't even fly over it because of the invisible shield. I can only show you a circle perimeter."

I looked below with great interest and tried to see anything that would give me more insight into my family, but I could only see trees. I made a silent promise that I'd be making a trip there the second I was able.

After we finished circling the land that belonged to my family, we headed further away from the castle. From a distance, I admired the picturesque fantasy. The multicolored foliage only enhanced the beauty and it was surreal that it was all *mine*. Even though I had no idea what it meant to be a monarch, I knew I didn't want to be the kind of ruler who claimed ownership of the world. These stunning views might be ruled over by the Fenix family, but I wanted every Solian to feel like they had ownership to its beauty as well.

"These are the nobles' lands. Everyone you saw at *Sun Eine* lives here in these estates," Theo explained.

There were rows of stately mansions, the lots of land large enough to leave plenty of space in between. There was nothing unique about this area and the houses were cookie-cutter. It was as if the whole development was recently built and with a quick economy that didn't match the architecture of the rest of Eluroom. There were some parks with no children or citizens occupying them, and that was about it.

As we passed house after house, I asked, "What do the nobles do?"

"Do?" Theo asked, confused.

"Do they have a profession? Do they work or contribute to Solis in any way?"

"Well, you met the Masters of Solis, they work hard to maintain the efficiency of our planet. Unfortunately, most of the others don't work since the majority of the other Masters Boards were disbanded and we have a vastly smaller population than we used to. Some try to be useful to me, but there's not enough need for all of them. To be honest, I don't know what most of them do to fill their days. Many frequent the shoppes and trades area just to be seen and kept busy. The workers of Solis appreciate the nobles in their spaces because they'll exchange power for goods or services. Power and energy are the big currencies of our world, so their monetary fortunes last them a long time as most payment is made with magic transfer. I can take you there now."

"Wait!" I yelled looking down below me at a particular estate. "Please go lower," I begged.

Theo nodded and gave the tablet commands to lower us.

"What. The hell. Is that?" I asked in horror. I saw four creatures working in the yard of one of the noble's estates. Their skin was afflicted with a sickly gray hue that was cracked and peeling. Putrid bruises were found in various parts of their body and their hair was different shades of gray with patches of it missing or falling out. They struggled to walk, and yet they were doing a noble's dirty work. The first word that flashed through my head was *zombie*, but I could tell they weren't the Earthly concept of the walking dead. But walking dead they did appear, and it took everything in me not to cry at the pathetic sight.

I looked at Theo and he still didn't answer, so I asked again. "Theo, what *are* they?"

"They're Voidlings," he responded quietly. I could tell it made him uncomfortable too, but he was choosing to ignore it.

"What's wrong with them? What are Voidlings? Can we help them?" I asked in a flurry of emotions.

"They're from The Void. It's a planet in Eredet that is nothing but a wasteland, and they live a horrible existence. We bring them here to work so they have a purpose since they don't live very long. They're affected by the curse, but I don't know why."

"You use these poor, suffering people as *slaves?*"

Theo winced at the word and I was glad for it. He should feel bad for letting this happen.

"Not slaves, they just aren't capable of doing anything else. We give them a comfortable existence with a purpose before they move on. I don't use them personally, but the nobles and the Guardians do," Theo explained.

"Take me down," I demanded. "I want to see them up close." My outrage caused me to stand, preparing to leave and help these creatures.

"I cannot do that. It would be a crime to enter their lands uninvited and they're this noble's property."

"Property? So they are slaves then." I was livid that anyone could use these souls to labor for their own laziness. As we continued over the noble estates, I saw them *everywhere*. It made me sick to my stomach that this seemed to be the status quo.

"Theo, why do you let this happen?"

"I don't like it any more than you do, Cyra. You must believe me. But they would rot away with no purpose on The Void, and the

Guardians like to stay in control of where they're allocated. Even if I wanted to, I don't have a say in the matter."

"I don't understand what our place is as Reina and Karalis then. If the Guardians have total power, what is our responsibility? Why hasn't someone...dealt with them?"

"We still govern the people on a daily basis even though, yes, the Guardians have the final say. As the Masters previously mentioned the Guardians are practically invincible, it's why the civilians lost the Great War. There's nothing we haven't tried to gain back our power. All you and I can do is help our people as needed and make sure things are running as easily as possible for them. Vish, Serin, and I have tried to heal the Voidlings but nothing works, we have no idea what else to do for them."

If there was one thing I'd learned in my short time on Solis, it's that the Guardians were on my kill list. I'd never had a kill list before, but I suddenly found it very necessary. "Can we please go somewhere else? I can't look at this anymore."

"I'll take you to the shoppes," Theo offered quietly. As if I'd care to go shopping after the gut-wrenching realization that those creatures existed and that they were being used.

We started heading in the opposite direction, but a large statue in the distance caught my eye by the water's edge. It was another gargantuan and absolutely stunning knight statue holding up a hemisphere.

"What's that?"

"Oh, you have good taste. It's the architectural gem of Solis, a gift from Amrel that he constructed with his unparalleled power. It's said that when the first Reina, Coralin Fenix, created peace in our lands, Amrel erected this in likeness of the first knights of Solis. It's seen as an ancient wonder and our people cherish it on a daily basis. If you look closely you can see some people picnicking around it."

Sure enough there were specs the size of ants on the greenery surrounding the massive structure.

"We hold special events there, such as weddings. If we were to wed, it would be in the Knight's Cup." A small blush donned his cheeks which was way too endearing to ignore.

"I see. So it's special to you too."

"Extremely. That treasure is a piece of home for all of us, and there is nowhere else I'd want to join myself to my bride."

The temperature in the vehicle seemed to rise and I had to stop my hands from fanning myself. It was unavoidable imagining myself in the stunning Knights Cup, committing myself to the man before me, and even though I barely knew him, the thought wasn't exactly horrendous. I quickly changed the topic before I said or did something I regretted. I wasn't ready to make that kind of commitment to anyone. "So the shoppes. You mentioned payments were made with energy, why would a shop owner want power instead of money?"

Theo looked bummed by our change of topic, but he answered. "With money you can only buy so much. But with magic you can grow your own field of produce to feed your whole family for a year. Magic stretches a bit further than a small amount of money. The Guardians only give bracelets out to the nobles, so they literally hold all the power. The working class is at the mercy of the nobles for the most part."

"How horrible. Are there not enough energy stores for everyone?"

"Once upon a time, yes, there was more than enough. Or so I'm told, it was before my time. Our energy sources have been dwindling for a millennium, it's tangible enough that we all feel it, even though we don't talk about it."

I wondered if magic would have come any easier to me when it was abundant, but I had nothing to compare it to. "What would happen if we got rid of all the bracelets and the power was distributed evenly?"

"I'm not even sure. But the Guardians control who gets power and when. They are the only ones who can wield our energy source in that sort of way. Nobody even knows how they do it."

None of it made any sense to me. If magical energy was naturally occurring in this galaxy, why were only some people able to access it? Why were bracelets needed? But with my small encounters with the Guardians, I wasn't surprised to see unfair advantages or decaying people used as slaves. There was beauty shining all around me, and below the people looked carefree and happy. Yet, there was something dark underlying all of it if you looked closely enough.

We spent most of the rest of the trip flying over farms and fishing villages. There was a surprising amount of both. Theo explained it was because Solis had to feed all of Eredet since we had the best growing conditions in the galaxy.

The vessel then crossed over lands with copious amounts of abandoned buildings and military style sites.

"These were the old training camps," Theo verified. "Solians used to be great warriors and our training program was the best of the best, but the Guardians shut it down seeing as they wanted to nurture peace and not war."

"That seems wrong, people should be able to defend themselves against the unexpected."

"Right or wrong, it's a ghost land of a time that is no more," Theo said sadly. His eyes were glued to the large statue of a female in armor with a sword in the air. It seemed as if he forced himself to look away with a frown. "We have one more place to see before I take you back to the castle to prepare for dinner."

We crossed back over some of the lands we'd already seen and came across a small island in the center of Solis West.

"This was known as your parents' favorite vacation spot. They came here frequently."

I looked down the clear floor and took it in, trying to connect with another piece of my parents long lost to me. The quaint island was mostly hidden from view just like their private lands. This was another place I'd want to revisit.

We started the trip back to the castle and I realized I was somewhat underwhelmed. Solis was a breathtaking place, but there was very little *life*. All this power, beauty, and immortality, and yet there was more booming life and intricacies on Earth by far. I'd thought Earth would pale in comparison to a planet with magic and immortals, but Solis seemed dead and flat beneath the external beauty. How the hell was there not enough energy for the miniscule amount of people living on this continent? Where was all the wildlife? I only got glimpses of small amounts of livestock on the farms. I suspected the Guardians were directly responsible for this widespread desolation.

We landed back at the castle and Theo turned to me expectantly. "So what did you think?"

"It was an eye-opener."

"Good." Theo had clearly intended for me to see the emptiness of the lands and the state of Solis in general. The brilliance of the sun the Solian's worshiped had made this society blind. After my meeting with the Guardians, the knowledge of the Voidlings, and a quick flight above the barren Solis West lands, I was convinced of the serious condition of Solis.

Theo brought me to him for a hug and I yelped in surprise. "Well, I didn't expect you to cry out for me this soon, but I must say it pleases me to no end." His boyishly handsome face turned devilish, a contrast from his usual professional and composed demeanor, but it made butterflies explode inside me while I squirmed. He bent down to whisper in my ear, and my senses went haywire. "I meant what I said earlier. I will be doing everything I can to win your heart. And the fact that I can empathically feel your lust is like being given a sinfully decadent dessert that you can smell, feel, and admire, but you cannot give in to your desperate desire to devour it." He rubbed his thumb against my lip before stalking into the castle without a backwards glance—like he hadn't just made my brain explode. It's true, I found him incredibly handsome, but it wasn't a fair fight that he *knew* it without me telling him. I was quite happy to live in my normal state of denial and that was impossible around an empath.

Still in a stupor, I wandered inside and ran into a man whose size was probably three of me put together. I'm not sure if he hit me on purpose or if I just wasn't paying attention.

"Sorry," I muttered.

"You lost, sweetheart?" the overgrown man asked.

"I'm obviously heading that way, so no."

"Oh, she's feisty. I like her. I know everyone on this planet and I haven't seen your face before, so you must be the new Reina."

I supposed it wasn't a surprise that everyone would know who I was. "Congratulations on being so popular. You should get an award for that outstanding achievement. Excuse me." I tried to step around him, but he held his arm out and knocked me back, so I stumbled and had to look up at him. He was hideous, pockmarked and mean.

"You might want to consider how you speak to me. We work for the Guardians, so we have autonomy over these lands. And if I don't like you, I'm free to make your life a living hell."

Get in line and take a number shit head. "I'll keep that in mind."

Thankfully he motioned to his five other equally ugly companions to leave with him. Great! More assholes to add to the growing list.

I ran up to my room only stopping about six times to rest, fan myself and catch my breath from the stairs. My anger was increasing exponentially about the lack-of-elevator situation.

Meili knocked and came in to find me dramatically lying face down on the bed.

"Are you okay? Did you have a bad day with Kara Theo?"

I blushed at the mention of Theo and his...confessions. The trip wasn't *all* bad. Meili's beautiful shining face was full of concern for me and I sighed. "There's so much happening to me, and I have nobody else to talk to."

I told her about Theo's offer about how he wanted me to be his, and about the Guardians and what they did to me and my 'fake family.' I told her about grandpa Amrel and how he was long gone, having died on Earth, without revealing his name or who he was, but I explained what he meant to me. Lastly, I detailed how the death of my Solian parents felt like it happened yesterday since I was still sifting through my real memories.

She moved closer and hugged me tight.

"Have you ever heard of a Voidling? I need to find out more about them and why they're afflicted. I can't see them suffer as slaves."

She stilled and her mouth parted, shocked by my question and I could tell she was trying to hold back some emotion.

"What is it? I'm sorry, what did I say?"

"I was born on The Void."

I was not expecting that at all.

"I escaped the curse because of your mother. She saw me as a child and took me back here to Solis and kept me hidden. She performed some kind of magic that blocked the curse from affecting me. She apologized profusely to me that she couldn't do it for everyone, and that the rest of my friends would be left behind. The people I was born with, they're long gone now, having died a horrific, agonizing death many, many years ago. I'm haunted everyday by the fact that I was given a chance at life while my people suffer intensely every single day of their short lives. The curse of the Guardians didn't just touch Solis. It touched our whole galaxy—some places more than others. None were more affected than my planet. They extracted all the energy and life from it so that it's a vast wasteland, and my people that are born to it are cursed to suffer and die. I am what a Voidling starts off as. I *would* have become a Voidling and died many years ago if it wasn't for your mother."

"Oh my God, Meili." I grabbed her hand and squeezed. "Does everyone know about this? Theo didn't seem to know how the Voidlings were so affected."

"I think it's one of those pieces of information the Guardians made sure were 'forgotten.'" She stood and began pacing and I could see her fighting to hold off tears.

"My people once had immense power, and I think that's why the Guardians targeted us. They literally drain our lifeforce, causing the Voidlings to decay and die. We are meant to be immortal beings with incredible power, which is why it takes so long to drain their lives until they're dust. To keep the race going, we are encouraged to mate and procreate to continue the cycle once we hit puberty. When we've served our purposes in breeding, the curse kicks in immediately, and we never come into real power. We're children when we're forced to give birth to more children, so we never have a chance to fight back. Even if we did fight, there's nothing we can do."

My hand was over my mouth in utter shock and I felt sick to my stomach. I beheld this unbelievably beautiful person before me that looked like she was always glowing under a sun that shined just for her, and I couldn't fathom her turning into the poor creatures I knew as the Voidlings. I wanted to murder the Guardians and rip them limb from limb for the injustices they delivered to this galaxy. *Oh, Grandpa. I see now. I see why I'm here.*

I knew I still didn't have the full story, but it was enough to make my blood boil in an all-encompassing anger like I'd never felt before. I was fully invested in seeing this through, whether I was really some prophesied girl or not.

"Do you know why my mother singled you out? How did she even find you?"

Meili shrugged her delicate shoulders and sighed. "Your parents often went to the Void to provide food and comfort to my people pre curse. They spent a great deal of time trying various medicines and magical tinctures to try to help reverse some of the effects of The Voidlings' curse, but the only thing that I ever saw work was when she freed me from the curse. She only said that she felt a strong connection to me, I wish I had asked more questions before she passed."

This time I stood and wrapped my arm around her, and she smiled sadly. "I'm so sorry, Meili."

"It's what you're here for. I have every faith in you that you'll succeed in restoring our lands to what they once were, so we can live in peace and freedom." Meili was the stronger one, dusting herself off and getting down to business.

"Would you like a different dress for dinner?"

"No, I don't think I ever want to take this beautiful dress off, I don't need to change."

Meili smiled and bowed. "I will leave you now, Reina, since you will probably receive an escort to dinner. I will be back later."

"Okay. Thank you, Meili. For everything." I looked at her meaningfully and she seemed to understand. It felt like the sunshine had disappeared the second she was gone. But I was left with more answers than I'd had yesterday... and also more problems.

CHAPTER NINE

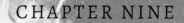

I grumbled when dinner time came and I saw Adelram's face at my door, but I was surprised that Kane was with him.

"Is there really no one else in the galaxy that can meet the menial intelligence level required to act as *escort*?" I said in response to Adelram's sneer.

"Your very own genius royal lap dog at your service. Only the best for the *Reeeina*."

"Oh my God, is he always like this?" I asked Kane as we made our way into the corridor, closing the doors behind me.

"Who is your God exactly?" Adelram asked, intrigued, putting his forefinger and thumb to his chin.

"It's just an Earth expression. I grew up there so it's still a part of me, I suppose I'll always say it. And what are you doing here?" I motioned to Kane. "If he's my lap dog, are you my guard dog?"

Adelram burst out laughing, but Kane looked less than amused, refusing to speak. The air surrounding him seemed to chill and I shivered.

"That about sums up my son pretty well."

I don't know why, but I was completely stunned. "Your son?"

Adelram responded by rolling his eyes, "I know, hard to believe, right? The kid has no sense of humor at all. He's quite the stick in the mud."

As we turned a corner I bumped into Kane and felt that static shock between us again. I yelped, convinced I was burned from the pain of it and looked to see if it left a mark.

Adelram looked at us suspiciously. "What just happened?"

Without missing a beat we quickly replied, "Nothing." We looked awkwardly away from each other until the static grew again and his green eyes latched on to mine like nothing else existed, sucking all the air out of the halls until it was hard to breathe. The second he turned away the spell was broken. *Yep, it must be magic.* Only explanation.

We arrived at the same ballroom that *Sun Eine* had taken place in, except everyone was standing and mingling with little to no tables in sight. The nobles were dressed like they were at the Grammy awards again and I regretted not changing. But when I locked eyes with Theo, I saw that he didn't care about what I was wearing. He beamed at me and stopped mid-discussion of whomever he was speaking to and headed straight for me.

"Cyra, I couldn't wait to see you again," he said and brought me in for a hug. I could get used to his kindness and enthusiasm. He put his hands on both my cheeks and simply looked at me with joy. I might have swooned...just a little.

After we parted, I looked up to inspect the room and there were eight sun statues near the ceiling with four on each side. They were on fire, and the flames shot from one sun to the corresponding sun on the other side in a constant back and forth display of flying embers.

Theo's turquoise eyes twinkled under the light of the flames and lit a glow on his face that made him look even more endearing. I hated the idea of an arranged marriage, but I could think of worse people to be tied to. I also had the prophecy to consider, it wasn't just my own happiness I had to think about.

He took my arm in his and led me to the buffet table. To my disappointment, most of the proteins were fish. It made sense, given that most of Solis was covered in water, but I was not a fan of fish, so I supposed I'd have to suck it up and get used to it. I took a piece, trying to hide my scrunched nose, and paired it with some greens. Just as I was about to take my first bite, a horde of people approached me.

The whole dinner proceeded to be an endless array of meeting the rest of the nobles I hadn't spoken to yet. After a few hours I started to get dizzy from the constant stream of new faces and I finally put my plate down, not having eaten any of it. Theo noticed me yawn and said his goodbyes to the room, mercifully leading me out of it.

"I'd like to show you something I think you'd be interested in seeing. Are you up for it?"

Thoroughly curious, I told him I was. He took my hand and folded his fingers into mine. I was not prepared by the intimacy of us holding hands, but I also wasn't disappointed. Being connected with someone again was a surprising relief, and his touch made me curious about this prince of the sun. Without warning, I felt an enormous amount of pressure, worried that my ribs were going to crack inward. A second later we were somewhere else in the castle. Theo had driven us to the top floor where my bedchamber was. Kane was right, there was much more resistance with this drive since I wasn't right against Theo. I had to stop and center myself because I was close to vomiting.

"I thought nobody could drive inside the castle?" I asked, choking back the rising bile.

"Only you and I can." Theo winked at me with a dimpled half smile that he donned frequently. He led me in the opposite direction of my bedchamber and opened two double doors at the end of the hall. "This was your old nursery. Nobody has touched it since you left, I thought you might like to see it. I'll leave you now to spend some time in it, if you'd like."

"Yes! I'd love to look around. Thank you so much for bringing me here."

He walked closer to me and held my face in his hand again. The way he looked at me without breaking eye contact was so sensual that my heart skipped a beat in response. It was as if he always tried to memorize every detail of my face in case he'd never see me again. Theo had a knack for making me feel cherished and I sorely needed it. I was vulnerable while still missing everyone I'd loved for sixteen years, and Theo's attentions were welcome.

"It is my pleasure, Cyra. I'll see you tomorrow." Theo leaned down and kissed me gently on the cheek, dangerously close to my lips, and it set my body on fire. My eyes fluttered shut and his kiss was so soft and slow that I thought we might be progressing to something else. I started to part my lips in anticipation, but he released me and left the room, closing the door behind him.

I stood there awkwardly for a moment, stunned at my body's response. It was becoming increasingly clear that I wanted him, and I knew for a fact that he could feel my lust through his emphatic ability. My horribly treacherous brain also pictured Kane and the buzzing energy I always felt when he was close. What in the hell was wrong with me? I wasn't man obsessed like this on Earth, did I have some crazy hormones bursting alive from magic?

I shook my head and my hands trying to physically forget all my nonsense and examined the room, eager to see a piece of my past that would hopefully tell me more about who I was, who my family had been. It was beautiful and surprisingly simple, like a nursery you'd see on Earth, full of toys and furniture I began to vaguely remember. What surprised me the most was a screen that looked like a television. I pressed the only available button and my parents' faces flared to life. I gasped and fell to my knees on the floor. Since my memory had returned I couldn't get a clear picture of my parents, but now, as tears fell down my face, I saw every detail of them like they were here with me.

My father said, "Now, Cyra, I know you know the rules, one story before bed. No staying up all night." I absorbed every detail of his face. The endearing laugh lines and crow's feet crinkling near his eyes, evidence of how much he loved to smile.

My mother chimed in. "Don't think you fooled us, we know you stayed up late all last week. If you keep doing that, we're only going to put history lessons on your television." I laughed because it was always my least favorite subject on Earth. I guess it predated that. It was strange how my eyes and hair didn't match either of my parents, but my face was a close replica of my mother's and it warmed me to feel that familial connection. Her blue-hazel eyes twinkled with love and amusement and I soaked in every bit of her love as if I were still a child basking in her attention.

I sat down on the floor and held a pillow to my chest as I watched an animated movie of a cuddly yellow bear and his friends. I couldn't believe it. It wasn't some magical, mystical space cartoon, it was

Winnie the Pooh. My favorite, only I didn't know it was my favorite *before* my time on Earth. I stayed and watched the whole episode. When it was over, I went to turn off the TV, but grandpa Amrel's face appeared and my heart jolted. This was not the grandfather I was used to. His skin glowed brighter than anyone else's I'd seen on Solis, and his eyes were fiercer and more authoritative, but not lacking his usual compassion. The usual crazy mop of gray hair was now a warm hazelnut brown, full falling to his shoulders.

"Now, Cyra, I told your parents that you're capable of listening and taking care of yourself. You don't want to make a liar of me, do you?" He winked and I melted a little at the familiar gesture. Even though he looked like a god, he was still his usual charming and playful self.

This jarred my suffering memory. My parents would load a program onto my TV every night with a message. I looked forward to it every single day and this message from grandpa Amrel was something I remembered.

"You're a good girl and I know you'll turn the television off now and go to sleep."

It was coming back to me. I did as I was told, never questioning grandpa Amrel's direction. I would try to test the limits with my parents, but with Grandpa I never dared. I knew when he told me to do something, it was time to do it. My connection with him was always something sacred to me, and my eyes burned with tears not being able to speak to him.

Before I could click the button again to turn off the screen, grandpa Amrel spoke. "Cyra, I know it's you."

I looked around me in confusion.

"I know it's you from the future."

Oh my God. Was this real? I stepped right against the television and ran my fingers down the screen, wishing he was in the room with me.

"Welcome back home, my darling. Your memories will come back to you in pieces, and you'll probably still need to learn a lot about your life since you were so young when you were taken away. Please know that this was the best way to keep you safe and whole. Earth was the best place for you to live a modest life away from power, greed, magic and danger. In the Creation Galaxy we sometimes forget that true magic comes from the simplistic joys that life offers, like a kiss from a loved one or the look in a child's eyes when they gaze at their mother...the sound of transcendent music performed by your most beloved granddaughter. These are the values that should be worshiped and gripped tight by both hands. True power comes from acts of forgiveness, altruism and supporting others. For when we make lives better for others, we gain strength in ourselves and our society. Earth was a setting to help teach you these invaluable lessons."

Tears were freely falling down my face now, listening to the soothing sound of his voice while committing every inch of his face and actions to memory.

"I'm so sorry about your parents. From Earth and Solis. My heart breaks when I think of all our pains and what we've had to endure up to this point and what is yet to come. More will be revealed to you when the time is right. By now you will have seen some of the conditions of Solis and have met the Guardians. You're smart enough to know not everything is as it appears. You must make it your top priority to find out more about the prophecy and how to restore the balance. Once you uncover more secrets, you'll know what this means."

"If there's one piece of advice that I could bestow upon you it's that we often feel we're right because our pain tells us so, but pain is a biased and disloyal friend that will stab us in the back. Never forget, I love you more than anything."

The screen went black, and I couldn't move for several moments, stuck in utter shock. Grandpa knew I'd be here watching this video in this exact moment. What *was* he that he could know so much about the past and future? My sweet, innocent grandfather that I got into mischief with and leaned on for advice was not all he seemed to be either. It was clear that he was immensely powerful, which made it even more confusing that he chose to spend his end of days with me. I was a nobody. I felt like an outsider on this planet who had less magical talent than a group of children. What the hell did I have to offer these suffering people? I continued my inspection of the room and, sat on a table in the corner, I saw a picture frame with my Solian parents holding me and kissing my cheeks while I laughed in between them. On the frame was a Winnie the Pooh quote.

If there ever comes a day when we can't be together, keep me in your heart. I'll stay there forever.

I sat down on the rocking chair and held the photo to my chest. The cartoons...this quote. It's as if my parents *knew* we would be parted and that I would end up on Earth. *Did they?* Were they preparing me for that? Seeing my parents and grandpa Amrel's faces so vividly again shattered yet another piece of my fragile heart. I doubled over and cried, unable to stop missing them and my adoptive parents from Earth. Pain and loss was the price you paid for unconditional love, and I realized I'd rather go through the heartbreak than never having known those extraordinary people.

I finally got the conviction to get up and head back to my room, but I took the photo and a few stuffed animals with me.

After an hour or so of sitting and absorbing the memories of my family, a knock sounded on the door. Assuming it was Meili, I yelled for her to come in and she joined me in my bedroom.

"Good evening, Reina. How was your afternoon?"

I detailed the tedious dinner, seeing my nursery, and getting a last look at my parents' faces.

"Your parents would be very proud of the woman you are today, Reina."

I wasn't as convinced as she was. My power was lacking, I had serious self-doubts, and I was doing everything imaginable not to let myself acknowledge how fucking terrified I was. Now that I was starting to accept being part of this prophecy, the details of it were finally sinking in. How was I going to save everyone? What did I have to offer anyone other than video game recommendations? And Adelram's words were always lurking in the back of mind as a venomous echo. *You're an utter disappointment.* But I wouldn't admit any of that to Meili. "Thank you, Meili. I just wish I had more time with them."

She gave me a sincere, commiserating look. "None of us knows how much time we are gifted in this life, so we must firmly grasp any cherished moments so we may revisit them when we need to. They gave you the love you needed to carry you through your darkest hours, knowing they did everything they could to protect you and give you a chance at life."

Now I knew why Meili always seemed so bubbly. She was the ultimate optimist. She left my side and walked to the armoire and picked a modest white nightgown that was soft and comfortable.

"I can see you're suffering, Reina. But we will get through this together. I won't let you grieve alone."

"Thank you, Meili. Truly. I think I'll go to bed now."

"Good night, Reina. See you in the morning."

I laid back on my bed and felt dizzy with everything I'd learned recently and everything I still needed to find out. Solis had few inhabitants and even fewer children to fill up its lands, and yet they still had a depleting energy supply for their magic. Maybe learning more about my family history could shed some more light on the state of Solis. It made me want to head to the Fenix private lands soon to see if there were any secrets hidden there.

CHAPTER TEN

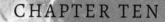

The brilliance of the sun awoke me the next morning and dread slowly filled me at having to play the part of ignorant *princess* all over again. It felt like everyone was assessing my every move, hoping for me to do something to make their lives better, which only made the pain of my failure so far unbearable.

When the grumbling of my stomach was louder than my thoughts I sat up, realizing I was dizzy from eating almost nothing at dinner last night. Maybe I could find the kitchens and try to steal some food instead of attending *Sun Eine*. The thought of the kitchens jostled a distant memory of someone very dear from my childhood which motivated me to get ready and head down there. I would have to ask Meili about where the kitchen was when she came.

I lazily slid off the bed and paused when I saw an overflowing bouquet of beautiful flowers with blooms I had never seen before, filling the room with a lovely fragrance. There was a hand-written note leaning against the vase and I unfolded it as I smelled each incredible blossom.

My Dearest Cyra,

. . .

ELRIC, Master of Fishing and Agriculture, asked to meet with me today so I will be tied up until the early afternoon and will come and find you afterward. I wanted to give you a chance to rest and sleep in. Let's plan to head to the shoppes to see some of the Solian working class now that you've gotten a taste of the nobles. I'll be thinking of the adorable blush in your cheeks until I get to see them again in person.

LOVE, Theo.

I SMILED and produced said blush at his sweet attempt to court me, but I wished he had awakened me so I could join them. I wanted to be more involved with the daily workings of Solis now that I was emotionally invested.

Meili entered the room after knocking and announcing herself, finding me still smiling sappily at the flowers. "Good morning, Reina. Did you sleep okay?"

"Yes, thank you. Can you call me Cyra? I don't think it's necessary for you to keep calling me Reina."

"I don't know..." Meili looked off to the side, biting her lip.

"How about you call me Cyra in private, and in public you can call me whatever you need to."

"Okay...Cyra..." she looked like she was going to choke on the words.

"So, what am I wearing today?"

Meili waved her hand and a raven black dress appeared on the bed. It was covered in black lace flowers with gold trim, and beads sprinkled throughout. The long, lace sleeves had a beautiful shoulder cutout. Two pieces of fabric with hints of shimmering gold lace cinched the waist, and were adorned with red sparkling jewels.

Meili helped me put it on and it hugged my body closely and flared out slightly at the bottom. I looked like a dark queen, and it gave me a small measure of strength to face the day. It's amazing how some cloth on your body can feel like protective armor.

"It's stunning, Meili."

"Just so you know, Reina..."

"Cyra," I corrected.

"Just so you know...Cyra...nobody on Solis wears black, so you will stand out. But I thought the color would suit you today."

"It suits me perfectly. Your intuition is remarkable and appreciated."

Meili styled my hair in two braids that led to a loose bun with two small strands of hair flowing down by my ears.

"Can you tell me where the kitchens are?" I asked.

"I would be happy to bring you some food if you're hungry and don't want to attend *Sun Eine.*"

"It's okay, I want to see the kitchens for myself."

Meili looked confused, but agreed to show me the way. We began the appalling descent down the stairs to the ground floor. Meili went in the opposite direction of the grand ballroom, then led me down another set of stairs that suddenly felt familiar.

I'd walked these stairs hundreds of times as a child, and the further down we got the more familiar it felt. The smells wafting from the kitchen, the halls, the chips in the stone that still appeared to be broken—I recalled all of it. And when we finally walked into the kitchen my heart leapt at the sight of the cook.

When he locked eyes with me he dropped his cooking utensil and flailed his arms with his usual endearing theatrics. "My goodness, is that really you?"

He ran to me and lifted me up into his arms as he twirled me around.

"Baduck! I remember you!" My goofy smile reached from ear to ear.

"Aye, how could you forget old Bad? You came to bug the piss out of me nearly every day, taking half of my ingredients to cook and bake your own creations!" He set me down and held me at arm's-length to look at me, tears filling his eyes. "I thought I'd never see you again, my dear. I'm so glad you're home." He pulled me close and gave me another suffocating, warm hug. "How have you been, girl wonder?" he asked with a huge smile plastered on his face. Girl wonder had been his nickname for me since I'd needed to know how everything worked when I was a child.

"Well, that's a loaded question. More importantly, how have you been?" The chef's assistants prepped food as they watched us with curiosity. I'd forgotten just how large the kitchen was, but I hadn't realized how outdated and run-down it was. I grabbed some diced fruit and a piece of warm, buttery bread and ate as we talked.

"Ah, it's been very quiet and lonely without you here. The day you disappeared was the day the life went out of Solis. The whole lot of workers agree. We've been grieving for over thirty years. There's been no laughter, no play, no music. The sun doesn't even shine as bright. We all noticed its sunshine dull a bit."

I imagined that was more from the energy draining curse than anything to do with me.

"Anyway, I only have Tulah to keep me company, but she doesn't talk to me. You must promise to come visit as much as you're able!"

He was always one of my favorite people and while his account of my absence was a little dramatic, I loved him for it. "You can count on that, Bad. Tulah... How has she been?" I extended my arm and the majestic bird came and rested on it so I could pet her soft, colorful wings. She was a maagaline bird, a highly magical creature that was thought to be able to do almost anything, like instant travel, communicate with all animals and were even known to have fierce magical offensive abilities. They're supposed to be immortal, but Tulah was thought to be the only bird of her kind left. She found Bad one day and never left his side, choosing him as a life companion.

"She's a little sad that she has no other maagaline friends, I can feel it from her. But I keep her busy, and nowadays I have her facilitating the crop transfers we do throughout Eredet."

"I'm glad she's busy. You'll be sick of me again soon. "

"Bloody likely of that happening, me being sick of you."

"I better go, I can see you're busy getting ready for *Sun Eine*, but I will be back soon," I promised.

"You better, missy, or old Bad will be coming for ya!" I laughed and kissed him on his forehead as we left.

I turned and joined Meili in the hall and walked further into the worker's domain curious what else was down here. We walked down a dark and mildew infested hallway, stopping at the first door I saw because I was floored by what was inside. There were three Voidlings picking up trash and sending them down a chute. I damn near fainted seeing them so closely, and the one nearest to me was crouched on the ground in fear of me.

"I'm sorry! I didn't mean to scare you—I'm not going to hurt you."

I walked over and helped him up. He very slowly raised his head to look at me and I struggled to hide that I felt sick to my stomach by the sight of him. His eyes had pools of blood in various places, and they were sunken so you could see the outline of his skull. Multiple open sores filled his face and body with extensive purple bruising everywhere. Patches of skin were flaking off, and the skin that was intact was wrinkled and sickly gray even though I could tell he wasn't old. A large patch of his gray hair was missing, and in its place was more bruising, like it had rotted. He looked like he was decaying while he still lived and breathed, and I was at a loss for words. This poor creature broke my heart, and the other Voidlings looked the same as the one before me. The foul stench of death permeated through the room and I forced myself not to gag.

"Are you...okay?" Sometimes I amazed myself at my stupidity. What a ridiculous fucking question. Of *course* he's not okay.

He opened his mouth, and all that came out was a long, painful sounding grunt. Just when I thought I wouldn't get anything from him, he tried again and he managed to say, "C... Curse. H... Help."

The other Voidlings moved closer, their eyes wide like they were also asking for help. It was as if this was the first time in their lives they felt hope, and they were reaching out to me for a lifeline.

"Meili, do you think it's possible to replicate whatever my mom did to you?"

Sorrow filled her eyes. "I'm not sure what she did and others have tried to save the Voidlings without success. I have no idea how to help. This is Mylo," she said, pointing to the Voidling closest to me.

I looked Mylo in the eyes and asked desperately, "How do I break the curse? What did the Guardians do?"

The Voidling looked like he was frantically trying to answer.

"There you are! I've been searching the entire castle for you. What are you doing down here?"

Stunned, I quickly turned around to find Vish with his hands on his hips looking at me with his head tilted in suspicion.

"I just...wanted to see all of the castle. I didn't know what was down here."

"Well, follow me. Theo thought it would be good for you to get some Solian history lessons, so I've come to teach you."

"Do we have to do this now?"

"Well, we could attend *Sun Eine*, but it worked with my schedule to do it now. Theo wanted to make sure you had more of an understanding of our world as soon as possible."

"Okay, fine." I was annoyed, but I recognized that any available education was vital.

I followed Vish, but before I left the room I turned around once more. The Voidlings were back shoveling garbage down the chute, but the one who spoke was still looking at me and all hope had drained from his face.

"I'll be back, I promise." And I left to join Vish, absolutely crushed that I had no idea how to help those poor people.

"HERE, WE CAN USE THIS CLASSROOM," Vish motioned, leading me in. He had taken me to the second floor of the castle which he explained held a few lesson rooms for the small number of children on Solis. He went straight for two lounge chairs near a fireplace. Why there was a need for fireplaces on a tropical planet was beyond me, but it surprisingly didn't add any additional heat to the room.

"So, tell me what you know so far about Solian history."

I didn't know if Meili would want me to share her history about the Voidling curse so I thought about what else I knew. "Um—Solians used to be great warriors, and our energy stores and power is dwindling."

"Anything else?" Vish asked hopefully.

"No. Sorry, not really. Can you tell me why there's so few people on Solis West?

"Yes, I can actually—at least the main reason. Most of our recent history stems from the events of the Great War a little over fifteen hundred years ago. Most of the events that happened before then, or even some of the particulars of what happened during the war, are hazy to all Solians. Many theorize that someone altered or deleted some of these memories so they could never be repeated."

"Isn't the point of history to remember what has transpired in our past so we can learn to avoid certain mistakes?"

"That's certainly one way to look at it. Have humans never altered their own history to suit whoever wrote it?"

Well, maybe I'd keep my mouth shut.

Vish smiled smugly. "I've spent a *great* amount of time trying to find more pieces of the puzzle to get all the facts of our history that were lost. So far, I've been unsuccessful. It turns out whoever wanted it buried did a thorough job. But I can tell you what I know. Have you ever heard of your grandfather, Dokoran?"

"No, I haven't."

"He was your mother's father, and he wasn't known as a kind person. In fact, by the end of his reign he was known as the Demon Reina. He gave a lot of Solians grief during his time. He expanded the training grounds and tripled the size of the Empire of Knights of Solis. But he forced all boys to be trained for a minimum of twenty years, and the training was hard and brutal. During his reign, he sought to harness our people's energy so he could use it as he pleased and control others' power. It was said that he banded the Guardians to figure out how to do just that. As I'm sure you've come to find, power and energy are the real currencies of Eredet, and Dokoran wanted to wield it all to dole out as he pleased, to be the most powerful being not only of Solis, but all of Eredet."

"So Dokoran is the reason the Guardians control our energy?"

"We're not sure. Dokoran killed many in his quest for power, and the people started fighting back. We were at war for many years as our people banded together to try to overthrow Dokoran and the Guardians, but the Guardians figured out the secret to harnessing our power. We don't know how they did it, or how they're able to access it or distribute it as they see fit, but it changed the game in the war. The Guardians eradicated half of Eredet's population because they continued to rebel, unwilling to be controlled. They showed us who had the real power, and they proclaimed all were to fall in line, or die.

More citizens were killed before we finally gave up and recognized the new regime."

"I guess that explains why everyone accepts the way things are now."

"People are terrified. The Guardians sealed the end of the old establishment by publicly executing Dokoran for treason, claiming he was trying to steal back the power source from the Guardians. Your mother was already married to your father, so they were sworn in as the new Reinan of Solis West *under* the Guardians' supervision. A number of people have disappeared since then and nobody knows where or why. Many say the Guardians are the most ruthless rulers since the dawn of time, and Dokoran was more preferable to them. As you know, years later your parents and Theo's parents were executed as well. It was said they were also guilty of treason, but there is no evidence to what happened. I don't think anyone even knows where they're buried. And as to the history of Solis *before* The Great War... we only know bits and pieces, but I've never stopped looking for the truth."

I sat quietly for a moment, trying to take it all in. It was very little history, yet a whopper of information at the same time. My grandfather's box came to mind and I figured I would see if he had more insight.

"I've seen portraits of people with wings but I haven't noticed any on Solis. What's the story there?"

Vish straightened, looking desperate and eager. "Where did you see this?"

I wasn't ready to tell anyone about grandpa's box yet. "Um, not sure, somewhere in passing."

His shoulders slumped in disappointment. "You're describing the Sunya Rei, often called the S'rei or Rei for short. They were immensely powerful higher beings that helped protect the galaxy and ruled over us all, but they're extinct, the last having died when our energy started waning."

"Are you saying that the Guardians are responsible for their extinction because of their curse?"

Vish looked around uncomfortably then leaned in closer and took my hand. "Cyra, be careful about what you say in public. I can tell you the history we know, but talking about the curse is dangerous, people have been killed for it."

"But we're not in public, we're alone in a room."

"Unless a room is secured and guarded against magical interference, you are in the public for anyone to hear."

"Is there anywhere in the castle that's guarded? Can you guard this room?" I asked.

"That's beyond my abilities. Your bedchamber and Theo's would be guarded against external magic."

"Then let's go."

"I...can't go to your bedchambers," Vish said defensively.

"Why not?"

"It would be...inappropriate, Reina."

I rolled my eyes. "Oh, please." I grabbed his hand and dragged him outside the room and started the long trek up to the top of the castle.

When we made it to my room, I let him in and threw my shoes off so they flipped away from me (a horrible habit I couldn't break from Earth) and sat on the couch in the main room. Vish walked around a little and came to a small desk with my framed photos.

"May I, Reina?"

"Of course, Vish. And stop calling me that."

He ignored my request and leaned in. He looked at the newest addition first, which was the photo of my parents and myself when I was a toddler.

"Your parents were wonderful people. They were always very kind to me and I loved being around them. I think everyone did, for that matter."

"I wish I could have spent more time with them. The only parents I really knew were my adopted ones on Earth. But they were wonderful people."

"What is Earth like? I would love to travel to see a world totally different than mine."

"Earth...is definitely different, but in a lot of ways it's just the same. On Earth, we're bombarded with technology, noise, and an urgent sense of *going somewhere*, and I'm not sure if any of us know where that might be. And Theo was right, humans *are* obsessed with time. They have to be since they have so little of it. They have to take a small flash of existence and either make it into something meaningful, bright and incredible before it burns out, or they risk wasting it before it's gone. Humans' greatest fear is that they will die regretting the way they lived their lives, and I can't imagine a worse death. With such few precious moments, we measure the seconds we have with the people we love. With our friends and family. We measure them by the memories we make and the experiences that make us grow. We have to learn very quickly how to make the most of it, and then when the time comes, we have to accept our end and the loss of the ones we'll leave behind to mourn us. There is no magic, but we create it in other ways, in music and art. In literature and passion. We love harder, we burn brighter, and we try as hard as we can to completely utilize the gift of life."

My loss of Earth was a physical ache and I missed it every single day. In that moment, I realized I understood Grandpa's wish to raise me on Earth. I *did* treasure simplistic beauty.

"Wow, Cyra. That sounds like a place I'd very much like to see for myself. I noticed you mentioned 'we' and 'us' when talking about the humans."

I hadn't even realized. "Well, it still feels like my real home, and I miss it very much." I sighed. "You seem to know something about the curse. You have to tell me. I know nothing and it's time I understand so I can figure out exactly what I'm doing here…why I was taken from my home."

Vish walked over and sat next to me and nodded his head. "I've heard whispers that the only way the Guardians were able to control our power was by cursing our people and trapping the energy in a *mikla*."

"What's a *mikla*?"

"It's the old language for puzzle. It's a vessel that can hold massive amounts of magical energy, but the prophecy says nobody but the girl with the mark of balance can open it and release the energy back to the people. The fact that the energy is trapped in this box and not released back to our sun is part of what's causing our sun to die and our power to wane."

"Why *me*? Where is this *mikla*, and why would the Guardians contribute to their own demise? They live here too."

"Those questions I cannot answer. The Guardians seem to want something, and they haven't found it yet. And the magic it would take to trap the massive amount of energy we have in our galaxy—it's unfathomable. It's not the sort of magic we're familiar with. I have no idea how they could even create such a curse."

"I don't know why I would be able to open this *mikla*. How do we go about finding it?"

"Well, don't forget, it's said that you *with* a ruler of Eredet will unlock the *mikla* together. That's where Theo comes in."

"Did I just hear my name?" Theo entered the room with a smile but it disappeared when he looked at Vish. "Ovishkar...what are you doing in here? I thought you were giving Cyra a lesson on the second floor." His brows were lowered in anger, and it wasn't a good look on him.

"I asked him to come to my rooms to be away from listening ears. He tried to fight me on it, but I insisted. Perks of being a Reina, right?"

My answer seemed to satisfy him and he went back to his usual bright, smiling self. "Vish, you're dismissed for today. Thank you."

Vish bowed and when he got to the door and Theo's back was to him, he winked and gave me a silent 'thank you' gesture with his hands. I tried not to laugh as he closed the door. I thoroughly enjoyed spending time with Vish, and I appreciated his candor. I would definitely be grilling him again later.

"Thank you for the beautiful flowers," I said. "My room still smells wonderful."

"You're very welcome, my Reina." He walked closer to me and took my hand and gently kissed it.

"Are you ready to head out?" Theo asked.

I was frustrated and annoyed that I was still so confused, but I figured the best thing I could do right now was learn more about Solis and my people and hope more would be uncovered in the process. So, I sucked it up, squeezed his hand back and said, "Let's go."

CHAPTER ELEVEN

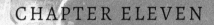

*T*heo drove again before I was ready and when we made it to our destination, I immediately threw up. It took way longer than I liked for the debilitating vertigo to lessen.

"Cyra, are you okay?" Theo asked, holding my hair back.

"I just feel sick after the drive." Even speaking made me dizzy.

"Do you want to go back?"

"No!" I yelled a little too loudly – the thought of doing that a second time made me retch again. "I mean, no, thank you. I think I'm better now."

Theo waved his hand and my vomit vanished. It occurred to me that I hadn't really seen him use magic before, besides admitting to his empathic ability. "Theo, what kind of magic can you wield?"

"I can make almost anything happen with the power bracelet, but my strengths are my empathic ability, as you know, and water."

Theo lifted his hands in the air and clenched his fists like he was squeezing something. When he opened his hands again, both were holding large water bubbles.

"Wow!" I was jealous of his level of control.

"Go on, touch them." His half smile was full of mischief.

I giggled and slowly touched the water bubbles and they both exploded open, the water spilling onto my dress. Theo reached out toward me and extracted the water from my dress and hair and then threw it back into the air to dissipate.

"That's pretty cool."

"Why, thank you." Theo bowed, his eyes sparkling with joy.

We entered the shopping center which was bustling with people. It was a town in itself, lined with countless boutique stores painted various colors among the cobblestone streets. We strolled down the main street of what Theo explained were popular shoppes and I was inundated with the wafting smell of sweet and savory food. I began to salivate over something that smelled dangerously close to chocolate.

"It smells so good! What is that?" My stomach rumbled greedily.

"Ah, that's a combination of Jessa's Delicacies and Blaze's Public House. Jessa makes the only sweet confections available on Solis and Vish practically lives there. Blaze makes some hearty Solian fare that the working class go nuts for."

"I'm starved, can we go to Blaze's?"

Theo looked puzzled. "You want to eat in the public house?"

"Yeah, why not?"

"I've never been in there, I suppose we can give it a shot if you're interested."

"In all your years you've never been in here?" How could he not have been inside every single establishment in Solis with how old he was?

He shrugged and shook his head. It was becoming clear that Theo was a little too uptight and needed to relax a little. He needed some fun in his life. I grabbed his hand and pulled him into the white and gray stone building, but the second we entered the lively chatter silenced immediately.

The hell with it. I hadn't even had a legal drink yet since turning twenty-one, so I walked to the bar, sat down and motioned for a slightly terrified Theo to join me.

It was an effort not to giggle, sitting in a tavern like Brendon and I only imagined in fantasy stories or video games. A little of my excitement was diminished thinking about him, and I took in the room that was a mix between what I imagined an old-time tavern would look like with some modern, unique flair. The stone floor was worn and dusty, but I could tell it had a golden shimmer to it in its heyday. It was dark inside from the ancient blackout curtains, providing privacy and protection from the outside, the only light coming from the fire hearth and magical orbs of light along the ceiling. This place seemed like an exclusive sanctuary—a world away from the plights just outside its doors.

I cleared my throat and looked at the bewildered bartender, trying my best to look competent—which of course only made me look ridiculous. "Um, I'll take an ale, please. And some food. I'm twenty-one." Oh good lord, that verbal diarrhea. Like they were going to card me. "He'll take one too."

"Cyra, are you sure that's wise?"

Theo's lips were slightly parted in shock and I rolled my eyes in response. "Oh, lighten up. Theo, you need to relax a little. I know we're in the middle of an apocalyptic situation, but that's all the more reason to sit for a moment and have a drink. Nothing's happening right now."

He smirked and shrugged, grabbing the beer that the barkeep handed to him. It's one thing I really liked about Theo, he seemed to be adaptable and ended everything on a positive note. With too much eagerness, I took my own beer. "Blaze, I take it?"

"You are correct, Reina." His sideward grin was full of baffled amusement and anticipation. Many of the other patrons stood to watch in disbelief as well, making my self-consciousness skyrocket. Why was everyone watching me drink a measly beer?

"Cheers." I raised my glass and took a large gulp, covering my mouth with my hand to stop myself from immediately spitting it out all over Blaze. Once I forced it down I choked, trying to make the horrid taste disappear.

Blaze's elbows were resting on the bar, holding his head with both hands waiting for my verdict with fluttering eyes. "Yeah, really good, Blaze. It's…tasty."

The crowd erupted in laughter as some of the men patted me on the back, causing some of the piss water to spill onto the bar. A patron yelled from the other side of the room. "No, it's not! It tastes like piss, but it's all we got!"

I joined in their laughter and gave Blaze a shrug while he nodded at me. "Okay, yeah, it tastes like piss. No offense."

"None taken, Reina. I work with what I got and we don't got a lot."

That comment broke my heart, because all of the succulent food and drink of the castle was heavenly and I keenly felt the division of this world more than ever. There was no reason that the working class had to live like this.

"Three cheers for the fancy Reina who had the balls to drink the commoners' ale!" The unease was gone from the room and a teenage boy started playing a guitar and singing about a rich girl who liked to slum it with good-time commoners. It was the greatest welcome I had ever received and, ironically, probably the first time I felt like I could be myself. A place where a royal or noble never deemed to visit.

"Blaze, get this little lady another on me." A burly man covered in dirt nodded at me with a friendly smile. I could tell he was a farmer by the soil under his fingernails. "I'm Derek and it's jolly nice to see you here with us. Just be warned, Reina, it'll take damn near every man in this room buying you a drink before you feel a buzz."

"Thank you, although I think that's enough for me. It wouldn't end well if I drank that much of this…delicious beverage." More laughter sounded as I shivered thinking of drinking that much disgusting beer.

When the beef stew arrived I was relieved that it was infinitely better than the ale and I devoured every delicious morsel, catching Theo watching my mouth more than once as he tried to hide his smirks. He finished his food before me and I made a quick decision.

"Would you mind going to Jessa's and getting me something sweet while I finish this? I'm eager to try the confections of Solis."

"Sure thing." He bent down and kissed my cheek and I melted into him, savoring his touch. But the second he was gone, I got down to business. I wasn't sure why I wanted him to leave, but I was tired of people telling me to be careful when I wanted answers.

I looked at Blaze, not able to hide my desperation. "What can you tell me about the Guardians and the curse?"

Almost everyone in the room gasped, and turned to watch. Many walked over to take part in the conversation.

"I'm surprised you're asking. Royalty has never bothered with our opinion before." Blaze straightened and crossed his arms, his brows pinching together with suspicion.

"Well, I'm asking. And I value what any of you might have to say." I turned to look at everyone in the room and could see the change in their demeanor, wide-eyed and eager—desperate to be heard.

"Most of us don't even have access to our magic anymore. Those fucking assholes stole something precious from this galaxy that wasn't theirs to take." There was fury in Blaze's eyes, and he rubbed his brown beard in frustration. The yells of agreement behind me grew louder as the crowd closed around me.

"We've been getting sick, we're used, we're killed and ignored. We're left to fend for ourselves in a dying land, and while the Karalis tries to help, it's not enough. We deserve a place in this society and we deserve to be heard without the fear of death." More cheers and agreements sounded around me and I took in every face I could—a promise to remember those who were forgotten.

A solar flare tattoo peeking out from Blaze's rolled up sleeves caught my eye and I damn near grabbed his arm when I read the small inscription under the sun.

Empire of Knights.

Blaze nodded solemnly when I looked back up at him. "You were a Knight?"

"Aye, for many years until they started killing our own under the direction of monsters."

"Blaze was a goddamn hero!" Derek cried behind me, and the other patrons chimed in with their agreement. "He is a Nobleseru."

"Nobleseru? What is that?" The grief on everyone's faces stabbed into my heart, making me dread what he was going to tell me.

"It's a load of nonsense, that's what it is," Blaze said dismissively, wiping the bar down with a washcloth and avoiding my gaze.

"It means he's a legend—a war hero," Derek explained. "The nobles of Solis...they're not just pretty faces with a large bank account. They are Nobleseru, war heroes of the Empire of Knights that were rewarded with riches of a hundred lifetimes. They were the best, the fiercest warriors in our galaxy...but they don't remember it." Derek crossed his arms and shook his head.

"No..." I was flabbergasted. The petty nobles were war heroes? "How is it that you guys remember then?"

"I rejected my wealth and status and opened this tavern to be with the struggling commoners and I've lived above the bar ever since.

Nobody remembered that I was a 'Nobleseru' so my memories remain intact. The Guardians made a mistake in dismissing the commoners as not being a threat and one day they will pay for it. Many of us meet here once a week at night to address needs and concerns and plot the demise of you know who. You're always welcome to join."

My interest was piqued at that, even though it was clear they didn't have any real information on how I could break this curse. Blaze was clearly a leader in his own right, and these people seemed to look to him for guidance. A crash at the door stunned us all and Theo raised his voice. "What is going on here?"

There was an almost imperceptible fear in Blaze's eyes which bothered me. He shouldn't have to fear his sovereigns. It was understandable why they were so angry.

"Nothing, just an innocent discussion. I'm done eating, so let's continue the tour." That seemed to appease him. Right before we exited I looked back at Blaze and my heart stopped, seeing that he had the same look in his eyes that the Voidlings had given me.

Desperation and hopelessness. Whether they knew all the details of the curse or not, it was clear in their faces that they thought I was their last hope, and I prayed like hell I would be able to deliver.

Theo and I walked for a bit down the beautiful cobblestone pathway as I stewed over what Blaze and Derek told me. It was clear Theo didn't know about the Nobleseru either since he couldn't tell me much about the nobles when I questioned him previously. I was brought out of my thoughts when a noble woman exited a dress boutique and lit up when she saw me and Theo. She preened like a peacock and made sure she was loud enough for everyone to hear. I couldn't help but wonder what kind of skills she had and what she had done to make her a war hero.

"My dear, Reina Cyra! What a pleasure it is to see you again!" I didn't recognize her in the slightest. Some of the shoppe owners came outside to see what the commotion was and I braced myself for an onslaught of attention.

"We had such a great time the other night at dinner, didn't we? I just bought a new gown for tonight! Is that what you're doing as well, Reina?" She looked me up and down in mild disgust and continued. "I say, that *must* be what you're doing. I've never in all my years seen a

Reina in a black gown in broad daylight when she wasn't in mourning."

Well, I absolutely was in mourning, and Meili knew it when she dressed me. Mourning a life that was no longer mine and for those that I'd lost.

"You know, Celestine, I was thinking the same thing. And have you ever seen anyone more radiantly beautiful? I think it really becomes the Reina, don't you?" Theo said with ease, his arms folded behind his back.

I don't think anyone could deliver an innocent insult like Theo could. He was a *pro* at petty politics and making other people think like him while having them believe it was their own original thought. I really needed to learn that trick from him.

"Oh! Yes, I do indeed. I was just thinking how I should like to have a black gown as well and start a new trend. Reina, will you come in with me and help me pick something new?"

"Why not, Celestine?" Theo put his hand on the small of my back in response and it sent a shiver up my spine. He rubbed his thumb back and forth slowly and it gave me courage, but it also drove me to distraction.

After the shoppe owner confirmed that she had no black material and Celestine was able to express her outrage, she paid the owner handsomely to acquire a dress before tonight's dinner. The cost was some coin and a transfer of a day's worth of energy stores, which, as I understood it, was a hefty payment. Celestine said her goodbyes to me and Theo and she promised to be back later to collect her dress. Before we left, the shop owner ran toward me and curtsied.

"Thank you, Reina, for coming to my shoppe. That payment will feed my family for another year with some to spare. I can never repay you."

My smile vanished at her serious words. "There is no need for thanks. I will come back again when I can if it will help your family."

"Indeed, it would, my Reina. Thank you for your kindness."

"I didn't do anything," I muttered to Theo as I turned to leave the shop and he followed me.

"Just having royalty in their shoppes helps them dramatically, everyone will be talking about them and your visit. Ah, here's where I wanted to take you." Theo led me a few shoppes down to a jeweler. "My good friend, Drit, has been keeping something safe for you for thirty years. His security safes are unrivaled in Eredet galaxy, so anything valuable can be kept safe here."

"I have it, Karalis," Drit said, swelling with pride.

"The time has finally come, Drit. Please go get it."

"Right away." He was gone for a few minutes then returned with a small package, holding it with reverence like it was pandora's box.

"Thank you, Drit. I have two items for you." He handed me a ring first. "This belonged to the Fenix family. It's a royalty signet ring of Solis, you'll notice I have one too, similar to yours. This one was your mother's."

I inspected the gold oval signet ring with a sun engraving that sparkled as I moved it in the light. It wasn't something I would pick out, but it was pretty and I longed to collect *anything* that was once my mother's. I put it on my right middle finger next to a ring Brendon had made me a few years ago. I had to fight back tears at the sight of my past and future colliding.

Next, he gave me what looked like a pocket watch, but when I opened the gold cover it was a beautiful, antique-looking compass.

"This was given to me by someone very dear to me, named Onna, during a dark time in my life. She told me when I felt lost, this could help me find my way. It's a magical compass, you only need to think of your destination and it'll help you get there. I know you must be feeling lost and lonely, so I want you to have this. Just know that now you are home, I will never let you be alone. I'll always be here to find you."

"Thank you, Theo." His sincerity and attempts to impress me was touching and it made me appreciate him just a little bit more.

A loud crash made the three of us jump in shock. We looked out the window and saw a commotion with two men yelling outside of a clothing shoppe. I put the compass in my pocket and ran out to see what was happening just as the shoppe owner threw a man to the ground outside his storefront.

"Stay out of my shoppe, you *filth*!" the owner spat.

"I have just as much right to buy clothing as anyone else!" the man on the ground yelled as he brushed off the rags that barely covered his body.

"This man is in rags. If he's willing to pay, why would you not help him?" I asked, trying to be diplomatic and not spew the curses I wanted to.

"He's a *Bellum*. That's blood money. He sells live decaying slaves to earn his money, and who knows what else. And his people steal from us constantly. I have no use for the likes of him in my store!"

"Hypocrite!" the Bellum yelled back through tears. "Most of you here have Voidling slaves. I have *no choice* but to sell them to feed my family and clothe myself and my children. What's your excuse for buying them?"

"Please sell him what he needs." I issued it as a command, not a request. If I was the Reina I had a duty to these people to set things right. The Bellum man looked up at me with bulging eyes and I helped him stand.

"And who the *grof* are you to tell me what to do?"

Theo walked up behind me and took my hand. "Is there a problem here, Reina Cyra?"

Everyone in the growing crowd gasped and bowed.

"Do I have money to buy this man some clothes?" I asked Theo, filled with frustration.

"You have an account in every store on Solis. You may spend it as you choose."

"Then if you will not accept his money, maybe you'll accept mine – and my advice to remember a little common courtesy."

The shoppe owner stilled in sudden fear, bowed and responded, "Yes, Reina. Right away."

After the exchange was completed, I gave the bag to the Bellum along with the candy Theo bought me and he bowed with true reverence and surprise in his eyes, like he had never seen an act of kindness before. I made sure it was clothing for an adult man, woman and children and then handed it off.

"Thank you, Reina. I only wanted to support my family." He walked away quickly with his head down in shame, desperate to disappear.

125

People started to disperse, and I noticed they were all as disgusted by the presence of that man as the shoppe owner. "What is a Bellum?"

"They're a mortal race of people in Eredet Galaxy. We think most of them live on The Void, where the Voidlings originate, but we have no idea exactly where. They hide themselves very well and nobody has ever seen where they live. They've been known to pillage and kill since their world is a wasteland. Many of them organize and sell Voidlings because they have no other natural resources to survive on. We give a ration of food to the Bellum king to divvy among his people, but we have no idea just how many Bellum there are. You don't see them on Solis often because they're not welcome. They have a bad reputation since they're so desperate to survive."

I was only just beginning to brush the surface of this world that I had been thrust into. A *mortal* race of people that lived on the same wasteland planet as the Voidlings? The Bellum man had looked so... well, human.

We walked down the strip gazing at more shoppes, but my heart wasn't in it and Theo noticed it too. A crack of thunder made us both startle and look toward the sky, the threat of a downpour imminent.

"Would you like to head back early?"

"Yes, please." He reached for my hand and I immediately panicked, moving away from him. "Oh, wait! Before you drive me back, this time let's try this."

I inched closer to him and hugged him tightly. His eyes glittered with amusement. "I could certainly get used to this," Theo purred.

"I think it might help with hitching a ride with you."

"You won't hear me complain." Theo looked down into my eyes and touched my face. "You really are the most beautiful woman I've ever seen."

I blushed profusely and looked away before we disappeared from the shoppes. Thankfully, I was right and the drive was much less sickening being so close to Theo.

When we arrived back in my room Theo didn't let go of me. He lowered his head and touched his forehead to mine and, unexpectedly, I grabbed his two hands and intertwined them with mine. He looked at me, startled at my gesture, and smiled.

"You handled yourself very well today." My hormones went haywire at the pride shining in his eyes.

"I wish I had your easy air of diplomacy. Everyone can't help but like you because of how confident you are. I don't think I could ever compare. You were born to be a leader."

Theo shook his head. "So were you, Cyra. I already see it emerging from you, you just need practice and patience. Soon, it will be second nature."

I wasn't so sure I wanted it to become second nature. I never wanted to become someone so obsessed with obtaining power that I could end up like Dokoran or, even worse, a Guardian.

"I'll leave you now to relax for a little bit before dinner. I'll see you in a few hours." He kissed my hand softly and stared deep into my eyes before leaving me alone with my thoughts of a galaxy of people whose home was deeply flawed and broken.

I was too disturbed to relax as Theo suggested. I decided to sneak out and try to get into the Fenix private lands to see what I could find. I wanted to go on my own since I was unsure what secrets my family had locked away.

After witnessing the suffering of the Voidlings and the working class Solians I didn't want to waste a single moment looking for more answers, and I was hopeful my parents' land had them. I changed into a casual dress and hooded cloak Meili had left for me in the closet, grabbed Theo's compass, rechecked my stolen switchblade was safe in my pocket, and made my way out of the castle.

It was the first time I'd seen it rain on Solis, and I realized this might be harder than I imagined. I'd only flown over the perimeter of the territory, and I'd never ventured into the lands beyond the castle alone. I was hoping Theo's compass would help me find it even though I didn't know how far it really was. But it was too late to turn back now, I was already fully committed. I figured it was as good a time as any to attempt driving there. I pictured the location in my mind and imagined myself appearing there. I only had an overhead view, but I could visualize it from the ground. I concentrated, trying to slip myself between the space of the two locations. I even repeated Oliver's instruction—closed my eyes, clenched my fists and imagined someone dying. After a few minutes I was frustrated and angry, but I tried one more time.

Slowly, I started to feel that familiar pressure engulfing me tightly, and I knew I had done it. I smiled with satisfaction and arrogance, feeling capable. When the pressure released, I opened my eyes and screamed, but there was no real sound. I was under water...with a horrifying amount of it above me. I panicked, thrashing and swimming as quickly as I could, terrified of drowning. I started to grow dizzy from lack of air—the surface was *so far*, but I could see the sun shining above me from a brief break between the rain clouds. I attached myself to it, and it was my guiding light as I endlessly kicked to try to bring myself to freedom and air. It was as if the rain had stopped to show me the way. Just when I thought everything was darkening around me, I made it to the surface, gasping for air.

I crawled onto land, soaked and exhausted, and as I looked around me, I realized I had no idea where I was. I could even be on Solis East, thousands of miles away. What the *hell* was I thinking trying to drive somewhere so far when I was inexperienced—not to mention I didn't really know where I was going. I didn't have much of a choice now but to keep going. I took out Theo's compass, silently thanking him for his gift as the hand slowly pointed away from me. Saying a silent little prayer the device would work I began to walk amidst the relentless rain. I passed the time by casually contemplating my own idiocy, hating the stupid decisions I made in life. I was really doubting this savior nonsense.

Solis was always warm—hot even. But after about an hour of walking in the rain I was frozen to the bone. I was just about ready to give up and go back when to my utter relief I saw an extensive gated area. I sprinted to it, and on a stone next to the iron gates, "FENIX" was etched. *Thank God, I found it!* I tried to open the gate door, but of course, nothing happened. I guess now I had to figure out how to open it, and Theo said only a Fenix was able to do it. I looked all around the gate and didn't see any locks. I tried touching various places to see if some kind of marking would show up. Tilting my head up in frustration, I sighed at my luck that I found the place and couldn't get in.

I doubled back to the etching of FENIX. The middle of the 'X' had a small oval indent that was almost invisible, but I had seen it before. My family ring! It had the same design! I took off my ring, placed it into the mold and the gate finally opened. With my heart racing out of my chest, I braced myself and walked inside, closing the gate behind me. I might have to change the way the gate was opened, because "X marks the spot" seemed a little too obvious.

It was entrancing when I observed the land, as if I'd walked into another world. It was bright like the sun was shining, with no rain in sight. I looked up and it seemed like there was another protective barrier keeping outside forces from getting in—including rain. Surrounding me was a fantasy garden, full of grass, flowers, bushes and trees. When I saw movement from the corner of my eye, I was stunned to find two maagaline birds. I thought Bad's bird, Tulah, was the last of her kind, but thank goodness it wasn't the case, hopefully we could breed these birds and return their population.

The private lands were much bigger than I'd expected and I made my way to a small cottage off in the distance. I noticed there was a second one in the opposite direction as well, but I opened the door to the one closest to me first.

Before I walked in, a stone arch in the garden caught my eye. I backed out of the house and walked over to take a closer look. I got a strange feeling of an intense magical presence, and I brushed my fingers over strange raised symbols. I ran into the house and found a pencil and paper on a desk and returned to trace over two of the markings and then headed back into the cottage.

Inspecting the dwelling didn't take long as there were only two bedrooms and a large study. I imagined my parents coming here to escape the nobility and smiled, knowing it's something I would do myself. I entered the study again and was filled with hope and excitement at the sight of hundreds of books that I was very eager to examine. A series of large, matching texts caught my attention and I looked at the spines. The first read *Solis: The First Age*, followed by *Solis: The Second Age*. And so on until *Solis: The Eighth Age*. I took the eighth book off the shelf and flipped through. Toward the end, I stopped at a photo of an evil looking man and a tortured woman in chains. The caption read: *Dokoran, The Demon Reina and his slave vordne, Lavinia.* I flipped to the chapter before it to find two photos of the most angelic looking people I'd ever seen. It read: *Torid & Isabaena Fenix, The Beloved Reinan.* Oh my God. These were history books. Here was the story of Solis's past, locked away where nobody could destroy them. I promised myself that I'd make sure Vish was able to read them all. I realized that those beautiful people, Torid and Isabaena, must be my great-grand-parents. How could two people whose reign was known as "beloved" give birth to the demon ruler? I needed to read these books, but I knew I couldn't take them from this place of safety. I put the book back and continued searching through the room to take in as much as possible before people realized I was missing.

There was another book that I couldn't draw my gaze away from. Some force was attracting me to it, almost begging for me to pick it up—so I did. It was oversized and the cover was thick and heavy like slabs of wood. The front of the book had a large symbol carved into it of a gold sun medallion that I swore I'd seen before somewhere. I stared at it for a while to see if I could jog my memory, but nothing came to me. I traced my finger along the rune-like mark, and every sense within me felt transfixed and connected to it. When I tried to open the text, it wouldn't budge. My skin tingled like the book was alive, and it started to slightly glow in my hands. I took out the pencil and paper again to trace the marking. I wouldn't have time to figure out how to open it, but when I got back, I could try to find out if anyone knew what it meant. Perhaps there was a library in the citadel that had the information. I still hadn't explored every inch of Eluroom castle yet.

I picked up a photo of my parents holding me as a baby with grandpa Amrel looking over their shoulder and I was stunned to see him with wings! He was absolutely stunning and ethereal, filled with a magical vitality and a youth that still screamed of ages of wisdom behind his fiery golden eyes. I longed to be in his arms again where I was safe and loved unconditionally. I would do anything for his strength and guidance and a wave of anger ran through me at the injustice of it all. If Adelram was to be believed and he did give his life for me, the guilt was debilitating. It wasn't fair and it didn't make sense for a nobody like me.

This version of grandpa was nearly unrecognizable and I imagined his level of power must be unparalleled based on his glowing aura.

Vish had called the winged beings of this galaxy the Sunya Rei, was that what grandpa was? A higher being that protected our people? If that was true it only compounded the guilt that he would die for someone who appeared to have no power at all.

The photo began to tremble and I jumped as the scene left the frame and became a life-sized 4D recreation in the room with me. It was like a scene from a movie, but I think this was actually a memory acting out right before my eyes. I stepped among these precious individuals like they were with me all together for the first time in sixteen years. I reached out to touch my mother's sorrowful face and when a tear fell I attempted to wipe it away, but my hand fell through the smoky image, not taking purchase. I sat on the sofa and watched in utter awe.

"WHO's the cutest baby Reina ever to be born?" Rhythen cooed at the baby. "That's right! You are, my darling. Did you know that 'Cyra' means Sun Throne? Yes, it's perfect for you because you will rule the people of the sun one day. I just hope I live long enough to see it," Rhythen whispered sadly.

"We'll fight to the end, Rhythen. We don't yet know what the Guardians plan for us," Brana said, touching Rhythen's shoulder.

"But Amrel has seen our deaths. You know he is never wrong."

Amrel moved beside Brana and his glow intensified, his large wings tucked behind him. He bent down toward the baby and got as close as he could without touching and looked longingly at her.

"The future is fluid and can always change. We have our backup plan. I will take Cyra to Earth to live a normal life if anything ever happens to you. She is the key to the destruction of the Guardians, and she can't be left unprotected."

Brana started crying and Rhythen held her. "I don't want to lose her, Rhythen. I can't be parted from her. She'll never know her people and her way of life. She'll never know how much we love her, and we won't know she's well cared for."

"Know now that she will never come to harm while in my care. You know this to be true. I have seen the paths of the future, and I have seen her succeed. I cannot tell you much more than that. We will start acclimating her to Earth culture now. I've put a television device in her room programmed

with childrens' entertainment along with toys from Earth. And when the time comes, we will adjust her memory and she will have a lovely life until adulthood," Amrel explained.

"No! Do not use that asshole Adelram to take my daughter's memories of us. I beg you, please don't take them from her," Rhythen pleaded through tears.

"We must, Rhythen. I'm so very sorry, but we must. And never speak of Adelram in that way, again."

GRANDPA and my parents faded from the room and I couldn't move from my utter state of shock. The look on my parents' faces over the thought of losing me would haunt me forever. I couldn't fathom how devastating it must have been to have a small baby and know you will never see her grow up. Tears streamed down my face at the amount of suffering this galaxy has seen because of the greed of the Guardians, and I had only brushed the surface of the pain.

I ran my finger over my beautiful parents' face one more time before I placed the photo back in its place and picked up the one next to it with another glowing winged figure—this one, female. Again, the subject from the photo leapt from the frame and was now life-sized in the room. I sat back down on the sofa.

"AMREL, I have had the vision of the girl and the king again—except I have more information. This girl will have the closest genetic make-up to yourself there has ever been since the beginning of time."

"Siare, are you telling me this girl...will essentially be—"

"Yes, Amrel. Based on her genetic makeup she could be considered your daughter. Do you know what this means?"

"Yes. I will protect her at all costs."

WAS THAT REAL? Was I genetically related to Amrel? How was that even possible? Another vision appeared breaking my chain of thought.

. . .

"I HAVE SEEN all possible paths. There is not one where you can defeat the Guardians by your own hand, Amrel. The girl and the Eredet king will be the only chance to bring them down. But there is a problem, the Guardians' use of dark magic is depleting our power at an incredible rate. You must find a way to slow the depletion, or we will all cease to exist before she is even born."

"What can I do, Siare? I've weighed the outcomes and I'm in an impossible situation. Anything I do from here out will only create more destruction. There is no path to take where I don't do more harm trying to hold off the end of days as long as possible," Amrel lamented.

"You must find the lesser of all the evils," Siare offered.

"Then we will proceed with the Battle of The Curses. I've never feared anything so much in my whole reign as the vision I saw of the devastating drain creating The Void Shift. May my people forgive me."

THE BATTLE OF THE CURSES. I'd seen that written somewhere in here. I rummaged around and found a small leather-bound notebook with that title written on the front. I took the book to the couch and opened it. The handwriting was unmistakably grandpa Amrel's.

THE BATTLE OF THE CURSES – Solis, The Seventh Age. Here is my account of my curse against Orphlam and his four companions.

Siare, the High Oracle, counseled me that life as we know it would collapse before the prophesized girl would be born. I was tasked with finding a way to lessen their use of our power since I could not defeat them myself. Any attempt to destroy them in their entirety on my own would end in them harnessing my power until there was nothing left, giving them the final access to an unlimited source of power or a catastrophic corruption of my own self. It would mean not only my death, but the death of all creation. They would not be able to wield and control such power regardless of their belief of their abilities. Orphlam, leader of the Guardians, managed to siphon our sun's energy through dark magic, and the draining into this siphon is constant and unending. At this time, it is unknown what he plans to do with this much energy, but he has a compulsive need in which he will never cease his attempts. The only way to slow their draining against our sun was to sneak into the Guardian temple and place a curse on their dark magic. I was

133

able to drain half of the energy they were siphoning and trap it in a mikla where it was unable to be accessed by anyone other than the one described in the prophecy. Orphlam almost destroyed me once he found me, but I was able to complete my curse before he had the opportunity to mitigate my actions. I was able to escape, but it was without the mikla. The Guardians have hidden the box and are trying everything to figure out how to open it. One small victory is that they do not know the secret to accessing it.

What I feared would come to pass, did. The Guardians found supplemental energy other than our sun to make up for the trapped energy in the mikla. They created their own curse, producing a devastating amount of ruin and destruction. An act like this calls for an extraordinary amount of power, and unfortunately, they still had enough to wield the curse with our remaining sun's energy and what they've already collected. They began by first cursing the Sunya race who held the most power of the lower beings in the galaxy, and secondly, by creating a Void Shift. My beloved first creations, designed to be the embodiment of life, turned into beings now known as the Voidlings, the embodiment of decay and death. Every choice has a consequence, and when you're a Creator, the consequences are monumental. I will have to live with their torment in my heart for the rest of my existence, which is mercifully not much longer. There is nothing I can do to reverse this curse other than rely on the chosen one to free us all. It is now certain I will have to retreat to Earth in two thousand years, and in my last act of desperation I created the race of the Bellum to protect my people in my absence. Even my own unlimited power has begun to weaken, and I could not make them immortal. As the years progressed the Bellum rebelled, they could sense their unnatural place in the galaxy and my intentions were ill-realized. I broke one of my cardinal rules, which is that creation must be organic and uninterrupted. Just because one has the ability to wield cosmic power, does not mean it should be done. The balance is a sacred covenant, and when it's tipped in an unnatural way, it creates a ripple throughout the entire expanse of the cosmos. This is why the Guardians are close to ending all existence in the blink of an eye, when it took me billions of years to mold. Our only hope now is the girl and the king.

HOLY *HELL*, Grandpa. What horrors had he endured in the span of his lifetime? And the fact that it was billions of years long didn't make it easier to stomach. At least now I had a few answers. But what did he mean when he said he was a Creator? Was it something to do with his magical strengths?

Grandpa mentioned the *Void Shift*. He knew that his actions would lead to the wasteland planet and the life being sucked out of the Voidlings. What a tremendous burden it must be to execute a plan you know will destroy so many lives. Did he make the right choice? Was there really no other way?

The light seeping through the window pulled my attention while trying to get a grasp on this information and I noticed a map on the wall. I walked over to investigate and there were three red 'X's' with the word, *Mikla*. I gasped, my hands shaking with adrenaline. Did my parents discover the possible locations of the *mikla*?

A noise steadily grew off in the distance, so I walked out of the cottage and closed the door behind me. I listened for a bit, until I heard a chilling voice. "Cyra…"

It was Orphlam!

I could feel a sickening thrum of power engulf me and it made my stomach churn with debilitating nausea. I didn't know why his magic affected me so much, but I began to perspire and the overwhelming dizziness made it hard to think clearly. My vision started to double and I wobbled forward, terrified I wouldn't make it out without him catching me. The invisible protective barrier began to crash and vibrate and I had serious doubts of how well it would hold even though I knew the Guardians had failed to get in before. The force of his power was terrifying and I was desperate to keep him out and guard my family's treasured land.

"Cyra, let us join you." The phantom voices were getting closer, like they were walking the perimeter of the barrier. I couldn't stay here since they could station someone outside of the entrance all day waiting for me to emerge. I began running toward the back of the land that I hadn't discovered yet. After what felt like an eternity I reached the edge of the property at the waterfront.

What was I going to do now? There was nowhere for me to escape to and I was unable to open the barrier before me. I started clawing and banging against the invisible wall until I screamed, "Let me out!!" in utter desperation.

As if the wall had sentience, it opened, and I quickly exited before it decided to close again. But where could I escape to? They were gaining distance and there was only the endless ocean before me or the way I came in, which wasn't an option. I inched closer to the water, trying to drive, but I was too sick and terrified, unable to activate the instant travel. Tears streamed down my face, utterly at a loss as to what I should do.

Out of nowhere, the ocean bubbled, slowly at first then quicker and more violent until a cascade of waves billowed into the air along with a massive beast that flew with a mind-blowing wingspan until it hit the sand.

I screamed and backed away as far as possible without going back into the barrier of the private lands.

"Holy *shit*. What the hell are you?" As if this day couldn't get any worse, I was about to be eaten by some kind of sea monster that looked like a dragon. My eyes widened in confusion as it tilted its head in a playful way and lowered itself until it was within arm's length of me as if the beast wanted me to touch it.

Sure, why not? I was already facing certain death and, if I had to choose, I supposed death by sea dragon was better than whatever Orphlam's horrifying imagination would conjure. Besides, I was strangely drawn to this creature, like its eyes held some kind of lure that made me want to reach out and touch it. The perimeter of the private lands boomed and shuttered so loud it sounded like thunder, making my heart pound out of my chest. I wasted no more time putting my hand to the beast's head and light shot from the point of contact down both our bodies.

The beast laid flat on the sand, wings outstretched on the ground and a serene voice entered my mind. "Climb onto my back and I will transport you to safety, Cyra."

"Did...did you just speak to me?"

"There is no time. Climb onto my back, now!" The creature wiggled tentacles on its back indicating where I should put my hands and feet. It hoisted me up with its wing and wrapped its appendages around me so I couldn't move and it flew back into the air. My screams were only heard for a moment before she dove into the water and swam at lightning speed.

Oh my God. I'm riding a sea dragon underwater. And...I could feel a connection to her now as if a small part of my soul had reserved itself for her–Laine. I somehow knew her name was Laine.

How did she know I was in danger?

"I will always be here for you in your time of need."

Did she just read my mind? I didn't have time to think more about it because I was running out of oxygen. I started thrashing against her, my screams making no difference in the depths of the ocean.

I never told anyone, but I was kind of scared of the water, and drowning was my greatest fear. Suffocating in general was a repeat nightmare of mine. My attempts to scream continued under the water as Laine swam at incredible speed.

"Laine, I can't breathe!" I yelled in my mind. It was made worse by my panic and desire to hyperventilate.

"Cyra, just breathe," she responded.

"What are you talking about? I can't breathe!" I screamed in my head.

"Breathe!" she commanded. I had no choice anyway since I had run out of oxygen and was getting woozy. I gave a sharp inhale and exhale. I was...breathing. *I'm breathing underwater!*

"Of course, you are. I told you as much," Laine communicated. I could sense her equivalent of rolling her eyes.

"Yes, I can read your thoughts. Your mind is open to me now that we've *Paeladoned*. And now you breathe through me. I give you the air you need, and you give me the voice I lack. We are one."

Wow. *I'm riding a sea dragon and breathing underwater and I might have found the location of the mikla.* The adrenaline surging through me was sky high.

I could feel her probing my mind to see what happened and where I needed to go. Without asking, she swam me to the castle shore. She emerged from the water and told me it was safe to enter land. When I dismounted, her massive head nuzzled me and she quickly disappeared before I got the chance to figure out what the fuck had just happened.

CHAPTER TWELVE

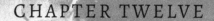

I needed to debrief everyone on what I had learned today and since they were currently off on their own, dinner was the perfect opportunity. When I arrived back in my room I sat on my bed for a few moments so my brain could process what had happened. I replayed the magical videos I saw in my mind and I tried not to break at the vivid images of my parents and grandpa Amrel *with wings*.

I looked down and saw that Meili had laid out another black dress for dinner and I was so grateful for her care and intuition. Celestine would be pleased, I thought, rolling my eyes with a smile.

A pleasant aroma hit my nose and I followed its trail into the bathroom to find a hot bath waiting for me. Did they give bonuses on Solis? Because Meili deserved all the riches in the world. She was quickly becoming my favorite person *ever*.

I sat in the tub and hummed in an attempt to soothe myself. On Earth, I would never have gone more than twenty-four hours without listening to music and I missed it terribly. It was still mind blowing to me all the things that I'd never be able to do again. I wouldn't play arcade games, go on roller coasters, ride an airplane, text my friends, write comics with my parents. I closed my eyes and pictured Brendon's face and I knew that acute ache would never fade. When I was pruned, I got out and wrapped a towel around myself.

Drained from the events of the day, I stayed in my towel and lounged in my sitting area. After a few minutes the back of my neck prickled and I looked up to see a dark figure hiding in the only shadow of the room. I yelped and fell off the sofa in shock.

In a glorious mess on the ground, I scrambled for my towel. "Kane! How long have you been standing there! Don't you knock?" I finally stood and then my towel slipped again and I screeched. It took me a few tries to grasp it and put it around me again. Why the fuck was I was so insanely clumsy?

Kane didn't make any attempt to leave. Instead, he walked closer with his hands behind his back, his eyes bearing into my soul and his muscles coiling tight like he was trying to restrain himself. His mere presence seemed to make the air thick and heavy, like his aura was too big to be contained. I could feel his power thrumming against me like a continuous pulse and it was slightly terrifying. Everything about him was *intense*.

"I did knock, but you didn't answer," he said with a sinful grin on his face. Ugh why did I let myself fall asleep, especially with no weapon within grasp. Not that I believed I needed around Kane, but anyone could have wandered in here.

"I came in to make sure you were okay after you didn't answer, and, of course, your door was unlocked. A simple oversight I'm sure, since you would never be dumb enough to leave yourself so unprotected when you're all alone and naked." Why did he seem to have the ability to know exactly what I was already thinking?

I pulled the towel up to my face as I grimaced, but then there was too much leg showing and I quickly lowered it again, flushing as his eyes snaked over every inch of them. His irises flashed with a menacing light and I was entranced by their beauty. I shuffled back into my bedroom, but he followed me.

Kane stopped when he was close enough to touch me and my whole body was on alert with that static sensation pulling me toward him. It felt like we stood there for an eternity, and I wasn't sure why I couldn't bring myself to move. I had an overwhelming desire to let my towel fall and touch myself, my body brimming with an unusual hunger that had me trembling and my mind conjuring up things it had no right to be thinking.

I was pulled out of my embarrassing daydreams when he turned away.

Holy shit, surely I was momentarily possessed by something?

He brought a hand in front of him, displaying a small figurine. It was my Dungeons and Dragons dark elf character from home! "What is this? Is this some kind of voodoo Earth magic where you rip off its head and I fall to my death?"

I burst out laughing because I knew he was serious. "No, it's just a toy. How did you get it?" I grabbed it from his hand and pretended the small brush of his finger didn't send lightning bolts through me.

"My father took it from your home because he thought it was suspicious," Kane said with a chuckle. He took his time examining my room like he owned the place, and picked up a sketch I had drawn of grandpa as I remembered him from Earth, his eyes narrowing. "Who is this? He looks familiar to me..."

"That's my grandpa Amrel," I said, smiling at his face. "He was the best person I've ever known."

Kane shot his head up and looked at me like what I said was impossible. "Did you say, Amrel?"

"Yes...why?"

"Amrel, as in The Creator of life?" Kane asked incredulously.

"Um, Amrel as in my grandpa."

"He looks a little different, but this is him. Are you telling me Amrel was with you on Earth?"

I didn't know what I was supposed to say. Adelram told me not to speak of Amrel to the Guardians, but I was beginning to trust Kane for all the pains he took to train me. I knew he was forced to work for the Guardians. And even though I didn't know all the details behind that yet, I could feel his desire for me to succeed was genuine.

"Yes. He was with me the whole time."

Kane looked utterly floored. "Nobody I know has ever seen Amrel in the flesh except my father. I've seen paintings and murals, but never in person. The Guardians are looking for him."

"I know, they asked me where he was."

"What did you say?"

"I told them I didn't know who he was," I said honestly.

THE DIVINE OBLIVION

"Good. If they got a hold of him…it'd be the end of all of us." He looked away, consumed with worry.

My eyes burned, knowing that nobody could ever get to Grandpa again.

"What is it? " Kane stepped closer, his eyebrows raised. He put a comforting hand on my bare arm and it was confounding how utterly and completely it steadied and comforted me. I had only experienced that level of protective peace from grandpa Amrel. I felt so safe-guarded that I allowed myself to come undone and feel the intensity of my grief.

"He's gone," I whispered, my eyes burning with the threat of more tears.

"What do you mean gone? Gone where?"

"He's dead. He died right before I left Earth."

Kane stumbled backward until he hit the wall in an uncharacter-istic display of weakness. He looked down at the chair next to him and sat.

"Then we're all fucked," Kane said, defeated.

"Grandpa swore that for some reason I would be able to break the curse. He told me more than once."

"Then let's pray that he's right," Kane replied with a broken spirit. He put his hand over his mouth then rubbed his square jaw.

"I found out some more information today, but I want to share it with everyone so I'll explain at dinner." This time I approached him and put my hand on his massive shoulder, and when his emerald eyes looked up at me I entirely lost my ability to breathe. There was so much unspoken passion and emotion behind his gaze and I realized I was desperate to uncover all of it. But it was probably smarter to distance myself. Things were feeling too intense in his presence and my destiny with Theo was always a constant reprimand back of my mind.

I cleared my throat awkwardly. "I'm just going to get dressed now…"

"Okay." He turned his head so he couldn't see, but he didn't leave the room. I decided not to admit to myself that I didn't mind. Or even that I secretly wanted him to peek. Fuck, why was life so goddamn complicated?

141

I dressed in the gown that was waiting for me on the bed and I couldn't reach the buttons in the back. I rolled my eyes and walked to Kane more eagerly than I would admit.

"Can you please..." I pointed to my back.

He hesitated for a moment, and I could see the muscles in his jaw clench as if he was at war with himself. It was a familiar feeling. "Sure." His voice was deep and gravely and the sound made something deep within me flutter.

Kane reached for the bottom button and the second he touched my skin, electric pulses whipped through my body. I turned my head to look at him and found his eyes already on mine. He didn't break his gaze as he slowly put his whole palm on my back and the buzzing became almost unbearable. The sensation drove me crazy–my heart raced, my breath quickened and my panties dampened with an overwhelming need for him. The rise and fall of my chest was obvious, and I bit my lip until it was almost bleeding. When I was thoroughly overcome, from the mirror I saw a bright light shoot from the point of contact on my back throughout my body and exited through my extremities.

He released his hand in shock and I turned around, wrapping my hands around myself. "What the *hell* was that? Did electricity just shoot out of me?"

"I don't know," Kane admitted quietly, clearly in shock as well.

"But you feel it too, don't you?" I spoke in a near whisper, fighting my bizarre urges to this man that was still practically a stranger.

I couldn't read the look on his face, he looked slightly desperate, but I could tell he didn't know what was happening between us.

He turned me back around gently and my treacherous brain wouldn't stop racing and my body betrayed its unexplainable desire. All I could think was that I wanted to rip the dress off so he could touch me all over. But Kane simply buttoned up the rest of my dress without touching me and I turned to him when he was done. "You look beautiful. Black suits you well."

His words did nothing to repress the firing hormones and electrical shocks rushing through me and I couldn't help but study him. He wore his usual attire of a deep hunter green sleeveless leather vest, showing off his toned arms and tattoos, and I wanted to reach out and feel every inch of them. The tattoo on his forearm looked like a flying deer with branch-like antlers flying over a moon. The wings spread far enough that the tips peaked to the front of his arm. The other two tattoos were on his bicep, one being two interlocked circles with the intersecting portion in black, and the second was of a moon covered by rainclouds.

I had to re-focus, before I did something the both of us might regret. I had a job to do and I had fully accepted that I would see it through to the end, whether I lived to see its conclusion or not. There was no longer any way I could live in this world while the Guardians lived and breathed.

"What did you mean when you said grandpa was the Creator of life?"

"It's exactly what you think. He created the Eredet galaxy and our races of people, and he created Earth. He's the first sentient being, and he created all life as we know it."

"No. You must be wrong. Or maybe it's just a coincidence. My Amrel isn't this creator –he was a simple, normal man."

"He is anything but normal. He is the deity of the cosmos."

I felt all the blood leave my face. That couldn't be who I'd loved and played with all those years. I thought back to Grandpa's favorite t-shirt that I wore the day I arrived to Solis, *If Grandpa can't fix it, we're all screwed.* Damn, if Kane was right then Grandpa really did have a sense of humor. I just hoped I could be what he was expecting. Creator of all life? What in the actual fuck? But those memories I saw in the Fenix private lands. They made a little more sense...

There was a knock at the door and Kane shot up from his seat, growling in the back of his throat, making me do a double take. I tried not to notice that his protectiveness had grown exponentially in the short time I'd known him. Meili walked into my room with a bright smile, but it disappeared when she saw Kane.

"I'm so sorry, Reina. I came to see if you needed help dressing for dinner, but I will leave you and Kane."

"Meili, wait! Please meet us downstairs toward the end of the meal, I have to talk to everyone together." She nodded and hurried out of the room quickly and Kane looked bemused.

"We should go, your *prince* will be waiting for you."

We made the debilitating trek downstairs and when we turned the corner, we bumped into each other yet again. I started to think it was that pulling force that made us repeatedly run into each other by accident. We both chose to ignore it this time and when we reached the entrance to the ballroom I gasped.

"Oh my God, half the room is wearing black!" I said under my breath to Kane.

"Looks like you made quite the impression." He looked down at me with a soft expression on his face and it made my insides feel like jelly. He always appeared fierce and primed for battle, so when that hardness melted away, he was even more breathtaking than I could fathom.

I saw Theo rushing toward me looking regal and Kane grunted before stomping away.

"You look radiant!" Theo put his hand to his heart and his look of awe was genuine. Powerful guilt overcame me, making me come back to reality. What was wrong with me? I had a fiancé I was destined to be with *to save everyone.*

My cheeks heated when I looked at Theo. "Thank you." To be honest, I felt pretty in the dress Meili made for me. It had a piece of fabric in the back that started below my shoulder blades and flowed behind me as I walked and there was a sheer portion of my back where black buttons trailed from my shoulder blades to my neck. The buttons that Kane had secured. I shivered thinking about our electrical interaction, but I quickly pushed the memory aside when I saw Theo's bright smiling face beam at me.

"Did you see what everyone is wearing tonight?" Theo laughed quietly and took my arm in his as Vish walked over to greet me as well.

"Yes! And look at you, wearing black to match me." I laughed as well and felt a swell of angry static from across the room that shot out and stung me like a slap. I followed it to see Kane indignantly grinning at me and I couldn't believe it—*I think he did that on purpose.*

I was so mad that I reached inside myself and envisioned smacking him back with that force I could feel engulfing me, until I felt a piece of it group together then rush out of me. I looked to Kane and he jumped in his seat, looking at me in stunned silence and I put my hand over my mouth trying not to laugh. I had no idea how I did that, but it seemed like my training was starting to pay off.

Celestine walked into my line of sight with all her teeth showing in a comical grin. "Reina, look at this movement the two of us started! We're quite the pair, aren't we?"

"We sure are," I said without looking away from Kane, the force between us seeming to swell until I forced my eyes away.

After we finished eating, I led Theo and Vish to where Kane and Adelram sat to fill them in on what I saw. We all relocated to a quiet corner and I waved Meili over when I saw her enter the room.

"Oh no, are we in trouble?" Adelram crouched in mock fear.

"Shut up and listen. I went to the Fenix lands this morning and found out more about the Guardians, the curse, and possible locations of the *mikla*."

They all had varying expressions of shock on their faces. "You went without help or protection?" Theo asked with hurt in his voice.

"I had to go on my own, I wanted to see what was in there for myself before bringing anyone else there. We already know that the Guardians are siphoning our energy, but what we didn't know is that Amrel had to slow down their siphoning or they would have already killed our sun. That is the energy that is in the *mikla*. The Guardians then placed a curse on the planets of Eredet to drain energy directly from them and from the Sunya race, which is continually making them into the Voidlings. Once a Sunya hits puberty and they've procreated, the curse from the Guardians sets in and they begin to wither away. In regards to the locations of the *mikla*, if I see a map I can show you where the probable locations are. Oh, and a bizarre side note, a sea dragon saved me."

Vish and Keeran looked at each other with bulging eyes, but Meili waved her hand and produced a map and all attention was steered to her.

"Okay, who's the chick?" Adelram blurted, finally suspicious enough of her.

"Hey," I chided.

"No, seriously, she's got some intense powers for a *criada* and she's listening to our private and dangerous plans. Either we know what we're dealing with or I don't trust her," Adelram reasoned.

I supposed he had a point. I looked to Meili. She nodded, giving me permission to tell her story.

"Meili is Sunya. She was saved from the horrible fate of becoming a Voidling."

They were utterly silent. "Meili is a Voidling?" Vish asked horrified.

"She *would* have been a Voidling. This is what the Voidlings are supposed to be, before the life is drained from them. My mother saved her."

"You can all trust me. I will die serving the Fenix family line," Meili finally spoke up.

"I'd like to look into your mind and see how Cyra's mother saved you," Adelram asked Meili with a raised brow, distrust coloring his voice.

"Oh. Um…okay."

"I'll do it later in case there's any strange side effects that will draw attention to us."

I glared at Adelram. "Make sure there are no side effects." He rolled his eyes and shook his head.

Vish gently took the map from Meili and handed it to me.

"Interesting. The marks were in these three places, but the islands are not here on this map." I pointed to the approximate locations.

"Then they're probably shrouded," Adelram said.

"I can detect hidden magicks," Kane offered.

"I will ready my ship and we'll go in person to search for these islands. It'll take a few days," Theo said, glaring at Kane with distrust.

"Well, baby *Reina*. You're finally fighting to test my theory of you being an utter waste of space," Adelram said before he turned and left the room. He was the most monumental dick I'd ever met.

The rest of the night passed uneventfully and I enjoyed my time with Theo while trying to ignore the demanding connection I had with Kane. Theo made me laugh more in one night than I had since before grandpa Amrel died and it hit me just how long it had been since I'd really enjoyed myself. Theo had given me a reprieve from my long-standing sadness.

After dinner, he drove me to my room as usual and he kissed my hand. I stopped him before he could go and gave him a tight hug, inhaling his soothing scent deeply. He held my face when I pulled back, looking deep into my eyes, and I could tell he was restraining himself. He reached to kiss me on my cheek, lingering for a moment, and my body responded to his gentle, sweet touch.

"I'll do everything I can to win your affections, Cyra. And I'm willing to wait as long as it takes. I could finally feel a little bit of joy seeping into you tonight and it made me so happy."

I believed every word, because Theo was pure. He was simply a joy to be with, and he was easy. I needed easy in my life more than anything. I leaned in closer to him, like a moth to flame. I wanted to see what more he had to offer and I wanted to be able to fulfill my destiny. I wanted to see what joy tasted like. Theo's eyelids slightly lowered, looking at me with anticipation. He leaned down closer, but waited to see if it was what I wanted.

I touched my lips to his and the softness of him made me weak at the knees. Theo was someone I could see a future with.

CHAPTER THIRTEEN

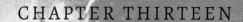

$\mathcal{I}$ woke up early the next morning and found a note next to my bed from Theo, telling me he wouldn't be available until late afternoon. If he was meeting with the Masters of Solis, I wish he would have brought me. I'd let him know next time I saw him.

There was another note with a plate of food from Bad telling me I had better eat since I was all skin and bones. I smiled at the meal he'd generously left me and how he'd remembered one of my favorite treats.

I sat quietly for a few moments unsure what to do with myself and feeling incredibly lonely. I gently brushed my fingers over where Theo had touched last night and felt a detached kind of confusion.

The only thing I could think of that could ease a little bit of my restlessness again was my cello. I got up and realized I didn't have anything to change into, so I put on my Darth Vader slippers and a white robe with blush pink lace trim that Meili had left me and walked back to the music room. Just seeing my cello again centered me a little and I let out a sigh of relief. I sat in the chair by the cello stand and picked up the instrument and bow and hugged them to my lap. I decided to play *Cello Concerto in B Minor, OP.104, B. 191:2.* by Dvorák. In my opinion it was one of the most beautiful pieces ever composed and it was just over twelve minutes long.

As I played, I shed a great deal of sadness as its energy was transferred into the song and ultimately transformed into the most beautiful sounds that echoed throughout the large open room. This was just what I needed and I gave the music all the dedication and emotion it required. When I neared the end of the song, I looked up and saw a golden light that quickly disappeared.

"Meili?" I called out. When I heard no response, I called out again, "Meili, I know you're there."

She slowly came into the room and there were tears flooding her face. I immediately stood. "Meili, what happened? Are you okay?"

"I'm more than okay, Reina. That was the most beautiful thing I've ever heard. I desperately love music and I haven't heard it in probably sixty years. It just moved me."

"Wow, sixty years is a long time to go without music. I'm happy to play for you anytime you like."

"I wish the castle workers could have heard this song. I think they would have the same reaction as me."

"Well then I'll play for them too. When can they come up?"

"Oh, they'd come up now if they knew they could hear music again." Meili was dismissive, but I was serious. How could anyone live so long without music? It would be a miserable existence.

"Then spread the word. I'll play here again in an hour. Invite all the workers you can find, and don't forget the Voidlings."

Meili looked at me like I had lost my mind.

"Oh, and if you can see if anyone from Blaze's Public House would like to come too. Make sure the guards in the back private entrance allow them. Well, I'd better get changed first. Shall we head back to my room?"

Meila stumbled over herself a little, a contrast from her usual perfection. "O-of course, Reina."

"Cyra."

"Cyra," Meili repeated with wide eyes. It motivated me even more to give the suffering working class people a little treat, and at the moment it was all I had to offer.

When we entered my room Meili held up a casual dress. "I've been studying Earth fashions, I thought you would be comfortable in something like this on an off-duty day."

"Meili, this is *wonderful,* thank you."

I was obviously capable of putting it on myself since it was a loose babydoll dress. Formalwear was nice and had surprisingly grown on me, but I had missed my lazy leggings and broken-in jeans. The babydoll was the next best thing.

Meili styled my hair in a high, loose ponytail and I smiled at the familiar normalcy. "I'll be back in that room in an hour for anyone who would like to hear some music, even if it's only you."

Meili flashed a big, sincere smile. "I wouldn't miss it for the world."

I still wasn't sure what an hour actually felt like, but I made my best guess then headed to the music room. I stopped short when I reached the threshold because there were probably fifty employees and another twenty patrons of Blaze's nervously standing around. I found Bad and waved as he bolted to embrace me.

"Cyra, I'm so proud that you kept up your parents' love for music. I can't wait to hear what you can do."

Blaze walked to me with an air of confidence and held out his hand. I shook it as some of the workers quietly gasped in surprise. I didn't understand why it was so foreign for a Reina to be interacting with her people. "I left a sign outside the house that we were closed for an hour. This is something I wouldn't miss, my first time stepping foot in the castle."

"You've never been here before?"

"Not a once. And a personal escort to your own private entrance. I'm impressed, Reina." His smile was genuine and I saw everyone looked to him as their representative.

"Well, it's not much, but I hope you all enjoy."

To my utter relief the three Voidlings had come too. I desperately wanted to give them something apart from their daily toil and suffering.

"Thanks for coming. I'm glad to see there's so many music enthusiasts. If you all like this, we can make it a recurring event. I won't keep you too long from your duties, this piece is twelve minutes. I hope you like it as much as I do."

I sat down, and began to play, performing with all the heart and passion I felt for these people who were dealt a shitty hand in life, and I didn't think anyone suffered more than the Voidlings who I watched with curiosity. They sat quietly with their eyes closed and to my relief, they looked like they *really* enjoyed it. Some small speck of their agony was lessened from their decaying faces and I tried not to weep at how painful their lives must be.

A static buzzing slowly grew in my body and knew that if I looked up I would find Kane nearby. In fact, I noticed a shadow in the corner of my eye toward the left part of the room, but I had to keep my head down so I could pay attention and give the music the justice it deserved. I wasn't sure when he showed up, but Vish was also there in the doorway, watching with curiosity and surprise.

As I neared the end of the song for the second time, I had to fight to hold back my own tears as I saw most of the room couldn't contain their own and, to my complete surprise, that included Vish directly in my line of sight. When I concluded, it was completely silent and I started to worry the performance wasn't what they'd hoped, but then the room erupted in applause. I observed the glowing faces and it filled me with joy, but then I felt like the breath was knocked out of me with the buzzing sensation crushing my windpipes. I turned to Kane's direction behind me, and he too looked like might have had a glisten in his eyes before he bolted out of the room in a hurry.

Bad approached me with his arms outstretched and he pulled me in for another hug. "That was incredible. We definitely need to do this more often, but I need to run and make sure the kitchen isn't burning down."

"You got it, Bad. I'll see you soon."

He kissed me on the cheek with his eyes still red and whispered, "I'm so proud of you," before he walked out of the room.

The other workers bowed to me one by one with their thanks as they left, but I didn't think it was for the sake of my title, but rather appreciation for the music. I approached Mylo, eager to talk to him after our last encounter.

He tried to communicate but was unable, so Meili came to his aid.

"I think he enjoyed this immensely, Reina. Thank you for doing this for us."

Mylo stepped a little closer to me as best he could, and he raised his peeling hand to point to me. "B...b...eautiful." He pointed again at me and repeated, "Beau...tiful."

I'd never fought so hard to choke back tears before. "Thank you, Mylo. I still have some questions for you so I will try to come find you this week."

Meili led him and the other two Voidlings out of the room and then Vish and I were alone.

"You know, I've never seen a Reina speak to a Voidling before and now I've seen it twice. In fact, I've never even seen a Voidling speak. I didn't think they could," Vish mused.

"You'd be surprised what people can do if you just give them a chance," I said, slightly annoyed by his comment.

"Oh, Cyra, I didn't mean it like that, only that I admire you for it. I appreciate what you did for all the workers, not to mention your talent blew me away."

"Shouldn't you be at *Sun Eine?*" I almost wondered if Vish was following me.

"I was going to ask you the same thing. It's why I'm here. When I saw you missing, I came to see if you'd like me to escort you, but obviously you had other plans. Once I saw you play, I couldn't leave."

"Well, I don't blame you, it's one of my favorites. It's really a beautiful piece. It gives me the chills most times I play it."

Vish smiled and nodded, giving the cello one last look before he walked away. I stood alone in the room for quite a while. The looks of pain, past betrayals and injustice on the people of the working class haunting me like reverberating echoes through the vast room.

CHAPTER FOURTEEN

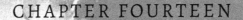

"*A*gain!" Kane yelled.

"I thought you said we were going to finish up an hour ago?" I whined with my shoulders slumped in exhaustion.

"We would have been done an hour ago if you had showed any signs of progress, but you insist on fighting me tooth and nail. It's as if you don't want to succeed."

"Holy shit, how many times do I have to tell you that I am trying everything I can, but it's not working!" Flames ignited all over my body and I yelped when I smelled burning hair.

Damnit! Most of my bra and underwear peeked through the destroyed portions of my dress and a part of my hair was singed. Why could I only produce a great amount of fire when I wasn't trying?

"Surely you will restore my clothing this time? I look ridiculous."

Kane circled me slowly and I raised my chin in defiance. I didn't care if he saw my disgrace. I think. When his sparkling emerald eyes looked at me, my resolve shattered to the winds.

"I think you look rather delicious, not ridiculous."

Holy hell, was he flirting?

"And a deal is a deal. You have not earned it yet. But I will restore your hair because it's too lovely a color to be left ruined." Kane gently ran his fingers through my hair and I thought I was going to keel over then and there. Looking down, I saw my long deep burgundy locks were no longer burnt and as his fingertips brushed the bare skin of my arm, my eyes involuntarily closed in delight.

When I realized I was giving myself away I snapped out of it. "Fine, I guess that'll do. I think we're done for today!" I ran away from him as fast as I could, still fearful he could smell my desire and I heard his stupidly wonderful laughter from a distance.

I was exhausted. It felt like Kane was trying to punish me in the last few sessions we'd had, and my thighs shook with every dreadful step back to my room. I sarcastically laughed to myself that Kane kept insisting that it was embarrassing how easy he was taking it on me and that of course only made me seethe in anger. The aches and pains of my body told me I had been working hard. My magic was improving, but only slightly. I couldn't find whatever connection I needed to master it the way I should. But I felt a small glimmer of achievement that I was able to steal another weapon, a spear head that was so dull that I doubted it would have any use other than chucking it at someone, but a win was a win. My growing collection made a sinister smile bloom on my lips.

Adelram had been conspicuously absent from my last few training sessions, which normally I wouldn't have minded, but if I wanted to get as much information as possible to break this curse and fulfill the prophecy, then I needed his expertise. Kane's father was something of an annoying enigma to me and the longer I thought about him, the dizzier I felt. I made it back to my room and immediately sat in the first chair I saw just in time for a vision to sweep me away.

"I'M SCARED," I cried in a child's voice. "I want my mommy and daddy back. Someone hurt them."

Adelram bent down to my height. "Don't worry, little one. I know you're scared, but these people will protect you. Remember your past happy feelings. Remember what it means to be secure by loving parents. Remember the love of friends and of bedtime stories that make you feel safe. Remember to fight when you need to and, above all, remember one day you will have a greater purpose."

A tear ran down Adelram's face as he continued, "Please, little one, when I take your memories— don't forget these things. They're very important."

"Are you going to hurt me?" I asked innocently.

"Never, dear Cyra. I would never hurt you. And I will do anything to keep you safe. Always."

Adelram kissed me on the cheek and another tear fell down his face. "Now close your eyes..."

OH...MY...GOD. That was why I always felt lost, like I had a higher purpose I wasn't fulfilling. That's why I'd felt like something was missing that I couldn't explain. Adelram wanted that feeling in the back of my mind and he planted it there. And what was this side of Adelram that I couldn't fathom was real? He had the highest hopes for me when he took me to Earth and wiped my memories, but when he brought me back to Solis, he called me *an utter disappointment.* What had changed between then and now? I needed answers, and I needed them now. I stood shakily and walked outside to the guard who was by his post down the stairs.

"Can you tell me where Meili's room is?"

"Certainly, Reina."

He directed me to the basement below the kitchens and I made the excruciating trip down and knocked on the door, not knowing if she'd even be there. Did she really walk that far up and down multiple times a day?

When Meili opened the door, she jumped in shock at my presence, but she curtsied and said, "Reina, what can I do for you? Are you okay?"

"I'm so sorry to bother you, Meili, I was just wondering if you knew where Adelram might be?" I had no idea how to find people on this planet—they really needed to invent cell phones (not that I thought for one minute that Adelram would ever answer me).

"I don't believe he's on any official business, which means he's probably at the Pogenemine. He spends almost all his free time there."

"Pogenemine? What's that?"

"You've probably heard people around here mention the Pog. It's a bar at the very end of the castle open to all, including the working class."

"Interesting," I mumbled.

"Would you like me to take you there?"

"No! Please don't trouble yourself, I'll find my own way there." Before I turned to leave, I peered over Meili's shoulder and saw a dingy room barely big enough to fit her bed. I curled my lip in disgust, "These are your quarters, Meili?"

She looked down and fidgeted. "Yes, Reina. It's okay for me. I don't need more, and I would have nothing to fill it."

I was dumbfounded. Meili was not staying in this dark hole if I had anything to do with it. I nodded and smiled easily. "Have a good afternoon."

"You too." She quietly closed the door and I let my smile drop, thinking about her cramped room with no windows at the furthest point from my own, but I would have to deal with it later. Right now, I had to go to the Pog and see if Adelram was there.

I ended up having to stop and ask about six guards how to get to the Pog, but I eventually made it after a long, *long* walk. I decided then that it was a matter of life and death that I learn how to drive.

I walked into the castle side entrance of the Pog and gaped at the sheer amount of people crowding the bar, it couldn't have been much later than mid-day. I started walking around the large room and focused first on the extensive bar in the center that held maybe fifty to sixty bar stools around it. It didn't take me long to find Adelram at one of the far ends that had a few empty spaces around him, as if nobody dared to sit next to him. I snickered to myself, understanding why everyone here would keep them empty.

Knowing I'd pay for it, I sat down in one of those empty seats.

"Ugh, seeing you here means I've had too little or too much to drink. Either way, barkeep! Get me three more and don't make me wait this time!"

"Do you really need to be drinking this early, Adelram?" I asked seriously.

"Yes, I do need. Nobody asked you to come searching for me."

"Adelram, a memory returned to me today. The memory of you

taking me to Earth when you asked me not to forget a few things. Why were you so sweet then, but such an overwhelming ass now? Is there something you're not telling me?"

"Why do you have to annoy the shit out of me during my time off? Can't you see I'm busy forgetting my own memories? I could care less about yours," Adelram spat, not even looking in my direction.

"What do *you* have to forget? Too many traumatizing escorts to the banquet hall?"

He banged down his cup and slowly turned to glare at me and his eyes raged in a fiercely bright moonglow. The entire bar darkened with shadows creeping from every corner, and the air chilled about twenty degrees. The other patrons went silent and looked around at the source of atmospheric change, and I didn't blame them. I started to regret my stupid decision to poke the quiet bear.

He said with more venom and disdain than I was prepared for, "That is *none* of your fucking business, *Reiiiiina.* Luckily for me, you can't come near my mind. If I were your pathetic self, I'd quickly avoid being the center of my attention. Now get lost, I'm sure you have some other poor soul to disappoint and a universe to destroy."

I wouldn't let him get to me. I would ignore the excruciating pang of inferiority and failure.

"Was Grandpa really the creator of life?" I whispered to him.

Adelram leapt off his stool with a look of panic on his face.

"Idiot child. This is exactly what I'm talking about, does this look like the place to talk about such things? You'll get yourself killed even earlier than I thought."

"Then when is the time, Adelram?" I shouted. "After you've had five more drinks and you crawl back to whatever dark hole you came from?" I shook my head in disgust as half of the bar looked in our direction. "And you call me the useless one. I doubt this is what grandpa had in mind for you. At least I give a shit. You're just pathetic."

I turned and walked away from him, bolting for the door and bumping into someone in my haste.

"Sorry," I mumbled, but the stranger had my wrist in a lock so I couldn't move.

"Didn't I tell you to watch yourself or there would be dire consequences?" I looked up and it was the Guardians' cronie I'd previously
ran into at the castle entrance after Theo took me on the tour of Solis
East. Shit.

"Like I said, sorry." I moved around him, but he damn near pulled
my arm out of its socket.

"I didn't say you could go. In fact, this is an opportune meeting.
I've got plans for you."

Everything immediately went black. I felt that familiar squeezing
pressure overcome me and thought I was going to suffocate to death
during the unexpected drive.

We appeared somewhere full of trees, rocks, and sand and I was so
sick from the instant travel that I was plastered to the ground uncontrollably retching, clenching my side.

"Aw, don't go and do that, you'll spoil some of our fun. Vomit is
just unseemly." The stranger laughed as an approaching crowd of men
laughed with him.

"Wh—Where did you take me? What do you want?"

"We're just a bunch of struggling folk, trying to make ends meet."

"Get your hands off me! I'm the Reina."

"And your point is?"

The men off in the distance started closing in on me and I struggled to try to get up off the ground as I saw that there were about
fifteen of them. Oh my God. I had no chance getting away from these
people. Despite my training, I couldn't take on all fifteen of them and
my magic was far from controlled. My breathing was erratic and
labored and I couldn't get enough air into my lungs. Not to mention I
still had nausea and vertigo from the improper drive.

The man who took me grabbed my arm and pulled me to him. His
stench was an overwhelming mix of stale alcohol, old sweat and body
odor. I pushed back, slapped him frantically and tried to run. He
grabbed me again and punched me hard, right in the middle of my
face so that my nose started bleeding and my eyes were temporarily
blinded from the blow. I could see nothing but stars flashing behind
my eyelids and I fell back to the ground face first, dirt filling my
mouth and my switchblade flying from my pocket.

"If you would just behave this wouldn't take long at all." He bent down and pocketed my blade and all my well-laid plans of protection died within seconds.

Tears began to fall from the pain and the realization that despite my training, I was absolutely *powerless* in this situation. Maybe Kane was right and I wasn't trying hard enough. I attempted to connect to my fire, but it was utterly silent. *What the fuck?*

I couldn't stop shaking and the feeling of utter helplessness despite the raging fight inside me was soul-crushingly devastating.

"Stop, guys, this isn't right!" someone said in the distance. With my sight returned, I looked over to a petrified teenage boy who seemed to have been dragged along for the ride.

"Shut up, Dax, we have a job to do," my abductor shouted. "If you want to get through your initiation into the Guardian's Sentry, you'll have to fucking man up.

"What kind of cowards are you that you need fifteen of you with only one of me? Are you scared, little bitches?" Bating them might not be the best idea, but I was trying to buy some time.

"We're just sensible. We have no idea what kind of power you have yet, and we've been tasked with acquiring some of your blood. A lot of blood, unfortunately for you," he said with a half-hearted shrug as if he couldn't care less if it killed me. A man walked up to the leader and handed him what looked to be at least ten large syringes.

Oh *hell no.* They were not taking a piece of me without the fucking fight of their lives. I jumped to my feet and slammed my fist into his face as hard as I could, and *fucking hell* it hurt much worse than I anticipated.

"Bitch!"

Two of the other men grabbed me and I fell to the ground again. My nails were full of dirt and blood as I tried to claw my way to freedom, making no difference at all. My abductor tied a tourniquet around my bicep and two more men held me so I was still.

"Get off me, you assholes!"

None of them paid any attention to me. I screamed in defiance as the first needle pierced my skin and I watched with horror as my blood filled the syringe. I had never tried so hard to quiet my mind, and I scoured desperately for my energy. I closed my eyes and the first thing I connected to was the sound of Kane's voice, instructing me to *believe* in myself and have confidence in my abilities. I pictured his forest green eyes, piercing me with their intensity as they usually did. A small amount of flames ignited in my hands and the men holding me there cursed and let go.

I managed to kick the others off one more time before my abductor stomped on my wrist and I heard it crack in multiple places. Blinded with pain, I screamed to the heavens praying for this to stop.

Enough.

I'd had *enough*.

An inferno ignited within me, bubbling and building rapidly until all I could see was fire. It must have been obvious what was happening because the men around me started to disperse and run as the blood-filled syringe rolled behind me, compounding my fury. I screamed at the top of my lungs, and a force of energy I didn't realize was hidden in my depths burst from me in an all-encompassing rage. Fire billowed and burst from every inch of me and I threw it with uncontrolled chaos towards anyone standing in my line of sight. Their cries of pain were a welcome symphony to my ears. No one would take something from me that I did not freely give.

My fire extinguished quickly, not used to expelling that much energy and I shook from being depleted as if I was hypoglycemic and in danger of passing out. But I smiled as countless beads of sweat ran down my face. Ten of the vile wastes of space that were employed by the Guardians were incinerated heaps of trash on the ground, smoking in the wind.

Suddenly, I felt a boiling hot sensation blasting through my body with unstoppable force. I looked up with my one eye that wasn't swollen shut, and Kane and Adelram appeared with murderous looks on their faces.

"Well shit, girl, I thought I was going to get to play a new role of savior," Adelram said, his brows raised with an impressed expression.

Kane was not amused. He walked over to the man who abducted me from the bar and in his attempt to run, he tripped and fell.

"I was just following orders!"

Adelram raised his hands and lightning burst from them at the three other men who were running away behind me. They fell dead instantly, joining the others, smoking on the ground. The small hairs on the back of my neck raised from his electricity and I shivered at his power.

Kane looked to me with his teeth bared and he growled. "Is this the trash that took you?"

I nodded. Kane picked him up by his neck and raised him into the air as if the weight was absolutely nothing to him.

"If you kill me, Orphlam will have your head! I'm the leader of his Sentry! I was just following orders!"

"This is how much I give a shit." Kane threw him to the ground and began to grow a ball of black wisps of energy in his hands.

"Oh, everyone watch, this is my favorite part," Adelram clapped. It was evident he was still probably tipsy.

Kane extended his hands so the black tendrils grew while the man stood and tried to get away. He didn't get far. When Kane snapped his hands open wide, my kidnapper was split into two from his head all the way to the bottom of his torso. I only felt a small amount of sympathy for the innards and gore that spewed from him and spread on the ground.

The boy next to me started crying at these two terrifying creatures that dealt death like a casual hobby, and they were heading right for him.

"Wait. Don't hurt him. He tried to help me."

Adelram bent down in front of the poor boy and said, "Well, it is your *lucky* day, boy. I thought you were dessert. Very well, I guess I'm full enough. Tell anyone what you saw here and I'll hunt you down and slit your throat myself."

Kane ran with a look of horror on his face as he knelt before me. He grabbed my non-broken hand. "I'm going to bring you to the healer," he whispered, as if the sound of his voice could hurt me.

Adelram quickly took off his shirt and covered me since I had singed my clothes away. I was a little surprised by the mindful gesture. Kane very gently picked me up and cradled me in his arms and I tried not to wince in pain in front of him. I looked into his eyes with an all-encompassing gratitude, and a tear falling down my open eye. "Thank you."

"Shh," was all he said.

"Remind me not to get on your bad side, *Reina.*" Adelram smirked with one eyebrow raised.

"Adelram, you *live* on my bad side."

"Oh. Good point." He looked at the full syringe on the ground and zapped it so the blood was destroyed.

Kane held me as close to his body as he could, being considerate of me hitching a ride, and we appeared in the private beach at the castle again. I didn't feel sick from the drive this time. Kane ran all the way upstairs to my bedchambers with Adelram following.

He laid me on my bed and Adelram said, "I'll get the healer." When he was gone Kane spoke.

"You did amazing, killing ten of those men. I'm so proud of you." He moved a strand of hair from my face and I held my hand to his so it stayed on my cheek. I shivered at his praise and closed my eyes focusing on what his touch did to me. The buzzing energy was alive within me and it felt as if my magic was being restored by his mere presence.

"It's all thanks to you and your training."

"No, it's due to you and your hard work. I see the power and potential within you. I truly believe that there's no limit to what you can do, Cyra, when you believe in yourself and realize your potential. You'll be utterly unstoppable. You're a bright star in the darkness of our galaxy."

A tear fell from my eye and I was filled with overwhelming gratitude for this man and how he made me feel like I could actually be the one from the prophecy. He made me a better person, believing in myself when I was at my lowest point in my life. His power, control and authority was terrifying but wonderful. He was beauty and brutality, and I wanted to embody that too. I was already well on my way to mastering my gift because of his careful guidance.

Adelram burst back in with Serin and I instantly sighed in relief. Serin's mere presence was soothing, and I relaxed as he said, "There now, Reina. I'm going to make you as good as new."

"You remember Serin, right? He's the best healer on Solis," Adelram offered, his eyes looking over me as if he was actually concerned.

Serin smiled sweetly and took both of his hands and ran them along my whole body as if searching beneath the skin. "Some bones in her wrist are broken, and her nose is fractured."

Serin then gently took my broken wrist and held it in his hands, and a warm comforting light seeped into my hand. It was a euphoric feeling, like he had pumped me full of morphine. After a few moments he moved to my nose and released the same calming light, and I could feel the shattered pieces fusing back together. He put his hand over my eye and healed it so I could open the lid again.

"You're all healed, but it could take a few days for the pain to completely disappear. Your body released a bunch of pain signals and now it'll be confused that the injury's gone. Sometimes it takes a little longer to disappear than if you had healed naturally on your own. But you will be okay."

"Will I be able to play my cello normally?" The thought had been plaguing me since I'd realized it was broken.

"You'll have full function of your hand as you did before."

"Thank you so much, Serin."

"And thank you, Reina, for giving me something to hope for. I look forward to hearing you play again soon." He nodded to me and left the room.

"What the hell do the Guardians want with my blood?" Any possibility sickened me, and I could only thank the freaking stars that they didn't get their hands on it.

"I don't know, but I do know that the Guardians like to perform… experiments," Kane said with his eyes down, unease overtaking his features.

"Oh God. What kind of experiments?"

"I have no idea what they were doing, but I was usually strapped to a table with sharp implements cutting me open like they were searching for something."

I gasped, grabbing hold of his arm as bile singed the lining of my throat.

"Let's just be thankful they didn't succeed and double down on our training sessions so you're protected." Kane looked back at me and his determination gave me strength.

"Get some rest. I have a feeling you're going to need it," Adelram nodded in my direction.

They both started to leave, but I stopped them. "Wait!" They turned around to look at me and I locked eyes with Adelram. "Thanks for doing anything to keep me safe...always," I said, referencing the memory.

He actually winked at me before he turned back and walked out of my room, still shirtless.

CHAPTER FIFTEEN

*T*he next morning Meili ran into my bedroom looking rattled, no doubt having heard what happened to me from Adelram after I'd asked him to fill her in. "Cyra, are you okay?" She sat next to me on the bed and held my hand. It was the one that was crushed and Serin was right, it *did* still hurt a great deal. In fact, it was excruciating, but I wouldn't let Meili know that.

"I'm glad you're here, I have something important to ask you."

"Anything, Cyra." I was beyond happy that she chose to use my name instead of a title. She was becoming one of my best friends.

"I need two daggers with a holster to strap to my thighs under my dresses. I'll be requiring that every day now." I needed something more secure than my pathetically concealed stolen weapons and it was time to change that. "Do you think you'll be able to find them? I know our weapons stock is low."

Meili looked taken aback, but she didn't question me and I loved her for it. "Of course. I'll get some for you as soon as possible, there are ways to find weapons."

I squeezed Meili's hand back as best I could despite the devastating pain. "Thank you for everything, Meili. I couldn't make it through these days without your help."

"It is my honor and my pleasure."

She quickly helped me dress then left to find me what I asked for. I was on my way to get my spearhead from Grandpa's box before heading to training, but I stopped short, feeling off. It quickly escalated until nausea overcame me while my organs felt like they were trying to escape my body. My screams were cut short when everything went black and I was transported to a place of pure darkness. What the hell? Someone had just driven me out of my room to another location.

"Hello! Help!" I slowly felt the walls around me since I was unable to see and came to a solid metal door, and when I pushed against it I knew it wasn't going to budge. To either side of me were bars, but I couldn't see if there was anything on the other side of them and when I reached my hands through the iron bars there was nothing to grab onto. I was in captivity, a jail of some kind, and the moment I realized that I was glued in place, shaking with my heart racing out of control.

"Help!" I kept screaming, hoping someone would hear me, and when I was able to move again I threw my fist into the steel door over and over until I was thoroughly bruised. All I could do was endlessly pace, trying my best not to cry. I banged and kicked every bar in the cell and ripped at every corner of the room I could reach, feeling the warmth of blood spilling from my efforts to break free. I continued my attempts to escape for what felt like an hour, then two, then three until I truly felt defeated by my terror alone. There was something inhuman (or whatever the equivalent to that was for a Solian) about being held captive, alone in the darkness that induced madness. Sitting on the ground, I held my knees to my chest and rocked, closing my eyes and trying to self-soothe to no avail.

It was unfathomable how long I was there, alone and confused, and the moments dragged on until I couldn't tell if hours or days had passed. Eventually I began to see things, and I convinced myself that Brendon was with me, his warm brown eyes and endearing smile bringing me a small amount of comfort before I fell into despair again.

"I'm so sorry I left you behind," I whispered into the void with tears streaming down my face. The guilt of being parted from him always crept up in the quiet moments of loneliness, remembering our pact that we would always have each other. But I had lost everything and everyone I loved, and being forced to sit alone and afraid with no vision I could do nothing but allow all my grief to flood my mind, crushing my soul.

The first disturbance came when I felt a blinding pain in my arm and I screamed into the vast darkness. *What is happening to me?* I was certain that my arm was broken, but after a moment the pain subsided like it was all in my head. But the pain continued, in my feet, legs, fingers, toes and I started to prepare myself that I would die in this room, alone and delirious. My death wasn't even my scariest thought, it was the failure of not having helped those who needed it if I died here and now. It was the thought of letting Grandpa down.

Mercifully the pain stopped and I jolted to my feet when I heard someone entering down the hall. "Help!" I screamed, but no one answered. The cell next to me opened and someone was thrown to the ground with a massive thump. "Who's there? Let us the fuck out, now!"

A slit at the metal door opened and I scrambled until my back was against the opposite wall. Orphlam's red glowing eyes peered through the small window and the evil that they emitted stopped my heart in its tracks.

"You have displeased me." As usual, his presence made me ill and it was hard to get my bearings when he was so close.

"I haven't done anything. Let me out!" I spoke with infinitely more conviction than I felt.

"That's not how this works. My Sentries were killed and you must answer for it."

"They attacked me, you asshole!"

His hum of power intensified in anger and I doubled over with sickness.

"Your disrespect will have consequences." The slit slammed closed and I ran to the door and pounded against it, knowing it wouldn't budge.

"Come back here, you coward! What did you want with my blood?" But he was already gone and I knew I wouldn't get answers.

With Orphlam's disappearance, I started to feel Kane's familiar static and my heart dropped realizing it was him lying unconscious in the cell next to me. I ran quickly and knelt down, putting my arm out as far as possible and was just able to reach his hand. I pulled it a little closer and intertwined my fingers with his so he knew he wasn't alone.

"Oh God, please be okay. Kane?" There was no response and I choked on my desperation. "Please. Kane, I...need you. Please wake up."

I sang quietly for countless minutes to fill the painful silence and to let him know he wasn't alone, until he finally stirred.

"Kane! Are you alright? What did Orphlam do to you?"

"Cyra, thank goodness you're safe."

I let out a small laugh. "I'm not sure safe is the right word, but I'm alright. Tell me what happened to you," I demanded. He straightened and sat against the bars and took both of my hands in his as we faced each other. I was able to make out the soft glow of his green eyes and his tattoos, which caught me by surprise. I had no idea his tattoos had a light to them since we were always under the brilliance of the sun, but they were truly beautiful this way.

"Orphlam was out for blood, I told him I killed all the Sentries because they attacked you and he broke most of my bones, Serin healed me after each break."

I squeezed his hands in anger. "Why did you do that? It's not the truth, I killed most of them."

He moved his hands from mine and leaned in and held my face. We leaned in until our foreheads touched through the bars. "Because he would have hurt you and I wouldn't have been able to stop myself from attacking him. Nobody will lay a finger on you if I have any say in it, and, if they do, they will answer to me." His thumb gently brushed over my lip in the darkness and I leaned into him, relishing his touch.

My heart fluttered at his words. "But he hurt you, instead." I stilled for a beat. "Did he start with your arm then move to your legs?"

"How did you know that?"

"I felt all of it. Probably not as hard as you did, but I felt all of it."

Kane became rigid and I reached out for his hands again. "What do you think that means?" Orphlam probably found a way to send pain signals to me so I suffered as much as possible.

"Turn around," he ordered.

I was in no mood to argue so turned against the bars and he scooted closer so his arms wrapped around me tight and I melted into his embrace.

"I'm sorry you felt any pain on my account," he whispered against my ear.

"I'm sorry you did too."

We stayed like that forever and the captivity was much more bearable with him at my side. But when I heard shouting from a distance we quickly broke apart. The door down the corridor slammed open and I heard Theo's voice.

"Cyra! Where are you? I've come to take you home."

"We're here!"

He opened my cell door and lifted me into his arms. "We?" he asked. But his question was answered when an unmistakable growl echoed from Kane's cell. Theo gave an almost inaudible sigh and opened his cell as well, but the second it was opened Theo had me in his arms and he drove us back to my room. My heart dropped, immediately missing Kane's presence.

"That will *never* happen to you again. I spoke to Orphlam. It was absolutely unacceptable!"

"How long was I in there?" My eyes were squinted because I still wasn't used to the light.

"I think it was about four hours."

"That's it?" I asked with horror. "It felt like days!"

"He probably messed with your mind so that it did feel like days. I'm so sorry, Cyra." He brought me to him for another hug. "Oh and I should only need another day to get the ship ready so we can journey out to the islands and find the *mikla*. The sooner we find it the sooner we can try to rid ourselves of them."

"It's not your fault. I think I just need some time alone to recover."

"Of course. Call for me any time and, if not, I'll see you at dinner."

"Okay, thanks, Theo."

He kissed my hand and left.

When I knew he was far enough away I screamed as loud as I could, letting some of my rage escape me. I paced with clenched fists, and fire erupted from them instinctively, so I used the time alone to work on my fire magic, unwilling to stop until I mastered it. There was nothing more important than that and finding the *mikla*.

MEILI KNOCKED a few hours later and had what I'd asked for. She showed me two beautiful, rich, brown leather holsters that buttoned shut, small enough that I could hide it underneath my dresses, but heavy-duty enough to hold two decent sized daggers. The daggers were old and rusty, but I didn't care. If they could find their way into an enemy's neck, I was fine with it.

Meili helped me put them on and I already felt more at ease, more in control. I wouldn't be without them again, but more than anything, I knew that *I* was the real weapon. If I could kill ten men at once, I had confidence that I would soon be able to achieve more.

Meili revealed my dress for the day and I was pleased by that as well. It was edgy and powerful looking. She helped me put it on and I was in awe of what I saw. It was an ombre dress that went from midnight blue at the top and gradually transformed to a deep brick red at the bottom. It had one midnight blue strap with lace that looked like small flames and the back of the dress had four straps that connected from one side of the dress to the other, leaving a bit of skin revealed. There was no sparkle or glamor today, just fierce authority. More importantly, there was no sign of what was hiding underneath my dress. Meili arranged two braids again, but this time they connected in a low loose bun that was tied slightly to the side opposite the strap of my dress. My bold purplish-red hair complimented the look well.

Adelram knocked and then burst in my room, as now seemed to be customary, before doing a double take in my direction.

"Hmm, Reina's come out to play, huh? Well, good. It's about time you started taking this seriously. You're going to need all the confidence you can muster."

For once, Adelram wasn't being snarky, just truthful. It was written on his face that he had heard what happened from Kane and that he was relieved we were okay.

When we reached the grand ballroom and Theo saw me, he rushed to my side. He kissed my hand and led me to the table. There were a lot of stares from the female nobles, but I think instead of all jealous glares, it was a mix of admiration of my dress *and* envy of my place next to Theo. He stopped in front of our table like he did during my first *Sun Eine* and I wondered what he could have to say.

"Good morning, Solians! I wanted to make a brief announcement about a very special event I have planned in honor of Reina Cyra's return. It's something many of you have never experienced before, so I think you'll find it a rare treat. Tonight, at sundown in the Knight's Cup, I will host our first symphony performance in over one hundred years."

The room exploded with noise and excitement and I turned to Theo with a look of confusion. What provoked him to do this now when music hadn't been commonplace for so long?

"I hope to see you all there. Enjoy the feast." An abundance of food appeared when we sat, and Vish wished me a good morning.

Theo squeezed my still aching hand. "I hope you'll come to the symphony with me. I heard about your performance and wanted to do something special for you. But you should be careful, the Guardians wouldn't approve."

"Are you sure this is wise after we pissed them off? I'm not looking to get locked up again."

"I told you that won't happen again." His eyes were fierce and determined, his mouth pinched closed tightly in anger.

I didn't know how he could guarantee that, but he seemed so certain that I simply nodded at him. To be honest, I *was* very interested in this impromptu concert. And as for my performances for the staff, I didn't give a crap about how the Guardians felt about it. Those people needed something to look forward to.

"I don't think you've ever seen anything like this before and I'm positive you'll love it," Theo said genuinely.

Vish's eyebrows raised as he nodded. "You should have seen her play, I cried like a baby."

"I'd be delighted to see it for myself soon." There was almost a tinge of jealousy in his voice, like he felt he had missed out. Theo took my hand again and whispered, "I'm so sorry about what happened to you yesterday and today. I hate that I wasn't there to help you."

"It's no matter. Turns out I don't need anyone's help," I said with a raised chin. Kane and Adelram only helped finish off my scraps. I was confident I would have walked away from my own merit.

Theo slowly nodded looking relieved that I seemed to be in one piece. I'm sure he could empathically feel my determination and sense of calm. It was genuine. He bent closer to me to speak in my ear.

"Also, my ship is ready so I'd like to leave tomorrow so we can search for the *box* as well as show you some special things about Solis East. Will you come with me? We'd be gone for about a week."

"I would love to!" That is exactly what we needed to be doing.

"Excellent! I'll make arrangements and alert your *criada* to make preparations."

"Kane, Adelram, Meili and Vish should join as well."

Theo stilled and folded his hands, his normal gesture when he was about to be formal. "I was not planning on Kane and Adelram joining us. They're a great help, but I don't entirely trust the Varjun."

Varjun. I guess that's what planet they're from.

"Well, it's time we started. It's a condition to me going, I will not fall behind in my training and it's time that we all started working together to find the *mikla*. We'll have a much better chance of success if we look to the future with hope and unity instead of dwelling on a past that's dead and gone."

Theo looked up to the ceiling and sighed. "Very well." He cupped my cheek. "If that is your wish, we'll go together."

"There's one other thing I want to speak to you about. I want Meili's room moved to my floor. It makes no sense for her to be where she currently is with how many times she has to go back and forth to me. Plus, if I need to find her it's easier for me if she's on the same floor. I'd like this done immediately," I said in my best Reina persona.

Theo looked like he was struggling with how to answer, but he eventually agreed. He was too caught up in formality and royal tradition, but I was going to break him of that as much as possible.

"Within twenty minutes I will have all of her belongings brought up to her new quarters on your floor," Theo promised.

I kissed him on the cheek. "Thank you, Theo."

He touched my chin and his dimples emerged in a smile.

After *Sun Eine* I went to the lesson room early to practice my dagger skills before Kane arrived. I was getting pretty dexterous, able to use both hands which made me show off as if I had an audience. Naturally I paid for it by dropping my dagger and slicing my arm so blood freely dripped onto the floor. I cursed my fragile ego and made my way to my room hoping Meili would be there so she could tell me how to find Serin, and luckily, she was.

"Reina! What happened to you?" She asked in shock.

"I was a little too presumptuous in my abilities. Can you tell me where the healer is? I want to get it fixed before I go to my lesson."

Meili looked around with uncertainty. "Come here." She took my bleeding arm and bit her lip. "Don't tell anyone I can do this."

Her warm hand began to glow as I felt the cut starting to disappear and my eyes widened in shock. "Meili, you can heal?"

"It's not a normal gift, Reina. It's something more common with the Sunya people and it would raise questions," she admitted with fear in her eyes.

"Of course, I promise, I won't tell anyone. I would never do anything to hurt you."

Meili looked relieved. "In case anyone questions you, Serin is on the same floor as me in the basement. Or rather, he was! That's why I came to see you. You had my room changed? I don't know what to say, it is a fantasy room...I don't know what to do with that much space!"

I laughed at the fact that a golden, shining goddess-like cherub thought a simple room upgrade was a thing of fantasy. "You didn't deserve to be in that pit of darkness." I shivered, feeling the walls closing around me after my own recent captivity in darkness. There was no way I would let her live like that.

"And I can't fathom how you made so many trips up and down those stairs multiple times a day. This is much better," I shrugged.

Meili ran and put her arms around me. "You are so kind and generous. I am lucky to serve you, Cyra Fenix."

"You're more than welcome. Did you hear the news about the symphony tonight?"

"Yes! I would give anything to be able to see it."

"So, what does one wear to a symphony here on Solis?"

"Oh, I have something very special ready for you. You will twinkle with the stars."

"Wow, you know what, Meili? I actually haven't seen the night sky here yet. I'm usually asleep before the sun sets!"

Meili giggled and walked over to the dead flowers that Theo gifted me a while ago, not having the heart to throw them out yet.

"I guess I should get rid of them, huh?"

"But what a shame that would be! This was the most beautiful arrangement I've ever seen. I can fix it for you."

Confused by her statement, I watched on and she wrapped both of her hands around the lifeless bouquet. Golden white light beamed from them while the flowers slowly started to reverse their shriveled state and straighten to full bloom. My mouth dropped open. Kane had told me about the special gifts the Guardians were looking for and, so far, Meili had two of them. Healing magic and reviving life from death.

"There, that's much better," she said, completely clueless to my utter fear for her safety.

The past few days had all been too much. The Voidlings, the working class, my attack, my captivity. I stood up, feeling a little uneasy and I fanned my heated face.

"Cyra, are you okay?"

My eyes closed and I shook my head trying to break myself out of this feeling, sweat pouring from my forehead as anger welled within me. I was overcome with a mix of anxiety and fury and I couldn't contain my anger. I literally—couldn't—contain—

Fire erupted from my hands and arms, all the way up to my shoulders, and I could tell my eyes were inflamed as well.

"Cyra! Take deep breaths. Breathe in and out slowly, over and over again. I'm here for you. We will get through this together, and you will defeat the Guardians. You will save us. Everything will be okay. Just take deep breaths."

Her voice was distant and muted and I wanted nothing more than to continue to burn. Meili's voice kept calling to me, and I attached myself to its sweet serenade. My breaths successfully slowed as Meili instructed, cooling my rage. The flames eventually subsided, and I began to feel like myself again.

"I don't know what that was. I'm sorry for losing control, it kind of came out of nowhere."

The floor was singed and destroyed and I was grateful that I wasn't near anything else that could have burned down. Meili easily fixed it with a flick of her hand.

"How far did my fire get?" I asked, not entirely sure what happened while I was lost in that state.

"Fire?" Meili asked, fidgeting with her hands.

Now I was beyond confused. Didn't she just see what happened? "That's what that was, wasn't it?"

Meili darted her eyes to the side like she was debating her answer. "... technically yes," she replied.

A thunderous knock on the door made us both jump. Meili ran to open it and was greeted by a dark warrior filling the frame of the door.

"I will leave you and be back when it's time to dress." Meili curtsied and began to leave.

"Meili, wait!" I ran over to her in the hallway and spoke so only she could hear. "I have a lot of time in between now and sundown after my training. Why don't you rally up the workers and invite them to another concert since they won't be able to see the symphony. Don't forget the Voidlings. How about in two hours?"

She flashed an angelic smile and continued the short walk to her new room.

"What happened?" Kane demanded.

"What makes you think something happened?"

"You blasted some strange force throughout the entire castle. Were you practicing magic?"

"Did everyone feel it?" I asked in horror.

"No…it was probably only me that could feel it," he said looking down, scratching the back of his head. "What happened?"

"I was angry, and I burst into flames that I couldn't control," I explained casually.

"What could you have heard that would put you in such a rage? How were you able to get out of it so quickly? Many will burn in such a state until they deplete all their energy and nearly die."

"I don't know, I just did."

Kane huffed and pressed his fingers to the arch of his nose. "Alright fine, keep your secrets. "

"Okay." I crossed my arms and raised my brows at him.

"Then we will focus on meditation and control today. Follow me."

He led me to my private beach at the back of the castle and I took my shoes off to let my toes sift through the soft, hot sands. I needed a moment to calm down after my blow up, and it was painfully clear that we all needed some reprieves from the horrors this galaxy was facing. I smiled at Kane's confusion as I ran to the shoreline and burrowed my feet in the damp sand. The silky texture of the cool, wet sand felt incredible, and I tilted my head back and greedily soaked up the sun with my arms raised.

"What do you think you're doing?" Kane was trying to chide me, but there was amusement in his voice.

"Oh, lighten up, drill sergeant." I kicked some of the sand toward him and clumps of it stuck to his face, arms and pants before unceremoniously falling back to the ground. I covered my mouth to keep myself from laughing, but it was no use. I bellowed at the sight of Kane's eyes closed in mock frustration and when he opened them the green in his irises flashed with mischief.

"Your faulty confidence will be your doom. I could have you buried under this sand in the blink of an eye."

"Not if you can't catch me!" I don't know what came over me, but I attempted a drive, and only moved about two feet to my right, closer to the water.

"Are you crazy! You're not ready to drive, you could end up at the bottom of the ocean."

"Been there, done that!" I teased, flicking more sand at him. He ran at me and picked me up, but I drove out of his grasp only to embarrassingly reappear exactly where I was and we fell to the ground. Kane's laughter made my heart sputter out of control, and the buzzing energy between us grew light and euphoric. He held me tight so I wouldn't fall as I laid on top of his hard body. My laughter quickly died when I looked into his mesmerizing eyes and I was overwhelmed with the desire to press my lips to his. I silently begged him to do so I could save face and blame someone else for my deep, hidden desires. He stilled, staring back at me, his face only inches from mine and my hand slowly felt over the curves of his shoulder and defined bicep.

The nearness was becoming unbearable and I was losing the war within myself. Kane moved his hand and I closed my eyes, ready for him to touch my cheek, but instead I felt the cold, wet smear of sand all over my face.

"Hey!" I screamed with mock anger and he wiggled free, running toward the water to get another clump of wet sand. I compiled my own and threw it at him, missing by a mile as his hit me in the hair. We chased each other for a while, running on the beach acting like kids and I relished the much-needed reprieve. When I was thoroughly tired out I huffed, "What an irresponsible tutor you are. Are we going to get down to business or what?"

I started to slide my dress up my thigh and he gave a mocking raise of his eyebrow. I kept going to reveal the holster with the dagger, then raised the other side of my dress to show the other.

"I see," he said with his rumbling bass voice. "So, you're ready to fight?"

"Yes," I said without hesitation.

"Alright fine, we'll do more dagger work before our meditation."

Our training was hard and focused since we had wasted an hour on Kane's silliness. I obviously had no hand in his slacking off.

When I was done, I fell back to the sand to rest. "Kane?"

"Yes, Cyra?" When my name crossed his lips like that, my stomach flipped. I pushed the feeling away, pretending like it didn't affect me.

"Sometimes when you look at me, you squint. Why is that?"

"It's your aura. Varjun are susceptible to aura and light in general, and you shine as bright as a star."

"Oh...I had no idea."

"My people can adjust and dim their eyesight so I have to do that when I'm around you."

I shuddered at the thought of being so different, wondering why my aura was bright, but I let it go.

"Can you make the trees dance?"

He looked at me, with a gentleness to his eyes and nodded. We sat together in silence for a few moments as I closed my eyes and listened to the leaves dance in the wind. Any lingering anxiety was swept up with it until it dissipated in the bright, unburdened sky.

CHAPTER SIXTEEN

*a*fter a quick bath that took me ten minutes to successfully turn on, I headed to the music room and saw that the crowd had almost doubled since the last performance.

"Wow," I said aloud when I saw the sheer number of people. I was pleased to see that Mylo was front and center, sitting directly below my chair ready to hear something that would help him escape some of his endless misery. After learning about what the Voidling had to endure, I couldn't help but wonder what he looked like before his curse set in. Who was his son or daughter? Where were they now? Did he ever mourn for them? I was desperate to do anything to help him and all the Voidlings, but for the moment all I could do was give them a small reprieve with the power of music. I hoped it was enough.

Blaze, Derek and some of his patrons were also in attendance and we nodded at each other in solemn recognition. How different would their lives be if they were given freedom and full use of their power? Would they be scientists? Would they travel the cosmos in spaceships? Would they reband the Empire of Knights?

Coming back to the moment, I started to play and you would have thought the room was empty from the utter silence. The only sound was my cello, and every pair of eyes were glued to me in awe.

The exhilaration filling the room from the workers was tangible as

I finished. It warmed my heart that I was able to bring them all together to relax and enjoy a few moments of freedom to just be themselves with no pretenses or expectations.

I had been eagerly waiting to speak to Mylo again to see if he had more information so I walked up to him as soon as I was finished.

"Thanks for coming again. I hope you enjoyed it," I said with a smile. "Where are the two others you work with?" I noticed they were missing since Mylo was the only Voidling there.

As usual, he struggled to speak.

Meili joined us and explained. "They've passed on, Reina. We're awaiting a few more Voidlings to take their place."

"How horrible," I said, saddened that I wasn't able to do anything for them. They died just like Mylo would.

Mylo slowly shook his head and said with difficulty, "No... more...pain."

"You mean they're at peace now?" My eyes widened in surprise.

Mylo nodded his head. He was happy for their passing. Happy that they no longer had to suffer, because he knew better than anyone how difficult their lives were.

"Meili, how long do Voidlings live?"

Mylo looked at me with unfathomable sadness in his eyes. There's no way I could understand what he had to go through or the guilt Meili herself felt.

"It varies. Some think it has to do with how much power the individual would have had without the curse. The other two Voidlings lived five years after the curse kicked in. Mylo is special, with fifteen years after the curse. The average is about five to ten years."

"Oh my God." I grasped my chest, worried that my heart would actually break.

"The immortal Voidling council teach a little about our people's history and explain what will happen to us after the curse. I wonder if they gave him any other new information that could be useful," Meili explained.

"Mylo, do you know how I break the curse? What do I have to do? Please, tell me how to save you."

Mylo grunted a few times. He was trying really hard to speak.

"It's okay, take your time," Meili said with her hand gently grazing his back. I imagined touching him anywhere would cause him serious pain.

"B... box. A... Aaamrel," Mylo said.

"Did you say Amrel?" I whispered. Box—Amrel. Was he talking about the box grandpa Amrel left for me when he died?

Mylo started to cry, either from the pain of just existing or from hope of a day he would probably never see. His tears had watery streaks of blood running through them and I had to look away so I didn't cry at the sight. I gathered whatever strength I had in me and turned back to face him.

"He might know something from immortal Voidling council. They educate us on some history and pertinent information before we succumb to the curse, but I've never heard them mention a box before."

I turned to Mylo to ask more questions, but he was struggling so badly that I decided against it.

"Thank you for the information, Mylo. Why don't you go rest?" I offered.

"Mylo must go back to work, Cyra," Meili said mournfully. "In fact, everyone must disperse before anyone notices they're missing."

And so they did. One by one they left and gave their thanks again for the performance and I promised I'd hold another event as soon as I was able.

The last one in the room was Serin. "How's that wrist holding up? Seems good as new based on that beautiful music it was able to make."

"I'll admit it still aches, but I'm able to use it just fine," I smiled at him. "Thanks for everything you did for me."

"It's my pleasure, one of the few I'm still allowed," Serin answered sadly.

"What do you mean?"

He lowered his voice to a whisper. "I'm a captive of the Guardians, forced into service for my ability to heal. It's a rare gift, so healers don't have much of a chance to live a normal life before they're sent to 'work' in service of the Guardians. Don't get me wrong, my ability to heal—my work—is my greatest joy. I never feel more alive than when I can repair someone's wounds, but I'm closely monitored and there's limits to what the Guardians allow me to heal. There's severe punishment for breaking those rules, like when I completely healed Kane after they tortured him."

My teeth ground together so hard I was worried they would chip. The memory of Kane's torture was as fresh and vivid as if it happened an hour ago, and I felt the heat of my fire tickling beneath my skin, ready to be unleashed.

"They use my gift as a tactical tool to get information. The things I've had to do and witness in order to survive the Guardians are barbaric. And I will continue to defy them because when we give in to evil...they win. This is my gift to share with the world the way I deem necessary. I'm not a pawn in their agenda. What you're doing here... there is *nothing* more vital than that. You have the chance to save us *all.* Whatever you need, I am at your true beck and call...not theirs." Serin winked at me.

"Serin, you must be careful. People need you and your precious gift."

"What we need is you, Cyra. Don't you worry about me, I'll be fine. Thank you for what you're trying to do and for the small kindness you're showing those less fortunate."

I looked toward the doorway and noticed Kane and Vish scowl at each other in the hall.

"Serin, do you happen to know why it seems like the Varjun and Solians can't stand each other?"

He looked at me with pursed lips, nodding sadly. "It started as these things often do, with fear and greed. The Varjun have magic that is somewhat different than what Solians can wield and it's still a bit of a mystery. Many, many years ago Solians sought to learn what made it different and perhaps adopt different ways of wielding energy. Some Solians inhabited their planet, attempting to learn their ways, trying to understand their power, but when it became clear that they wouldn't find out the secret behind some of their abilities they became angry. Tensions grew, and when the Varjun asked them to leave they refused. Eventually they had to force the Solians to leave with violence, which only led to retaliations by the Solians. They fought for many years, both sides at fault and the history is so long and bloody that generations today still feel the echoes of it."

"How sad. I wish they would let it go since we have a worse enemy than each other."

He touched my hand and squeezed with hope shining in his eyes. "I believe there is someone here that will help them see that."

Serin started walking out of the door, but I stopped him. "Serin..."

"Yes?"

"Take care of yourself."

"You too, Reina. And when you can't...I will be there."

I rushed back to my room to get the box that grandpa Amrel gave me, inspecting the items inside, but nothing gave me any clues as to how to break the curse. I looked at the details on the outside of the box and I was stunned to realize that when I first saw them, they made no sense to me. But now...

There were warrior knights who had to be the Solians because of their cherished Empire of Knights. Dark creatures with bursts of light coming from their hands, which were the Varjun using magic. And the bright angelic creatures represented Amrel and the Sunya Rei.

All three races were fighting an obscurity, which now I saw had a faint hint of an outline of hooded cloaks. I hadn't noticed that before, you had to look closely to see it. From a distance it just looked like phantoms shrouded in darkness.

At the back of the box was a girl with flaming red-purple hair holding a globe that matched the design of my birthmark. That had to be....me. When I first saw this box, I thought it was a beautiful design of some fantasy story. But now I wondered—was this a depiction of Eredet's past—and future? I believed Mylo's information was regarding this box, but I was clearly missing something since it didn't help me any further in figuring out how to break the curse.

Taking a seat at my desk, I grabbed my sketch pad, pencil and watercolor paints that I had asked Meili for shortly after I arrived. I started drawing Mylo's face, giving him a look that told the viewer that he held the sorrow of the world hidden beneath his tainted eyes. It was important to me to make the viewer feel the same despair I felt just by looking at him. My brush touched the paper and I painted his shredded rags where you could see his decaying flesh peek through in various spots. I captured his gray withering skin and hair, and the blisters and open wounds that plagued his entire body. And, finally, I included a single blood-streaked tear starting to fall from his eye. His body was putrefying and his eyes had pools of blood in them from burst vessels. He could barely speak or function properly, but behind those eyes were knowledge, intellect and emotion. He was a prisoner in his own body—suffering from the curse inflicted upon him.

He sat on soft grass with a backdrop of a setting sun, with a cosmic star-filled night sky above it. Mylo was at the twilight of his life, his sun was setting, and he would soon be free among the infinite cosmos, and I wanted his end to have a beautiful, reassuring view. His past was bleeding into his inevitable future that I would do anything to change. I included a tree with broad leaves that flowed in the wind so he would have a comforting sound to carry him on his journey. It's exactly what I would want to hear.

Looking at the finished product caused my eyes to burn and I had to take deep breaths to avoid igniting the pages of my book. I wanted justice for Mylo, for Meili, for all the Voidlings. For Theo's parents and for mine. For the Solian workers and for Serin who were also basically kept as slaves, for grandpa Amrel—forced to make a choice to end his life. Walking away from my desk, I felt the flames threaten to burst again. Fire erupted from my arms and I tried to remember Meili's sweet voice telling me to breathe. I remembered Brendon's voice telling me he loved me and Theo's voice telling me he'd do anything for me. Anger was obviously my biggest trigger, but love was my relief. I calmed down and promised myself that I *would* get justice for everyone who deserved it. And I would find a way to destroy the Guardians.

I sat back down and did another watercolor of a golden, glowing Meili in a backdrop of darkness. She was a virtuous beacon of life and purity, trapped in a world suppressing her grace. Right on cue, I heard a knock at the door which I knew must be her coming to dress me for the performance.

"Come in, Meili!"

She opened the door and came inside. "You skipped dinner, Cyra?"

"I'm not at all hungry. In fact, I still feel sick to my stomach. I've kind of felt sick ever since I came here."

"Well, Bad will make you something anytime day or night. If you're hungry later, we'll make sure to feed you," Meili smiled. "Would you like a bath before dressing?"

"I already took one before. You should have seen me battle the dreaded bathtub faucet!"

Meili looked at me with amusement as she opened the closet and revealed one of the most stunning gowns I'd ever seen. She helped me into it and I went right to the mirror to admire it in all its splendor. It was white with sheer lace three-quarter length sleeves, an open-back 'V' with a white satin ribbon that trailed the length of the dress and a flowing, sheer white tulle overlay that lightly sparkled. Finishing it off was a short train so the dress swept behind me. I knew that under the night sky I would stand out like small pieces of fallen stars. Meili styled my hair in loose bouncing curls and finished with just a touch of makeup.

There was a knock at the door and I wondered if it was Adelram, coming to escort me, but when Meili opened the door I was surprised to see Theo.

"Cyra, you look...stunning." He put his hand to his chest and his mouth parted as he took me in. "You literally took my breath away. I've come for the honor to escort you to the symphony myself."

I looked around and realized Meili had already quietly slipped out of the room.

Theo moved closer and gently touched my hair and my heart skipped a beat at his tenderness. "Are you ready?" he asked.

I nodded and he put his arms around me, pulling me close. This time he remembered to be mindful about driving with me, but he also made it incredibly sensual by resting his cheek on my head and opening the palms of his hands so his fingers pressed firmly into the bare skin of my back. His soft fingertips grazed slowly up and down, feeling my skin and sending all my senses on high alert. I melted into his embrace and took in his warm jasmine smell. When I opened my eyes we stood beneath the Knight's Cup statue, and from this vantage point it looked like the knight was holding up a full globe. There were numerous people there, lining up to touch a plaque on the side of it.

"As I mentioned, this is a sacred piece of architecture for our people. It's been many, many years since we've held an event here and I can feel an overwhelming rush of excitement from everyone!" He pointed to the plaque that read 'Loyalty. Unity. Hope.' "That was the creed of our first defenders, the Sun Guard, which are the same knights you saw at the castle entrance the day you arrived. The ancient Sun Guard later became The Empire of Knights, but you'll notice most of our decor and motifs are of the ancient Sun Guard armor since it's one of our last connections to Amrel the High Creator."

"How wonderful." I walked up to the plaque and touched my hand to it like the Solians before me and it tingled as if I could feel some of the love passed down through the generations. I could only pray that there was enough hope left to save us from the Guardians.

Once inside the Cup, I noticed that the curvature of the edges was high enough that we couldn't see over the walls which made me feel safe. The orchestra was already seated in the center of the cup, waiting for the audience to fill up and sit down on all sides. They were quite a distance away from us and I wondered how we would hear them in the open with no visible speakers. Floating in the air were stadium lights, allowing everyone to find their seats and settle in, and when every seat was filled the lights started to dim until it was utter darkness. Was this supposed to be a blind performance? I wasn't sure I liked that idea since I enjoyed seeing the passion of the musician's faces as they collectively created an audible work of art.

Theo grabbed my hand and squeezed. "I hope you enjoy it." Even though I couldn't see him, I could tell he said it with a smile, excited for what was to come.

The symphony began a sound check and from their instruments tiny twinkling lights started to float into the air. At first, I thought there was a random invasion of fireflies, but I realized it was coming from each of their instruments. The tiny lights grew in number as the sound continued and it lit up the musicians just enough so we could now see all their faces. When the first few lights were right in front of me and Theo, I heard the sound of the orchestra as clear as if they were right in front of me and when they floated overhead and behind us, like it was a 4D experience. I was utterly captivated. When the orchestra stopped their sound check, the twinkling specs stopped coming from their instruments and darkness fell again. When they began playing the actual symphony piece the magical twinkling lights once again sprang to life and continued to permeate the crowd. I couldn't help but gape as they continued to float up into the night sky until I couldn't tell what were stars and what were the mysterious little pieces of sound. I could hear the entire orchestra as a collective in every spec of light that circulated, and it consumed the entire space of the arena. When one reached my lap I was hesitant, but I cautiously held out my finger and touched it. It felt like warm, vibrating energy that mimicked the waves of the music. It occurred to me that in this world of sunshine, color and magic, I had the ability to physically touch and see music for the first time in a way that I couldn't by merely playing or listening to it on Earth. This was a whole different experience that blew my mind.

I sat back but stilled as I recognized the piece. *How could that be?* They were playing an orchestral piece that I had written on Earth. The only person I had ever shared it with was Grandpa. When I'd played it for him, it was the one time I had ever seen him cry, explaining it was because it reminded him of home. How did this orchestra have something I wrote on Earth when I was a teenager?

Theo reached for my hand and held it in his. He leaned toward me and said, "It's okay. Just let it out." And I saw a tear running down his own cheek.

I didn't know if he was feeling my own emotional turmoil with his empathetic ability, or if he had his own problems he was contending with, but I yielded to his sentiment. Tears ran down my face and into my lap, in the opposite direction of the musical lights that continued to float into the night sky.

The music lasted about an hour and I spent half of it in joyful astonishment and half in poignant release. When the orchestra stopped and the flood lights went back on, I jumped from my chair in applause. Everyone looked at me in confusion for a moment, until Theo stood and joined me until the entire audience followed suit. I didn't care who thought I was crazy, these musicians deserved some recognition.

I damn near bowled people over like a fan girl to reach the musicians and congratulate them on the performance. "What was that first piece you were playing? Where did you find it?"

"Ah, you have good taste. It's called *The Sun's Progeny.* It's been a classic staple of Eredet for thousands of years. It's said it was a favorite of Amrel's and the piece came to him in a vision. It's one of our sacred songs."

Nobody knew why I was wiping tears off my cheek, but I wasn't going to elaborate. It would be another shared secret between me and him. "I love it. How do the lights work?"

"Well, it's something I can feel more than I can understand, but sound waves are just another form of energy. We can use the energy of our magic and act essentially as transducers, connecting to the sound waves we feel from our instruments and converting its energy in a way that we can see in the form of light. It also acts as a sound magnifier with the enhanced energy we give to it. There's a bit more behind the inner workings, but I'm more interested in the magic behind the music than the mechanics of it."

"Cyra is a talented musician herself." Theo beamed to the group, wrapping his arm around me.

"That's wonderful! Then you should be able to do the same when you play. Don't think about how it works, just feel it. As a fellow musician, you'll understand when you practice it."

The musicians packed up and Theo readied me for the drive to the ground. When we landed, I almost fell over at the sight before us. All five Guardians stood waiting for me and Theo, eerily still and silent. No winds rustled their cloaks, and there were no chirps from birds or hum of insects. Orphlam's familiar sickening power made the air around us quiver and it caused my body to feel frail and sickly like I'd been suffering from a long-term illness. I *hated* them.

"We must have misplaced our invitation to your little event." Orphlam didn't waste a second of time voicing his displeasure or beating around the bush.

"I didn't think you were a fan of music," Theo said evenly, his hands tucked behind his back.

"And yet you thought it was a good idea to host this ridiculous event when it was disbanded many years ago under our direction. Why the sudden defiance, Theo? You've always followed the rules." Orphlam very slowly slid his foul masked face to my direction making the hairs on the back of my neck rise. I festered with hatred for this abhorrent creature who was too cowardly to show his face. I wanted to take my two hidden daggers and stick them right into the burning red eye slits. I think Theo felt my rage and rubbed my back to calm me down.

"Miss Fenix, we gifted you the power bracelet, but I have yet to see it grace your person." Orphlam sneered at me.

"Cyra is still learning about her powers and abilities. Once she gets a handle of them, she'll wear the bracelet, no doubt." Theo smiled easily and I kept my lips tightly sealed so I didn't say anything I'd regret.

"Well, we've been disappointed one too many times."

It was silent for a moment and anxiety whorled through me at what they were going to do. There was still a small crowd of curious onlookers, closing in on the scene.

The musicians appeared from thin air, gagged and tied. The blood drained from my face in horror. "Let them go!" I screamed, shaking from head to toe with dread.

"I don't think so." Orphlam twisted his hand in the air lazily and I heard the sickening crack of each of the musicians' necks before they thumped to the ground. Screams and disarray flooded the field, but the torment didn't end there. He raised both of his hands and small chips started to break off of the Knight's Cup as it rumbled.

Theo's eyes bulged in panic and he pleaded with Orphlam. "No! You can't do this! The Knight's Cup is an ancient treasure, one of the very last ones we have. Please don't do this, punish me instead. It was my fault."

"This is your punishment. You and everyone else who think they can defy us." Orphlam turned his head to me one more time before he released a tremendous amount of power. Theo grabbed me and we drove a distance away to safety, but we were close enough to watch as the gargantuan Knight structure, a sacred piece of history, tumbled to the ground in a billow of dust. Citizens of Solis reappeared when it was gone, kneeling by the wreckage, yelling and sobbing. The damage was loud and catastrophic enough that the Solian working class began showing up and joined the others in their horror and despair. I demanded to be taken back, to see the effects of the consequences our actions. Theo reluctantly agreed, and when we reappeared Kane and

Adelram were also there, looking on in shock. The Guardians were nowhere to be seen.

"What the fuck have you done?" Adelram wasted no time grilling Theo. "Amrel himself gifted this architecture. It's been around for thirteen thousand years! It was priceless!" I was floored when I saw a small glisten in Adelram's eye, his pain just as heavy if not more so than the citizens of Solis. Theo lost his composure and knelt to the ground with his people in mourning.

Blaze came up behind me and touched my shoulder. "We're relying on you to save us from this. Please tell me you're doing everything you can." I looked at him and nodded, unable to speak. I bent down and took a few pieces of stone and held them to my chest.

The scene before me was horrific and sound momentarily disappeared as I lost my bearings. Would these people's suffering ever end? Was I really even capable of helping them, or was I only hurting them? When my hearing returned I noticed the cold pieces of rock in my hand that now resembled nothing, and I traced my finger over them, knowing that Grandpa once touched some of it as well.

We needed a way to keep going, we needed a reason to believe. I looked to Kane whose brows were raised, his eyes heavy. "Is there any way to restore this?"

He shook his head. "It would take a lot of energy and it wouldn't be the same, I feel dark magic in the stones and I wouldn't face Ophlam's wrath again."

Accepting defeat, I nodded, feeling the sickening magic as well. I began to speak and Kane waved his hand so that my voice was amplified. The people of Solis turned to hear what I had to say. "There is nothing that is going to make the pain of this loss any better, but this precious piece of history belongs to all of us. Everyone take a stone home with you tonight so we remember what happened here and the gift that Amrel gave us."

With tears still in their eyes, they eagerly picked through pieces of stone, there being plenty for everyone in attendance. I turned to Blaze who was still at my side. "Do you think we can organize everyone here to have a small ceremony for these poor musicians?"

"Leave it to me, Reina." He gathered his usual patrons from his

Public House and they wrangled everyone together, the crowd having grown to approximately three hundred or more people.

I spoke to the crowd and Kane amplified my speech again from a distance. "These musicians died giving us a small reprieve from the pain we've endured. Let's honor them together and give them thanks. They will not die in vain as we have not given up here tonight. This is a setback, and a tragic heartbreak, but it is not the end of our story. There is life left in Solis and we will see that it once again becomes a land of loyalty, unity and hope–the creed Solis was built on." I put down my stone as Kane stepped into view and his eyes were full of softness and wonder. A small appreciative smile appeared on my lips and I instantly felt bolder with him at my side.

Closing my eyes, I gave myself a pep talk, praying that I could rise to the challenge and provide an honorable fire service for these musicians I admired so much. My energy swelled, and I was able to effectively connect with it, releasing fire so that every dead body lit aflame. An extraordinary amount of heat was needed to burn the bodies and when I started to fatigue too early, Kane put a hand on my shoulder and it instantly boosted my reserves so that I could continue until they were ash. It was strange that I always seemed to have significantly more power when Kane was near, but maybe it was simply because he trained me and I felt more capable in his company.

Blaze bowed his head to me, which was surprising. It was the first time he'd made the gesture. "I will be happy to dispose of the ashes property, Reina."

"Thank you, Blaze, that is most helpful." The people of Solis began to disperse with their precious pieces of rubble and it appeared Adelram and Kane had already disappeared.

Theo held my hand as we walked toward the castle for about an hour in silence and I clung to my own piece of stone. "I'm so sorry. I just wanted to give everyone a special night."

"Our best course of action is to find the *mikla* and end this."

"Yes, and that is what we will do tomorrow." I locked eyes with him and it appeared as if he was struggling to remain upright.

"The emotions of the night have me in a chokehold."

I nodded with realization. "How do you make it through everyday feeling everyone's emotions?"

"It's not easy, by any means. There's still a great deal of fear, but I do my best to help people overcome it. Many of the nobles are past their fear and are simply empty shells. I think it's a defense mechanism, how they're able to survive. But when I visit other places, I do have to sometimes turn my ability off as best as I can, or I wouldn't be able to do my job. And since you've arrived, your emotional fortitude is so strong that some days I find it hard to even get out of bed in the morning. And it's because I can feel your lingering pain radiating in waves through the castle. I try not to turn off my connection to you in case you're in trouble, but sometimes I'm forced to so I can focus. If I'm far enough away though I can't feel the connection."

"Wow, I had no idea. I'm sorry I make your life so difficult."

"Don't apologize, Cyra. We all have grief to work through, some more than others." He looked off to the side and I could tell he would need some time to recover from this night's events.

"What do the Guardians feel like?" I wasn't sure I wanted to know, but curiosity won out.

"Like all-encompassing darkness. Like a black hole. Sometimes I don't feel *alive* in their presence." Theo shivered.

"And Kane? What do you get from him?"

Theo looked at me with pursed lips and I looked up at the sky, pretending not to take notice of his disapproval. "He's a steel vault. He and Adelram are so well guarded I never feel anything from them whatsoever." Interesting. I remembered Kane telling me I could block people from my mind and emotions, I would definitely be adding that to our next session.

"What does a Voidling feel like?" I whispered.

Theo's eyes widened. "I've only felt them once and I won't open myself to them ever again. It was the single most painful experience of my life. It felt like being burned alive, like never getting a real breath of air – it was a constant state of suffocation and agony. I felt like I was screaming at the top of my lungs for help, but nobody could hear me. It was a pit of despair so great that I had an overwhelming desperation to die, and the desire didn't disappear for quite a while after I turned off my power." Theo looked blankly off in the distance with a glisten in his ocean eyes.

"Then why do you allow them in the castle and condone the use of them as slaves?"

"Because I don't know how else to help such a creature. They would be left on their wasteland of a planet to shrivel up and die. At least here, just *maybe* a simple task might help take their mind off their perpetual agony."

"Adelram said he would search Meili's mind to see if we can replicate the cure my mother used on Meili. We must find a way to help them."

"I agree. I hope he *can* find a cure for them."

We walked hand-in-hand much of the way back to the castle, letting the quiet darkness meld with our pain.

Loyalty. Unity. Hope.

Orplam had managed to destroy every one of those values and everything the Solians stood for.

CHAPTER SEVENTEEN

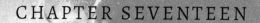

The next morning, still running on fury, I didn't balk at the fact that I'd only had a few short hours of sleep. Bad had left me some food again on my nightstand, so I scarfed it down quickly before I jumped out of bed and asked Meili for an outfit for my first day at sea.

We met Theo, Vish, Adelram, and Kane by the front doors to the castle and it felt odd to see all of them together.

"Ready for a new adventure?" Some of the lightness returned to Theo which made his face glow with even more beauty than usual. I had a curious desire to squint, sometimes it was hard to look at that much perfection head-on.

I gave a smile and nodded, trying to leave some of the extraordinary heaviness behind in Eluroom. I followed Theo and Vish to the exit and Theo explained as we exited the castle that we'd be boarding at the dock below the water bridge where I'd first arrived. I recalled the various sail boats that were floating by the shores of the castle beneath the shadow of the colossal warrior sculpture.

"I just want to make a quick trip first to the triage Serin set up for the sick," Theo explained. "Will you join me?"

"Of course, I will. I remember you and Serin speaking about some illness affecting Solians during my first *Sun Eine*."

"Yes," was all Theo said before turning to nod at Vish and glance suspiciously at Adelram and Kane. "We'll meet you back here." He drove us to the triage and I immediately saw why he had been so concerned and distracted this morning. I could tell we were in the farmlands of Solis West and there were about fifty tents set up, with some people in cots outside in the sun and some laying in the shelters. We approached Serin who had his hands over a patient, scanning his body.

"How many new patients today?" Theo asked.

"Ten," Serin sighed.

"It's getting worse by the week." Theo breathed deeply and looked to me like the weight of the world was on his shoulders. "This illness started about ten years ago and there were maybe two patients the first year, then it gradually escalated until there was one infected per month and now there's five to ten new patients per week. The fact that there are ten complaints just today is not good."

"What are they sick with?" I frowned

Serin looked weary. "It's not a contagious disease, it's directly the result of...the situation of our galaxy. The people of Eredet galaxy thrive on pure, clean, natural energy. The Guardians have been using dark magic to drain our energy and fulfill their curse. Large amounts of consistent dark magic is like a disease, it can corrupt us and change us on a cellular level."

"What is dark magic?" I had felt the strange magic every time I was in the Guardians' presence even though I couldn't identify what it was.

"It's any type of magic used by unnatural means, or forcing magic that wouldn't normally occur in nature. Cursing a race of people to drain their energy is not a natural occurrence and it's negatively affecting nature."

Theo knelt next to the man on the cot who was sweating profusely and unaware of our presence. He grabbed the patient's hand and they both started to glow as he transferred some energy to the sick man, similar to what I'd seen in the shoppes where payment was made in energy.

"Did you just heal him?"

"No, I am not a healer, and Serin who *is* the healer doesn't have the ability to cure these people either. He can ease symptoms, but the only cure for this illness is to restore the balance in the galaxy."

"Theo gave him some *natural* energy," Serin confirmed.

"I assume there's also dark magic in those bracelets?" I asked

"I believe so," Serin agreed.

"But it looks like most of the patients here are working class, and they don't wear bracelets."

"Yes, the patients are all working class. The nobles somehow haven't been affected. My theory is that there's something else that's in those bracelets that's protecting the nobles from the side effects of dark magic," Serin explained. "But the effects of whatever is happening to our energy is spreading throughout all of Solis and the working class are not protected."

"Why aren't they in the castle being treated? Why are they out in farming fields hiding?"

"Remember what I told you about what I'm permitted to do with my healing gifts?" Serin asked. "The Guardians have forbidden it. They don't see it as a real disease or a castle matter. Theo and I have arranged for this triage in secret."

I shook my head in disbelief.

"Show me to the rest of the new patients and I will give what I can. It doesn't completely cure them, but they can get back to their lives for a few months until they feel sick again. Since we'll be gone for a week, I want to make sure everyone is safe before we go."

We visited the other nine patients and their symptoms varied from mild to moderately severe. One patient was vomiting and in clear distress, but once Theo gave her his natural energies it looked like she'd never been sick. He explained that some patients needed multiple offerings of energy to feel better again, which is why they had to stay on the campsite.

Right before we decided to leave, Bad showed up with a bag full of food for the patients staying at the triage. I was so pleased to see there were people in vital positions who cared about the welfare of Solis and its people. I still couldn't fathom why the Guardians needed to control the galaxy's energy source. It was clear that they were guarding nothing but their own agenda.

We drove to the seaport and even with the heaviness of the past few weeks, I smiled when I saw what awaited us because it looked like nothing less than a pirate ship.

"What a cool ship!" I was practically jumping out of my skin with excitement, knowing that this would be a completely different experience than I'd had thus far on Solis, and I was happy to get away from the fear, formality and ceremony of Eluroom for a while. More importantly, I was happy to be away from the toxic Guardians and I was ready to hear any new information Theo wanted to share with me.

"This is no ordinary ship. It's the only one like it in Eredet," Vish replied.

"Is *anything* ordinary here?"

"Well, to us it is. I suppose it will take quite a while for anything to feel normal here for you." Vish shrugged.

Waiting at the top of the boat's entrance was a glowing Meili and I was so pleased to see her out of the castle and under the rays of the sun where she belonged that I almost didn't notice Adelram and Kane standing behind her, scowling at the sunshine.

"Reina. Karalis." Meili curtsied out of duty, but even she couldn't contain her excitement.

"Welcome to the Eventyr." Theo said, trying to overcome his melancholy. "This ship belonged to my parents and it's been unused for quite some time. Driving makes travel easier and more efficient, but sometimes the journey is more important than the destination and we can forget to appreciate the world around us. Plus it'll be easier to sail around looking for shrouded islands."

I could get behind that sentiment, especially if this world was dying. Nobody here seemed to enjoy *living* because they weren't given the chance to. The past few days had been evidence of that.

"My people's passion on Solis East is the sea. They'd live in it if they could, as they used to. We had bungalow houses over the water, aquatic sporting events, water shows, etc. Our way of life revolved around it," Theo explained.

I looked around and realized the others were gone. The ship started to back away from the dock and we quickly took off into the unknown. A small burst of excitement rushed through me which I felt guilty about.

"What changed?"

He led me to the front of the ship to watch the open sea ahead of us. There were two cushions on the edge of the boat where one could sit and dangle your legs freely. The missing railing surprised me.

"Don't worry, there's an invisible protective barrier in front so you won't fall off."

I gave a mental sigh of relief and accepted his hand to sit with him. It was exhilarating and I felt like I was flying above the seas. My breath caught in my chest as I took in the breathtaking view. Water sprayed off the sides of the ship and there were tiny bits of rainbow in each droplet just like the color of the clouds in the skies. The heated air and the smell of the briny water put me at ease instantly, and I couldn't imagine why anyone would want to drive so often when this was an option. The balmy breeze ran through my dark magenta hair and I absorbed the prickling warmth from the sun with a hunger that was surprising. It felt as if the sun was providing long overdue sustenance, feeding my soul and dissolving some of the darkness that clung to me for weeks. The sun seemed to speak to me and I opened myself to its blaze, letting it infiltrate my body until I felt something igniting within, growing until I pulsed with an unknown vitality.

I was brought out of my trance when Theo continued to speak. "Things changed after the Great War. Solians were in such bad spirits by the enormous loss of our people that many gave up on their past. They didn't feel like there was much to celebrate anymore. Many nobles and workers went to live in Solis West where the greater power resided, so they had a better chance at survival. The ones who stayed behind lived a smaller, simpler life, and there weren't many left to uphold our traditions. You'll see for yourself how different Solis East is."

The castle was far behind us and I already felt like a burden had been lifted, even if I knew it wasn't forever. I thought about Brendon and how much he and our friends would have *loved* to be on a ship like this. I smiled until something shook me out of my tranquility.

"What was that?" I could have sworn I'd just seen something out of the corner of my eye. A small movement from the side of the ship made me turn my head in that direction, but it disappeared again. I felt a mental nudge and smiled. My beast friend was back to see me.

"I didn't see anything."

"I think you're in for a treat." I got up and walked gingerly over toward the edge of the ship. I slowly moved my head closer to peer over and a familiar, gigantic head that was terrifying yet sweet, popped back up in front of my face until we were nose to nose. She jerked her massive head toward mine and back like she was bopping my nose and then disappeared back below the ship. I laughed so hard I doubled over, clenching my stomach.

"Holy shit!" Theo screamed directly behind me. I stood up and then the creature peeked over the edge again, resting its head on the deck and tilting it like it was studying us. Theo moved slowly closer, eyes widening.

Adelram, Kane, Vish and Meili joined us after hearing Theo yell.

"I...I don't believe it. That's—a Paela," Theo said with his jaw to the floor. "I almost couldn't believe you when you said you were rescued by a Paela, but there she is!"

"Is this for real?" Vish asked desperately, like a fanboy who realized his favorite comic book hero was real.

The creature nodded its head like it was in agreement. It must indeed be rare if both Vish and Theo reacted this way.

Kane walked beside me and looked down at me with a twinkle in his eye and half a smirk and I could feel a small tingle of awe rush through me. I quickly looked away with my cheeks burning to a crisp.

"Our Reina is *Paeladoned,*" Vish said with his eyes bulging out of his face.

"*Paeladoned?*" I asked.

"One who's bonded with a Paela," Vish answered. "I thought it was a myth. My parents read me stories about *Paeladoned* warriors who had extraordinary abilities. They were the ultimate fairytale stories of the Solians—I *dreamed* of being a *Paeladoned* warrior." Vish bowed down before me like he was seeing me for the first time.

"Vish, stop it. Nothing has changed, I just have a new buddy following me around like a little puppy."

"Not even close. It's said that Paela sightings increase if there's a threat to life on a grand scale, and they seek extraordinary fighters who can survive their bonding process and restore balance. Who knows what is truth and what is legend, but it is still precious to witness," Vish responded. "And one thing I do know for sure is that you truly must be special to have been chosen. It is the utmost honor of our people."

I walked closer to Laine and tilted my head. I asked silently to her, "Why me?"

Not expecting a response, I jolted in surprise when I heard her majestic voice in my head. "Your friend is right. You are special." I stepped back and stumbled a bit. Vish and Theo ran to steady me.

"The first time I saw her I thought it was the Lochness monster," I laughed.

"I'm unfamiliar with that creature, but I thought the Paela were a myth because I've never actually seen one. They're said to be incredibly intelligent creatures who are playful and friendly, and can form a bond with one chosen person. They're also known to be magically powerful and can have a dangerous temper if you threaten their loved ones. I've read that ancient Solians would ride their bonded Paela in the water and they gave their human the ability to breathe in the seas."

We'd already proved that to be true.

Theo moved closer to the creature, but she moved away from him and looked directly at me. She made a silly noise then ducked again.

"Looks like she wants to play with you," Theo said, laughing.

I smiled, only on Solis could a sea monster want to play peek-a-boo with me. I walked to the edge again and Laine shot her head up and bopped my nose again, which made me uncontrollably laugh. I could hear her own laughter in my mind and I relished the sweet sound. She rose up to a great height that made me stand back a little in fear of her enormity. Her smooth eel-like skin shimmered in the sun in a multitude of colors and her wings were massive, shaded beautifully in red, orange and yellow patterns that resembled flames. She began to flap her wings and hovered higher into the sky to reveal a long tail with red and yellow tipped fins at the end. The dazzling, twisted horns that sat at the back of her head came to sharp points a few feet in length and I gaped. Laine was *stunning*. She looked graceful, but dangerous, like she had the potential to rip you to shreds in seconds if she so desired. Since our first encounter was short, she was now showing herself to me so I could take in all her glory, before she sank back into the water.

I could feel exactly where she was and every movement she made. She sent pulses of fondness to me and I watched her grace with awe as she maneuvered the seas as if she owned them.

"I've also read that they can sense great power and pure souls. You must have called out to it without knowing," Theo said. "I've known you were special since I first laid eyes on you, but now I know you're the missing element to bring this galaxy back to life. That was truly incredible, thanks for letting me be a part of something so special, Cyra. That was a once in a lifetime event."

I giggled. "It's certainly something I will never forget. I can feel her right now following us behind the ship. Her name is Laine, by the way. She's approximately five thousand years old, and she's been lonely for most of it. That's all I've gotten a glimpse of so far."

"Incredible. I can only hope to have a Paela bond one day," Theo said wistfully. "Let's get some food, shall we?"

"Yes, I'm starved."

Kane and Adelram disappeared so the rest of us sat in the dining room below the deck for a few hours, eating and enjoying each other's company without fear of being watched. It was a joy to simply spend time with these people I was growing close with as if our troubles were mere memories.

My lightness faltered when the entire boat shook and I felt a lifting sensation.

"What the fuck is happening?" I yelled and shot from my seat. Meili looked worried as well, but Vish and Theo were grinning.

"Right on time. We're taking off," Theo said casually.

"Huh?" As far as I knew we had taken off hours ago.

"Come with me," Theo said to everyone in the room. We headed back upstairs, and I stopped short when we reached the deck. The ship was floating in the air.

"Are we—flying?" I blinked around in confusion.

"We are indeed!" Vish chimed in. "This baby can sink, swim and fly."

"That is correct." Theo smirked.

I ran over to the edge of the ship and the water was already miles away. "Is there any kind of advantage to flying over sailing?"

"Nope, it's just neat." Theo laughed.

I felt Laine trailing behind us, so I walked over to see her. She was diving into the air and flying for a moment or two before falling back into the water. She gave me a little mental nudge as if to say, *what the hell?* I laughed and assured her I'd be back down for her. It seemed to appease her and she informed me she was going to find food. When she disappeared far enough into the depths of the ocean I couldn't feel her anymore. I didn't know what kind of abilities Laine had yet, but I pitied whatever poor creature she considered food.

We played cards on the deck for a few hours, and I was happy to report that I wiped the floor with everyone. It was beyond satisfying that at least some things didn't change. I looked at the stack of Jessa's candy before me that we had wagered with.

"What am I going to do about my sugar addiction? That was supposed to last me months! I've never lost this much – and she's never even played *Reina's Deck* before. I don't get it!" Vish exclaimed, throwing his cards down to the table and rising from his seat.

"I've had a lot of practice in the art of game play. I'm just good at it," I smiled with smugness. My Earth parents had always called me a 'sore winner' because I was merciless when I won.

"Yeah, well, don't expect it to be like that forever!" Vish laughed as he left and I was thrilled at his competitive spirit. I understood it completely, and I knew he wouldn't get too many chances to beat me. When I played a game, I made it my life's mission to win—it was just the aggressive gamer in me. I couldn't help but think that he'd be part of my misfit crew of nerdy friends on Earth.

The sky darkened as the sun hit the horizon and I walked over to the edge to watch it set. Theo followed me and took my hand in his and I rubbed circles on his soft skin with my thumb.

"My grandfather's favorite thing in the world was to watch the sun rise and fall. He told me there was great power in the sun and that he cherished every day it gave us life. Now that he's gone and now that I'm here—knowing what I do—I will never take that for granted again."

"Wow, he sounds like a Solian," Theo said.

I nodded and blinked back the burn in my eyes. "I wish he was here to tell me what to do. I don't know how to help everyone, and it kills me. I feel guilty enjoying myself when people are suffering and I should be helping them."

"We will do it together. I will help you no matter the cost. I've loved our people my whole life and I will do whatever it takes to help them with you at my side," Theo said, unblinking, with his head raised.

He led me up to stand and cradled me in his arms so I could rest on his hard body. His long-sleeves were rolled up to his elbows and I held his forearms. As I felt the brush of his soft skin, I realized how incredibly lonely I'd been feeling since losing the most important people in my life. I craved that special connection with someone and Theo was here, desperate to be with me. Despite my guilt and my doubt, I reached behind and caressed his hair and looked back into his eyes. They really were stunningly beautiful and full of an aching longing. I pressed my head up against his, so we were cheek to cheek, the wind bustling through our hair so our strands twined together. I reached behind me again and grabbed his toned arms from biceps and trailed down to his hands where they interlocked with mine. We stood there together on the side of the magical ship and watched the most incredible sunset I'd ever seen in my life, with a multitude of colors filling up the sky—and he never stopped holding me against him, content to just be there for me.

When the sun was gone without a trace, Theo bent his head and held mine in his hand in a sweet caress and whispered against my ear, "You never have to worry about me leaving you."

That simple, caring admission was exactly what I needed to hear at the exact right moment. The feeling of his breath on my skin with me in his arms made me melt into him. I lifted my face toward his again and I inched my lips closer to his. With a look of need and infatuation, Theo leaned down to touch his lips to mine. He was so soft, and gentle and he tasted like sunshine and hope. I wanted to bury myself in his intoxicating jasmine scent.

Theo bent to my neck and kissed me, his hot breath a sweet caress and warm shivers surged through my body. He traced the goose-bumps on my arms with a tickle of his fingertips.

"Hate to break up the love fest, but the wretched laser in the sky is gone and I'm ready to party!" Adelram yelled in an attempt to scare the shit out of us. It worked. We jumped out of our skin and parted ways. Adelram belted out laughing before he opened his flask and downed half of it. I couldn't see Kane in the distance behind his father, but I knew exactly where he was because of the burning rage I felt pulsing directly toward me and Theo.

"Well, Cyra. I'm off to bed." Theo said with disappointment lacing his voice. "Unless you would feel more comfortable with me by your side." He looked toward Adelram and Kane.

"No, I'm fine. Goodnight." I touched his hand in reassurance and he walked away, stopping in front of Kane. They both straightened and Kane took a step toward Theo as if daring him to say something. I cringed, able to hear Kane's unmistakable guttural growl. Adelram stood there literally twiddling his thumbs with a smirk on his face as if enjoying a show. I ran my hand down my face and walked closer.

"What the hell are you so smug about?"

"Good lord, you're never happy, are you? I scowl and you're annoyed. I smile and you're annoyed. Can't a man live his life in peace with his precious flask? Our galaxy has gone to shit and this is the first vacation I've had in who knows how long. Things are looking up for Adelram." He plopped down on a lounge chair and spread his arms behind him with his flask on his chest as if he were soaking up rays on a beach.

"I will never understand him," I said to Kane as he approached, Theo now gone.

"It's better that way. He was born to be an enigma."

My arm was wrapped around the mast, and when I removed it I cursed when a splinter embedded into my finger. "Goddammit!" My attempts to dislodge it were unsuccessful since it was buried too deep.

Adelram huffed and rolled his eyes. "Dear lord, save us. The mighty prophesied savior felled by a half-centember long splinter." He lazily raised his hand and the splinter vanished.

"Did you heal me? I didn't know you had that power."

"No, I can absorb others' injuries and pain. Obviously, you won't see me do it often because I like my sanity."

"You call yourself sane?" My brow raised with disbelief.

"It'll be touch and go, but I shall endure your unbearable festering wound for the good of the galaxy."

I gaped at him. He had some freaking nerve.

"There's something unnatural about a planet with no moon!" Adelram said with his arm flailing above him. Clearly, he was already drunk.

"I was going to ask you for some training on mental blocking, but it seems you've lost your faculties."

Adelram sat up straight and faced me. "Have you ever met me? It would take me a lot more than that to lose it. Like a tiny spaceship ride with a girl from Earth. That might do it."

"Very funny, asshole."

Out of nowhere my head started to ache and a random memory flashed before my eyes from five years ago. It was of grandpa Amrel and Brendon dressed up in Halloween costumes. Grandpa was dressed as the devil and Brendon was dressed as a werewolf. They both jumped out of hiding spots and scared the daylights out of me as they did every single year.

I yelled out loud since the memory was so fresh it was if I had just lived it again. "What the hell!"

"That's for calling me an asshole. You could push me out, you know."

"How about you tell me how?"

He invaded my mind again a few times in succession and I was unable to block him. First, I was under a rainbow eucalyptus tree with Brendon as we laid on hot summer days and talked about what we would do if we had magical powers. Next, I was writing the song that was played at the symphony while Grandpa watched. The last memory was of my parents and I playing video games together like we did every Sunday. Adelram withdrew quickly.

"You wrote *The Sun's Progeny?*" he asked with his eyes bulging in genuine shock. "That was the old man's favorite song. He said it was his hope for the future and I never knew what he meant by it."

"Why can't I block you?" I asked, deciding to ignore his shock.

Adelram laid back down, clearly done with his tiny lesson. "Because you're not trying hard enough."

I looked at Kane with my brows raised. "Did you tell him to say that?"

"No. I suppose there's a reason we're related." Kane stood closer to me and folded his arms. I had to look up to lock eyes with him and the stars and nebulae in the sky gave the most breathtaking backdrop for his stunning face. I attempted to swallow unsuccessfully.

"Stop focusing on the white noise that's in here," he said pointing to my head, "and remember what's readily abundant in here," he concluded, putting his hand to my heart. I wasn't sure if he could feel it, but my pulse had doubled its pace. "Your heart will guide you until your mind is ready. And when they're in sync, you will be unstoppable." He put his hand to my lower back and walked me back to my bedroom, my body shaking with adrenaline from his touch the entire way.

I stewed over his words, but it was still hard for me to believe in my abilities when it didn't come easily. When we were outside my door I silently looked back up at him, my chin quivering with self-doubt.

His face was soft with tenderness and his hand reached up to cup my face.

"Promise me you'll start believing in yourself the way I do."

I placed my hand over his and nodded, still unable to speak.

"Don't forget how bright your light is because it will illuminate your way." He began to walk away and I stopped myself from begging for him to stay. He turned around once more and his smile took my breath away.

"Goodnight, Star."

CHAPTER EIGHTEEN

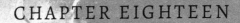

Sweat dripped down my face as I ran my hundredth freaking lap around the ship.

"You call this running? You're shuffling around not picking up your feet. We should have tied wash cloths to your feet, at least then you would have been productive, cleaning the deck. Looks like we'll be adding distance training to our schedule. This is pathetic!" Kane boomed in my face. He was the picture of tidy perfection while I was most likely beet red, sunburned and drenched from head to toe.

"Just when I thought I was beginning to like you," I said through labored breaths.

"You'll be thanking me when you can run away from someone who could destroy you."

"Someone like me?" Adelram said with a saccharine smile.

"Ugh, I hate you all." I plopped down on a chair next to Vish and dry heaved, trying to ease the burn in my lungs.

"Ah, good morning, Cyra! You're just in time for a treat!"

"Oh God, what now? I'm so done with surprises."

"You'll see shortly!"

"Who is actually steering this ship?" I asked, rubbing my chest as if that would help me.

"Theo's magic controls the ship."

"Theo is doing this? You know he's asleep, right?"

"He's already instructed the boat what to do and where to go, now the energy just flows from him without him having to do anything. Don't forget Theo has water strength, so sailing this ship is as easy as walking to him. His bracelet probably gives enough boost that he doesn't feel the drain of energy at all."

Interesting. "So, you're saying a worker on Solis West wouldn't be able to power this ship to Solis East?"

"It depends on their level of magical ability, but it would probably drain all their energy stores before reaching their destination and many wouldn't be able to make it even halfway. With the dwindling energy around us I'm certain most wouldn't even be able to start the boat sailing from the dock. Theo already has a little more than average magical ability and the bracelet substantially boosts his abilities."

"What does the bracelet do for you?"

Vish fidgeted like he was uncomfortable. "I don't have a great deal of innate ability, so the bracelet significantly helps me. I would never be able to power this boat like Theo does, even with the bracelet. I'm able to do lower vibrational magicks like drive and everyday necessities. I have more than average strength for a Solian, and that is my gift."

I wondered how that made him feel in Theo's shadow, but I didn't dare ask. "Tell me how you came to be friends with Theo, you seem really close."

"It's not a happy tale, really, but I'm willing to tell it if you want to hear it."

So much for making him feel more comfortable. "Yes, please tell me." Kane and Adelram disappeared below deck.

"As you know, we met fifteen hundred years ago. What you don't know is why. My family all died in the Great War. They were once simple shop owners and farmers, happy and loving. When the war had infiltrated our territory, my parents had created an emergency escape plan for me and my two younger brothers. We practiced it countless times and our alternative option was a trap door hiding spot in the back of our house. In the end, none of it mattered. The Guardians' troops found us all—traitors to the new regime and loyalists to the natural order of Solian life. My parents hated what the Guardians and Dokoran represented, and they met with fellow Solians trying to find any weaknesses of the Guardians to overthrow them. My parents were active and respected in the community, so they were seen as unofficial leaders in the resistance."

My thoughts went to Blaze and his followers. I knew they talked about rebellion during their weekly meetings with the other working class Solians and his story was scaring me.

"Were there many that fell in line with the Guardians instead of fighting back?"

"Oh, yes. But they're not to be blamed, millions were killed during that time. Everyone lived in fear, much as we do now, we just hide it better."

I shook my head, unable to fathom what it must have been like.

"I was seven years old when they found us. My little brothers were five and one. They busted down our door and dragged the whole family out of the house. Trap doors and escape routes didn't save us. They made an example of my family to all who would oppose the Guardians, and one by one, killed us all. To make my parents suffer as much as possible, they started with the youngest of us and worked their way up. I watched as my little brothers were murdered before me, starting with my one-year-old baby brother. They succeeded in their wish to make my parents suffer, nearly dying from grief alone, experiencing the murder of their children. Mercifully, all their deaths were quick."

"Mine was not. I fought like hell to try and save my brothers, but the guards held me in place so I could do nothing but watch, helpless and broken. When they were dead, I was not afraid for my turn. I was happy to join my brothers, so they weren't alone. One of the Empire of Knights stabbed me in the gut, and it felt like I laid there in searing agony forever, forced to watch my parents killed next. I prayed for it to end, I begged Amrel The High Creator to have mercy on me. Tiny boys, devoid of life and my loving parents, pillars of our community and Solian way of life...gone so pointlessly."

"Oh, Vish." I grabbed his hand and squeezed, my heart breaking for his and all of Eredet's injustices.

"And that's when I first saw Theo. He was young then, fighting against the Guardians and their Empire of Knights. His parents had abandoned the castle and left Theo there alone to defend his people. He killed the Bellum and Knights that murdered my family without much effort. That was the moment I knew I would be forever in his debt, as long as my life lasted. When he saw I was still alive, he immediately drove me back to his castle and had a healer mend my wound. I begged for him to let me die, but he wouldn't allow it."

"Why does Theo work with the Guardians now if he once fought against them?"

"We lost the war and Theo and the remaining Solians surrendered to the Guardians. Later on I heard whispers that the Guardians spiked my parent's heads outside of Eluroom castle along with many other poor souls who resisted them. Luckily, I never made it there to find out for myself, I was with Theo in Meri Kardem. He's been my only family for the past fifteen hundred years. I still have our old family farm on Solis East and try to visit when I can."

I was frozen in place, horrified at his tragic past. When I could compose myself, I said, "It seems like strength is definitely your gift, Vish. And I'd love to see your farm sometime. I'm so incredibly sorry for what happened to you and your family, and my greatest hope is that I will be able to help set things right." I took both of his hands and squeezed, trying to somehow will my sympathies and earnest intentions into him. He untensed a little and smiled back at me.

"I'm glad you're here, Cyra. Life isn't the way it should be."

"There you both are!" Theo smiled toward us. "I was finally able to get some sleep and now I'm starving. Anyone else hungry?"

Vish and I both nodded, pulled out of the intense atmosphere. After Vish's gut-wrenching story, the last thing I wanted to do was eat. All I wanted to do was rip out the hearts of the Guardians one by one, though I doubted they even had hearts at all.

"Let's find Meili and–"

An echoing blast shredded through the air and the entire ship shook violently, knocking us all to the deck. A second blast erupted, and I could hear groaning creaks from the ancient wood as the ship dipped to one side. The three of us started sliding, and furniture was tossed to the other side of the ship in a crash of vicious sound. Vish grabbed hold of a plank and reached for my hand, but I slipped through his fingers and screamed as I knocked my head on something hard and fell toward the open water.

My stomach was in my throat from the velocity and I closed my eyes for the terrifyingly long fall to the sea, but I brutally landed, making every bone in my body throb with intense pain. I groaned and opened my eyes. I was about to scream since it looked like I was laying on air, but I remembered Theo explaining that there was an invisible barrier around the ship to prevent us from falling. Not a second after I got my bearings, the ship began to level out and I fell again, back to the deck of the ship.

"Cyra!" Theo yelled and ran to me. "Are you okay? Are you hurt?"

Meili, Adelram and Kane ran up the stairs. "What is happening?" Kane demanded, his swords drawn and his teeth bared.

"Yeah, what the fuck is going on?" I asked, rubbing my back. Vish ran to me as well and touched my face, looking me over.

"I'm fine," I said to everyone. Theo helped me stand and we all walked to the edge to investigate.

"I don't believe it. They *never* give up." Theo ran a hand through his hair as he looked at another ship positioned below us.

"Bellum Raiders," Vish said through gritted teeth.

"We're seriously outnumbered. Why are they attacking us?" I could hear my heartbeat in my ears it was beating so hard.

"Don't worry, they can't penetrate our shields, they're only mortals. They've been trying to steal this ship for hundreds of years — they'd be at a great advantage with a vessel such as this. But how did they know we'd finally taken it out again after all this time?"

"Lower your ship!" a Bellum screamed.

"Leave now and we will let you escape with your lives," Vish boomed with an amplified voice.

I could hear the Bellum laughing even with the great distance between us. Despite Theo's confidence that they weren't a threat, I had a bad feeling in my gut. "Theo, maybe we should drive out of here. Can we drive with the ship?"

"It would take too much of my power to drive the ship, I would be completely depleted and I'm already greatly diminished after treating the afflicted Solians—even with my bracelet."

"This is your one and only warning! Bring down the ship or we'll take it by force!"

"What gives them such nerve?" Vish asked, seething with anger.

A strange light left their ship, aimed directly for us. Theo's eyes bulged. "Duck!"

We all jumped to the ground, bracing ourselves, and the light energy hit our shields. Kane was shielding me with his body, and I felt the impact of the attack down in my core as our shields sputtered out. There was another blast into the ship, and we started falling out of the sky. This time there was no barrier to protect us from falling to our deaths. We were in the open air and I couldn't see Kane or Adelram anywhere. Theo kept driving over and over and I could tell he was trying to catch me, but driving vertically was much harder to do, especially while falling. He and Vish were unable to get to me and Meili, and I heard Theo scream for me as I plummeted into the water and the vast depths of the ocean.

I WAS NOT A GREAT SWIMMER, but mercifully grandpa Amrel taught me the basics. I was able to make it to the surface, gasping for air right before I was about to pass out from lack of oxygen.

"Meili!" I looked around, but couldn't find her. The Eventyr was still surprisingly intact, standing firm on the water. The enemy ship was a distance away and I realized they wouldn't destroy the Eventyr since they intended to take it for themselves. I didn't get to think any further because I saw a flash of a wooden object before everything went dark.

"Ouch." I moaned into the darkness. "Where am I?"

"Cyra!" It was Meili. I turned as best I could, but I realized she was bound to me. I tried to reach her hands behind me, but I couldn't budge an inch.

"Meili, thank goodness you're okay. Do you know where we are? Do you know if the others are safe?"

"I haven't seen them. I woke up here, like you. This is the lowest deck of the Eventyr, I scoped out every inch of the ship when we arrived." Thank the heavens, unlike me, she'd had the good sense to prepare and use her brain.

In a panic, I tried to ignite my flames but nothing happened. I squinted and tried again, but I felt completely empty, like there was no magic at all living within me. Even if I could summon fire to break free, it would burn Meili in the process. "Meili, can you drive us out of here?"

"I already tried, it's as if there's a block on driving."

I remembered Oliver's ability to block drives, so I knew it was possible. "What about magic? Do you have any abilities to free us? I tried and I don't feel anything."

"I'm not sure, my powers are more geared toward cultivating life, not combat."

"Ugh, if only I could reach my knives." Meili and I braced ourselves as we heard footsteps coming down the stairs.

"Oh, good you're awake," a Bellum man said. "I'm Scott." Two other men accompanied him and one young woman who sauntered to the corner of the room and started examining her nails. She looked like she couldn't be bothered with the whole situation.

Scott knelt down before Meili and whistled. I could smell his gnarly breath from where I sat. "Hot damn, you are the loveliest creature I have ever seen." He stood and walked toward me, the piercing on the bridge of his nose the first thing I noticed. His hair was completely shaved on one side and fell to below his brow on the other. I was able to see a plethora of black skull and weapon tattoos on his arms since all three men wore sleeveless wife beaters and combat pants. All of them were filthy, covered in dust and I imagined the cowls around their necks were to fight off dust storms. While I seethed at these abductors for their gall, a small part of me despaired. It was obvious by their appearance how difficult their lives were and how often they fought to survive.

"And you...you're not as pretty as that one, but still quite the looker. But there's something else interesting about you, isn't there?" He squinted like he was trying to read something within me. Bellum are only mortals, I reminded myself with uncertainty.

"Hey, you don't get dibs on both of them. I'm the one who caught them, I'm taking at least one."

"Settle down, Jenkins, there's enough to go around. This is perhaps the luckiest day of my pathetically short, mortal life. Not only have I finally gotten my hands on the famed Eventyr, which will make me wealthiest Bellum besides the king, but it came with two pretty little things." Scott knelt down again, and I turned my head as best I could as I watched him put his disgusting lips on Meili. Her squeal sent me over the edge, and I thrashed against the cords tied around us and could feel my hands burn. Meili cried out even louder and I knew I had burned her. I calmed myself down, so I didn't end up melting her arms away.

"Oooh, feisty. Just how I like my women. Perhaps you will be my favorite after all."

"Touch her again and I'll fucking kill you."

"Don't worry, darlin', you'll get your turn too. No need to be hasty," Scott said laughing with his two men. When he crouched before me again, I spit in his face and he yelled in anger as he punched me so hard my lip drew blood.

It took everything in me to calm down, I was shaking from head to toe with rage and magical energy desperate for escape.

"Ugh, you guys are so boring and predictable. You're only capable of thinking with your tiny dicks," the girl in the corner grunted.

"Oh, shut it, Kaia. I don't know why your father insists on you coming. You never lift a finger, and you suck all the fun out of every-thing. I am *entitled* to my earned spoils. This ship and these women are mine by rights," Scott seethed.

"Yeah, yeah, yeah. The king forces me to accompany you idiots because you have zero common sense or reasoning skills, and you can't be trusted with anything."

The Bellum King? Was she a Bellum princess? She appeared loathed to be here. In fact, her angular, almost monolid eyes, were hollow and unfeeling like she had never experienced joy. She spoke with no enthusiasm either, like it was an effort to even produce words. She seemed so…broken.

"You're just bitter because no man would ever dream of touching you and taking you away from your father. You're stuck, and you resent everyone else for it, Princess Kaia Gessaine."

"Don't you ever tire of hearing your own sickening voice?" she said in a quiet monotone. These men didn't rile any emotion out of her, and it obviously annoyed them to no end.

I wondered at Scott's words. Kaia was beautiful under the dirt, the ragged mis-matched clothes and dusty goggle type glasses on her forehead, presumably to fend off dust storms. She hid beneath a sooty hood like she was trying her best to stay out of anyone's attention.

"Just hurry up. You dopes tend to stroke yourselves so long for successfully completing one tiny job that you end up fucking everything up while you're too busy with your hand down your pants. So, I'll save us some time. Good job, big boys! You did it! Now wrap this shit up so we can go home." Kaia walked up the stairs and disappeared.

"I *hate* that bitch," Jenkins spat after her.

"I pity the bastard who ever sticks it to that black hole," Scott agreed. "Now, time for one quicky before we leave." Jenkins and the other man laughed with him.

"What the hell do you want from us? Why do you want this ship? There's still time to do the right thing and just go back home," I reasoned.

The three men belted out laughing. "You idiot, Solian. You're truly all the same, aren't you? You think you're so superior to everyone else in the galaxy and won't lift a finger to help anyone else but yourselves."

"What are you even talking about? Are you working with the Guardians? Did they give you some kind of ability?"

"The Guardians? Fuck no, I don't work with that scum. Some Bellum do—shit, some just don't have a choice. You're all a joke, living a comfortable life in your sun-filled fantasy land. But your time will come."

"Our time for what? What is it that you want?"

"We're done asking. You'll find out soon enough. Now, about those spoils…"

I tried to hold onto Meili, but I still couldn't move. She bent down her head and I noticed a soft glow in the room. The three men moved toward Meili and started to separate her from me.

"No! Don't touch her!" I screamed. Meili didn't say a word or make a noise. Jenkins held me down, so I was facing her and Scott. Her head was still down like she was concentrating, and I seemed to be the only one who noticed the soft glow in the room. Before Scott could get his hands on her, the three men in the room started coughing. Lightly at first, then hacking and gasping for air. One by one they hit the floor and passed out.

"Meili...what just happened?"

"I noticed some mold in the corner of the room. I was able to extract some spores and plant it in their lungs, so they had difficulty breathing. I don't think they're dead, but they'll be out for a while," she smiled at me.

"Meili, you're a *genius!*" I smiled and tried to ignite my flames. "You've got to be kidding me. I was able to summon the fire before but now nothing is happening!" I panicked.

"Anger seems to help you. Just close your eyes and imagine what that man was about to do to me." She healed her own wounds from where I burned her, and I blushed with shame.

I obeyed and closed my eyes. I imagined poor, sweet Meili and that man even *thinking* about hurting her. Flames burst from my hands and it took a mere few seconds to free myself. I ran to Meili and cut the rope at her feet with one of my daggers. I gave her my second one for defense.

"Stay behind me," I whispered. It wasn't like I could save either of us, in fact, she was obviously more equipped in a desperate situation than I was. But I felt protective of her, and as long as I was alive, I'd do my best to keep her safe.

We inched quietly up the stairs and passed by the mid-level quarters straight for the deck. The first thing I saw was Theo and Vish tied and gagged. The Bellum must have bound their powers somehow because there's no other way they could have kept them constrained like that. There was no sign of Kane and Adelram and I prayed that they were finding their way back to us. If they had hurt Kane I'd find a way to burn them and their ship until everything was nothing but ash.

There were about twenty Bellum on the deck, investigating the ship and taking inventory. It made my blood boil that these people thought they could simply take Theo's cherished family ship. Like me, he had so little left of his family, the loss of this ship would be devastating for him. My blood was boiling, but no fire came. It was the most frustrating feeling in the world. I knew there was something ready to strike within me, but I couldn't access it. What did it say about me that I couldn't manage to use my magic when my friends were in imminent danger, while the children in Solis were able to summon theirs barely trying?

"Meili, we're going to have to fight...my magic's not working. Keep your dagger close. I'll go for Theo and you run for Vish. We'll have a better chance at survival if we have them free, and there's twenty or more Bellum on the deck, we can't make it without them. Vish and Theo are straight ahead, so when I count to three, you run as fast as you can to cut them free." Without question she nodded in silent agreement, and I was momentarily taken aback by her bravery. I was shaking from head to toe in fear, but Meili, who'd probably never fought a day in her life, who valued life above all else, didn't flinch. It gave me slightly more courage than I could have mustered on my own.

"One...two...three!" We ran as fast as we could, but it wasn't fast enough. Theo was yelling in his mouth gag, but I ignored him and knelt, starting to cut his ropes. I didn't get far, before I was knocked over the head causing me to fall to the deck.

I was in and out of awareness, and when I touched my hand to my head there was an abundance of blood. I saw Theo wriggle free from the small tear I made on his rope and he started to fight the Bellum that struck me. They had taken his sword, so he was stuck with his fists and his cunning. He was able to disarm his opponent until they were both engaged in melee combat.

I did my best to sit up, still disoriented by the multiple blows I'd received. Vish stood, still tied, and head-butted another Bellum who had Meili in a choke hold. It sobered me up enough that I managed to wobble to Vish and free him. He was a fearsome thing to behold. He picked up the fallen Bellum's sword and I could see hundreds of years' worth of battle training in every move that he made. He easily took down two more Bellum, and Theo was wrestling another with a rapier he had stolen. He moved with surety and strength, but so did the massive Bellum he was fighting, and Theo was badly bruised and bleeding while still holding his own.

I caught movement in the corner of my eyes and said a silent prayer as Kane and Adelram climbed onto the ship, unharmed. Adelram knocked the heads of two unsuspecting Bellum and Kane beheaded another. He sheathed his swords, and began growing the dark tendrils of energy I'd seen before, but it was subdued and I couldn't feel the massive thrumming of power. Kane threw his energy at two Bellum across the ship and they screamed as they exploded in two leaving a macabre scene of gore.

Three more Bellum ran up the stairs and I realized they were probably scoping out the middle of the ship. We were seriously outnumbered. I ran to Meili to protect her, but stopped dead in my tracks as a Bellum knocked her to the deck and pinned her down with his knee. He raised his hand and my heart dropped as I realized he was holding her dagger.

"No! Meili!" I ran at top speed even though it felt like slow motion, but an enormous wave stopped everyone on the deck and knocked me to my back as the ship tipped sideways once more. The fighting ceased as everyone was knocked around. I heard an other-worldly piercing cry come from the water and some of the Bellum covered their ears from the intensity of it. As soon as the ship leveled out, we ran to the edge and I couldn't believe what I saw.

Laine was there, massive and terrifying—a promise of a painful death glinting in her eyes. She cried out again, and her mammoth tail rose to the air and fell down onto the Bellum's ship cutting it clean in half. I saw about twenty Bellum from that ship fall to their deaths into the water. Laine swam toward us and raised as high as she could, so she was towering over us like a sea creature goddess, wings spread to their full capacity and eyes glowing yellowish red. She roared again, and the Bellum that were left on our ship squealed and jumped over-board to escape. Princess Kaia was the last Bellum on the ship, and she looked slightly stunned and confused before locking eyes with me, letting her overwhelming sadness take over once again. She touched her neck and disappeared. She just *drove*. A Bellum mortal.

I turned to face Laine and she lowered down until she was face to face with me, her eyes now soft and full of affection.

"You saved us," I said aloud as I gently touched her head. She basked in my appreciation.

"We fight together, Cyra. I am now a general in your army, and will always hear your call. This war is only beginning to reach its apex and the beasts of this galaxy that have stayed hidden and dormant for thousands of years are awake...and waiting."

I quivered at her words. *My* army? Hidden beasts?

"Yes, your army. You are the one of the prophecy, Cyra, and you *will* unite these fractured worlds to face the end of days. And I am honored to assist you until the very end."

My blood ran ice cold in my body as I stood in disbelief, and her words echoed softly in my head as she turned to leave, waves responding to the demands of her massive body. "We are waiting..."

I believed.

The last threads of doubt that clung to me snapped and flew away, replaced by fear at the overwhelming responsibility this acceptance would bring. A galaxy—multiple words of people suffering and dying, relying on me to bring the peace they cried for.

"Are you alright?" Theo asked, and I flinched back to reality.

I nodded my head in silence. Laine and I had more to talk about later. "I'm fine. How about we go clean up?"

We all started to walk away, and I turned around once more to watch Laine swim away. "I'll be here when you're ready, Cyra." Her words softly echoed again in my mind as she traveled further into the Solian seas amongst the floating dead bodies of her kill.

CHAPTER NINETEEN

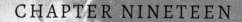

*W*e cleaned up and inspected every inch of the ship to make sure all the Bellum were gone, and then ate to replenish our strength and energy stores. We decided to eat on the deck to keep an eye on things and make sure there were no more threats.

"I think it's time for the next phase of our trip, it'll be safer this way," Theo said.

"I agree. Cyra, remember I said you were in for a treat? Well, to be clear, I didn't mean the Bellum attack." Vish chuckled. "*This* is the treat."

An invisible field launched and created a dome effect above us. There was a tremble on the ship, and I stood in a panic.

"Oh God, what now?" I asked.

"Don't worry, this is supposed to happen." Theo winked.

As we began to sink below the shore, my breath sputtered out. The invisible force was keeping the water out and there was an incredible view of the ocean all around us. "Um...we're not going to suffocate down here, are we?"

Vish snorted. "Do you really think Theo and I would be so relaxed if we were in danger? Theo's magic is recycling the air in this protective dome, it requires almost no energy from him."

I slowly let myself sit down and relax. I was already entranced watching the foreign fish swim by, lulled by the soothing sight. It was like my own personal gigantic aquarium—except I was the one in *their* natural habitat. The creatures swimming before me were whimsical and I walked toward the edge taking a closer look.

The first thing I saw was a beautiful sea turtle that had a mother of pearl shell. I noticed a large school of tiny fish, but on closer inspection they looked like butterflies with semi-translucent wings of all different colors.

I zeroed in on a tiny creature floating by, and when it noticed me, it swam closer to inspect *me* a little more. It looked like a seahorse, except quite different from the ones I knew on Earth. It much more resembled what a land horse looked like with front hooves and the same shaped face. A transparent fin adorned the top of its head that reached to the back of its neck like an adorable mohawk and it had a horn in the middle of its forehead that immediately made me think *unicorn*. It was black and white striped with strange fins wrapped around his bottom torso that kind of looked like he was wearing a skirt, and he had a tail that curled up just like an Earth seahorse. There were others in the background swimming toward him, and they had all different kinds of colors and patterns. I squeaked out loud and giggled at the adorable tiny creature who seemed just as interested in me. And then the whole boat started to rock back and forth as a gigantic creature swiftly swam behind the seahorse and out of sight.

"What was that?" Vish asked.

"I don't know, it was so fast I couldn't see it," Theo replied.

"It's Laine." She was still hidden from view, but I felt her mentally reaching out to me, keeping close to make sure there were no further threats.

"She's jealous that I was playing with another sea creature." I laughed at the wonderful absurdity that a massive sea beast would feel envy, especially of me. "Don't you worry, girl, nobody could ever replace you."

She then appeared before us, a massive presence that would make any unknowing person mess their pants at the sight of her so close. She tilted her head, viewing the invisible barrier.

I turned to look at Theo and Vish. "She wants me to go swim with her since I'm under water."

"I will *never* get used to this. It's too amazing for words," Vish said in a stupor.

I could agree with him there. I wasn't sure I would ever get used to this new life. Just a few short weeks ago I was a nobody in Arkansas whose biggest worry was if the private rooms in our arcade would be available for Dungeons and Dragons. The death of my beloved grandpa brought much more pain than the simple act of his passing, it came with an unknown binding contract to save everyone from impending disaster. I'd give anything to go back to that simple and safe time—and yet, knowing what I do now and seeing others around me suffering, I didn't think I'd ever be able to make that choice if it was given to me. These were my people, and our world was dying. Even the hidden creatures of the world were screaming for help. Not only that, but the desperation in the galaxy turned everyone against each other. Solians and Varjun hated each other, and everyone hated the Bellum. The Bellum attacked anyone out of opportunity, yet nobody seemed to really know them at all. All of this reminded me that my training was important. No, I wasn't a warrior, but I knew I needed to become one. I had to protect myself and my people – both on Solis and Earth.

Theo looked at me, noticing my eyes were glazed over in thought and said, "Well, I'm stuffed. Why don't we retire and get some last relaxing hours before bed? I think we earned that today, plus we'll reach the first shrouded island tomorrow."

I smiled at him, and his dimples sent a rush through me forcing me to look down so he wouldn't see my blush. He quietly chuckled, knowing what he had just done to me despite my efforts to hide it. Damn his empathy and my betraying body.

Theo walked me back to my room and he didn't wait for an invitation to follow me in. I rushed over to the window to see another live aquarium right outside my balcony. I would never get bored of the sight of these fantastical fish swimming by like I was living among them.

Theo came up behind me and caressed my arms. "Are you okay?"

"Yeah, I'm fine, I just have a lot flooding my mind. I'm still a little lost."

"That's understandable, but I promise I will help you find your way."

I turned around to face him and got lost inside his kind eyes. "I believe you." I leaned in and wrapped my arms around him and breathed him in. His presence was soothing and the aching hole in my heart was somewhat suppressed.

"I was so worried about you when I didn't know where you were," I said, fighting off the stinging in my eyes. "All I could think about was that I would never again see your beautiful eyes gazing at me like they are now." I *could not* admit even to myself that I had the same worry... about Kane. I buried that monster of a realization deep down because the alternative was too much to bear. Theo was the future king blessed by the sun that I was destined to be with. While a part of me ached with that fact, I could think of worse fates. And it was no longer about me and my petty whims. It was never more important for me to be strong and think with my head.

Theo gently touched my face and I melted into his hand that I loved so much. "I was going out of my mind not knowing where you were. I was consumed because all I could feel was your fear, it took over every other sense in my body and drove me mad. I could feel you so completely it was as if they were my emotions, but I had no idea where you were. It was one of the scariest moments of my life," Theo said in a quiet voice he couldn't stop from cracking. "I was bracing myself for the worst, terrified of feeling that moment when the fear ended. When all your emotions... disappeared. What made it all worse was that the majority of my power was drained, and they managed to somehow stifle the rest of it."

"The Bellum said they're not working with the Guardians, but how else could they have power like that? The Bellum princess was able to drive!"

"It seems like there's even more about them that we don't know. I'm just glad you're okay. I would be lost without you, Cyra."

"Well, we're all safe. That's all that matters." I squeezed his hand in reassurance.

We ended up laying in bed together as he held me for a few hours watching the fish, and I told him about my childhood on Earth and how much I missed it. I told him every highlight reel of my time from my days in Arkansas until I yawned and fought to stay awake. I turned to face him and his eyes glowed an intensely bright blue that took my breath away.

"You really are a beautiful man, how have you not been snatched up by an equally beautiful woman by now?"

Theo looked surprised by my comment, but smiled and kissed my forehead.

"My dear, Cyra. Haven't I made that clear by now? I've been waiting my whole life for you."

CHAPTER TWENTY

*T*he next morning I dressed and made my way to the deck where everyone was already convened.

"Have we found the shrouded island?" I asked, filled with hope.

Adelram's fingers tapped against his lips while he rolled his eyes. Kane's arms were crossed and his scowl let me know they had been arguing.

"It's here, we've just been looking for the right place to enter. There's no telling what could be on the other side of the shroud," Theo huffed, staring at Kane with disdain.

"I don't feel any magical presence, but your *prince* thinks my word isn't good enough," Kane growled. "But instead of standing around with our hands up our asses, let me volunteer to be the first to enter."

Without warning Kane leapt off the ship and I yelped in surprise. I sprinted to the side with my heart beating out of my chest, worried for his safety. When I saw him emerge from the water and open the shroud as if opening an invisible curtain I let out a huge sigh of relief. Theo looked at me with a fierceness in his eyes I'd never seen directed at me before. I calmed myself realizing he could feel every bit of my emotion and he *did not* like it. He walked away with his hands clenched and my face burned with embarrassment—and utter confusion. I shook out of my stupor when Kane yelled from the island.

"It's desolate! You're safe to enter."

"Allow me, my *liege*," Adelram cooed with sarcasm, grabbing me close and driving me to the opening Kane made for us. Theo, Vish and Meili joined seconds after and Theo stalked toward Adelram with his teeth bared.

"What's the problem, princeling? I'm merely carrying out one of my tasks as an indentured servant. Protection duty," he said in a mocking tone that only fueled the anger in Theo.

"Everyone calm the fuck down! Can we please search this island? There's more pressing matters at hand than male ego." I walked to Meili and hooked my arm with hers and she gave me a commiserating look. I was promptly getting off the testosterone train.

We walked around the island for hours, only coming across rubble from destroyed buildings and decaying plant life. It shook me to my core realizing how much extra care Solians had been giving their farms and wildlife, witnessing what would have naturally occurred with no interference. The island was dead. The silence in particular instilled a sickening terror within me noticing the blaringly obvious lack of sounds from birds or insects. The trees were shriveled and brown and the stench of decay was like a poison to my nose.

We entered the only building that was still standing with a sign that read "Solian Detention Center." The first thing we saw inside was a large painting of a maniacal looking man and a woman next to him with her hands cuffed and chained.

"I had no idea Solis had a prison," Vish said softly.

"That's Dokoran, The Demon Reina and his slave *vordne*, Lavinia. This detention center must have been used during his reign," Theo said to me with his brows raised.

The smell of mold was overwhelming and I scrunched my nose from the acrid aroma and the thought that my Solian grandfather was so evil.

Adelram walked into an open cell and bent down to pick up a pair of beads with a crimson and violet flower pendant. When he turned around his moonlit eyes were glowing with vehemence and his hand fisted the necklace so tight it broke and scattered throughout the ground. Lightning danced all over his body and I felt the hairs raise all over me from the electricity. His face was mangled in rage and a hiss escaped his throat. I thought I had seen Adrelram's anger before, but I was dead wrong. The powerful being before me made me take a step back, my eyes wide in fear.

Kane stepped into the cell to see what Adelram had dropped, and he picked up the flower pendant, put it to his forehead as if performing a silent vigil. Then he turned to glare at Theo and Vish. "This is a Varjun pendant. You kept Varjun people in these fucking cells!" His deep voice reverberated through the empty, putrid walls. I could feel his power thrumming so wildly I wondered at how it didn't explode from him and I somehow felt irrationally irate out of nowhere.

"We knew nothing about this place and it clearly hasn't been used in thousands of years. You can't blame us for that. Besides, don't act like your people are blameless in the history of our feuds. The Varjun have just as much blood on their hands."

"That's enough!" I cried, my voice cracking from the tear that fell down my cheek. I couldn't help but feel partly responsible for this fight because it was clear Dokoran was a big part of the reason the Solians and Varjun warred for so long.

"This place is deplorable and I can't pretend I know everything Solians and Varjun have suffered, but Dokoran ruled twenty-five hundred years ago. Please, let's try to keep the peace and figure out how we can save our futures."

Adelram cursed and his lightning died. He turned and walked down the row of dark, damp stone cells and we followed behind him. We inspected every one, and it was clear that people from all over the galaxy were kept here, including Solians. There was no rhyme or reason to Dokoran's madness and everyone was subject to his cruelty.

But there was no *mikla*. We returned to the ship and sailed to Meri docks, silent the entire time. There were too many open wounds for the people of Eredet that still had not healed. That detention center was an ugly skeleton of the horrors these people had endured for thousands of years.

After an hour or so we reached the docks and Theo led us to the small, stone castle, holding my hand so tight I thought it might lose circulation.

"Welcome to my home, Meri Kardem. Kardem meaning kingdom

as you would know it. On Solis West where royalty is known as Reinan, your kingdom is Eluroom Reindem."

Vish breathed in deeply then exhaled beside me. "It's great to be home."

The first thing I noticed when taking in my surroundings was the wind. It was glorious and I absorbed the wondrous sounds of the trees swaying in the breeze. I never really thought about it, but the air was completely still on Solis West. The only time the wind moved was when Kane willed it to. It was as if the planet was holding its breath near the vicinity of the stench and horror of the Guardians.

Theo took my hand. "Are you ready?"

I nodded as he held me tight to him like we were an official pair, and I supposed we were. Destiny already proclaimed it so. I looked over my shoulder at Kane and the inner corners of his brows were raised instead of their usual fierce downturn, and his eyes were dull and empty. It took everything in me to face forward and pay attention. *I had a destiny to fulfill. I couldn't let everyone down. It wasn't about me.*

The castle was much less grand than the sky-scraping glittering white and gold castle of Eluroom and there were no intricate statues or architecture, but I think I liked this better. It was homely and inviting, like the inhabitants actually wanted to open its doors to its people.

"It's beautiful," I smiled at Theo.

"It's not overly glamorous, but it's home."

A short, clean-cut man came rushing out of the castle doors. "Welcome home, Kara! Meri has missed you."

"Thank you, Frederik. Please meet Reina Cyra."

Frederik straightened and began acting overly formal. "Welcome to Meri Kardem, Reina. We already have a room prepared for you."

"That's very kind, thank you."

Theo took my hand and Frederik's eyes widened as if he'd never seen Theo touch a woman before. *I've been waiting my whole life for you.* I didn't doubt his words and it made shame heat through my body with how much I'd been thinking about Kane. It was becoming more and more difficult to steer my thoughts away about how much I felt for him.

Frederik rushed over and opened the doors, and Theo gave me the full tour, which didn't take too long since the castle was modest, and I adored every bit of it. Instead of the monochrome, stately and ostentatious décor of Eluroom, Theo's home had bright, warm colors while still feeling majestic. There were also countless nods to the sea, and it was clear Meri Kardem worshiped their water life. Theo looked right in his element and Vish was visibly at ease, happy to be home. Meili was her normal, smiling self while Kane and Adelram were the picture of annoyance.

"Frederick, please see that our guests are comfortable and fed."

"Of course, Karalis."

Theo turned to me and spoke quietly. "I know we just arrived, but there's an urgent piece of business I'd like to show you that I think you'll want to see."

"Then I'm ready to leave now."

"I was hoping you'd say that."

Theo held me close, and we instantly appeared on a small, completely empty island.

"Um...Theo, there doesn't seem to be a lot of urgent business here."

"That's because you're not looking hard enough dear, Reina. You must promise not to speak of this to anybody."

Instantly intrigued, I nodded my agreement.

Theo approached a large stone, almost his height, and held out his hand to it. I realized he wasn't wearing his power bracelet for the first time since I'd met him. When he touched the stone, a glowing rune-like marking materialized and a massive temple appeared before our eyes. It was ornate white stone, much like the architecture on Solis West, with winged beings I now knew as the Sunya Rei, grasping large swords on various pedestals of the building. Intertwining knot designs adorned the building in between the statues.

"This is another uncharted island, boats and visitors can't visit unless they know it's here. Most of my people work together to keep this whole island shrouded. It takes a tremendous amount of energy to sustain the shroud, and they choose to dedicate much of their power to it anyway."

"How wonderful." I was relieved to hear that there was still some level of camaraderie between our people and it filled me with hope.

We entered the temple and it felt like I had walked into an opulent church in Rome, complete with colossal stained-glass windows, sculptures and a plethora of gold and jewels. There was a crowd of people gathered around hundreds of portraits and murals of people's faces—most of them children. I walked over to them intrigued, wanting to get a better look.

"What are these images?" I asked Theo quietly. People were knelt before them with candles lit, and they looked as if they were in silent prayer. Most were overcome with grief and crying. Who did they pray to? I couldn't believe the similarity between these immortal powerful Solians and the ordinary people of Earth. Everyone needed help, and sometimes—salvation.

"They're images of the *lost ones*," Theo put a hand on my shoulder as if bracing me.

"Lost where?"

"Nobody knows. After the Guardians came into power and the war was officially over, we started to notice that people were disappearing, and it hasn't stopped to this day. Nobody talks about it in public, but here is a secret place the families can come to grieve, post their loved one's picture to report them lost and to pray for help.

"Oh my God—so many children."

"There's plenty of adults taken, but most of the abductees are children. Thousands of souls have disappeared over the millennia never to be seen again, and that's after the devastating loss from the war. It's why you see very little children on Solis and why the lands are barren."

It was obvious this was the Guardians' doing. I thought back to Kane admitting he was held captive and was only released because of his father's interference. That, paired with their attempts to take my blood without my permission, made my mind go to dark places. "Who are they praying to?"

But when I looked off into the distance my heart stopped, I saw my answer. I didn't walk. I dodged as quickly as I could through the crowd to the largest effigy in the room with people knelt before him. His stone wings were open and spanned half of the width of the temple and I couldn't help but also fall to my knees and weep with the others.

Kane did tell me that grandpa was a creator of life—but something in me didn't take him seriously. Didn't comprehend the magnitude. And I'd never expected he was the center of Solian life. He was their...*deity*—and I'd never had *any* idea. He was my silly, loving, and eccentric grandfather who doted on me. He was my mentor and my best friend. It was completely blowing my mind and, even worse, my heart ached for these parents and family members who had no clue that their deity was dead. My cheeks were on fire in disbelief and confusion. Everything I thought I understood about life dissipated along with my sanity. I understood *nothing*.

"A new face and even she feels the healing power of our great Creator, Amrel."

I jerked my head up and a striking woman with white-blonde hair in a white robe was smiling at Theo. "Is she a new recruit of yours, Theo?"

He grabbed my hand to help me up. "Eleri, I'm pleased to introduce to you, Reina Cyra, returned to us. Cyra, Eleri was once the Master of the Divine when it was still an operating board."

Eleri's pleasantness vanished instantly. "Are you sure we can trust her? We don't know where she's been for thirty years."

"Eleri, please. I trust her completely or I never would have brought her here."

"I wish you would have at least had the courtesy to consult me first. I'm not okay with this."

"Well, if you can't trust her, at least trust me. Or have I now lost your trust after all these years?"

Her face softened a bit, and she batted her eyes at him and blushed. What a shock — this woman was in love with Theo. I sucked up the unpleasant greeting and the unfamiliar pit in my gut and tried to be congenial.

"Nice to meet you, Eleri. It's a beautiful temple."

"It's not meant to be beautiful. It's meant to be a haven for those who need guidance and help in these dark times. It's meant to be a token of our gratitude to our High Creator."

"I meant no offense, only that I appreciate this place."

"I'm so relieved I now have your approval."

Woah. This woman needed to relax.

"Cyra, Eleri is our *silta*. She's like a bridge between the divine and our people. It's said that Amrel has touched her with the ability to communicate with him."

"That's right, I speak to him almost daily. I try to ease the suffering of our people by asking Amrel for guidance and help."

Unable to control myself any longer I snorted a laugh. Unbelievable. This fraud was making a mockery of the situation. Grandpa would have thought she was ridiculous and pompous, and wouldn't have blessed anything of hers.

"You come into our safe haven and mock Our Creator?"

Oh, everyday woman, you have no idea. I joked with that old man every single day.

"Let's just calm down," Theo stepped in. "Eleri, I'm sure Cyra meant nothing by it, and I was really hoping you would show her around the temple and explain some of our beliefs and history. She is our *Reina*, and she is here to help us."

I watched as Eleri clenched her fists beside her. "Fine. This way."

I followed them as she explained what I already knew about Grandpa being the Creator of Life, but she couldn't explain *how or why* which would have been the useful information. She told me that a lot of history was lost so they only had bits and pieces of history plus their faith. We passed statues of more winged people and Eleri went on to say that they were also higher beings like Amrel, but not as all-powerful.

The Creator of the universe protected me on a mortal planet for sixteen years and died so that I could live. I still could not fathom the magnitude of that realization and I wasn't sure I would ever be able to get rid of the crushing guilt of it.

"It's believed that all the Sunya Rei died out long ago and that Amrel reigns alone," Theo chimed in.

It was painful to listen to this. I felt like I knew very little of Eredet, the prophecy and grandpa's past, and yet I somehow knew more than these people who had lived here for thousands of years. I didn't dare correct this woman, though, unable to betray Grandpa's secret to a judgmental fraud like her.

"This is the wall of the *lost ones*. Here our people display images of their missing in hopes that Amrel will bring them back safely where they belong."

I reddened in shame and looked at the ground, so I didn't betray my emotions. It destroyed me that I couldn't tell anyone the truth, and yet it was probably the greater kindness to not kill their hope.

We passed a floor-to-ceiling stained-glass window and I stopped short in shock. "What is this scene?" I asked desperately.

Theo looked at me with confusion. "Cyra, do you recognize it?"

"I'm...just curious."

Eleri smirked and looked pleased that I asked. "This is the first piece of art to be put into the temple. It's said to be a direct message from Amrel himself, foretelling the future. It tells of the apocalypse— the end of days, and the secret to how we can avoid this disaster is hidden in the art. Some say the end is here, and the darkness is winning."

I stared at her sense of melodrama, but I walked closer to examine it. The mural was the same one on the box Grandpa had given me, except it had even more detail. That box had to have something to do with the *mikla*.

I noticed Theo looking back and forth between the girl on the mural and me, and my dark magenta hair. *Way ahead of you, Theo.* I just didn't know *how* this all fit together yet.

Eleri showed me a few other places in the temple, but I was too distracted to pay attention. She brought us outside to show us one final thing. "This is our *lost garden*. A flower is planted for every soul who goes missing."

I gasped at the enormity of the garden. It put another visual to the sheer loss of Eredet's people, and this didn't include the losses from the war. There were thousands of flowers flowing in the wind, giving a visual macabre beauty to the souls they represented.

We said our goodbyes to Eleri, and she disappeared back inside. I wasn't going to miss her.

"Man, it's always painful going in there. The anguish of the families of the lost is overwhelming for me. It attacks me like an infestation, experiencing each person's pain all at once, and it feels like I'm drowning under water. Even when the temple is empty, I feel the echoes of pain like the energy is so strong that it lingers long after the suffering have left, hiding in the darkness unable to escape." Theo shivered and I was horrified at the true impact of his gift. I would never wish to be an empath, it seemed more like a curse.

"Theo, is there somewhere private we can go to talk where we won't be overheard?"

He nodded, not asking me why, and drove us to another island that appeared completely abandoned. There were empty buildings, unkempt foliage and not a sound to be heard. Neglected huts rotted in the water and I remembered Theo explaining that they were once commonplace in Meri Kardem. I got the sense it was a shell of a past life that was once bustling with activity and life.

"What is this place?"

"It's a collection of islands we call the Schools of the Seas. It once hosted thousands of children and vast amounts of schools where you could learn just about anything. It was one of the gems of Eredet galaxy, and now…it's completely dead. There's no one left to learn and no history to remember. It was one of the first things the Guardians destroyed. We won't be overheard here and, as you can see, I've left my bracelet behind."

I wondered if the horrible blows of this tragic galaxy would end, but it seemed the fates weren't anywhere near finished delivering them. But If Theo was part of my destiny, it was time to tell him the truth.

"First of all, you know that woman is a phony, right? I highly doubt she's ever spoken a word to Amrel *at all,* and secondly, she obviously hates me."

Theo laughed, but said seriously, "How can you be so sure she can't speak to Amrel? I'm not convinced either way, but I can't rule it out. More importantly she gives our people hope, and for that I'll let her convince anyone of her beliefs."

"I agree, it's good to have hope. It's just…"

"What is it, Cyra? You can trust me."

I couldn't help the tears falling down my cheeks. Theo came closer and wiped one away and held my face. "It's just that in this case— there really is no hope."

"Cyra, don't say that, there's always hope."

"No. Theo...Amrel's dead. There's no one listening to those poor mothers' pleas."

"What are you talking about? Nobody's seen Amrel in millennia, but we believe—"

"He's my grandfather. Grandpa Amrel raised me on Earth himself for sixteen years—well thirty-something years in Solian time. I was there with him when he died. He left me a letter saying that things would be happening to me that I wouldn't understand, but would become clear as time went on. He was everything to me, but he's gone now. We're on our own."

Theo clutched his chest like I had crushed his heart. His eyes were wide with fear, and it was only the second time I saw him lose his composure. He bent over and grabbed his knees.

"I'm sorry, Theo—I wasn't sure if I should tell you and now, I see you are worse off for it."

Theo belted a sarcastic laugh. "*Grandpa.* I can't believe you've known our deity—our High Creator—as Grandpa. I'm glad you told me. Ignorance kills, and I have a Kardem to keep safe. But you're wrong about one thing, Cyra. There *is* always hope, until the end. I believe in us, and I still think we can bring the balance back to Eredet together, with or without Amrel. The thought of us being alone in the universe is absolutely *terrifying*, but we're not yet alone in this galaxy. There is someone listening to those mothers' pleas. We are."

Theo and his abundant optimism, determination and confidence was really something to admire. After over a thousand years of hardship, he was still unwilling to give up, and he did it with a smile. There was a lot I could learn from this prince of the sun. I walked up to him and hugged him tightly, and I relaxed slightly as he returned the embrace.

"I'm due to meet someone back at the castle. Will you join me? There's someone else I'd like you to meet."

"I'm right by your side."

Theo smirked and playfully rubbed my chin before driving us back to the castle.

"I don't want anyone to know I'm here. Only I can drive right into the castle. I'll make sure you are able as well when you've mastered the ability. This is my private study."

I looked around the room filled with luxurious wood and elegant, masculine furnishings and noticed there was already someone there by the window.

"Theo, there's someone here," I said, pointing to the unknown man. He had on a hooded cloak so I couldn't see his face.

"Cyra, this is Urien Norshade. My spider."

"Spider—as in spy?"

Urien took off his hood and bowed to me. His short mahogany hair complimented his hooded, dark hazel eyes. He looked primed for a fight with long-sleeved fighting leathers on under his cape, and he was rough around the edges. His scruffy, unshaven face was interesting, more than traditionally beautiful, and it was obvious that he was most definitely lethal. He fidgeted with a stunning jewel around his neck which looked odd on someone so gruff.

"It's an honor, Reina. I served your parents long ago. I'm out in the galaxy gathering intelligence and reporting daily activities to the Karalis."

"Have you ever wondered where I go every day when I'm in my 'meetings'?" Theo smirked at me.

"Well, sure, but I assumed you were sitting in a stuffy conference room with the Guardians discussing which living sacrifice Orphlam demanded that day."

Theo and Urien chucked. "I'm usually here. Helping my people with their farms and livelihood, healing the afflicted, gathering intelligence and planning an offensive. We've been searching for the *mikla*, and now we're closer than ever thanks to you."

"Do you know what it looks like?" I asked Theo.

Urien stood up straight, like he knew I was hiding something. "You say that as if *you* know something about it. Do you?" he questioned.

"Mylo told me the key to breaking the curse was grandpa's box, so I'm wondering if the *mikla* looks similar."

"Who's Grandpa?" Urien asked.

"Who's Mylo?" Theo asked, bewildered.

"The Voidling in Eluroom castle," I explained.

"You spoke to a Voidling? They can *talk*?" Urien said with disbelief on his face.

"How did you not know this? You know almost everything in the galaxy, and you didn't know the Voidlings can communicate?" Theo directed at Urien, who simply shrugged.

"Theo, Grandpa left me a box when he died, and I haven't thought much of it until now." Urien and Theo both stood straighter now with keen anticipation.

"The scene in the stained-glass window in the temple—it's the same depiction that's on my box. I feel like it's connected to this *mikla*, although there's nothing in the box out of the ordinary, I've studied it multiple times."

"And...who is her grandfather, exactly?" Urien looked to Theo.

"Amrel. Creator of Life. He raised Cyra on Earth, I only just found out myself." I stilled, surprised that he blurted it out so freely, but I reminded myself it was time to include those we trusted. More support only increased our chances of success.

"Holy *shit*," Urien blurted, playing with his glittering jewel. "But that's perfect! He can help us end this bloody curse and defeat the guardians. He must have returned with the Reina. He must have a plan!"

Theo shook his head. "He's gone. Forever."

Urien looked sick. *"Holy shit."*

"Grandpa told me it was up to me and the King of Eredet to save our people. We must somehow find a way—without him."

"Then that's what we'll do," Urien said, sounding defeated.

"This must remain a secret except for those of us that already know. Knowing that Amrel is gone during this devastating time would cause mass hysteria among the people," Theo lamented.

"Not to mention the Guardians are desperate to capture him. I still don't know the reason. Most likely they want to harness his power in some way. They're very careful about mentioning their intentions with him every time I've spied on them," Urien contributed.

"How in the world are you able to even get remotely close enough to the Guardians to spy on them?" I asked, horrified at the thought. What kind of person could successfully escape the Guardians notice? From what I've seen so far, they are aware of every tiny detail happening in Eluroom.

"Very carefully. And because of this." Urien pointed at the door behind me so I turned around to see what he was referring to.

"I don't see anything." I turned back around and Urien had vanished. "Wait, where did he leave? Did he drive away?" Theo smiled and shook his head.

Then from the corner of my eye I saw movement and the barely noticeable outline of a person. It was Urien, but he was completely blended into the wall behind him until he came back into focus as himself.

"Woah," I said, impressed.

"I have the ability to camouflage myself. It's not complete invisibility, but if I'm careful it's almost impossible to detect me."

"That's incredibly handy and a unique gift," I said with a smile.

"Now you know why he's my spider," Theo agreed. "That and I just can't seem to get rid of him." They both laughed.

"Yes, I was blessed with a special talent. I have a distant Sunya relative and they're immensely powerful with unique gifts so it likely stemmed from that."

Urien walked to me and took my hands in his. "Cyra, with Amrel gone you are now the most important being in the galaxy. You *must* be careful. Don't go out alone, don't upset the Guardians. Stay quiet and inconsequential—pretend you're they're puppet. We need you for this fight, and the fact that Amrel personally protected you for so long, means you're probably incredibly vital, even beyond the curse. And if you can help it, don't wear the power bracelet."

Theo nodded in agreement. "I wouldn't ever wear it if I could help it, but the Guardians expect it of me. They can track us with those bracelets. They know exactly where we are and how much power we're using when we wear them. I can get away with short bouts of not wearing it so they're not suspicious, but when I'm here I take it off. I couldn't risk them knowing the location of the temple and I'm not even sure how *much* they can track with the bracelets. When I'm meeting with Urien, I take it off and hide it just in case they can hear through it as well."

"They're disgusting. I can't wait to end them." I almost smiled thinking about all the grueling hours of training I now had under my belt.

Urien beamed at my conviction. "I must depart. I'm meeting with a

Bellum contact on The Void, and if I don't show exactly when he expects he will not come back."

"You work with the Bellum? We were just attacked by them."

"Not every Bellum has the same agenda, just as not every Solian is virtuous." I thought of my attackers on Solis and heat warmed my cheeks. Urien continued, "It's vital that I have contacts in every corner of the galaxy, especially because we know next to nothing about the Bellum, even my contacts there won't give up certain information. I've been cultivating relationships with some of them for years to try to gain their trust, but I haven't been successful. And they're mortal beings with a harsh existence. Just when I make the most progress they pass away."

Urien walked up to me and knelt to the ground and bowed, holding my hand. "I pledge myself to you, Reina Cyra, as your sword and your eyes. I will do anything I can to keep you safe and to see that balance is restored to our galaxy. If you ever need to reach me, write my name on a piece of paper, burn it and speak my name. I'll know it's you. I have fire power just like you."

My eye was twitching at the fact that he was kneeling down to me, gestures like this still made me incredibly uncomfortable. I swallowed, ignoring my feelings and replied, "Thank you, Urien. I really appreciate it."

He exited the room, and Theo and I were alone again. Theo took my hand and led me to a comfortable couch before a fireplace and sat close beside me.

"I'm still stumped how the Bellum got to Solis with a ship and planned to take two back to The Void."

"I've wondered that myself," Theo admitted. "They have ships that were given to them many years ago, but I don't know how they maintain them. They also make deals and do random jobs for passage from a person with magic. I imagine they planned to live on the Eventyr on Solis —for them it would have been a getaway resort. If they can get ships here, I bet they can make the ship invisible. They would have been able to live among us on the Eventyr in a planet that is still functional." I saw both sides of this and I felt so conflicted. Bellum had a right to live and try to thrive, but Solians merely saw people who consistently stole from them.

Theo sighed, leaned back and stretched like his whole body was aching and the weight of the world was on his shoulders. Unfortunately for him, it was. Seeing him vulnerable made me cling to him, leaning close and putting my head on his shoulder and wrapping my arm around him. He gave a quick look of surprise, but smiled and leaned into me. We sat in silence for a few moments just trying to decompress from all the recent daunting events, and the realization of what we would have to do in the future. Defeating the Guardians would be no small feat, and we were both going to have to find a way, together.

"Your home is so comfortable. And that's a beautiful portrait, is that someone you know?" Above the fireplace was a painting of a woman in chest and leg armor sitting on a stone ledge of some kind. The backdrop was of the ocean and sailboats approaching a dock. Her head was down studying a flower, her face mostly hidden by her dark wavy hair.

Theo smiled sadly. "That's my dear cousin, Brayln. She was the favorite of my family—the crown jewel who made our family proud, and my own favorite as well. We were best friends—inseparable. She was a fierce warrior with a fiery spirit. You didn't want to get on her bad side since she'd make you suffer for it, but you'd never find anyone who was more fiercely loyal either. She commanded the Solian Empire of Knights for many years."

I smiled, loving that a woman led the most impressive army in the galaxy, overseen by the most ruthless Reina in Solian history.

"There was no other being who could command the loyalty and dedication of the entire army like that woman. There's a monument to her in the training camps, but as usual, there's no one there to see it, and her memory died along with our people."

I remembered Theo's despair as he looked at the monument of the woman when we flew over the training camps. I squeezed Theo's hand and he looked overwhelmed with sadness now, his lower lip slightly quivering.

"I'm certainly not unique in this. Every family has lost someone during the Great War and this endless strife with Orphlam. But her death broke me—for *many* years. The Guardians spiked her head in front of our castle until it was completely decayed. I can't handle even thinking about the loss of her."

A single tear escaped that he quickly wiped away.

"I keep this portrait to remind me of why I'm fighting. This was her at her most beautiful, a formidable, ruthless warrior taking a moment from the brutality of her life to appreciate a little piece of Solian beauty. It still affects me so much because she felt like the only real family I had. My parents were indifferent, having no great love or attachment to me. I barely existed in their life. Their great love was power and trying to win the favor and good graces of your family who had most of the control and esteem from our people."

"There is nothing worse in the world than being an empath and feeling the disdain, the sense of burden and annoyance of your own parents simply by your existence. With every word I spoke to them, I could feel the regret and irritation ooze from them like a poison. It clung to every inch of me and each encounter with them just added layer upon layer of venom that I was never able to peel off. I never told them I was an empath since it would have made things even worse—them having to tiptoe around me trying to hide how they really felt."

"Brayln was the only reason I made it through. She saw the deep pit I had fallen into and I was close to ending my own life. I couldn't live on with the overwhelming liability and disappointment I was... even if the beliefs didn't originate from me. She taught me to control my ability and to differentiate between what was my emotion versus what was an external one."

"Oh, Theo," I said, choking on the lump in my throat. I had always envied his cool confidence and poise. I assumed he was born the regal leader I met, but I was wrong. He had a past full of trauma, and he was still able to overcome it and bloom into someone a whole planet of people could admire.

I took his hand and led him back to my quarters. We slept in the same bed again, doing nothing but reminding each other we might both be alone, but for now at least—we had each other.

CHAPTER TWENTY-ONE

The next two days Theo showed me the rest of Solis and I got the pleasure of seeing Vish's family farm. Just like on the west continent, there was an endless array of empty land and abandoned buildings, including the noble estates. Most of the nobles had moved to Eluroom to try to secure a place of importance—meaning a greater chance of survival. With the strange disappearances and the dwindling energy, many believed being recognized and known would keep them off the list of the *lost ones*. We visited an island that I recognized immediately. It was where the Sentries had tried to steal my blood. Theo explained that it was called Sea Horse Island, and it was a frequent haunt of the hired help of the Guardians and the nefarious deeds they carried out. It saddened me that those adorable creatures in the Solian seas would now be associated in my mind with the place I was attacked.

Theo took me to a large farm where it was obvious that every crop was drying out. That was a common theme among the poor of Solis, the plants had trouble surviving on their own. To look at Solis you would think there was nothing amiss with the abundant sunlight and the state of the soil. But the plant life knew their land was dying.

"There's someone very dear to my heart I'd like you to meet," Theo said, his eyes alight with excitement. "Remember I told you I had a caretaker growing up?" I nodded and saw a beautiful middle-aged woman step out of her farmhouse. She appeared to be in her fifties by Earth standards, with silver-gray hair, freckles scattered across her heart-shaped face, and kind marigold eyes. She put her hands to her cheeks in happy surprise, first to see Theo and then who he was with.

"Could it be? My Theo has come home with a girl?" She ran to me and took my hand in both of hers. "My dear, you are just *lovely*. I'm Onna, and it's a pleasure to meet you. I have been waiting a thousand years for my boy to bring home a girl, I just about gave up on the idea. I told him he better hurry his royal behind because at my age, things just can't wait." Immortals looked young for thousands of years, so she must truly be old to look middle-aged. She started walking me into her house, leaving Theo still standing outside and laughing to himself.

"I'm happy to see you missed me, Onna!" Theo yelled with a smile from the distance.

"Oh. Hi, honey!" Onna responded not looking back. I laughed, liking her immensely already. I suspected most of Theo's warmth and sincerity came from this woman.

"Come, sit! Make yourself at home. Can I get you a drink? Of course you want one, you wait here, I'll be right back." She rushed into the kitchen, fussing around, and Theo walked into the house with that beautiful smile still on his face, his clearwater eyes sparkling with joy. I couldn't explain what it was, but some ice that was still frozen around my heart preventing me from letting Theo in melted a little, and I felt his glowing warmth start to seep into my cold crevices. It felt...nice.

Onna put some drinks down on the table, then turned to Theo. "Oh, this beautiful boy. Come here." She walked to Theo and held his face in both her hands and kissed him on each cheek. He looked down, relaxed and exposed, and I saw it. This woman was his real mother, not the unfeeling woman who gave birth to him.

"I've missed you. You've been quite busy the past few weeks."

Theo blushed and looked down again. "I know and I'm sorry. Your farm is suffering because of me."

"Nonsense! It'll come back after it rains. Don't you dare take the credit for that."

"I'm going out there, I'll be back in about an hour."

"Theo! Please sit, let's just enjoy the day together."

"You *need* this farm! I'm not sitting until every inch is restored. I'll be back in a bit." Theo rushed out and didn't look back.

Onna sighed. "That boy makes too many things his problem," she said sadly. "He uses every bit of his power saving Meri's farms and healing the afflicted. He keeps Solis alive single-handedly." She looked out the window after him, filled with worry.

"Well, he's not alone anymore. I'm here to help him."

"That makes me beyond happy. Theo has a heart of solid gold and he deserves some happiness after the life he's had. You must be Cyra, the one everyone's been talking about!"

"Oh, yes, I'm sorry. I'm Cyra, it's a pleasure to meet you. Theo said you were his caregiver?"

"Yes, I was certainly the one doing the caring."

"Theo told me about how difficult it was growing up around his parents."

"That's an understatement, and I bet he didn't even tell you the half of it. He doesn't like being the center of attention or the cause for worry."

"That just astonishes me. I see him speak in a crowd of a hundred nobles and he's effervescent and charming. He thrives as a leader, as opposed to me. While standing next to him I'm shaking from head to toe from nerves. I can't stand so many eyes on me."

"It's all an act, darling. Not the love for his people or planet, that is very real. But that is why he puts on that face. He becomes that leader because we need him to. He wasn't born that way, and his parents damaged him so severely that it took many years and lots of grueling hard work for him to become the man he is today. He worked his behind off for all of us."

Onna shook her head in disgust and some of the vibrant marigold in her eyes lost its luster.

"It is such a shame that his folks missed every piece of his life because he is the bravest, kindest and most selfless person I've ever met. And none of it is due to them. If they had just opened their eyes to what was right in front of them, they'd be filled with immeasurable pride."

"No, it wasn't due to them. It was because of you. Brayln helped him with his gift, but you showed him what it was like to be loved. He's the amazing man he is today because of you. I saw it in his face when he looked at you."

Onna's eyes turned watery. "I love that boy like I did give birth to him. I've taken care of many children throughout the long years of my life, but Theo is my son."

I nodded. "I hope you don't think I'm rude for asking this, but I'm still learning about this galaxy. You insinuated that you don't have time because of your age…do immortals die of old age?"

Onna laughed with a bright smile. "No offense here, dear. I have never known of anyone to die of old age, but many have not gotten the chance for the past few thousand years. I won't die of old age, but I am probably more susceptible to that illness going around, and my powers aren't what they used to be, which is why I can't keep up with this farm."

"What is your power?"

"It's hard to describe, but for simplicity's sake, it's light. It's not a powerful gift, but it has served me."

"That makes sense. You are filled with light."

Onna looked touched and put her hand on her heart. "Oh honey, you and I are going to be great friends," she beamed. "You know, you and Theo were sort of betrothed since you were born. He never lost hope that he would find you again after you went missing."

"He did tell me. How could he have so much faith in something that was improbable?"

"That's just who he is. He believes in the good of life and the good of people. Come, let me show you around the house, I have some excellent baby portraits of Theo." I smiled and followed her. She took a framed image off her wall and handed it to me. Theo was beaming with his fist in the air in triumph, wearing a swimsuit next to Onna who was just as excited.

"This is one of my favorites from when we still had water games in Meri Kardem. Theo was about ten years old, and this was a sort of water obstacle race. You had to find certain objects and bring it to the designated location while swimming through a few hundred meters. It wasn't easy, but he was such a natural in the water. He didn't even have his powers yet, but he destroyed the adults, winning the race."

"Here, this one he was six months old," Onna said, passing the watercolor to me. She was holding Theo as an adorable drooling baby and even then, she looked like his true mother with a prideful smile on her face.

"Ah, and this was one the proudest moments of his life. This was the day he was awarded the medal of completion for Empire of Knights training."

There were two paintings, and one of them was shocking. I studied it closely. It was an ornate rendering of Theo in golden armor and a matching crown. What gave me pause was the fierce look on his face. It was as if the military training had stolen some of the goodness in him and replaced it with violence. It made me strangely uncomfortable, my heart racing in confusion. I had to look away, so I took the second painting.

"Is that Vish and Brayln next to you and Theo?"

"It sure is. His father told him he would never pass training because he was too sensitive, and the Empire of Knights were brutal warriors. So, when he completed his training and was labeled an official warrior, he felt validated. And he did have to work harder than some of the other boys, but that made his efforts all the more worth it."

"Oh no, you're not showing her baby images, are you? At least don't show her my super awkward adolescent years for goodness sake!" We turned around and Theo was standing there as handsome and charismatic as ever. I walked to him and put my arms around him tightly, trying to reign in my emotion. He hesitated and put his arms around me too.

"Onna...what have you been doing to Cyra?"

"Who, me? You know I'm innocent."

"Yeah, sure."

I wasn't going to embarrass Theo, so I didn't bring up anything Onna had told me. "So are the crops thriving?" I asked

"Every last one of them," he said proudly. I noticed the dark shadows under his eyes, and I knew it was from depleting so much energy in the past week. He took the responsibilities of the world to heart, seeking that endless validation he never received.

"Theo Beaurdlaux! You've exhausted too much energy," Onna chided.

"I'm fine, just a little tired. No need to fuss."

"Fine, then go eat and drink something." He smiled and we all headed back to the living area and sat for refreshments. We talked for hours, and I was happy to just sit back and watch how atease he was with Onna. Before we left, she gave me a huge hug and asked me to take good care of him. I promised that I would.

"So, what did you think of Onna?" Theo asked.

"She's absolutely delightful. I can see why you cherish her."

"She's everything a person could want from a mother," he said with a smile. He may not have had the birth parents he wanted, but in every way that mattered, he had the mother he deserved.

CHAPTER TWENTY-TWO

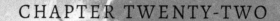

The night before we planned to set sail again, I went to bed early to try to prepare myself for the journey. The second I fell asleep I started to dream.

"MAXILEN AND LARA BEAURDLAUX, thank you for accepting our invitation," Orphlam said artfully.

There was no mistaking who these people were. The stunning blonde woman covered in jewels and extravagant attire had the same turquoise eyes as Theo, but hers were duller and lifeless. Theo's father was regal and handsome with a well-groomed beard. How could this stunning couple be so dead inside?

"We are most honored by your invitation. What can we do to assist the Guardians?" Maxilen asked with a deep bow.

"I have noticed both of your fiery ambitions in your stewardship of Meri Kardem. It is a passion I could only wish of our Reinan, Rhythen and Brana Fenix. As you know, a Karalis is still not the ultimate authority of this planet, as they still answer to a Reina. Rhythen and Brana are traitors, and we need assistance in carrying out their sentence. In this quest I am also seeking a particular sword, I am sure you understand the one I mean.

Knowing the extent of your valuable aspirations, I have asked you here to see if you'd be amenable in helping me carry out these tasks."

"Consider us at your disposal, Orphlam," Maxilen responded. "But we would require something in return for our efforts."

"Please, elaborate."

"We want the Beaurdlaux family to be the new Reinan in Eluroom from now on," Lara answered without hesitation.

"So be it," Orphlam agreed with a chuckle.

THE SCENE CHANGED, and Maxilen and Lara were chained against a wall in the Guardian temple, blood and bruises covering their body.

"I am dissatisfied with the outcome of our arrangement," Orphlam told the whimpering couple on the ground.

"We did exactly as you asked! It wasn't our fault how things turned out!" Maxilen shouted.

"Please! If you need a scapegoat or a traitor for appearances, take our son...Theo. Spare us," Lara begged.

"You would end your son's life to save your own?" Orphlam asked in surprise.

"Yes," they answered in unison.

"There is not much that surprises me anymore, but perhaps I could find use for your ruthless will."

I WOKE up with a sheen of sweat covering my forehead from the nightmare. Actually, I wished it was just a nightmare, but this was a vision of a real piece of history. I started crying immediately. It was clear Theo's parents had a hand in my parents' deaths. Were they the ones I saw in the flash of light? And how...*how*...could those horrible people offer up their own son to die. I couldn't fathom that level of betrayal, and I knew I could never tell Theo. It would *destroy* him. But how would I be able to look into his honest, beautiful eyes, the same as his mother's, and keep this from him? There was no way I could go back to sleep. I was on the verge of bursting into an inferno thinking about Theo's past.

Despite Urien's advice to never wander alone, I decided to take a walk to the waterfront to clear my head and get some fresh air. I laid down and gazed up at the stars with wonder, the Solian night sky was quite different than Earth's. I could name almost every constellation on Earth just by sight, and they were obviously nowhere to be found here. These clusters of stars were completely foreign and I wondered if they gave them names and shapes like humans did. One constellation stood out to me, brighter than all the others, and I felt drawn to it like there was a secret it was trying to whisper to me in the dark. It looked somewhat like a crooked bow being pulled back, ready for an arrow to be released, so I decided to call it The Bow. I stared at its brilliant beauty for quite a while since there was something about the shape that seemed strangely familiar.

Theo told me that Solis had no natural satellite, so it had no moon like Earth did. The details in the sky were much more visible, but I wasn't sure if that was my fresh immortal eyes that could see more, or if there were more objects that were visible from the planet's position. I could easily see a spiral arm of the galaxy in the sky as well as multiple colorful nebulae. The stars were bright enough to create the lost light from a missing moon. It was truly a magical display, and I wished I had the time to see it more often. I could only imagine how often I would have slept on my balcony on Earth with this kind of awe-inspiring tapestry of wonder before me. Only then, I didn't know that we weren't alone in the universe. Looking out to the cosmos now had a much profounder depth to it, and the potential hidden secrets within it held possibility and hope. What else was out there? Would we survive this to find out?

I sat up quickly because I felt an approaching presence in the water. "Laine?" I whispered like someone would overhear me. "Is that you?"

The sea began to ripple and spew onto the sand as Laine emerged in a crash of misting water, crawling onto the beach. I screeched and backed away as fast as I could, still laying on my back. Laine emerged until she was completely on land and her face was hovering right over mine. It probably resembled an elephant standing over a mouse.

"Why do you fear me, Cyra? We are one." She communicated telepathically as usual, never moving her mouth.

I, however, responded out loud. "I'm not afraid of you, I was just taken aback by your sheer size. You're *much* bigger than you appeared from the ship."

"All the better to destroy our enemies."

I laughed at that. She was the size of a medium sized building, but she had a sense of humor. "Thanks for that by the way. Your help with the Bellum raiders."

"No thanks is needed, it is my sacred duty."

I stood and ran my hand along her head and long neck and felt her internally smile. "Wow. You are beautiful, Laine." She nuzzled me as I rubbed her face.

"Will you come with me?" Laine asked.

"Go with you...where?" I asked apprehensively.

"A place with no name. It was a secret place of Amrel The High Creator."

My heart started pounding in anticipation. "Then I will go with you."

Laine laid down flat on the ground. "Climb onto my back."

I jumped, and she boosted me with her wing lifting me up. She wiggled two tentacles at the base of her long neck and two lower tentacles where I could secure my feet. She wrapped them around me so I couldn't move. "Hold on, Cyra."

She turned around slowly and started walking back into the ocean. I was hoping to see some of the adorable creatures I witnessed while on the Eventyr, but Laine was swimming so fast I couldn't see any of my surroundings underwater except for a bright glow in the distance. She slowed down using her wings in the opposite direction to fight the water and she gave one final dive and we fell onto a flat, dry surface. It was amazing to me that her magic was able to keep me dry.

"I'm so confused, are we on land again or are we at the bottom of the ocean?"

"It is both things. This was Amrel's place."

"How did you know Amrel? Were you *Paeladoned* to him?"

"No. A Paela only goes through one *Paeladon*. They die along with their mate once the bond is broken. Amrel was a friend to all Paela, and we mourn his loss."

"So, do I, Laine."

"He asked me to show you this place a few hundred years ago. He knew we would be bonded one day."

I didn't know what to say to that. My life continued to get stranger and stranger. There was next to nothing in this bubble under the ocean. A bed with a seashell and a bunch of rocks in the shape of an arch against the invisible wall of the ocean barrier. I walked to the bed and grabbed the ornate seashell shaped like a conch. It was encrusted with various colored crystals and embossed with artwork on the exterior of the shell. The interior was mother of pearl, and the elongated tip was plated with a silver mouthpiece. I was instantly entranced by it, like it was made of magic itself. Mesmerized, I leaned toward it, swearing I could hear whispers coming from its hidden depths. I put my lips to the mouthpiece and blew into it, but no sound escaped. I placed it back on the bed and walked to the arch.

"What is this?"

"I couldn't say."

Couldn't or wouldn't say, I wondered. When I stepped closer the stone melted away and became what looked to be a portal and I could see nothing but darkness beyond it. I hesitated and looked back at Laine who nodded gently in reassurance.

I gingerly stepped into the gate and instantaneously felt as if all the blood had left my body and I morphed and melded into the space until I was something else, and I couldn't define what that was. I was no longer myself, but something celestial, unconnected to the mortal coil. It was the strangest and most terrifying sensation I'd ever experienced, and tears abundantly fell at the shock and awe that I couldn't process. When I screamed no sound escaped my throat. I was transported into a place that felt like a void of existence, and yet was the definition of life. There was no end and no beginning, and I existed amongst an infinite realm of the divine, where worlds were born and laid to rest. It was as if I was weightless, floating through the vastness of the cosmos as it flowed through me like I was forged from it. I brought my hands to my face, but there was no flesh, I was merely a blazing energy.

I tried to calm myself to understand what was happening. How long had I been here? It could have been days or seconds; time had no bearing here. I searched through the vastness, and I heard a whisper of sounds, cries calling to me from afar. Once I connected myself to it, I was transported, and I began to *see* so many different visions it was hard to focus on them all. As I was thrust through the vastness, as I witnessed world after world, thousands of civilizations lost in an unnatural pocket of space that didn't allow them to exist. They were frozen in time, unaware of their being, yet screaming for help so loud it pierced my soul.

There was an intuition I possessed in this place, and I *knew* what I was seeing even though it shouldn't be possible. I needed to leave, I needed to tell the others what I'd discovered. I needed to *leave*.

I was thrust from the gate, back on the bottom of the ocean floor of Solis and I laid on the ground, uncontrollably shaking. I had to adjust to having a body again, to a place with petty squabbles and desires that seemed almost insignificant now.

"How long was I gone?" I asked Laine.

"But a few seconds."

I laid there, still catatonic. It only took a few seconds to feel so detached from the world that none of our daily concerns made sense. I forced myself to stand, and I slowly remembered what I'd witnessed.

The *Void Shift* that Grandpa mentioned from the curse wasn't referencing Looma at all. Yes, the Guardians cursed the planets of Eredet galaxy to drain their energy, but it was so much worse than that. I held my stomach to try to stop the bile that singed the walls of my throat.

There were thousands of thriving, inhabited worlds out there, and Orphlam had locked them all into a pocket of space, so they were frozen in time, not living—stealing their energy. If I didn't find the *mikla* and a way to break their additional curses, trillions of people would cease to exist.

LAINE LAID NEXT to me so I could climb onto her. "You now know it is here. I will bring you back."

I grabbed the shell before we plunged back into the water.

"Be careful who you tell about that place. Some things should only be for The Creator."

"Then why did you tell me?"

"You will know soon enough."

I was too shaken to care about her cryptic words. I had seen a lot of horrors since I'd arrived on Solis, but that experience alone had irrevocably changed something within me, like I could see beyond the plight of men. But it still terrified me so deeply that I was unsure how to handle myself. I needed the feeling of comfort and safety, and there was only one thing I could think in that moment.

Kane.

My eyes closed for the whole trip back to the shore and I said his name in my mind on repeat, imagining myself in the safety of his arms. I didn't give a shit that he was in the service of the Guardians or what it meant in regards to the prophecy. My whole being told me it was the only thing in that moment that made sense, and that was all I needed.

When Laine crested the water and let me down, I could already feel his presence closing the distance between us. Before I could even see him I started running, and when I witnessed him running toward me as well there were no Guardians, no prophecy, no threat of annihilation. There was only him, and I jumped into his arms and wrapped my legs around him as he held my head tight to him.

I was still trembling out of control, but the intense relief I felt breathing in his essence and feeling his strength against me was exactly what I needed to come back to reality.

"Shh, it's okay. I've got you," he whispered tenderly against my ear.

He carried me back to the castle and into my bedroom, tucking me into bed. He knelt on the ground and took my hand in his and my heart beat so hard that I was sure he could hear it.

"You came for me," I whispered with my eyes down. I didn't know what my connection to him meant and I was too scared to acknowledge it.

He put his finger under my chin and lifted it until we locked eyes and it made a fire blaze within every inch of my body.

"There is nothing in this universe, mortal or divine, that could keep me from you if you're in need."

I squeezed his hand, barely able to catch my breath at his words. The buzzing sensation that linked us was filled with warmth, gratitude and peace. It felt like...home.

Despite all that, I wasn't sure what to tell him about the gate since I still didn't know how to put it to words myself.

"Kane–"

"Just get some rest. Whatever it is, you can tell me when you're ready." He rubbed his thumb along my cheek before getting up and leaving me alone. Once he was gone I wished more than anything he had stayed with me the rest of the night. I laid in the quiet dark, finding it impossible to sleep now that I knew the true definition of fear.

CHAPTER TWENTY-THREE

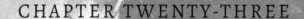

*W*hen Meili woke me the next morning I tried not to show how shaken I still was by my journey inside the terrifying gate, so I quickly asked her about the shell I found.

"Meili, do you happen to know what this is?" I slept with the shell on the bed, so I dug it out from under the pillow next to me and handed it to her. She turned it over and inspected every inch of it with wide eyes.

"Oh, wow, I think I do. Where did you find it?"

"Laine took me for a swim and I found it at the bottom of the ocean." I wasn't ready to tell her about the gate.

"I've read about this and seen a picture of it before. I believe this is *Coralin's Song*, a divine relic made by Amrel The Creator. The shell belongs to an incredibly magical sea creature known as the merikarp, which is now long extinct. The merikarp was said to instill euphoric calm and peace to anyone that ate its flesh, and the shell had similar healing properties. It used to be ground into tonics and magical remedies until they disappeared."

"It's said that he gifted this to your ancestor, Coralin Fenix, the first Reina of Solis who united a broken world with no clear leader. We should try to find out more about it when we have the chance. Keep it safe, it could be invaluable one day."

"Thank you, I certainly will."

"I'll get you dressed, they're ready to depart immediately."

We packed what little I had brought and set sail to search for the next shrouded island in hopes of finding the *mikla*. I gathered everyone to tell them about what I saw in the gate, the strange space where I was able to see and sense things that weren't normal. The fact that there were thousands of worlds in a state of non-existence, relying on us to save them. Adelram stared at me straight-on with wide eyes, his face drained of color until he almost lost all the grey to his skin. His hand covering his mouth in genuine fear and it was incredibly unsettling to see him so affected. Kane looked at him in confusion and when his mouth parted it looked like he was somewhat hurt as well.

Meili cried for the first time since I'd met her and I sat next to her and held her hand. "The thought of so many suffering people because of a greedy few," she said between sobs.

"How could I have no knowledge or memory of this?" Theo asked, his mouth parted with astonishment.

"Yes, that is extremely curious," Vish spouted, glaring at Adelram. "You work for the Guardians and are able to alter and delete memories. I supposed you're to blame for this."

"I don't give a fuck *what* you think of me, entitled asshole." Adelram's sneer had even more anger to it than usual.

Vish made a dash for Adelram, but Kane held out his hand and Vish ran into it.

"Enough!" I rubbed my eyes that were throbbing with an epic pain behind them. "Once we find the *mikla* we're one step closer to fixing everything. So let's focus our energies on looking for the shrouded island before we miss it completely."

Theo and Vish stalked off to the edge of the ship to look for the island, mumbling to themselves.

Adelram rubbed his face with his hands and his color and attitude returned to normal. "Hey, Blondie, while you're here let me get into that head of yours and see how Cyra's mother saved you. Maybe it'll give us some insight," Adelram said with his hand outstretched.

Meili looked at me, clearly hesitant to step any closer to him which I didn't blame her for, but I wanted to know this information too. I nodded to her and her shoulders dropped and she picked up her head and stood before him. Adelram put his hands on her head and closed his eyes. There was only a moment or two of silence before he let out a small noise of surprise and stepped away.

"What?" I asked desperately. "What did you see?"

The sorrowful look Adelram gave me instantly made me queasy. He rubbed the back of his neck and cleared his throat with obvious discomfort.

"What?" I demanded.

Kane walked closer to me and put his hand on the small of my back, calming me instantly.

"I could only see what was witnessed through Meili's eyes so I don't have all the answers. I only know what happened because I could recognize the actions that took place. Your mother, Reina Brana, gave up her immortality to save Meili."

"No!" Meili belted, looking aghast, and she ran and took my hands with tears running down her cheeks. "Cyra–I...I'm so very sorry. I had no idea she did that."

"You couldn't have known, Meili. Don't blame yourself," I said in earnest despite my overwhelming shock.

"My guess is that based on what you told us about the vision in the Fenix lands, is that your mother knew she was going to die anyway, so she gave this gift to save Meili. I don't know why she chose her, however." Adelram put his arm on my shoulder and I looked up at him with a mix of shock and confusion, but I accepted his show of comfort nonetheless. "Looks like the *criada* is even more important than we thought."

I almost wished the secrets would stop coming. It felt as if each piece of information that was revealed cracked another portion of my sanity and I was dangerously close to shattering completely.

"Here!" Theo yelled from the other side of the deck. We joined them and Kane made quick work of breaking through the shroud like he did last time. The island was even smaller than the previous one, so it didn't take much time to examine all of it, and we quickly realized it was a royal cemetery.

"I had no idea the Reinan of Solis were buried," Theo said. "I always assumed they were burned, the ashes scattered as is the custom in Solis East."

The first two graves were of Coralin and Bendel Fenix, rulers of the First, Second and Third Age of Solis.

"Cyra, this is the ancestor I told you about who used *Coralin's Song* to unite the people of Eluroom," Meili explained.

I put my hand to the surprisingly plain and unadorned tombs and wondered if her past was as trying as the times we were in now. The next set read Clara and Drake Fenix, rulers of the Fourth and Fifth Age of Solis, followed by Torid and Isabaena Fenix, rulers of the Sixth Age of Solis. The next tomb was solo and the stones were broken and scattered on the ground, but I could tell what was etched in the stone. Dokoran, ruler of the Seventh Age of Solis.

"Dokoran was a disgraced, Reina, so he was burned at his death," Vish explained.

"Why is there no grave for his *vordna*, Lavinia?" I asked, remembering her name from the books I saw in the private lands and the prison.

"I have no idea," Vish shrugged.

I knew what stones must be next and my breath became erratic and strained. It appeared we had found their final resting place and I couldn't stop the tears that fell before I even read the tombstones.

Brana and Rythen Fenix, rulers of the Eight Age of Solis.

I dropped to my knees and dug my fingers into the dirt, sobbing with the unfairness of it all. What I'd just learned about my mother made the pain of their loss fresh and new.

"Excuse us." I heard Theo dismiss everyone and when I looked up I was crushed that Kane left with everyone to give us a moment alone. He locked sorrowful eyes with me then turned and returned to the ship. The tingling in my body grew with an affectionate warmth before he disappeared. I was overcome with a strange bout of anger, but it melted away when I saw Theo's concern.

He knelt beside me and held me while I dried my eyes. I thought about how intensely brave my parents were, sending me away regardless of the loss they felt. My mother giving away her immortal power to save Meili. Them both knowing they were going to die, yet facing it head on. It sobered me and gave me the strength I needed to stand

and dust myself off. It was clear the *mikla* was not here, and we had no time to lose. There were countless people waiting throughout the vast cosmos, holding their breath for the right to live.

THE JOURNEY back to Eluroom was somber, and I trained tirelessly with Kane, determined to perfect my control of my fire, my defensive techniques and my skill with my dagger. We decided to regroup and send scouts out to look for the third shrouded island, and when we disembarked there was a castle worker already waiting for us.

"The Guardians would like a word with you alone, Karalis," he said with a bow. Theo turned to me and rolled his eyes. "Sorry, Cyra, I guess I'll have to catch up with you later." I glanced down and saw his bracelet was back on his wrist and I inwardly groaned knowing we were back to the dangerous vicinity of the Guardians.

"Should I come with you?"

"Definitely not, especially if they want to see me alone. Better to do as they ask."

"Okay, please be careful." I wanted to be part of his meetings, but I had no desire to see the Guardians again.

"I'd say it's been a pleasure, but it's safe to say you're the worst vacation buddy imaginable," Adelram said with a sarcastic smirk. I couldn't help but laugh at the asshole as he raised an eyebrow at me and disappeared.

When Kane approached, I had to work at swallowing. "Let's pick up tomorrow morning with our training."

"Okay. And...thanks, for everything." Kane nodded his head and looked at me for a few elongated moments before he disappeared as well.

I made the god-awful trek from hell back to my room drained of energy, and Meili was already there waiting for me in all her perfection and loveliness having brought back all of my luggage. Yes, I *definitely* needed to master my driving so I didn't have to walk everywhere.

"Happy to be home, Reina?"

"Cyra. And I suppose that's one way to put it."

"I'll start your bath and get your night dress."

Thank God for Meili. I soaked in the tub for a long time, haunted by everything I'd seen on Solis East, and I still hadn't recovered from those few seconds in Grandpa's gate. I shivered despite the heat of the water.

I was ready to accept that my chapter on Earth was over and start writing a new one as a Reina of Solis, destroyer of the Guardians. The one who would do anything to save the people of this dying galaxy, and the whole universe.

CHAPTER TWENTY-FOUR

I woke up very early the next morning, before the sun even rose. The haunting events that had occurred since I arrived on Solis wouldn't leave my troubled mind. Anxiety and anger made it impossible to go back to sleep.

The watercolor I painted of Mylo caught my eye and it did nothing to lift my mood. I paced my room for a long time and I grew so livid I decided to practice my fire until I mastered it.

I took a deep breath and reached inside myself and tried to light my hands in flame. Nothing at all happened. Sweat was abundant all over my body from how hard I'd tried and failed. The power bracelet sat on my desk and glistened in the light as if mocking me. I'd sworn I'd never touch it, but would it really be so bad if it helped me? Fed up with my lack of control, and the constant reminder of feeling power-less, I grabbed it and quickly shoved it on before I changed my mind. The glow of the bracelet intensified and I began to feel…strange. Vertigo overcame me, the room spinning slowly at first, then so fast that I trampled off to the side and had to brace myself on the chair. With a burning rage inside me and an overwhelming sickness threat-ening to make me retch, I screamed as loud as I could and let go of every little piece of pent-up fury I'd been carrying. Billowing fire erupted from me in a frenzied burst, shattering all the windows and burning the entire main room in an all-encompassing storm. This release felt good. Oh, it felt *so* fucking good.

I laughed with abandon at the wonderfully free release—there was no way I was going to let go of this power and feeling of unburdened freedom. In fact, I wanted to let it all burn down and relish the menacing conflagration. I raised my hands, amping up my flame until it escaped the destroyed windows, illuminating the world in a fiery chasm. I leered and tilted my head back in sweet release, ready to burn it all away. This whole miserable fucking big dick energy castle. The burdens I'd been carrying were *gone*. The guilt and pain and death were gone. I didn't give a shit, and it was the best feeling of my fucking life. I ramped up the blaze even more, my command a sure and easy thing. Why had I ever struggled before? This was *beyond easy.* I knew without a shred of doubt that I could keep going for hours. For *days*! My power was endless. Infinite—and mine.

My door came crashing down, and there walked in the hateful duo. Interesting, I didn't feel Kane's presence this time. Didn't I really like him? Like *really* like him? Well, I didn't anymore, I couldn't care less. Good riddance, asshole.

"Cyra! Stop this!" Adelram screamed as loud as he could over the roaring blaze. He ran into it without hesitation, burning as he came closer. He lowered me down to the ground and took me in his arms. I didn't even realize that I was floating off the ground. Neat.

"Cyra! Calm down! You must calm down!" Adelram's skin was singing right off of him at a rapid pace, yet he still held me. The stench of burning flesh singed my nostrils more than the fire.

"Getting your rocks off, Adelram? Burning in misery? That's your thing, right? Allow me to assist." I laughed with abandon and released a bolt of more fire while Adelram screamed in agony.

Meili appeared outside the door and shrieked. "Cyra! Please don't! You can control this!"

The sight of the angelic Meili was like a blanket on my fire. It shook me out of the dark tunnel vision and the blaze died within moments. Kane ran up and grabbed the bracelet off my wrist and threw it to the corner of the room. Meili rushed in and returned the room to its former state and healed Adelram completely of all the severe third-degree burns. He tried his best not to scream in pain as the burnt flesh repaired piece by piece. I imagined it was unbearable—and I had done that. Wha...what had I done? *What did I just do?*

My body began uncontrollably shaking, and I lost sense of reality. I heard their exchanges like it was somewhere off in the distance.

"They're coming." Kane said. "What are we going to do about her? They can't see her like this."

"I'll take care of it," Adelram said.

I felt the trembling quell from within me. With no energy left, I succumbed into Adelram's arms.

The last thing I saw was a demon sun god's golden mask before everything went black.

ADELRAM AND AMREL were playing Reina's Deck as they usually did once a week.

"Ha! Full suite. Sorry, loser," Adelram boasted unapologetically.

"I don't get it. I created all life, and I can't seem to ever win at cards?" Amrel asked, genuinely distraught.

"I believe the score is now one million to twenty. You really need to learn when to throw in the towel and give up, big guy. Let's get a new hobby."

"Never! I do not yield until I emerge victorious!"

Adelram rolled his eyes and threw up his hands. "Are we still going to that new planet of yours—Earth?"

"Yes. I'd like you to take some notes, document the local's behaviors, interact with them slightly. Maybe teach them easy things to understand that could help their society. You know, like rubbing sticks to make fire—that sort of thing."

"Don't terrify the fragile, primitive mortals. Got it."

Amrel chuckled. And they disappeared.

"AMREL, that is the last time I'm going to that forsaken planet. I'm done! I'm tired of being portrayed as a devil while you prance around as a savior angel. They're idiots and all I've ever done is spend countless hours trying to teach

them science, survival, language and the written word. I've gotten nothing but accusations of being a demon threatening to corrupt their children's souls. I'll show them hell! Let me use some magic on them and I'll have them fleeing in terror!"

"Now you're starting to sound like the devil they think you are. I'm sorry this experience didn't turn out how I thought it would, Ad. I thought it would be beneficial for both sides with your extensive academic knowledge and language skills. I'm also sorry to tell you, but I have a feeling you'll be back there one day."

"Like grof, oldtimer."

"Remember that day I told you you'd be taking a trip back to Earth, Ad?"

"Nope, pretty sure you're going senile, old man."

"If I'm senile, you're an old leather shoe. You know exactly what I'm referring to. I have something serious to ask of you. A time is coming when something will happen to me."

"Excuse me? What could possibly happen to you? You are forever."

"Even forever has an end, my friend."

"You're not saying what I think you're saying..."

"Yes, Ad. It's about the prophecy..."

"Oh, that damn prophecy again. You really need to stop."

"You don't want to hear it, but that doesn't stop it from being true. My end is near. You must protect the girl at all costs. I need you to take her memories and replace them when the time is right..."

"Ugh, come on, Amrel. You know I hate doing that. That power is really a freaking curse, I could possibly get stuck with a piece of that person forever in my memory, it's torment."

"I know, my dear friend. I am asking as a favor to me and our very long friendship. When she comes back home to Solis, she will be in more danger than ever. I need you to watch out for her until the curse is broken, because...I won't be there."

Adelram held his head in his hands and when he raised it there were tears in his eyes.

"And who am I supposed to play cards with when you're gone, huh? You ever think of that, you jerk?"

Amrel reached to touch his hand, but refrained and bowed his head, trying to hide his own grief. He wasn't able to touch other living beings or they would burn away to dust.

Adelram sighed in defeat and spoke in a whisper. "You know I will do anything for you, even after you're gone."

MY EYES OPENED, and everything was blurry. It took a moment for the view before me to come to focus. I'd just been dreaming about Grandpa and Adelram, and an Adelram I didn't know. But I felt a pit in my stomach when everything became clear. I was able to feel the true devastation and grief from Adelram when he had to acknowledge that Amrel was going to die. They were close friends, inseparable, and the fact that Grandpa gave up his life for me was why Adelram resented me so much. When he came to Earth to keep his word to Amrel he must have been beside himself knowing his friend and High Creator was gone for an ignorant girl who looked like a beggar off the street. His constant lashing out made more sense, and I made a conscious decision to forgive him.

When the room came into focus I saw that very person along with Kane, Theo, Vish and Meili all sitting beside my bed.

"Where am I? Why am I in bed and why are you all here...watching me?"

"Oh, I don't know, it was all so sudden, but I believe you attempted to serve up roast Varjun. Except I taste terrible, so the *criada* helped nip that in the bud," Adelram said.

"Are you okay, darling?" Theo asked, taking my hand. I felt a buzzing rush swoop over me and I looked at the direction of the energy to find Kane glaring at Theo.

"I'm fine, I think?"

"Why would you ever put on that stupid bracelet?" Kane seethed.

"It was a mistake," I said, trying to hide my face in shame.

"Next time, don't attack your teacher and burn alive your protector. It's bad manners," Kane replied.

I winced as a chuckle escaped me. "I'm sorry. I don't know what happened to me."

"I do, it's that bracelet. You have too much power to be able to wear that thing. It could consume you and become something unnatural, it's why I don't wear it."

I snorted. "Sure, so much power that I still sweat turning on my bathtub."

Kane let his guard down and smiled and it took my breath away. "That's what lessons are for. I'll see you then."

Kane and the others left so I could rest, and the air was finally silent and calm. The room felt as if it withered slightly, missing the presence that Kane filled with his potency.

Meili popped her head back in. "I will leave you now, Reina. Come find me if you need anything."

CHAPTER TWENTY-FIVE

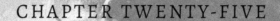

I slept an entire day and only woke when Meili entered my
room the next morning, her smiling face glowing through
my bedchamber. "I'm sorry I woke you."

"No, it's alright, there's too much to be done. I need to get up."

"Would you like to attend *Sun Eine* this morning?"

"Am I a bad Reina if I don't?" I asked earnestly.

Meili smiled at me. "Considering you're trying to protect our
people I'd say it's okay to skip the morning meal."

"Thank goodness," I said, dropping back onto the bed.

Meili came and sat beside me and spoke almost in a whisper. "The
castle workers have all been asking when the next performance is.
The mood has changed greatly with them since you've arrived."

"That's wonderful, but I fear performances after the Guardians'
retaliation of the Knight's Cup. But spread the word anyway, we can
play it by ear and if nothing else we can simply enjoy each other's
company. We could all do with a little more innocent magic right
now. I have a lesson with Kane, and I don't want to be late, I could end
up torching another floor of the castle."

Meili laughed. "Yes, let's try to avoid that. Please don't be late."

After getting dressed, I opened the door to leave and Theo was
there about to knock.

"Oh! Hi."

"Good morning, beautiful. I came to make sure you were okay."

"Yes, I'm better now, although yesterday was a bit of a whirlwind."

"It sure was."

"I was just on my way to the second floor for my lesson with Kane."

"Okay, I'll walk with you," Theo said, taking my hand in his. It was already a comfortable feeling, like we had done it a million times. A twinge of joy surged through my belly at the thought. I could get used to his steady comfort.

"I've spoken to Urien, he's been searching for the last island, but hasn't found it yet. He shrieked like a little girl when he realized he'd get a chance to help find the *mikla*."

I smiled. "I hope he finds it quickly, the sooner we find the *mikla* the better."

"I agree."

"Good morning, Reina," a castle employee curtsied as we passed. I recognized him from one of my cello sessions.

"Good morning, Raynol," I replied with familiarity.

We began our descent to the second floor.

"Reina," another worker curtsied as he passed and I nodded back.

On the second floor we made our way back to the end of the hallway and another worker paused to curtsy. "Have a wonderful day, Reina."

"You, as well, Jeb."

"Well, aren't you miss popular today? The workers usually completely ignore the royalty. You know all their names?" he asked with his brows raised.

I just shrugged and smiled, it really didn't take much effort to bond with these people we see on a daily basis. We reached the classroom and Theo took my hand and kissed my cheek making my core fire up. "I'll find you later. Good luck today, don't burn anything down. It's a lovely castle."

"I'll do my best." I felt a powerful humming coming from inside the classroom, alerting me that Kane was already waiting for me.

When I entered I stopped short, taking Kane in all his massive intensity, glaring with glowing green eyes. His arms were crossed so his muscles bulged to their max, and he was standing with his feet apart like he was bracing for something unpleasant. I continued walking until I was directly in front of him, nonplussed, and looked up into his eyes, wondering what he could be thinking about. He'd been pretty private since the day I met him, and I still knew very little about this person. His demeanor finally softened, and he unfolded his arms.

"I think we should work exclusively outside from now on. You seem more comfortable and more in control when you're outdoors."

"Sure, whatever will help me master my control."

"Great, follow me." He didn't wait to see if I followed so I ran to keep up.

He led me to my private back beach outside of the castle and there was no sign that it had rained the day before, it was simply gorgeous outside.

Kane released his wind and the trees started to sway, instantly calming my nerves. I guess I never thought about it before, but I was more relaxed out in nature.

"Clear your mind. Forget the events of the past few weeks and focus on your breathing and the sounds outside. Focus on nature instead."

Doing as he bid, I breathed in deep, taking in that wonderful Solian air—letting it reach every part of my body. I took a few more cleansing breaths of fresh air and my mind started to empty. I soaked in the rays of the sun and it filled me with a warm glow, making me feel almost transcendent. My eyes fluttered shut, and I felt the sunshine seep into every crevice, bonding with me on a cellular level until I was no longer alone in my body. I felt connected to the world around me like it was a part of me. The warm radiance within me gave me inner peace, and it was unlike my previous attempts at magic —hectic, sporadic and disjointed. I knew I held the real connection I'd been looking for so I commanded the force inside of me to move its way to my hands until they gently became flame—controlled and contained.

"Now *that* is what we've been looking for," Kane said with a look of relief on his face. "Now move the flame up your arm, to your elbows."

I closed my eyes again and felt the energy within me, guiding the warm glow from my hands, slowly up my arms and to my elbows as Kane directed. I knew that I could command the fire to do exactly as I wished because it was now a part of me.

"Good. Now extinguish."

This time it was easy, and innate instinct took over. I doused the fire, releasing the energetic connection.

"Your comfort resides in controlling with your hands, it's always the first place your power manifests. Make the flame appear at your feet."

Reaching out, I connecting with that energy again until it filled me with its power. I summoned the flame again, but it ignited in my hands. I immediately shook my hands, extinguishing my accident. Kane nodded his head to me to try again. I closed my eyes, focused on my surroundings again until I felt interconnected with the world around me. It was as if I could feel the buzzing of life and energy in every part of my surroundings. I felt the breath and heartbeat of nature, and I concentrated the energy, moving it toward my feet. When I knew I had complete control, I released the energy and my feet became flame, disintegrating my shoes.

"Excellent!" Kane said with enthusiasm. "Now raise the flame all the way to your knees."

I concentrated and was able to slowly guide the flame to my knees where my dress rested. It singed away to my upper thighs revealing my daggers and *almost* my undergarments, but there was no way I was going to quit my control.

"That's more like it." Kane gave a full smile, and my legs went weak, almost making me lose control of the fire. I didn't know if he was referring to the control of my power or the fact that I was almost naked.

"Extinguish," he said with authority.

I relinquished the energy and the flame dissipated. I felt alive and refreshed, like I had unlocked a part of myself that was sealed shut. I knew that this was finally the start of my new life.

"Well done. We will meet here from now on for your lessons. We shouldn't overexert your magic after your episode so we'll end early."

"I feel like I could do that forever, I feel a well of energy with no end when I tap into it."

Kane looked at me, confused and almost concerned. "Regardless, let's save your energy."

"Last night was different. I don't know how to explain it, but the magic came from a different source. Today it felt—right."

"I'm glad to hear it. But for now, let's move on to your daggers," he said pointing at my thighs.

"Are you going to restore my clothing?"

"You know the drill."

After two hours, I hobbled back to my room all but naked.

I KNOCKED on Meili's door and she gaped when she saw my appearance—singed and mostly missing dress, missing shoes, my hair coming out of my tie and shredded knife marks at the top of my dress.

"Goodness, what happened to you!?"

"Kane," I growled with vengeance in my voice.

"Ah," she nodded knowingly.

"Meili, you should have seen it!"

"Oh, your poor dress and shoes." She brought me into her room and closed the door. She waved her hand, and my shoes and dress were restored.

"I need to learn that trick."

"It's a bit complicated, so that will probably take you a while to master. What should I have seen, Reina?"

"I finally learned some control. Kane took me outside for our lesson and it made all the difference. I felt everything around me, it was much easier to access my power!"

Meili smiled at me and grabbed my hand. "That's so wonderful, Reina! Mastering your power will only help all of us. But I'm not at all surprised being outside helped you."

"Why do you say that?" Meili always seemed to know more than she led on.

"Because fire isn't your power," she said without thinking.

It was like a punch to the gut. Just when I thought I was getting to know myself; the façade was ripped again.

"Meili...what do you mean by that?"

She looked uncomfortable for a moment and stayed quiet as if considering whether or not to elaborate.

"Meili?"

A bang on the door interrupted the serious direction our conversation was going. Adelram busted in not waiting for an invitation. Heathen.

"You've been summoned," he said with boredom.

"Are you going to elaborate?"

"Oh, of course, my liege, my deepest apologies," he said with sick sarcasm. "Your shenanigans led to a gaping hole in the castle that the Guardians could feel from a planet away. Which almost killed me, by the way, still waiting on *that* apology. Yes, I think that about wraps things up. Now as I mentioned before, in an inevitable consequence... YOU'VE BEEN SUMMONED," he said in my face.

I reconsidered my choice to forgive him. I didn't care how much Grandpa liked him, one day I was going to finish the job I started yesterday. Ugh!

I turned to Meili. "We'll talk later."

"By the time the Guardians are done with you, I wouldn't count on it." I wanted to punch the sneer off his face. Foul, miserable creature.

CHAPTER TWENTY-SIX

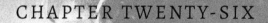

We made the normal trek up the walkway with the masked men and entered the temple with no issues. When we walked into the grand room, Orphlam was standing in the center of the room, rather than seated with the other Guardians like usual. He stood unnaturally still as we walked closer slowly, bracing for any kind of attack. We stopped with plenty of distance between us, but it didn't prevent Orphlam from inching closer in his strange, unnatural way of moving. He was now inches from my face, his putrid odor making me struggle not to gag.

"Cyra, you've become of great interest to us," he started circling, and it sounded like he was sniffing me. I hated him with a passion. I remember Urien urging me to stay unimportant to the Guardians. Shit. And for some reason Orphlam seemed...thrilled. Excited.

"Oh? I don't see why that would be," I said with venom.

"I think you do. You finally tried on your bracelet, but took it off. Why?"

"It wasn't the right fit."

"Then we'll get you another. What happened yesterday? We felt an enormous power surge come from your bedchamber. An amount of power that no person in Solis is capable of." I seized up in fear at him knowing where I slept at night.

"Adelram pissed me off."

"Doesn't he always?"

Adelram looked between me and Orphlam with incredulous disbelief.

"I felt ill, so I lost control."

"You have more power than we initially thought..." he said, still sniffing me. Was he trying to assess my power level by the smell of magic?

"Then you should see me try to turn on my bathtub. It's impossible."

"Did you happen to take a little stroll through Eluroom before your little trip?"

"I don't know what you mean."

"Again, I think you do. Maybe to some iron gates that say FENIX at the front?"

"Again, I don't know what you mean."

"You and I could do great things together—if you join me."

"What kind of things?"

"Join me and find out."

"I'm a little busy with common Solian affairs".

"Pity. We'll be keeping a *very* close eye on you, Cyra. Even during your trips to Meri. We'll see if that sardonic attitude of yours keeps you safe. And your family on Earth."

Shit. Shit. Shit.

I went back to my room after that disturbing visit and stayed alone the remainder of the day, with Orphlam's threats echoing in my head. I cursed myself for being so weak and foolish as to wear that bracelet. I knew in my gut that there would be more consequences coming because of it.

THEO and I ate dinner alone together that night. It was incredibly romantic and thoughtful. He had a table set on the private beach and we had the whole shore to ourselves. Nobody to bother us, no worries about the Guardians or prophecies. Just us amongst the splendor of Solis. Feeling the energy from my surroundings seeping through me, I showed Theo what I could do now, and he admitted he was relieved I had an extra layer of defense. To be honest, I was too.

"Dance with me?" Theo asked. He got up and took my hand leading me closer to the water. He took off his shoes and gestured for me to do the same.

"There's no music," I giggled.

"I can hear it," he said pointing to his heart.

He led me until we were knee deep into the ocean and suddenly the water erupted from under us propelling us into the air. I screeched and grabbed on to Theo for dear life, and he bellowed with joy. Still leading me by the hand, he walked and the water beneath us followed our steps, still carrying us high over ground.

"Theo—are we...walking on water?"

"Technically, yes."

I couldn't help it, I laughed as well. We ran, racing each other to see who could outrun the water. His control was so on point that the water held us the entire time even when I ran away from him. With my fear of drowning not even playing a factor, I realized I trusted him completely and I was able to be relaxed and free. I ran and jumped and dived on the water a hundred feet in the air. When we slowed down, he pulled me close and swayed with me. Mist in the air was dampening our hair and faces and the rainbow color within it was visible all around us. We danced on top of the world as the sun set in the distance and the night touched the day.

"You don't have to respond, but I want you to know—I love you," Theo said softly.

My knees felt like they couldn't hold my weight anymore and Theo picked me up into his arms, leaned down his head and kissed me as the mist surrounded us. I opened my lips, letting him in with curiosity. With the romantic scene all around, I couldn't fight it. I wrapped my hands around his neck and thought about a possible future together. I tasted him, and I immediately felt all that Theo was. His kindness, his bravery, his love. The water started to bring us down to the sand and my tongue continued to caress his, joining in physical need. When we were firm on land again, I planted my feet and I stared into his eyes, which looked so like his commanding power over the ocean he loved. I saw potential there. A man who wouldn't betray me, who would do anything for me.

"This has been absolutely magical, but I have an appointment to keep with Meili."

I could see the loss and disappointment in his eyes, but he did everything he could not to show it. "Of course. Until tomorrow, Cyra."

I cursed myself for my stupid sense of duty and guilt. I started to head back into the castle, and I slowed as I saw a figure standing in the shadows. But I knew who it was even though I couldn't make him out in the dark. Kane was there, alone, watching. I couldn't see his face, but I sensed the immense static force that felt an awful lot like devastation.

I THOUGHT about Theo's confession all the way back to my room. He loved me...and I was fated to be with him. But there was always that whisper in the back of my mind, trying to creep its way to the forefront every chance it got. When I entered my room I stilled as a vision overtook me.

"HERE HE IS. His name is Kaanan," Adelram said with a radiant smile.

"Oh, he is a looker, isn't he?" Amrel beamed.

"Did you really think I could produce an ugly child?"

Amrel rolled his eyes.

"Will you just bless him already, old man? We've been waiting for weeks."

"I apologize that my urgent attention caring for all of the cosmos is troublesome to you, Ad."

Adelram held Kaanan close to Amrel since he couldn't hold him.

"Hey, look at that, he likes you. He's cried when anyone other than Ilus holds him or is even close to him."

"Ad, every baby likes me. I'm The Creator—they can feel that. Come to think of it, every being in the universe likes me but you."

"Especially when you prolong this blessing..."

Amrel shook his head at his friend. "Alright, let's take a look at the boy." Amrel bent down as close as he could to Kaanan, careful not to touch him lest he burn him, and looked deep into his big bright green eyes as Amrel read his soul.

"Oh. You're quite the special one, aren't you?"

"What? What do you mean? Why is he special? What did you see? What is his fate?"

Amrel raised his hand over the baby and his hand glowed.

"Kaanan Distira, son of Adelram Distira, I bless you and instill you with my light. May you know peace, love and happiness." He then leaned closer to the baby and whispered, "And thank you, dear boy, for being extraordinary —for me."

"Amrel? What's going on, what do you mean by that?"

"You've asked for my blessing and you got it. You didn't request anything more, my work here is done."

"Amrel, I swear, if you couldn't kick my ass here to next week as The Creator, I swear I would–"

I WAS DYING to know what Grandpa saw in Kane that he thought was so special. Fuck my life.

CHAPTER TWENTY-SEVEN

$\mathcal{A}$ few weeks went by in monotony, I trained with Kane and became faster to summon my magic and it became a little easier to control. I was also getting quite adept at handling my daggers, although I still ended up leaving the sessions all but naked since I still couldn't block Kane's attack, and he refused to restore my clothing until I did. In all due credit to myself, he was probably one of the deadliest warriors in the galaxy, so it wasn't really a fair fight. But I supposed there was no better way to learn.

Urien tirelessly continued his efforts searching for the missing island to no avail and Theo and I visited Solis East a few times to meet with the residents, helping them when we could and healing more of the afflicted. Two more people went missing and we went to the temple to post their portraits amongst the wall of the lost and plant two more flowers in the painfully overgrown garden. I surprisingly didn't see much of Adelram and didn't know what he was up to, I could only assume he was spending his time at the Pog considering I hadn't seen him at any of my sessions with Kane.

We were also preparing for *Hvala* which was fast approaching, Solis's holiday celebrating Amrel and Creation. One day when Theo, Vish, Meili and I were planning decorations in the castle, Kane and Adelram approached us with the news we'd all been waiting for.

"I found it," Kane said simply, like he hadn't just found the holy grail.

We all gaped at each other, wondering if he meant the island.

"Should we go talk in my room?" I asked.

"Yes," Adelram responded.

We all rapidly made the trip up to my room and scattered throughout the main quarters.

"You found the island?" Theo asked, his eyes wide with hope.

"Yes. There are multiple guards on the outskirts of the island, as well as two others guarding what appears to be nothing. I took a closer look and noticed a hidden entranceway which must be where the *mikla* is being hidden. The guards were all Bellum mercenaries so I can easily take them out."

"You scanned the whole island? How did you go undetected?" Vish asked incredulously.

"Carefully."

Vish squinted his eyes with annoyance. "Well, what are we waiting for? Let's go get it!"

"If they have guards there, we need a plan," Adelram said with a sneer.

Vish glared at him, but thankfully didn't respond.

"The only time the Guardians leave the temple is for large official Solian events—and extenuating circumstances, like Cyra accessing the coveted private lands. Their ability to monitor from the temple is *why* they never leave for long. We won't have much time to retrieve the *mikla* before they realize what's happening."

"Then why don't we use *Hvala* as a diversion?" I suggested. "We invite the whole Reindem and honor the Guardians for... 'protecting us'." I tried not to gag getting out the words.

"They certainly wouldn't miss a chance to be worshiped," Theo volunteered. "I think it's perfect. We all attend so the Guardians witness our presence, and we disappear one by one to the island. With the whole Reindem in attendance it will be very difficult to keep tabs on all of us, even with their hired muscle."

"Who will go?" Vish asked.

"All of us," I insisted. "Except for Meili, I don't want to chance the Guardians finding out about her, so she will remain in the castle."

"Reina, please—I can help. If someone gets injured, I can heal."

"Then help us by staying safe and healing us once we're back."

Kane chimed in. "I will need to drive you there one by one since I'm the only one who knows where it is. There's a rocky cliff on one side of the island close to where I believe the *mikla* is. I will drop you off there to hide until we're all present. We'll then climb up when the coast is clear, and once we're on land I will take out the guards all at once so nobody has the chance of running or alerting outside help."

I shivered, wondering at Kane's level of power to be able to wipe out an entire island of guards in one fell swoop, *I'm the most powerful being in Eredet, after Orphlam.* "Will Urien be joining as well?" Vish asked.

"No, he should stay here, in case something goes wrong. If we're captured he might be able to save us, and keep an eye on our people. It sounds like we have a plan. I will arrange to have the invitations sent today. Cyra, we should go all out decorating the castle, so it looks legitimate. We haven't made much effort in many years for *Hvala*, but this year we will," Theo directed with a smile.

"I'd still like all of you here on *Hvala* before the ball—one last chance to be together since we won't know what will happen after we retrieve the *mikla.*"

Everyone looked at each other uncomfortably, and Adelram looked like he was filled with complete repulsion, but they all agreed. It was all I could ask for.

MEILI and I spent the next few days decorating the castle in splendor. Golden tinsel and gilded shimmering globes hung from walls and ceilings. White, soft wings were incorporated everywhere, in honor of Our Creator. There was a lovely statue of Grandpa in storage that was used as decoration in the past, but we thought it best not to annoy the Guardians by the sight of what they couldn't find. Golden suns glittered in every room emitting fire, along with a plethora of shrubs, flowers and greenery that made every part of the castle feel booming with life.

The mood had finally shifted amongst everyone in Eluroom. The decorations and preparations for the holiday were infectious, and I noticed quite a few more smiles around me. The staff went out of their way to help me and Meili until the castle was brimming with *Hvala* celebration. The castle grounds were adorned with full, plush wreaths with gilded accents and breathtaking floral arrangements. I basked in its resplendent grandeur even though I was missing my parents and Brendon. We went crazy at Christmas time and every piece of decoration I placed, I imagined I was doing it for them.

It was hard to imagine that in a few short days we'd all be risking our lives in hopes to finally find the *mikla*. The next step would be figuring out how to release the locked power, since I doubted it would be as easy as me simply *opening* it. And once unlocked, how did we stop the Guardians from absorbing or trapping all of it for themselves? It still greatly bothered me that I didn't know *why* they needed so much power. Nobody knew anything about the Guardians or their agenda, and it made for a much more terrifying opponent. We had no idea what to expect.

I decided to try to let myself thoroughly enjoy and embrace this holiday. It was entirely possible that the Guardians could intercept our efforts retrieving the *mikla* and destroy us. Life was too precious to spend in constant fear, anger and mental anguish. That was the whole reason for risking our lives to rebel against the Guardians, they kept all of Eluroom cowed. This holiday was a reminder that there was life to be had beyond the rule of the Guardians. I wanted to hold onto it with everything I had.

The Guardians had agreed to the *Hvala* ball we'd proposed to them in their honor. I think they had been waiting for it since they came into power. Even a formidable demon had its petty weaknesses, and we were ready to exploit them.

I made my way to the Solian shoppes to get gifts for my new friends—who were just about as wildly different as possible to my friends on Earth. My human friends were so easy to buy for, a game here, a book there...anything nerdy. What in the world did you get deadly immortal beings of various races? I thought about the nobles

I'd likely face in the marketplace. I hadn't been diligent in my role of Reina and interacting with the nobility, and I'd realized that it was wrong. They were my people too and, as far as I knew, they were only doing what they needed to survive. I hated it, but it all came down to power. From the poorest working class Solian, to the nobility and up to the Guardians. It's all that mattered here—the Guardians craved it for some unknown reason, but the people of Eredet sought it for survival. The more power a noble had the more recognition and the more value they held. The more power a worker had, the more chances they had of feeding their families and impressing the nobility. It was a vicious cycle I intended to break if I ever had the chance.

I finally made it to the shoppes after a grueling two-hour walk and, sure enough, as soon as I was spotted a horde of noble women rushed over to greet me.

"Reina! We've missed you lately, it seems you've been rather busy of late," a woman I'd come to know as Meglyn said.

I figured it was time to accept my role and become friendly with these women. Avoiding every public event such as *Sun Eine* was cowardly, and I felt ashamed at my childish actions. I'd have to make time for *all* of the people of Solis if they desired it. It's something Theo would do.

"Yes, I do apologize, ladies, you can imagine that Theo has been keeping me a very busy woman."

They all squealed in excitement to hear more about the impossibly handsome Karalis.

"With what sort of things, Reina?" Giorgima giggled.

"You know, I am parched after my very long walk here. Would you all like to join me for refreshment and I can tell you all about him? You pick the place."

They almost fell over in excitement and I remembered Theo's words, *it's a great honor to be seen spending time with the royalty.* I regaled them stories of Theo's superior talent with water and our dance in the sky, and how he swept me away on his magic ship that sailed over rainbow-colored waves. The ladies swooned at the details, and I was happy that the air seemed to change from the one of envy and suspicion when I first arrived, to excitement and curiosity. They filled me in on the latest noble gossip and we reveled in the upcoming holiday ball. To my complete surprise, I actually enjoyed myself. I wish I had given them more of my time during the months I had been here. Now it might be too late.

"Ooooh, I do believe we'll be seeing a royal wedding soon!" Meglyn said with delight and the other ladies agreed. I couldn't bring myself to disagree with them. It seemed likely to happen—and soon. No matter what thoughts I had for anyone else, I didn't want to let my people down.

We parted ways and I was surprised when I was left alone during the remainder of the time I spent purchasing my gifts. I gave each shoppe owner a holiday tip and they were gracious enough to send all my bags back to the castle. There was no way I could travel back two hours with them.

I grumbled as I left the final shop, preparing for the grueling journey back, and to my utter relief I ran into Vish.

"Vish, thank goodness!" He looked around his vicinity to make sure I was talking about him, and I laughed.

"Would you be willing to help a girl out? I walked a full two hours here and I'm really not looking forward to doing it again. Could you help me get back?"

"You *walked* here?"

"Well, unless you can teach me the secret to driving consistently every time, I have no other choice."

"I'm afraid I don't have the answer for that one. Driving is not easy to learn. It took me probably fifty years to master."

"Fifty years! I don't have that long! It's a handy skill to have when you're fighting evil."

He laughed. "I was able to drive consistently much earlier than that, but to be able to do it on point every time without fail took the full fifty years."

I stared off into space with a look of dread on my face. He put his arm around me and smiled. "Come, it'd be my pleasure to drive you home."

CHAPTER TWENTY-EIGHT

The morning of *Hvala* I woke up clammy and uneasy. The day I had been eagerly anticipating yet dreading for months had finally arrived. I had a jam-packed day ahead of me which I was thankful for, so I couldn't dwell on the danger we faced later. I got out of bed the same time that Meili announced she was coming in.

"What perfect timing you have, Meili, I was just about to come to you."

"Happy *Hvala*, Reina!" She beamed at me and drew me in for a hug.

"Happy *Hvala*, Meili."

"Here, I want to show you something."

I got out my sketchbook and showed her the watercolor I did of her likeness.

"You did this?" Meili looked utterly shocked.

I nodded. "It's how I see the tragedy of your circumstance, a glowing angelic woman who's a radiating positive energy, forced to hide in the shadows."

"Nobody's ever noticed me like this before. Thank you, Cyra."

"I hope we're successful tonight, so we all have a chance to live the lives we deserve, Meili."

Meili nodded seriously, wiping a tear. "Well, now. Onto more important matters, I have your dress ready for tonight. You can't put it on yet because you have a lesson with Kane before our little get-together. But I couldn't wait to show you."

"Oh, I can't wait to see it!"

Meili headed over to the closet and brought out a gown that even on a hanger made me gasp. I wasn't an expert at dress fabrics, but it looked like the skirt was made of soft white organza. The top was a semi-sheer lace corset with a sweetheart neckline and champagne and pastel colored flower applique that trickled down into the top of the skirt. The skirt was slightly fuller than any previous dresses Meili had made for me, but it was still elegant and tasteful.

"Check here, Cyra. It has hidden pockets in the skirt, only they're not ordinary pockets. They're open so it gives you stealthy access to your daggers."

"Meili, you're an artist and a genius. It might be disturbing how thrilled I am about my dress giving me such easy access to implements of death."

"I will feel much better knowing you are able to defend yourself, and you weren't hindered by a piece of clothing I made for you."

"What would I do without you?"

"You'll never have to find out."

My stomach turned to lead as if I just received a bad omen. I'd heard that sentence before from Brendon and it didn't end well.

I MADE my way to the private beach for my lesson and was stunned that Kane wasn't there yet. Although, I felt a faint humming of energy in the vicinity—was that him?

I circled the area for a few moments checking behind trees and noticed no tracks in the sand. When he still hadn't showed, my brain started going into its usual dark places, so I took my rusty dagger out to prepare myself. Kane had only ever been late the first lesson and someone else was there to fill in for him. My crippling fear had made me panic until I was nearly unable to function, but now I closed my eyes and tried to *listen*.

I listened to the gentle waves of the water and the motionless still trees that still seemed to hold sound for me. A small smile crept onto my lips as I felt the web of energy connecting to all the elements on Solis and it was available for me to borrow. The emissions of the sun coursed through me like I was a conduit, instantaneously igniting the power within me until the well of energy was immeasurable and I began to see with a different kind of sight. Imbued with a soothing, powerful light, I was one with the world and at utter peace, nothing else existing but me and the constructs of energy. Without needing to use my eyes, I could see all things through that interconnecting matrix, whisps of shining electric color that flowed like liquid currents–each strand connected to its own source. I reached out to twine my fingers through the shades of magic, and it tickled my senses, responding to my presence like it was waiting for me all this time. In that moment it felt as if I had finally unlocked a part of myself that was begging to be unleashed.

Amidst the endless activity of life, I sensed an almost undetectable disturbance above me in the nearest tree. I crouched down, bracing myself, and the presence dropped behind me. Before it touched the ground, I somersaulted around it and pinned it from behind. When I opened my eyes, my dagger was at Kane's throat and his eyes were bulging in utter shock as I laid on top of him.

"Does this mean I get to watch *you* limp back to the castle half-naked today?" I purred with a long-awaited victory.

Much to my sheer delight, Kane was speechless for a few moments. "Well, it's good to see some of your lessons are finally paying off, and not a moment too soon. Don't expect me to take it easy on you anymore." He spoke with authority, but there was a levity hiding beneath the gleam in his eyes.

I laughed with sarcasm. "Don't get all butt-hurt because I wiped the floor with you." I clenched my thighs around him and squeezed with wicked intentions. "Literally."

He moved so quickly that I yelped in shock, but didn't process what he did until I was flat on my back and he was on top of me, my dagger still at his throat. He ignored it and leaned into it, only an inch or two from my face, clearly unaffected by my scare tactics. "Let's not let one moment of triumph get to your head, shall we? You may shine as bright as a star, but I can still fell you back to the earth." His breath danced over my skin as his eyes trailed to my lips as if he wanted to taste them.

"Well aren't you just the cockiest little devil?"

"You have no idea."

My eyes bulged out of their sockets, knowing he wasn't talking about ego, but the hardness that I could feel through his pants. He laughed and stood with his arm outstretched, but I stood on my own, ignoring my glaring disappointment.

"You've greatly improved. You'd still perish pathetically quickly on a battlefield, but you can at least keep the dagger in your hand most of the time and occasionally light a fire in your hands."

"Praise, indeed. I'm glad after months of grueling practice my death will be prolonged all of five minutes."

Kane laughed with earnest and damn it to hell if it didn't make my nether regions drenched. "That's what Adelram and I are for. Hopefully we can help prolong your death up to an hour."

I rolled my eyes as we began heading back into the castle.

"Oh, and Cyra?"

"Hmm?"

"If you want to see me naked, you only need to ask."

My shock was so great that I stood motionless and gaped at him. His laughter echoed throughout the beach and the tingling was tangible in the space between us. I absolutely *did not* envision his broad, bare tattooed chest, rippling with unrivaled strength. Not. A. Chance.

Back in my room I bathed and finally dressed into the work of art Meili had created.

"Meili, it's absolutely stunning. I don't even know what to say."

"That is praise enough, and you are the one that makes the dress stunning."

She braided two loose French braids again and tied it off at the back of my head off to the side. She left two small strands of hair to fall at the sides of my face with gold ornaments and real flowers tastefully throughout the braids. Meili topped it off with a hint of gold shimmer on my eyelids, with just a touch of color on my lip. She had made me into a living masterpiece.

Meili was dressed in a beautiful plain white flowing gown with no adornments, not that she needed any. She *was* the adornment—one of the greatest beauties I'd ever laid eyes on, inside and out.

All the gifts had been stacked in my room ahead of time and arranged by who was giving them. Kane was the first to arrive. When I opened the door my heart stopped, unable to think of anything but our "training session." I gave my best genuine welcoming grin, hoping everyone would be as excited as I was to be here to celebrate. He looked me up and down with delight on his face that slowly disappeared as if he remembered he was supposed to be miserable. He nodded but stormed inside and plopped on the sofa forcefully. What the hell was that about? We were off to a *great* start.

Vish and Adelram came next, clearly appalled to be arriving at the same time and standing in each other's vicinity. I rolled my eyes. This wasn't getting any better. Adelram pushed me aside, and plopped in the space by his son. I sighed and outstretched my arms to Vish.

"Welcome, Vish. Thank you for coming and happy *Hvala*!"

He hugged me back tightly and gently picked me up off the floor. "Happy *Hvala*, Reina!" He entered the room and stayed as far away from Adelram and Kane as possible.

Theo finally arrived a few minutes later and put his hand to his chest when he saw me. His look of love and pure joy was infectious, putting me at ease.

"Cyra, my goodness. You are the most beautiful woman I've ever seen." He leaned in and kissed me softly on the lips and I relaxed until I felt an actual magnetic force pulling me away from him. It yanked me back so hard it was awkward and abrupt.

"Sorry, I tripped a little." I heard a laugh off to the side and shot a glare in the direction Kane was sitting.

Theo held my hand and walked into the room with me as Meili handed a glass of champagne to everyone. I nervously walked to the center of the room and faced the band of misfits. "I just wanted to thank everyone for coming today."

Adelram sucked back his champagne in two gulps then took Kane's glass and knocked that back too. "Got any more?" he asked after belching. To my horror, Meili filled both glasses up again and I clenched my jaw.

"Uh, yeah, like I said, thanks for coming. It's evident none of us want to be here in the same room at the same time, but I believe that fate has brought us together for a reason. Tonight, we fight for the same cause, with one common enemy." Theo beamed a smile at me as Meili and Vish nodded their agreement. Kane and Adelram were still and silent, stoic and unreadable.

"I'm thankful for each of you in this room, and for the fact that we can finally come together to celebrate without jumping down each other's throats. So, let's open these offerings of appreciation and celebrate the gift of life. Cheers."

"Here, here!" Theo applauded and took a sip of champagne as Vish mimicked the sentiment. Adelram was now holding his own bottle of champagne and drinking directly from it, already half-finished.

I approached Adelram and gave him the first present, shoving it into his free hand.

"Here, this is for you. Since you are *so* ready to party, I think you should go first."

"Ah, no. I don't want to go first. And I don't do presents."

"Too bad. Open it."

Adelram looked completely petrified that I'd dared to give him a gift, but he did as he was instructed. When he saw what was inside his horror turned to pure terror. You'd think the ultimate forces of evil were boxed inside and he had just unleashed them.

"What in the bloody *grof* is that?"

"Well, I was going to commission a monument in your likeness, but they couldn't find enough stone in all of Eredet to create something with that massive of an ego. So, instead, I got something that reminded me of you. It's a teddy bear in armor, Adelram. Because you're my valiant protector that gives me the warm fuzzies on a daily basis."

Everyone was struck stupid with looks of shock and utter confusion, then erupted into laughter, including Adelram. The immensely powerful, dark and miserable Adelram, sitting on my couch with a bottle of champagne and a fuzzy teddy bear was too much ridiculousness in one package. It was also the first time I had ever seen him genuinely smile with no sarcasm. Much less *laugh*.

"Next *Hvala* I expect that monument, no lame ass excuses." Was that another smirk on Adelram's face? I felt like I had just performed a small miracle.

Vish opened his present from me next. I painted a picture of his farm and got it put into a Solian designed frame. "So you never forget who you are," I said to him.

"You made this yourself?"

I nodded at him, smiling.

"It's perfect—absolutely perfect. Thank you so much." I could tell Vish was incredibly touched, and it warmed my heart.

I gave Meili a state-of-the-art sewing machine with all the bells and whistles money could buy, complete with countless fabrics and sewing accessories. I spent the most on her gift by far, but she deserved it more than anyone. Meili's delight was at an all-time high when she squealed in excitement.

I approached Theo next. "I've made a copy of your cousin's memorial from the training camps and I've arranged to have it placed in the castle gardens where she'll always be remembered by the Solians. She doesn't deserve to be left in a place that's lost and forgotten. It'll be next to a bed of flowers filled with the one she was admiring in your painting."

"Cyra, I don't know what to say." He gently touched my check and I saw genuine reverence in his eyes. He leaned toward me and his kiss was featherlight and tender, sending waves of ardor throughout me. "Thank you." His appreciation and adoration were gift enough for me.

Everyone began handing out presents to each other to speed up the process. I went and sat by Kane since Adelram had gotten up to use the restroom after a gallon of champagne.

"I must admit, I struggled with what to get you. Crochet is one of my hobbies so I made you a blanket. The thread shoppe owner told me this was Varjun silk and I chose green to match your eyes. He also said that this patch was your people's emblem, so I sewed that onto the blanket." I had also embroidered his name on the bottom right corner as well.

"I...uh...thanks." His demeanor had totally changed, what was going on with him?

"Happy *Hvala,*" I said, throwing up my hands in confusion. I tried not to let my frustration at his behavior sour the festivities so I walked away, inspecting everyone else's gifts. I opened my own as well.

Vish gave me his copy of the fairytale book *The Paeladoned Warrior* along with a very close replica figurine of my Paela, Laine. I laughed with delight, but I would be secretly studying that book in great detail later.

Meili presented me with a beautiful hair brooch that she said was an emblem of her people, the Sunya. It meant so much to me that she would give me a piece of her beloved culture.

Theo gave me a toy rendition of the Eventyr that could magically fly and he assured me it could swim underwater as well and I absolutely loved it. He also gave me a ridiculously expensive diamond necklace, which wasn't too shabby either.

Adelram gifted me with a few moments of utter peace and quiet with no complaining which I accepted with relieved appreciation.

I was pleasantly surprised to find that this incompatible group was enjoying themselves. The room was loud with talk and laughter, the *Eventyr* continued to fly around the room and Adelram was off by the window dancing solo with his second champagne bottle and teddy bear that he'd named Poopsie. The only one not engaging was Kane, who was still sitting on the couch staring off into space like his puppy had died.

We eventually said our goodbyes as we all had to ready ourselves for the ball and the danger ahead. Theo kissed me goodbye and promised to meet me by the ballroom entrance. Adelram wobbled over and frowned at me.

"What, did you and Poopsie have a fight already?"

"Yeah, I told her I needed a nap and she said she wouldn't sleep with me."

"Well listen to her, you don't have much time before the ball. If you do take one, make it quick."

"Yes, mommy Reina."

Meili said goodbye, thanking me profusely for the fine gifts. I handed her a piece of paper with an envelope and said, "You can open this later. It's how I really see you...free to be who you are." I gave her the second piece I'd painted of her. She hugged me and walked out.

That left Kane, still sitting on my sofa. I couldn't tell if he was even aware that everyone had left.

"Is everything okay?"

He stood and looked down at me with his attentive, unique eyes. "No, but that's life, right? Look, here's your gift," he said, shoving it out unceremoniously before me.

I hesitantly opened it, but was stunned by the contents of the dark wooden box. Nestled in fine purple velvet was the most stunning dagger I had ever seen. Infinitely more elegant and precious than the rusted and chipped daggers I carried daily. The black leather scabbard was braided and detailed with vined leaves and flowers accented with dark jewels, each end capped with polished silver that complemented the indigo leather grip. I traced my finger over the glowing pommel, a replica of what I assumed was a foreign cerulean blue moon. But I was mesmerized by the unique blade which shimmered with opalescent color and I could feel it humming with a silent and deadly power. It was safe to say I was blown away by his gift.

"It's a magical dagger made by my people. You need only deliver a tiny scratch to your opponent, and it produces whatever poison is most deadly to them, so you don't need much skill to wield it."

"Perfect for someone like me who would die upon stepping onto a battlefield, huh?"

"And now you don't have to keep stealing the minute amount of training weapons we have." His forehead mockingly creased, giving me a knowing look.

My cheeks reddened a little at my antics, but he chuckled. "I would never stop you from feeling safe. If you needed me to move the entire armory to your bedchambers to feel a sense of comfort I would have done it."

He took a step closer, examining the gaudy necklace Theo had given me, his brows furrowed in either disapproval or disappointment and I had to look away, unsure why I felt somewhat embarrassed. The air was heavy with friction and his formidable power, and eventually I was forced to raise my head to meet his gaze which was full of unspoken words that I desperately wanted to know. "It's the best chance at keeping you safe. That is more important than anything else."

After clearing his throat he shifted his weight and began fidgeting, clearly uncomfortable and it only made him more endearing if that was even possible. "The giving of a gift is an extremely personal act, displaying a great deal of admiration and respect for the recipient. It's not something that's done lightly where I'm from."

I nodded with understanding. "That's why you and Adelram looked so panicked when I dared to give you gifts." My stomach immediately began doing somersaults when I noticed the faintest hint of pink beneath his shadow gray cheeks.

"The rarer and more valuable the gift, the more it shows the giver's respect or love. This dagger is one of the few of its kind left in existence and was a highly coveted tool everywhere in the galaxy."

I swallowed, my mouth instantly dry. It was hard to keep my composure since his potency always made my head spin. What did this gift mean then? What kept me sane recently was my constant self-assurance that it was his job to make sure I was safe, and that he didn't really have any more interest in me than that. But this gift...sounded infinitely more intimate than my assumptions.

"Well, thank you Kane, that means a lot. I will cherish it, always."

He leaned down so very slowly and I was glued in place, unable to move, shocks of adrenaline and energy coursing through my veins. Whatever magic there was between us made it feel as if he was already touching me even though he was hovering right before my face. I was caught in an endless moment of bliss that I never wanted to end until he kissed me on my cheek so close to my lip that my mind short circuited. His soft lips sent electric pulses through my body with heat simmering in every inch of my skin, burning alive with fierce energy. There was an unexplainable connection there and it drove me wild, inwardly begging for more. My breath became rapid and labored and my eyes fluttered shut in anticipation, but he didn't give me more. When I opened my eyes he was gone and I was left damn near devastated. It was for the best, anyway. Right?

What the fuck was I thinking pining after a man that I wasn't destined to be with? Everyone made it clear that if I didn't follow the decree of the prophecy I would doom everyone to death. I shuddered, realizing it made me selfish to want something different. Even if I would deny it to hell and back. There was nothing wrong with Theo and I admired and respected him. I knew I could grow to love him, and royalty married all the time for the sake of their kingdoms, love having no place in the bargain.

CHAPTER TWENTY-NINE

The moment we had been waiting for had finally arrived, and we would soon find out if our plan could fool the Guardians long enough to steal the *mikla*. Theo was waiting for me at the entrance to the ballroom and I could hear the room behind him was filled to the brim by the level of chatter. He looked absolutely regal and beautiful as he stood waiting with his signature one-sided smirk and his hands behind his back. He had changed, and he now wore the most formal royal suit I'd seen him in, and a golden cloth off one shoulder. On his head was a small golden crown, but it only peeked through the center of his hair, looking like small rays of the sun.

"You look wonderful," I said to him and he beamed back at me.

"Thank you." He brought his hands forward and revealed a golden tiara that looked similar to his, but there were small diamonds throughout the sun rays. "This was your mother's." He reached to put it on my head, careful not to disrupt Meili's creation.

"Thank you, Theo." I realized Solis was starting to feel a little bit like home, and I had become attached to its people and my role here. I was honored to wear my mother's crown and I fought the tear that threatened to escape.

"Are you ready to go save our people?"

This is what I came for, and I wouldn't let Grandpa down. "I'm more than ready."

He took my hand in his and we entered the opulent and crowded ballroom. The room erupted in thunderous applause and every person of Solis bowed as we passed. It was unfathomable to me that most of the inhabitants of Solis were in this ballroom and out in the courtyard on the castle lawns. There were so few people left on this large, beautiful planet. They needed our help, and it emboldened my spirit so that I felt no fear.

We reached the center of the room and there were five chairs in the shape of a 'V,' just like I'd seen at the temple. There were no seats for Theo and I, the Guardians were the feature of honor for tonight.

We stood in front of our people who were silent, waiting for us to address them. I looked to Theo who was so eloquent and confident and waited for his speech as well, but I saw that he was looking to me —waiting for me to address our people. The fear returned, threatening to throw me into an unruly panic, but looking at the hopeful people of Solis again, it quelled the fright inside me. I looked back to Theo and he nodded. It was time for me to show our people that I accepted my role as their Reina.

"Happy *Hvala*, everyone!" I said outstretching my arms to the crowd. They applauded and cheered with an enthusiasm and happiness I knew they hadn't experienced in quite some time.

"As you know, I have very few memories of Solis and its traditions from when I was a child, but one of the few ones I do have is the feeling of magic and awe I felt during the *Hvala* holiday. My father Rhythen Fenix, once said to me, *life, love and family are our most cherished possessions—and the only ones worth fighting for.* And he was right. That is why we celebrate *Hvala* and the creation of life. We remember what it means to be loved, and we express our gratitude for all those in our life that make it worth living. Thank you all for coming so we might celebrate together as one people. I, for one, am grateful for Solis and its citizens, and I'm filled with hope standing with you all that we will continue to enjoy our way of life for eternity."

The room erupted in cheers, whistles and applause. Theo squeezed my hand and wrapped his fingers through mine before giving me a soft kiss. This time he spoke up to say a few words.

"This *Hvala* we recognize and honor the Guardians for protecting our way of life so that we might preserve Solian culture. Please join Reina Cyra and me in welcoming the Guardians to the *Hvala* Ball." The room was silent with tension and I was glad I didn't have to be the one to welcome the Guardians because I wouldn't have been able to get the words out without vomiting in disgust. I held my breath when they appeared, materializing in their seats of honor—Orphlam front and center. The crowd hesitantly applauded and I tried not to grimace.

Orphlam stood and looked as menacing as ever with his creepy gold mask and black cloak in a room of people wearing finery. "By my gracious generosity, we'll allow a few hours of music for dancing on this special occasion. Proceed."

Profound and gracious, indeed. Music erupted throughout the room and the people of Solis cheered in shock, most of them hearing music in this castle for the first time in years. Theo led me to the center of the room, and we were the first to dance.

"May I have the pleasure?" Theo asked, extending his hand.

"Every moment with you is a pleasure," I responded, taking his hand in mine.

I wrapped my arm around his shoulder, and he wrapped his around the small of my back. He started twirling me around, and we looked into each other's eyes like there weren't thousands of spectators. There were no Guardians or masses of people. It was just Theo and I and the beauty of music in the elaborately decorated hall. It only lasted a few moments, but it was enough. Everyone else joined in the dancing and the crowd was so congested with people it was hard to pinpoint anybody—and that's exactly what we were hoping for. We had positioned Vish, Adelram and Meili in set points so they were seen by the Guardians and we knew where to look for them as they exited the hall. Adelram was the first to leave, discreetly followed by Vish and, so far, nobody had noticed their departure. I was to be next, so Theo and I parted ways and he made a point to be boisterous, laughing with some of the nobles off in the opposite direction from where I was leaving. I turned and looked for Meili. She locked eyes with me, and they were filled with sorrow and worry, but I nodded my goodbye and slipped out of the room. I went to our agreed meeting point on the private beach and Kane was already there waiting.

"Do you have your Varjun dagger?"

"Yes."

"Good, let's go." He pulled me close, and we appeared on a rocky cliff that way farther than I'd like from the island. We were supposed to climb this monstrosity?

"I'll be right back with *your prince*." Even in moments of imminent danger Kane managed to throw in a dig. He disappeared, but didn't reappear when we expected him to. After about fifteen minutes they both finally joined us.

"Thank God, I was getting really worried." I had picked almost every cuticle raw and bloody waiting for them.

"Sorry, you know how the nobles are. It was very difficult getting away, Meili had to invent a matter that 'needed my immediate attention.'"

"Everyone's bracelets back in Eluroom?" Adelram asked.

"Yes," we said in unison.

"Let's climb up, I'll go first and stake out the position of the guards," Kane instructed.

The climb wasn't as difficult as I feared since there were plenty of jagged rocks that I could grip and stand on as we ascended. I was sandwiched directly beneath Kane and above Theo in case I slipped. We spotted a guard directly above us, and Kane moved so silently I studied him to make sure he was actually moving. He jumped onto the ground beside the guard, slit his throat and threw him over the edge before I could blink. When we were all on land Kane closed his eyes, raised his hands slowly while a ball of black light grew to a massive size between his arms. When he opened his eyes, he threw the energy forward and the darkness followed the curves of the island to find its targets. We heard yells off in the distance, but Kane stopped short and the color seemed to drain his face.

"What is it?" Adelram asked, putting his hand on him for support.

"They're all shielded! The Bellum all have magic shields."

"How is that possible? They have no magic," Theo panicked, running his hand through his hair.

"Could the Guardians be protecting them?" Vish frowned.

"Magic shields must come from within unless the Guardians were here shielding them. They wouldn't be able to shield them from Eluroom," Adelram said. "Are they here?"

"No," Kane answered.

"How many guards?" Adelram was all business.

"Thirty. And they're coming—fast."

Oh my God. I wasn't expecting this. There were only five of us against thirty guards. I quickly closed my eyes and tried to find the energy I had tapped into before, but something happened that I didn't expect. I could actually see the essence of the guards approaching.

"There's five over to the left, two straight ahead and seven coming from the right. The remaining men are still too far away."

Kane looked incredulous, but didn't discredit me. "Theo and Vish go left against the edge of the island. Adelram and I will go right. Cyra, stay here."

I was left alone with two guards approaching me at full speed. I reached inside my pocket and took out my Varjun dagger before moving away from the cliff's edge and studying my vicinity. I ran to the nearest tree and climbed onto a lower hanging branch, pulling myself up as fast as I dared.

The two guards came into view, one with a sword and one with a bow and arrow. When they were directly underneath me, I jumped onto the guard with the sword since the longbow had a smaller chance of attacking me at close range. They both yelled in shock, and I managed to dislodge his sword and throw it from him. I raised my poison dagger to him, but the other guard pulled me off and it went flying. I tried to push Kane's comments out of my mind. *You'd die within moments on a battlefield* and *that dagger is your best chance of protection.* Well, I had managed to fuck that up in a matter of seconds, just like he'd predicted. Goddammit, I hated when he was right.

I reached for my other dagger and stabbed backward into my captor's thigh. He screamed, and I used the opportunity to remove it and stab him in the throat. The fear and adrenaline helped me over-look the blood that was spewing from his neck. The other guard pinned me to the ground, and with both of his hands he grabbed me by the hair and started to drag me toward the edge of the cliff, likely to throw me to my death. With no more weapons, in desperation and agony, I prayed for my last line of defense to work. I screamed in pain, losing dark burgundy strands of hair as he continued to pull me to the edge, so I could now view the resting place of my imminent death. Despite my overwhelming panic, I slowed my breath as I reached inside to search for any power I could grab hold of. I was only able to feel a small reserve of energy, but it was enough. I put my hands on the guard and ignited them with every ounce of fight I had. Despite his magical shield, he screamed and let go of my hair. My dingy dagger was close enough that I was able to run and grab it while he was on the ground rolling in agony and I stabbed him in the heart, his eyes blown wide that someone like me was able to defeat him. I didn't relish killing anyone, but as I watched his eyes lose their light, I was filled with a power I was wholly unfamiliar with. Confidence and strength. He'd underestimated me, and I had been guilty of doing the same for far too long.

Without wasting time, I ran for my Varjun dagger and sheathed both knives. I closed my eyes and tried to pinpoint where everyone was. It looked like they were all in the center of the small island battling the rest of the mob of guards. I ran like hell to meet them, and when I arrived a guard had sliced Vish's arm and knocked him to the ground.

"No!" I yelled as the guard raised his sword to deliver the final blow. In a fiery and controlled wrath, I quickly soaked in every available ounce of energy I was able to and blasted it toward the negative force I felt. My flames whirled with beautiful precision, adhering to my command and dancing through every remaining guard until they were engulfed in a blaze of fury. I could feel every scream, every breath they took through the fire, and it was only mere seconds before they burned to dust. I shook my head in confusion, almost unsure of where I was and it took effort to come out of my trance and return to the present state, out of my plane of power. When my eyes adjusted and refocused my party was staring at me, stunned and speechless.

I shrugged one shoulder. "Nobody fucks with my friends."

"Have I ever told you that I'm tickled pink to be your bestie for life?" Adelram asked.

"No, you haven't."

"Oh…must have slipped my mind."

"They had magical shields. How were you able to kill them?" Theo asked, bringing us back to reality.

"Our first lesson…you didn't harm me, but you penetrated my shield. I didn't think anything of it, but shields must be void to your magic," Kane surmised.

"And good thing too. You saved my life. Thank you, Cyra." Vish said, rubbing my arm.

"As much as I'd love to stand around and hold hands with you all, we have limited time before we're discovered. We don't know if the guards had a chance to alert anyone to our presence," Adelram urged.

"He's right, we need to go. Wait, did I just say Adelram was right?" Vish asked.

We made our way to where Kane indicated the invisible doorway was. We still couldn't see it, but when it was opened a veil was lifted and we clearly saw stairs leading underground. Adelram went in first and Theo held my hand as we made our way down.

"Ugh, it's absolutely rancid in here," Vish said through coughs, and we all cringed at the stink.

After we somewhat adjusted to the stench, I gasped at the sheer size of the underground cavern. It looked to be half of the size of the island. As we walked down the dimly lit corridor, we noticed small captivity cells. Many of them. They were mercifully empty, but I had a sickening pit in my stomach knowing that they were all used at some point.

An unnatural darkness in the corner of my eye caught my attention and my whole body tensed. Something innate within me felt echoes of a presence in the shadows, and I wanted to call it evil. The party continued to walk on, not having noticed. I wanted to do the smart thing and follow them so I didn't venture off to my death, but I couldn't pry myself away from that disturbance. I inched closer, and the feeling of dread intensified as I got closer. It was so dark it looked like the room was empty, so I enflamed my hands, instantly regretting it as I screamed at the gruesome sight.

The group ran back to see what had happened, but I was too in shock to say anything.

"What happened, Cyra! Are you okay?" Theo grabbed my shoulder and I pointed to the cage of carnage before me.

Nobody made a move, so Kane was the first to walk over without fear, peering inside and immediately stiffened. His sharp inhale and uncharacteristic distress immediately put everyone on edge.

"What is it?" Vish asked, clearly too afraid to go look for himself.

"Bones. Thousands of them."

CHAPTER THIRTY

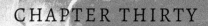

"*The lost ones...*" Theo said, pulling on his shirt like he couldn't breathe. He took my hand and we walked closer to inspect the area. I ignited my fire again so they could all see the devastating sight. Countless souls lost to the evil of the Guardians, and there were more tiny bones there that I didn't dare look at too closely. These were thousands of Eredet's people locked away in a dark, festering, putrid pit like yesterday's waste.

"Cyra, we must move on. We must find the *mikla*," Adelram said gently. He put his hands on my arm and looked me in the eyes. I searched his soft moonlit irises and found they could be tender and soothing when they weren't full of hate and anger. "This is why we're here—so this never happens again, we must keep going." Adelram turned away from the room and I numbly followed suit until we all began to walk down the dark corridor once more.

We reached a gigantic open room that had a large wooden chair with arm and leg straps. It looked like a chair of torture. Surrounding it were hundreds of jars, boxes and books. Off in the distance were ten stone archways just like the ones I'd seen before.

"Look! Those are like the stone archways I saw in the Fenix lands!" I looked at Kane and he was frozen in place looking utterly terrified. "Kane, are you okay?"

"What is it?" Adelram asked.

"Guys, look at this! This is a log of some sort. It documents experiments they performed on thousands of people from all over Eredet. This must chronicle why they abducted so many people and what they did to them." Vish flipped through the pages of a book and slowly his excitement dimmed to disgust the further he read. "This shows most of the procedures involved. They were trying to extract a being's essence and transfer it to another living body. This is vile, utterly vile. They took people with both high and low magical ability to perform these tests. Children were frequently used since they wanted the implantation to take place among youth, and they thought they could be more resilient to an invading essence. This is unbelievable." Vish looked pale as he continued to flip through.

"Why? Why were they doing this?" Theo asked through clenched teeth. He knocked some of the items off a nearby table.

"So that's what they were doing," Kane said quietly.

I paled next to him, remembering he had been abducted.

"I was taken here...about fifteen hundred years ago. I was kept captive for approximately five years. I thought they were just torturing me for information or even just for the fun of it, but I guess they were trying to rip out my soul. It certainly felt like it."

My stomach churned so wildly that I had to breathe deeply to keep from retching. I observed the chair that had countless bloodstains now permanently seeped into the wood. How many screams of horror and pain had that chair seen? I was violently angry at the thought of anyone even coming close to inflicting pain on someone as quietly altruistic as Kane. It was hard for others to realize the virtue and kindness of Kane because he didn't boast about it or look for affirmation. He simply did what needed to be done for others. Flames burst from my hands involuntarily.

Adelram hissed and turned away with his arms folded in front of him, visibly hurt seeing the place his son had spent five years of his life being tortured.

"How did you get away when all the others were never seen again?" Theo asked suspiciously.

"That doesn't matter!" Adelram yelled, deliberately changing the topic away from Kane. "Do any of you idiots see the *mikla?* You know, the whole damned reason we're here?"

He was an asshole, but he had a point. We kept on our search, but Vish had found something else and summarized the text.

"Guys, listen to this. This is an account of the Guardians' rise to power by Amrel himself! *In the wake of certain death is when one feels the most alive, and will do anything to remain so.* It claims that they are actually beings from another *galaxy* that invaded Eredet because their planet was dying. Their people were becoming mortal and dying off, so they came to the source of the greatest power in the cosmos to try to capture some of it to bring back home. Once they were here and began the process of siphoning our energy, they started doing these experiments so their people could transfer their souls and obtain immortality. After absorbing too much power themselves, the Guardians became even more corrupted, and wanted permanent access to it. They banded with Dokoran, knowing he was the perfect opportunity to watch a society crumble and infiltrate it from within. They pretended to be Solians as they became the ultimate power in all of Eredet. He continues to explain what we already know from Cyra, that Amrel locked most of our power away and cursed it so they wouldn't kill our sun. They found another way to regain the lost power by creating a *Void Shift* that drained energy from other worlds."

"Oh! This one's titled *Sild Gate,*" Vish offered.

"Let me see that!" I said, ripping it from his hand. "Let's walk over and take a closer look as I read this. Oh, there's almost nothing written here, they must not know anything about them. It simply states that it can only be opened by one with the mark of the *Sunya Reina.*"

"That sly dog," Adelram said with a smile.

Before anyone had time to question him about his typically vague comment, I looked over to a sea of shelves that held hundreds of various boxes.

"Look!" I shouted. "These all look similar to the box Grandpa left me."

"Cyra, look for one that's identical. Maybe he left you a clue on how to find the right one!" Theo said.

I started carefully scanning the sea of boxes and I felt something pulling my attention. An energy signal was pulsating towards the middle of the long row of boxes and I followed the trail of energy until I stopped in front of one that was emitting a soft glow.

"Do you guys see this?" I asked.

"See what?" Theo asked.

"I don't see anything. Kane, can you? You can see hidden magicks," Vish questioned.

"No, I don't," he admitted.

I picked up the box and it looked identical to the one grandpa had given me, and my hands shook at what this meant.

"Guys, this is it. It's identical to the one grandpa Gave me and I feel immense power emanating from it."

We all looked at each other for a few moments in silence. All our worries could disappear. Were we really on the cusp of freeing our people from the terrible curse of the Guardians?

I placed my hand on the lid and pulled—but nothing happened. Maybe it was stuck after a millennium in dust. I tried again, pulling with all my might, but it wouldn't budge. I heard various exhales and groans of annoyance.

A pop sounded, jerking us from our concentration and out of nowhere four people appeared before us.

"Bellum!" Theo yelled. "Is that…a meige?"

One of the men with the Bellum wore a cloak and was holding a large glowing staff. What I didn't know was that there was a man behind me, and they thrust a knife to my throat and grabbed the *mikla* from my grasp.

"Cyra!" There was wild panic in Theo's eyes and I braced myself for the worst.

"Halt, or I slice her carotid. I wouldn't bother with magic either. My meige is shielding us. We've been watching and waiting for you to come and pick up the box. I bet you didn't know Amrel also cursed it so that you would have to be the first person to take it. Even the Guardians didn't know why they couldn't approach it, they've been searching for him forever to force him to open it – and to kill him and steal his power, of course. With our meige, we'll find a way to open it and harness its energy. The Bellum are done being a pawn in an immortal galaxy that treats us like the shit on their shoe. Spread the word that you've been bested by the Bellum King."

Just when I didn't think it could get any worse, Orphlam appeared and I felt the wrath escaping him like a sharp slap in the face. Flames erupted from my hands, but it was too late.

The Bellum and their meige disappeared leaving us alone with Orphlam and all my hopes floated away to be replaced by fear. I never even got to see what the Bellum king looked like.

Screams erupted in my mind. I'd had the box in my hands and now it was gone. *I'd had the box!*

The bones in Orphlam's fingers made a popping sound as he clenched his fists together in anger. The air began to vibrate with a phenomenal amount of energy, making me dizzy and nauseous. My thoughts became fuzzy and I couldn't think straight, as if Orphlam's power was a poison seeping into every inch of me. Beads of sweat started to form at my brow and I hunched over, unable to act.

Theo was the first to action. "We need to leave, now!"

I grasped all the energy within me, but my flames sputtered. I tried again and only produced a flickering kindle. Orphlam tilted his head with that golden mask of his perfectly intact as if daring me to try again.

"Did you think it would be *that* easy?"

Orphlam lifted his hands and a force I couldn't fight started dragging me to him. I was in the air before him, and as he choked the life out of me I knew it was likely the end. I kicked and fought and threw any energy I could at him with no effect. I could see Adelram and Kane attempting to fight Orphlam, but he shielded himself with magic.

Suddenly, Orphlam looked away from me, startled. Something was happening to him...someone was affecting him. I turned and saw Theo staring at Orphlam, not moving an inch. He was doing something to him and Orphlam was struggling. Was it Theo's emphatic power? Was he affecting Orphlam mentally? Whatever it was, it was working!

Orphlam dropped me as his attention turned to Theo and he twisted his hand in the air and Theo went flying. A loud crack echoed through the cavern as Theo hit the wall and it felt like my heart stopped as he lay unmoving on the ground.

"No!" I screamed. Adelram held me back and I fought him with everything I had to run to Theo's side.

Vish knelt beside him and held Theo in his arms.

Kane threw a dagger toward Orphlam, but he stopped it with ease and sent it flying back to Kane stabbing him dead center in his torso. Kane stumbled back and fell to his knees.

I clenched my chest as if there was a dagger in my own heart. I could almost feel the sharp sting embedded into my skin and the pain was unbearable. I screamed with tears flowing down my face and it took me a moment to realize I wasn't mortally wounded. I ran to his side, but before I reached him, Adelram raised his hands out toward Kane and the dagger fell from his body and landed on the ground with a crash. Blood started to pool on Adelram's chest and he fell to his knees, clutching the wound. With his other hand he used the last of his energy to hold off Orphlam, electrifying him with lighting.

"Father! No!" Kane's voice cracked with pain.

"Go!" Adelram demanded, coughing up blood. "I can't hold him off!"

He ran to pick up his father, but Adelram stopped him.

"No! You must go, all depends on it! Take her and get out —NOW!"

Kane rushed to me, swept me up to his arms and I stopped him. "Not without Theo!" He only hesitated a moment before kneeling beside him. Kane raised a hand to his chest and I saw a glow emit from beneath his vest. I got one last glance, watching Vish drive away and Adelram, who I realized had absorbed Kane's injury and sacrificed himself, gave up his fight and laid his head to the ground.

CHAPTER THIRTY-ONE

This drive was different than my previous ones. The squeeze was unpleasant, like we were traveling an extreme distance, and when we arrived at our location, I was in a place I'd never seen before. Kane dropped me and Theo carelessly to the ground as he fell to his knees.

"Kane, are you okay?" I wiped away the tears that continued to fall. I still couldn't fathom what was happening, but now I was alone in a place unfamiliar to me, and my knees buckled under the magnitude.

"Don't *touch* me!" he boomed so loudly the surrounding area vibrated.

I flinched at the venom in his voice, shocked at his tone even though he had just lost his father. Instead of pushing him further, I put my fingers to Theo's throat to feel for a pulse, but felt nothing. I didn't know if he was alive.

I cursed with fear and frustration at how this whole plan had gone haywire. Thankfully, I saw Vish drive away to safety before Kane and I disappeared, but he was alone now on Solis along with Meili. She was vulnerable now that there would be a hunt for us and the *mikla*.

The *mikla*. I couldn't believe I'd had it in my grasp and then lost it within seconds. The Bellum who were never considered a threat, who were never treated as a part of Eeredet, who were constantly starving, struggling and hated—were now seizing their opportunity and seeking revenge. We now didn't have just one enemy to contend with, we had two. More than that, they had a weapon nobody knew about—a meige. Nobody had ever mentioned meiges to me, did Kane and Theo know what they were? The worst part was, nobody knew where the Bellum hid on the Void. The chances of finding the *mikla* and breaking the curse while on the run from the invincible Guardians now seemed like a pipe dream.

And Adelram—he might have made me want to punch him more than once, but he had the right intentions. I always felt it somewhere, even without the visions I had. He'd promised grandpa Amrel he'd always do anything for him, and that alone made me love him. The Guardians had destroyed most of Eredet, the thousands of other planets stuck in limbo and almost everything I cared about, and I was more lost than ever on how to come out of it with the few remaining souls left alive.

I fell to the ground behind Kane, shaking from fear, adrenaline, and loss. It was dark outside, but the moon was so bright I was able to see most of our surroundings. *Wait—Solis had no moon.* I looked up and saw a dark castle off in the distance.

"Where are we?"

"Home," Kane said gravely.

"Home? Is that...*your* castle?"

Kane touched the two tattoos on his arm, and they glowed in response. Seconds later, two massive and frightening looking Varjun appeared before us, rushing to help Kane stand.

One looked like death incarnate with the same shadow-kissed skin as Kane, but his hair was long and white with two small strands of tight braids. He was the same height as Kane, maybe six-foot-five inches, and too many bulging muscles.

The other Varjun male had lighter gray skin and a full head of black hair to his shoulders with bright violet eyes. The gleam of mischief in his eyes made him seem like a wicked creature and his smirk directed at me on the ground validated my thought. His slender figure moved like a slippery serpent and he appeared beyond amused by the sight of me quivering.

The one with the violet eyes laughed and said, "Good, she's scared. Welcome to Varjutus."

"What's going on?" I wiped my wet face and Kane's jaw clenched as he looked back at the castle in the distance.

"The castle… it was my father's, and now I guess it is mine."

"Are you–a Reina?" I braced for his next words, already anticipating them as all the color drained from my face. If it were true it meant that Theo had blatantly lied to me, and the thought of that betrayal was devastating.

"No," Kane laughed bitterly as he clenched his hands into fists. "I was born a prince. And now… I am a king."

ACKNOWLEDGMENTS

First, I must thank you, dear reader, for taking a chance on this debut of mine that has been in the works for many years. I truly appreciate your interest in the world I live in on a daily basis.

A special thank you to my husband for all the extra time he spent entertaining our imaginative princess while I'm one hundred million lightyears away.

Thank you to my alpha readers, Jenn K. and Kim C., who made me believe I might be able to pursue this dream of mine.

And a very special thank you to my beta readers, Sarah Wise, Heather Creeden, Amber, Ducle and Charley (@theliteraryreviewjournal, IG). Your feedback was invaluable, and the story wouldn't be the same without you.

Lastly, thank you to my editor, Jade Church, who took a hot mess and made it into something I can share with the world.

ABOUT THE AUTHOR

Clare's goal in life is to make you laugh, cry, scream and squirm (hopefully leaving you begging for more). She enjoys writing about fantastical journeys with characters you love, or love to hate, with a plethora of spice mixed in. When she's not writing, she's spending time with her husband, daughter and floofy cats.

Instagram: @clare.archer.author

Tiktok: @clare.archer.author

Website: https://www.clarearcherauthor.com

email: clare.archer.books@gmail.com